ETERNAL LOVE

Alice Alfonsi

J

JOVE BOOKS, NEW YORK

8436198

HAUNTING HEARTS is a registered trademark of Berkley Publishing Corporation.

ETERNAL LOVE

A Jove Book / published by arrangement with the author

PRINTING HISTORY
Jove edition / January 1998

The Putnam Berkley World Wide Web site address is http://www.berkley.com

ISBN: 0-515-12207-6

A JOVE BOOK®
Jove Books are published by The Berkley Publishing Group, a member of Penguin Putnam Inc., 200 Madison Avenue, New York, New York 10016.
JOVE and the "J" design are trademarks belonging to Jove Publications, Inc.

PRINTED IN THE UNITED STATES OF AMERICA

10 9 8 7 6 5 4 3 2 1

Old Flames Burn the Brightest . . .

At the other end of the room, the fire was catching and the darkness was alleviated somewhat by the glow of rising flame. Hannah began kicking off her bedcovers. She twisted toward him and settled down a moment, her face relaxing. Tendrils of dark blond hair now framed her cheeks, long locks spread out on the pillow around her, looking more golden in the firelight, as if they'd caught fire.

Neil swallowed uncomfortably.

"This is nuts," he murmured. Yet, as his eyes strayed back to her face, and, more specifically, her rose-colored mouth, Neil felt an overwhelming sexual curiosity rising in his veins. A voice seemed to coax him to do what he most wanted—at least at this moment.

He wanted to bend down low, lean his weight in. Just the thought brought him a little closer to her. His shadow covered Hannah's face. After all these years, a part of him wanted to know what it would feel like to kiss his girl again . . .

Praise for Alice Alfonsi's
Eternal Vows:

Acknowledgments

It's a turbulent world we live in. Without my family, I would be lost. A thank-you to them for their love and understanding through the years, especially my dad, my aunt, Mary Capaccio, and my sister, Grace Alfonsi Capaldo.

This book would never have hit print without the firm faith of one editor and one agent. I thank my editor, Gail Fortune, for her belief in this story and the opportunity to write it. And I thank my agent, Alice Orr, for her unflagging support as well as her service to so many women who write.

The many eras of Newport's history are still leaving haunting impressions due to the hard work of some very dedicated people. My sincere thanks for assistance in research goes to the Newport Historical Society, the Preservation Society of Newport County, and the Newport Chamber of Commerce Visitor's Information Center, as well as the flamboyant guides of Belcourt Castle. If there are any errors in this book, they are entirely my own.

Last but never least, I thank you, Marc Cerasini, for being my muse as well as my love.

For my father,
Antonio A. Alfonsi,
who gave me the courage to believe
in things that aren't always visible
to the rest of the world.

The private eye is a knight-errant
in a corrupt world.

–Lee Server
Danger Is My Business

—For love is heaven,
and heaven is love.

—Sir Walter Scott
The Lay of the Last Minstrel

ETERNAL LOVE

Prologue

MAY 1928

"I love you."

Mrs. Daisy Channing Hunterton closed her eyes. "Oh, please, Dan, don't tease me . . ."

The dark-haired Pinkerton detective pushed back the brim of his brown-felt fedora and turned off the car engine with an agitated twist of his scarred wrist—broken more than once in the line of duty. His battered Ford was now parked beneath the rain-soaked leaves of Daisy's elms and oaks, stately sentries on her grand Newport estate.

Tonight the Women's Tennis League was holding its annual summer bash, to which the Channings had been lending their mansion's ballroom for years. A dance band's jaunty brass and tinkling piano echoed hauntingly through the freshly washed night air.

Even though it was late in the evening, guests were still arriving. Fifty yards away, the parade of smartly tuxedoed men emerged from late model cars and lent their arms to ladies in drop-waist pastel dresses. Swinging pearls flashed in the night below bobbed hairdos expensively capped or banded with fashionable feathers.

Earlier in the evening a light summer shower had descended, but now the rain was thinning to a drizzle and the stark moonlight shone down with stunning clarity. From the heavens, it seemed to part the dissipating clouds, then aim its pure radiance directly through the streaked windshield of Dan Doyle's weathered black Ford.

Funny, thought Dan, although he'd always had his eye on a late model Sport Phaeton, he'd never bought it. The Ford had been more practical for his line of work, and tonight it had earned its keep, making the safe, surreptitious journey to Boston then back to Newport with Daisy right beside him.

It was the first time a wife had asked to accompany him. But then, Daisy was the kind of woman who didn't shy away from the truth. In fact, she seemed absolutely absorbed by the entire idea of detective work. Like him, she found it both fascinating and exhilarating. It was just one of the reasons he'd fallen for her. Take last week: He'd presented Daisy with enough evidence to divorce her husband, yet she'd insisted on seeing the *whole* of it for herself. Eyewitness reports were not enough, she'd said. She wanted to see exactly how Dan did his job.

Flabbergasted, he'd tried to talk her out of it, but Daisy had a mind of her own. So tonight, after the start of the Tennis League party at her mansion, Daisy slipped out with him. They tailed Randolph Hunterton, her husband of one year and one month, as he left the party on "urgent business," then drove to Boston and rang at another woman's town house.

Dan himself flinched when Hunterton groped the woman in the doorway, but Daisy didn't move a muscle. She watched without emotion—like a professional—waiting patiently till the perp emerged like clockwork sixty minutes later to head for the back alley door of a mob-run speakeasy.

Now sitting next to her in the car, Dan could see that a street sense of survival had already begun thrumming through Daisy's veins. It burnished her skin and brightened her eyes, giving her a newfound sense of clarity and self-awareness—qualities that few young women of her class ever came close to possessing.

Over the months of work on the case, Dan had come to

admire Daisy's reserves of inner strength—not to mention her irrepressible passion for life. There were other things he admired about her, too, but right now he was admiring how the moon's ghostly essence draped along her pretty cheek, caressing it in a veil of unsullied silver.

She looks like an angel, thought Dan, and something inside of him lurched. How he wanted to sidle closer to her, reach an arm around her shoulders and pull her against him. How he wanted to love her, protect her, and, as impossible as it seemed, just be with her forever.

"I know this is a hell of a time to say it, but it's true," he whispered in the silent still cocoon of the car. "Somewhere in the middle of this ugly mess it just happened. I fell in love with you."

Daisy turned her face to him, and he saw a damp droplet glistening on her face. "I guess you can't love me for my money," she said with a bittersweet sound, between a laugh and a cry, "because you know Randolph's nearly spent it all."

"I shouldn't have said anything," said Dan quickly. "I'm sorry. Just forget I opened my big mouth, just forget—"

"No, Mr. Doyle . . . don't you understand? I love you, too."

Dan held his breath a moment. She couldn't be serious. Not a gal like her with a bum like him. She had to be toying with him. The idea tightened around his heart like the cold dark of the midnight alleyways he practically lived in.

A rushing pulse of blood pounded in his ears and suddenly he was transported back to the damp gloom of his foxhole, hearing the unrelenting shelling of the Great War, the guns and grenades ceaselessly booming. The desperate feeling seemed tragically normal to Dan now. Like he'd spent his whole life in that muddy hole—and never left it. Like he'd been buried alive.

If only her words *were* genuine, he murmured to himself. A little prayer sent quickly Heavenward. If only he could be granted this one last chance of climbing out, seeing the light again.

Quietly Dan watched as Daisy's hand moved toward the steering wheel to cover his. And still, he dared not believe.

"It's true, Dan," Daisy finally whispered into the murky

chasm of silence between them. "I think we're two of a kind, you and I . . . a pair of torn-up hearts with missing pieces in exactly the places that make them fit so right together."

Dan closed his eyes. Then a sound like a moan came from his throat and he was drawing her into his arms. It felt so good, so natural, this powerful pull of two people so deeply in need of each other.

Daisy felt the strength of this man's embrace, the honest longing in his arms. And when he kissed her, it was the kind of connection that told her everything that should exist between a man and a woman—and had never existed between her and Randolph.

Far from being painful for Daisy, the truth she'd learned tonight was profoundly liberating. A great relief to know she hadn't been "delusional" or "overwrought"—as her society friends, and even her older sister Ernesta, kept insisting.

What a vindication it was for her! All the deceptions beneath the slick charms of Randolph Hunterton had become apparent enough to Daisy after their gala society wedding. But none of her so-called friends or even her family had wanted to listen.

"You're just imagining things," Daisy had heard over and over again. "Randolph's family practically started the New York Stock Exchange for Heaven's sake!" and "He's *so* handsome and *so* generous. You're absolutely the luckiest girl in the world!"

At the end of her rope and out of tears, Daisy had finally called Pinkerton's. They'd assigned her the best private investigator in their Boston office—an ex-cop with a busted-up marriage, a tenacious nose for trouble, and a shell as hard as a macadamia.

Over the months, Dan Doyle had systematically documented not only her husband's cheating, but also his reckless involvement with bootlegging and an extortion scheme targeting some prominent Rhode Island families. Daisy now had the evidence of crimes that would make Randolph Hunterton leave without a fight. As it was, he'd nearly dwindled her inheritance down to its last reserves. If he forced her into a protracted legal battle, she'd surely be forced to sell her beloved *Château du Coeur*, the family mansion that had been built by her grandparents in the 1890s. And Daisy hated to even think of being parted from her "House of the Heart."

Earlier tonight, Daisy hadn't hesitated a second on that dark wet street outside the speakeasy alleyway. She'd marched right into the low class gin joint and told off her red faced husband, assuring him that their marriage was over and she'd be filing for divorce.

Perhaps, without Dan looking on, she might have acted differently. But with Dan there, she felt more than herself—and, oddly, more *like* herself than she had ever before in her life.

Daisy now sighed with satisfied pleasure as Dan thoroughly kissed her, his sure fingers tenderly massaging the tense muscles of her back. But, as he deepened the kiss, her need for him grew to an impossible level.

"Let's go upstairs," she whispered into his ear, realizing how much she loved the scent of his pipe tobacco, a woodsy masculine aroma that lingered on his clothes and hair. "We can slip in from the side, and take the service staircase . . ."

"Daisy, are you sure?"

"I love you, Dan," she said softly. "Even before I met you, I think I loved the idea of you. I should have believed in myself and what I wanted most. I should have waited for you instead of listening to my family and marrying Randolph. But then, if I hadn't, I might never have found you. And now that I have . . ."

"Daisy?"

She turned and looked directly into his eyes. "Please, Dan. I just need to be near you tonight."

Dan nodded and left the car. Slamming the door, he closed his eyes a moment in disbelief, certain this was the work of some misguided spirit, blown in his direction by a wayward wind from Heaven. Somehow it had mistaken him for a man who deserved one last chance.

As he came around to the passenger side, he saw that Daisy had been in such a hurry, she hadn't even waited for him to open her door. She'd popped the handle herself and emerged, smiling at the sound of the squeaky hinge before shutting the door behind her.

Daisy relished this moment. She regarded Dan, standing there beside his banged-up Ford. He'd often told her that detective work required the kind of car—and the kind of man—

who could shadow suspects without suspicion, blend into the background in the blink of an eye.

She supposed Dan Doyle was like the Ford he drove, an average sort, the kind that careless young women routinely passed their fickle gazes over in favor of flashier models. But Daisy knew that when trouble came, Dan was the kind that by far had the highest value. He was the kind that pushed on through the worst roads, no matter the ferocity of the storm. The honest, stubborn kind that stuck by you. The kind that never gave up.

Daisy smiled up at him through the dark copse of tall trees, their shoes and feet dampening as they moved across the rain-washed grass. Nearing the side of the mansion, they heard the party's music more clearly. In front of the ballroom's band, a male singer had picked up his megaphone to croon a popular ballad. The sentimental words echoed through the mansion's air as couples danced cheek to cheek.

"A dreamer can awaken to a Heaven on the Earth, when the heart is finally taken by a love that knows its worth . . ."

"That's it, Danny. That'll have to be our song," said Daisy gaily. She laughed out loud as she took Dan's hand and pulled him inside. This deserted side entrance led to a hidden private stairway. As she suspected, there wasn't a soul in sight.

"Come on," she whispered.

Dan didn't need any urging. He was right behind Daisy's powder blue drop-waist skirt and white leather shoes as they flew up the narrow staircase. Within minutes they were striding quickly down the third-floor hall to the far end of one wing, where her large bedroom suite was located.

There was no shared marriage bed in this sham of a marriage. Dan had known that early on. Randolph maintained his own bedroom at the other end of the huge mansion—hadn't even expressed an interest in sleeping with his wife in months.

Once inside, Daisy shut and bolted the door. She leaned against it with closed eyes and an excited smile.

Dan stepped up to her. "I want to marry you, Daisy. But . . ."

Daisy's brown eyes opened, and her smile disappeared. "But?"

His eyes wouldn't meet hers. "But . . . you need to know

something about me. During the war . . . there was an injury. It's why my wife left me. . . ."

"Dan?"

"I can make love, but I can't . . . make children."

Daisy's gaze caressed the hard planes of Dan's rough features—a face she'd come to know so very well. Her slender hand reached up to remove his felt fedora and she ran her fingers through his thick dark hair.

"I love you," she said finally, as her palm moved to touch his cheek. "And I want to be with you."

"Daisy, you're young, you could have a family with another man—"

"Perhaps I could, but I don't want another man. I want you, Danny."

"Oh, honey, are you sure?"

"I want us to be together, no matter what. I want us to be together for all time."

Dan doubted her for a moment, but then her lips touched him and he knew he could trust the truth he felt there. Bending down, he swept her up into his arms. She let out a soft cry of surprise but hung on tightly as he carried her across the Persian carpet to the large bed. As he gently laid her down, she kept her arms around his neck, silently urging him beside her.

"I want us to wait," said Dan softly, "until your divorce goes through and we're married. I want us to do it right."

Daisy searched his face a moment then nodded. "Whatever you say. But will you just hold me tonight?" she asked softly.

Dan smiled. "Just try to get rid of me."

Daisy laughed and snuggled closer, nibbling his ear. "You know, I think I'd like doing detective work."

"You would?" he asked, kicking off his shoes.

"I think I'd be good at it."

"Yeah, somehow, I think you would be, too."

"So, perhaps we could open our own office right here at the mansion and, you know . . . do it . . . together?"

Dan's low chuckle miffed her for a moment. "What's so funny?" she demanded.

"Well, I already hoped we'd 'do it' together—as often as possible."

"Oh, you are just too fresh, Dan Doyle. And you've got way too many clothes on . . ."

"Well, then, I'll just have to take care of that."

"No, wait. Let me . . . investigate . . ."

As they talked and kissed, the rain started up again, and the music downstairs continued. For hours, they listened to its jazzy rhythms; and, when the band did quit for the night, they sang "Love Eternal" over and over to each other until they drifted off.

Their sleep was deep and happy, blissful in the knowledge that they'd each found the person they'd been looking for all their lives. To both Daisy and Dan, it felt like Heaven, like finally coming home. And somehow both knew in their hearts that it would be a home they would never, ever leave.

Even after death.

Chapter
One

LATE APRIL, PRESENT DAY

The special edition Mercedes sedan pulled out of the Burger World drive-thru and resumed its speedy course, flying along the dark Rhode Island roads like a golden bullet. The specially contoured seats had been crafted by one of the industry's leading leather manufacturers. Their butter-soft feel and hand-stitching had added a small fortune to the luxury car's list price.

Its present driver, however, could not have cared less.

Mrs. Hannah Daisy Whitmore Peabody, known to cable television viewers as *Homemaking* Hannah, the "new Martha Stewart," needed a place to put her Burger World bag. The posh leather seat next to her was summarily elected.

Without pause, she plopped the greasy bag down, then rummaged inside for a handful of the just-out-of-the-vat fries. Murmuring a little prayer, she shoved them into her starving mouth: *Thank Heaven for fast food.*

After swallowing the divine union of salt and grease, Hannah reached for the chocolate shake she'd ensconced in the car's ergonomically designed cup-and-cell-phone holder. She sucked on the straw, pulling the rich creamy chill into her mouth. Despite her recent show on "Cooking Healthy at Home," a sigh of pure satisfaction followed.

"Ecstasy," she pronounced before she sighed again. This time with pathetic dejection.

Ecstasy.

Satisfaction.

Any other woman her age would be associating such suggestive adjectives with sex, thought Hannah glumly. Not fast food.

"Sex," she announced to the Mercedes' dark interior.

Beneath her round, wire-rimmed glasses, her large gray eyes blinked. Just the thought of those three little letters was enough to make her grit her teeth. It had been *much* too long since she'd even come close to having sex.

By rights her wedding night nearly four years ago *should* have been one of those times. But it hadn't. It had been . . . well, an unnatural disaster.

Okay, so maybe it wasn't the Hindenburg, she conceded—after all, people weren't actually killed or anything—but if she was forced to put a word to it, *disaster* did come to mind. A step aerobic workout probably would have been a better idea, she'd have burned off more calories, and it certainly would have been more emotional.

Now why was she digging up the archaic artifacts of her wedding night, anyway? she asked herself. The answer was obvious: *Because your little sister is going to have one in two weeks.*

Holly Lilian Whitmore had been abroad for the last year, completing studies in art history. And now, according to Holly's heartfelt letters and her impassioned—and obscenely expensive—long-distance phone calls, she'd met the man she wanted to marry. He was a Brit named Sir Reginald Carraway, some kind of prince charming—or *knight* charming, anyway—who'd swept her sister off her trendy Italian sandals.

Charming schmarming, thought Hannah, all that really mattered was that Reggie was a good and decent person. And that he had a brain in his head. *Oh, the hell with it. The man could be a half-wit, as long as he loves Holly. And she loves him.*

Hannah just didn't want her twenty-two-year-old sister to make the same mistake she had. Marrying the wrong man for the wrong reason could only lead to extreme regret. It certainly had for Hannah. She'd just turned twenty-seven and yet she was living like a nun.

Oh, she knew what she *should* do when it came to her failed marriage. She and Greta Green, the show's head writer, had won a Cable Ace Award for the *Homemaking* installment they wrote titled: "Re-creating Your Home After Your Love Moves Out."

"Don't spend your life grieving," she'd advised her audience in the opening segment. "Get on with your living. Open your eyes and you'll see the endless possibilities that stretch out before you for finding love, fulfillment—and maybe a good buy at your local antique shop."

Sure, on the perfectly cozy "home" set of her *Homemaking* show, Hannah said all the right things to make her audience believe in a wonderful world that they themselves could create—and re-create. But when it came to inspiring herself, Hannah wasn't so successful. The truth was, Hannah had gotten through these last few exhausting years by accepting the idea that life wasn't going to get any better.

She'd come to the decision that the best way to be happy was to keep from being wretchedly *un*happy. No more chances on men. Instead she would focus solely on her work, and what was left of her family.

The ring of the car's cellular phone interrupted her depressive thoughts—and drive-thru dinner. After licking the French fry grease from her fingertips, Hannah pushed the speaker button.

"Mrs. Hannah Peabody here."

"Will you accept the charges for '' '' came the operator's robotic voice. "Holly Whitmore," finished the message with her sister's own recorded voice.

"I accept," replied Hannah.

God, everything's automated these days, thought Hannah. *The downsizing of America continues.* It made her wish she could do the kind of shows she really wanted to, like "Surviving with Style: Living on a Limited Budget." That was one theme that Hannah had become an expert on after her husband had left town. That and "Which Heirlooms to Hock to Stay Out of Court."

Unfortunately, the cable channel that aired her show had insisted on strictly traditional "homemaker" themes. Those were the themes that advertisers of laundry detergent and diapers wanted, or so said Chip Saunders, Hannah's boss.

With the exception of that Cable Ace Award–winning show on losing a spouse or lover, which she and Greta Green had slipped past him, most of the *Homemaking* shows were constrained to conventional approaches to cooking, decorating, and entertaining.

Chip, the executive producer and the venture capitalist who owned all interest in the show, kept a tight rein on Hannah's appearance as much as the show's themes. "Stay away from glamour," he'd insisted after she passed the audition. "Keep your hair in a bun. Very little makeup. We want you to appeal to Mrs. Average American. Within a year or two, if we position you right, you should be getting offers for product endorsements—and that'll mean bigger exposure for the show. My goal is to take us to a major network within five years."

Hannah had no problem with Chip's "packaging" requirements for her image. After all, she'd long ago accepted the simple fact that she wasn't anything special physically. So there really was no point in trying to pretend otherwise. In fact, it was amusingly ironic to Hannah that her *lack* of attractiveness was the very thing that paid off in her current career.

So far, it really was working. The focus groups and survey takers had summed her up as "knowledgeable, articulate, intelligent, and warm." And, as for her looks, well, nobody actually had the nerve to call her *plain*, at least not to her face. But they did confirm that her "average, everyday" look made people feel they could trust and identify with her. It was exactly what Chip said he wanted for her show's "home" themes.

"Hannah! Where have you been?" Her sister's exasperated voice finally came over the car phone's speaker. "I've been calling your apartment for twenty-four hours. Then I tried Greta at the studio office, and she said you were on your way to Rhode Island!"

"I *am* in Rhode Island, Holly, and just about there."

"I didn't have your company car's phone number. And I certainly didn't know you were leaving so soon! What about your show?"

"*Homemaking* is on hiatus for a month," said Hannah, continuing to steer with one hand while the other reached into the drive-thru bag for her burger. "We're finally moving to a network morning slot—"

"What!? Did you say *network*?"

"Yes."

"Oh, Hannah, that's fantastic!"

Hannah sighed uneasily. "Now's the chance for everyone to take a break before we start taping again. Till then I'll be working on a book."

"Another one—"

"Guess the theme?"

A short pause was all Holly needed. "Oh, no—"

"Yes!"

"You're going to do a *wedding* book, aren't you?"

"Why not? I'm about to live through a gala one I planned for you."

"God, Hannah, you never stop. I really worry about you. And when I couldn't reach you—"

"What time is it in Florence?" interrupted Hannah, taking a bite of her main course. "Morning?"

"Yes, it's after seven, which, by the way, means it's after one in the morning there. Hannah, *what* are you doing on the road alone?"

Hannah swallowed then yawned. "Holly, do you know what the *rates* on car-phone calls are? I do love you, but for the price of this call, I'd much rather be talking to 1-900-STUDLEY."

"You're the one who ordered me to always reverse charges—and *don't* try to change the subject, you should *not* be on the road so late, and all alone! You really worry me—"

"Don't start doing the mother routine, *I'm* the older sister here—"

"Come *on*!"

Hannah smiled. "And don't have a cow, I'm almost there."

"Why did you just take off like this, anyway? The wedding's not for another ten days. I thought you had a plane ticket for next week.''

"I did, but I called Maura Ryan last night. We talked so much that it brought back all these memories—'' Especially *one* particular memory, thought Hannah, a memory of Maura's eldest son. But, chickenheart that she was, Hannah couldn't even summon the nerve to ask how he was doing these days.

"Anyway," continued Hannah, "this little voice in my head just said, *Go, Hannah. Go now.*''

"That doesn't sound like you at all. You always plan everything down to the smallest detail—''

"Control, control, control, that's me.'' Hannah laughed, but it was hollow. Her own wedding had been the last spur-of-the-moment decision she'd ever made. Ever since, she'd decided that predictability was tantamount to bliss—after all, nothing could hurt you if you knew what was coming.

"I guess I just don't know what came over me,'' said Hannah with a little shrug. "I just decided to grab my laptop and go. Besides, what better place is there to begin work on a wedding book than at the site of my sister's upcoming nuptials?''

"Oh, Hannah, I am *so* happy you're doing this for me. Grandmother Edith never leaves her town house these days, and she's much too old to take on wedding plans.''

Hannah rolled her eyes at the mention of her grandmother, Edith Channing Williamson. From her well-upholstered throne on Boston's exclusive Beacon Hill, the grande dame of New England society had already cast her regal shadow over the wedding. Two months ago she'd faxed Hannah a twenty-page guest list of names that were a virtual who's who of the Yankee upper crust—Hannah wasn't even sure that Holly *knew* some of those people, though she was certain Grandmother Edith did.

"Holly, the truth is, I enjoyed doing this for you. And I've been looking forward to visiting Newport again, anyway— it's been so long—and I can use the R&R.''

"Seeing to the final arrangements for a gala wedding is not exactly R&R.''

"It is compared to what I've been doing for the last few years.''

"And you've done so much, Hannah, Mom and Dad would have been so proud of you . . ."

"Oh, I don't know. All I do is regurgitate their knowledge of art, antiques, and tastemaking, repackage it for the masses, then peddle it on television—"

"Stop running yourself down. I know you love what you're doing. You won an award doing it, for Heaven's sake. You're just being cynical again—"

Hannah sighed as she braked for a stop sign. It seemed pointless. There'd been no cars on this long stretch of road for miles. She listened to Holly berate her, but that seemed pointless, too. Hannah had been berating herself for the last few years.

"Okay, Holly, I admit they would have been proud of me," said Hannah with a small smile, "but I'll bet my hot glue gun *and* my garlic press that they would have been more proud of you—"

A quiet descended in the darkness of Hannah's car.

The two sisters knew that *parents* were supposed to be the ones to say things like "I'm so proud of you," and "Everything will be all right," and countless other banal-sounding sentiments.

Owing to a lethal wind shear at a Swiss airport, Lilian and Lawrence Whitmore were no longer around to convey such sentiments to their two daughters. And, during the last five years, Hannah finally discovered what children without parents heard instead of such sentiments.

Silence.

With deafening clarity they heard it. At Thanksgiving dinners and on Christmas mornings. At graduation ceremonies and Cable Ace Award banquets. And . . . at weddings.

Hannah could not bear for her sister to notice any such silence at her own wedding. So she vowed to distract her by putting together the kind of glorious picture-perfect occasion her little sister had been dreaming of all her dreamy life.

"Well, call me this weekend and tell me how things are going," said Holly finally. "My exams will be over next week, and then Reggie and I can fly to the States."

"I know, Hol." Hannah's only recurring prayer was that "Reggie" was good enough for her sister.

"Will you be okay tonight?"

"Of course," assured Hannah, "I'm almost home."

"Home?"

Hannah shook her head. "I mean at the *hotel*."

By rights, Hannah had once called Château du Coeur home. Long before every major bridal magazine in the country had ranked the place "*the* most romantic spot in America for a wedding," the spectacular seaside mansion had been the private summer home of Hannah's late parents.

"Okay, Hannah," said Holly. "Call me if you have any problems."

"I will," said Hannah, "but I still wish you'd given me some idea of your expectations for this wedding—"

"Forget it," she reiterated for the tenth time. "To second-guess the newest tastemaker for America's middle class would be sheer folly."

Hannah smiled. "How do you know I won't serve Burger World fries and shakes?"

"Be my guest," challenged Holly. "In fact, I *dare* you—"

"Well, maybe just steak tartare and pomme frites," Hannah quipped as she made a sharp turn on the dark road and lightly tapped the Mercedes' power brakes. "Gotta go, cutie."

"Okay, love you, Han. *Ciao*."

"Love you, too, Hol. See you next week." With a yawn, Hannah pushed the button to disconnect.

Chapter Two

The twisting roads were darker now as Hannah neared the Atlantic Ocean. The buildings were fewer and farther between until finally only the occasional turnoff appeared, where long private drives eventually led to elegant mansions with exclusive beaches, stables, and tennis courts. But Hannah never paused once. She continued her course, right, then left, then right . . .

Funny how you never forget the way home.

Hmm, thought Hannah, there was that word again where it shouldn't be. *Home.*

It had been ten years since she'd been back to this house. And yet, something inside Hannah remembered. Her arms turned the steering wheel so certainly that it almost felt as if an invisible force were guiding her movements.

But Hannah knew it was simply the phantoms.

Phantoms of memory. Ghosts of recollection. Whatever you called them, they were the reason she'd been able to dredge up a sense of dead reckoning—long buried perhaps but in reality far from truly dead.

Yawning again, Hannah recognized the turn ahead even

before she saw the tasteful sign reading *Château du Coeur*. With a relaxed motion, she turned into the long, ground-lit drive, barely slowing. And then abruptly she slammed her foot down on the power brakes.

She felt her body lurch forward, restrained instantly by the shoulder harness. The Burger World bag didn't fare nearly as well and landed hard on the car floor.

Hannah took a calming breath, hardly believing she'd nearly crashed the company Mercedes into a small brick booth beside a pair of closed gates.

Where the heck did this come from?!

When the Whitmore family had lived in this Newport mansion, the tall wrought-iron gates had been ornamental only—and they'd *always* stood open. The gatehouse was definitely a new addition.

Uneasily, Hannah noticed the blond, blue-eyed security guard sitting inside that very gatehouse. He was staring unhappily at her, quite understandable since she'd almost tattooed him with the Mercedes' front grille.

After a moment's pause she hit the button on the car's armrest and the window descended.

"Name?" asked the young guard in a clipped militaristic tone.

Sir, yes, sir, she almost replied, but chewed her lip instead. The guy didn't look like the jocular type. Plus, he was wearing a side arm.

Hannah tried not to squirm as his sharp eyes inspected her and the vehicle as if he were a Cold War border guard reviewing her credentials. She got the distinct impression that he had the ability to memorize every detail at a glance.

"Mrs. Hannah Whitmore Peabody."

The guard nodded efficiently and turned to a small computer console in his booth. As he punched in her name, Hannah noticed security cameras just behind the locked gates.

Those were new additions, too.

"Thank you, ma'am," said the guard, and in the next instant the tall wrought-iron gates were swinging silently open. "If you'll drive up to the front, I'll ring for a valet to meet your—"

"No," said Hannah. "Please don't bother. I'll park in the hidden lot and have my bags dealt with tomorrow."

"If that is your wish."

"Thanks, it is."

"Very well then, pleasant night."

Hannah returned the guard's nod and guided the Mercedes through the gates and up the long drive. She knew the turnoff that would allow her to park the car in a lot, discreetly hidden by a trimmed line of tall topiary in the subtle shape of hearts.

She shut off the ignition, opened the car door, and then gasped at the sight before her. The dome light had illuminated her face in the rearview mirror. *Ghastly.*

At times, traveling could be hell. It had certainly taken its demonic toll on her appearance tonight. Behind round wire-rimmed glasses, her usually luminous gray eyes—her one attractive feature in her estimation—were shot with scarlet lightning. Her long dark blond hair was a tangled mess, barely tamed into its usual conservative bun, and the little bit of makeup she'd bothered to put on this morning was long gone, leaving a greasy mess that could only be compared to an Exxon tanker oil spill—those French fries certainly hadn't helped, either.

To top it off, her tailored gray pantsuit was a rumpled disaster, displaying stains from every course of her less-than-gourmet dinner.

Thank God it *was* one in the morning, thought Hannah. Nobody to scare but this obviously crack security staff—and by rights, they were being paid *not* to be squeamish. So what did she have to worry about anyway?

After grabbing her tan leather briefcase and cellular phone, she slammed the car door and retrieved one of the smaller bags from her trunk. It wasn't until she began walking toward the seventy-room Newport "cottage"—transformed six years ago into a luxury hotel renowned for its spectacular society weddings—that she found her usually brisk steps slowing to a standstill.

"My Heaven," she breathed as the remaining bit of air slipped from her lungs. "My . . . Heaven . . ."

Lit as elegantly as ever with hidden ground lights, the white marble gleamed in the night like a Narragansett Bay beacon to a world-weary sailor. The two wings jutted out now like welcoming arms.

It was *exactly* as she remembered.

Hannah's lips tilted with astonishment as her eyes sparkled in the darkness; perhaps a reflection of the mansion's grandly romantic luster, or perhaps the glistening sheen of unshed tears. Either way, Hannah hadn't been prepared—not one bit—for the emotional impact.

"Château du Coeur," she whispered. "You're still a stunner."

With her elegant alabaster balconies, paired Ionic columns, and crystal chandeliers winking through arched French doors, this "House of the Heart" had been patterned after Rosecliff, a grand Newport "cottage" designed by Stanford White. Like that wondrous mansion, this Beaux Arts beauty was a monument to romantic dreams.

Hannah was certain that over its century of existence, Château du Coeur had inspired countless such dreams in every young girl who'd ever looked at it. She herself had been susceptible, although her own romantic dreams had involved only one young man.

"Neil."

The name felt creaky on her lips, like the rusted hinge on a jewelry box opened after years in an attic. Hannah knew that a dozen questions had been rattling around inside for years, like where was he these days? And what was he doing? Was he happily married? He had to be. A man as handsome and intelligent as Cornelius Patrick Ryan would never have his marriage fail after only one disastrous year—like her's.

On the phone last night, Hannah *could* have asked Maura Ryan all about her eldest son. But what was the point, really? The man was long gone from her life—and this place. Dusting off that particular antique was certainly a waste of time. Instead, she concentrated on the sight before her. The structure that the family's financial advisor had once called "a white elephant" now gleamed like an ivory palace.

God, she'd never before realized how much she missed this place. This *home*. And that's how she thought of it, too. Much more than the various blur of hotel suites her high-powered art dealer parents had moved into and out of, or the European rentals they'd taken. Château du Coeur had been the one consistent home in her life—every summer through her childhood, then later in her teen years, when she attended all-girl boarding schools during the rest of the year.

It wasn't until she'd gone away to college in Chicago that her parents had finally decided to relocate permanently to Europe and give up their summer home, selling it for very little money to some very worthy buyers.

The household staff had come to her parents under the leadership of the beloved head housekeeper. It was Maura Ryan's idea to have the staff pool their life savings and turn the place into an exclusive seaside hotel.

There were other offers for the mansion, some for more money, but Hannah's parents had gone with their *heart* for their "House of the Heart." They'd placed Château du Coeur, a home they'd loved, into the hands of people who loved her, too, and saw a wonderful useful future for her.

Hannah loved and admired her parents for that—and so many other wonderfully generous things they'd done. She closed her eyes for a moment and a part of her pretended the place truly *was* welcoming her home now. Even after ten long, difficult years. Even after her parents' untimely deaths.

For a moment, she believed that her mother and father were still inside, waiting to wrap their arms around her and tell her to hurry and dress for the party. Because at this place—like no other—there were always parties, with a corps of caterers and an army of fashionable crowds.

Standing here on the front lawn, in the chilly night air, her eyes closed, Hannah could almost hear the music.

"Wait a second—?" she murmured. "I *do* hear music."

Slowly, Hannah opened her tired eyes. And then she gasped. In no more than a few startling moments, she saw a strange tableau across the grounds: crowds of arriving guests, all in 1920s styles, just as they'd been every year at her mother's annual summer Jazz Age party. Pastel-colored dropwaists with long, swinging pearls; headbands and feathers on bobbed hair.

Hannah's hand flew to cover her mouth. She suddenly felt dizzy. A line of antique cars, five deep in the drive, had abruptly appeared. And *music*. She heard a band's lively strains clear as a bell, playing a sentimental old ballad.

"A dreamer can awaken to a Heaven on the Earth . . ."

And then it was gone. All of it. Except the song, which echoed hauntingly through the elms and oaks that lined the grounds, then vanished into the night's darkness like a fleeting wisp of sentimental smoke.

"It can't be . . . I must be . . . tired," murmured Hannah, stumbling back a step.

She took a deep breath, trying to keep herself steady. The emotional impact of coming back here after so many years was obviously taking its toll. She rubbed her eyes for a long minute, then started again to cross the mansion's front lawn.

"I need to rest . . . that's all."

After climbing the mansion's steps, she was relieved to find the heavy double doors unlocked. Quietly she walked into the small entryway that led directly into the grand main hall of blushing marble.

With a ceiling that reached three stories high, the vast room had been cleverly converted into a lobby, with colorful Persian rugs and potted palms nicely defining comfortable seating areas.

At the far end, Hannah noticed a new feature—an elegant rosewood and mahogany bar. It had been set up near the mansion's Gothic-style hearth, an immense white Caen stone fireplace whose mantle had been carved with scenes of an errant knight's travels.

The room was still flanked romantically by a double set of steps that descended from opposite directions into Hannah's absolutely favorite feature in the entire mansion—the heart-shaped stair. The draping moldings above provided an elegantly subtle creasing effect, which formed the top of the heart. The bottom was completed as the two staircases angled together from opposite directions. They flowed like tributaries into the final single river of long, red-carpeted steps, leading down to the vast marble floor.

Opposite this grand stairway was a wall of paneled glass doors that provided an unencumbered view of the ocean. In warm weather the panels could be folded back to allow the outdoors in.

It was a stunning room in a stunning palace of a place. Hannah stood there alone, gazing about, letting memories assail her from her youth, especially her coming-out party.

"What a disaster that was . . ." murmured Hannah, shaking her head at the memory. Her grandmother Edith had insisted Hannah take part in the silly society ritual along with two dozen other seventeen-year-old girls who were connected to one of Edith's exclusive Newport "summering" clubs.

"Miss Hannah Daisy Whitmore, escorted by her father. . . ." Hannah could still hear the announcement. Then she'd proceeded to trip somehow. Her father's arm had held her up a moment, but she'd tumbled down the mansion's grand heart-shaped stairway anyway, her white gown billowing like a runaway meringue.

Yes. It was true. To the astonished faces of everyone who was anyone in Newport, Hannah Daisy Whitmore had made her societal debut by landing directly on her pedigreed butt.

Her mother had accused her of falling on purpose so she could claim a sore ankle, then sit out the rest of the party in her room. Maybe a part of her *had* done it on purpose, though she still swore it was simply a bizarre accident. But she *had* hated the whole idea of her "debut."

What Hannah had truly preferred was reading in her own room until precisely midnight, when she'd slipped away and found Neil Ryan, son of the hired help, just where he'd said he'd be in his note to her—behind her mansion, on Newport's famed Cliff Walk.

The two-mile path along the rocky cliffs of the Atlantic caressed some of the most ostentatious backyards in America—from the Astors's charming Beechwood to the Vanderbilts's majestic Breakers. They were the mansions that had made Newport a playground for the 1890s filthy rich—and the 1990s curiosity seekers. Halls that once heard the footsteps of railroad magnates and tobacco barons now heard the echoing voices of tour guides and sightseers.

Hannah had been all too happy to meet Neil on that famous Walk. She'd already developed quite a crush on him over the previous few summers. He'd just turned twenty that week, and he'd been working as a waiter at the party when he saw Hannah fall. Neil knew she'd left the party before the dancing, so he decided to make it up to her at midnight by taking her in his own arms and swaying with her in a splash of moonlight, to the music of the ocean waves.

Every particle of her being had been happy in that moment. But their little bit of paradise hadn't lasted.

Hannah blinked her eyes and shook her head clear. It was much too late to start daydreaming about yesteryear. She was sure to start seeing and hearing things again if she did.

She looked around once more and noticed a Louis XVI–style desk tucked away in a corner near a door that led to an anteroom. A phone and leather ledger sat on the desk next to a gold pen, and she realized this was, for all intents and purposes, the registration desk.

She could see through the partially open door of the anteroom that it held the modern necessities of a functioning hotel—computers, safe, copy machines, fax. It was very clever floor planning on the part of the staff. But then again, where *was* the staff? Surely at least one person would be left to look after late-arriving guests?

Her head turned at a noise from across the empty hall. It was a voice just outside. She noticed shadowy forms by the large alabaster cupid fountain, just off the back patio.

Hannah stepped toward them and then stopped.

Something about one of those forms felt familiar. Disturbingly familiar.

Chapter Three

"Miss, would you mind getting down from that fountain?"

The request was made calmly, with total and complete self-control.

It didn't matter that Cornelius Patrick Ryan had been making such *requests* for the last three days. It didn't matter that it was well after one in the morning in a Rhode Island April and the wind was whipping off the Atlantic like a slave driver's lash.

All that mattered to Cornelius—or rather "Neil" as he'd preferred to be called ever since he was old enough to discern syllables—was that he did his job, and did it well. And at present his job was to prevent Miss Tiffany Ashton Townsend, a former Junior Miss semifinalist and current heir to the throne of Townsend Real Estate—"Your Neighbor, Your Realtor, Your Friend"—from falling off the hotel's cupid fountain and landing herself a whopping lawsuit against his boss.

"I don't want to get down! I love it up here! Weeeeee!"

Drunk. Drunk as a skunk. Neil never should have left the military police. Never in a million years. He glanced up at the stars and considered the idea of a million years. How far could he travel at the speed of light?

25

"He's such a party pooper, isn't he, Cark, honey?"

"Cark-honey"—or more precisely, Master *Clark* Von Devon, of the Greenwich Von Devons—was blacked out at the base of the dry fountain on an evening's worth of potato martinis, the latest New York trend imported to the hotel's own martini and cigar bar.

Miss Tiffany hadn't drunk hers so steadily. As far as Neil could gather, she'd alternated them with cordials and diet colas, which was why she'd even been capable of climbing up fifteen feet to hang on the alabaster cherub with the upraised bow.

"I'm going to count to three . . ." threatened Neil. Not that counting had worked with her before—he had tried counting to ten two days ago when he'd found her luring five yacht-club preppies to her room for a game of strip poker. And then last night after catching her locked in her Jaguar with two giggling cousins and a bottle of bourbon, insisting that he reattach the distributor wire so they could drive drunk to the Newport bars.

"Corny, honey, don't get all *parental* on me—"

"One . . . don't call me 'Corny.' "

"—besides, Daddy always lets me do what I want and—"

"Two . . . your 'daddy' hired me to look after you."

"—you're not even my father. You're just a stupid hotel security gua—"

Three didn't even make it out of Neil's mouth. He figured the effect on the girl was subliminal. Somewhere in spoiled Miss Tiffany's dizzy twenty-one-year-old brain was the recognition of authority—and the inevitable realization that somehow, someday, she would have to grow up. That alone was enough to give that prettily pickled prima donna a brain blackout.

As she dropped through the brisk night air, Neil considered, for a split second, letting the girl get what she probably deserved—and he'd inevitably endured—a few of the bruises life had to offer the average person.

Of course, Miss Tiffany, like so many of the wealthy people he'd grown up around, did not think of herself as an "average" anything.

No. Far from it. Money was an interesting elixir. It made

life easy for these people—and eventually, for the less en-
lightened of that class, gave them the mistaken notion that
they were being treated with deference and flattery not because of the overabundance of green bills stuffed into their
fat bank accounts but because they were somehow "special"
people, deserving of respect and admiration by birthright.

Wisdom, discipline, courage, ingenuity . . . such virtues
might or might not earn you a moment's civility in their
world; it usually depended on your family's name, or your
bank account.

Tiffany had clearly been a party to the good life from the
beginning of her life, and the cushions it provided. Case in
point: Vincent Townsend's blank check. It was an insurance
note against any damage his careless daughter might cause at
her favorite hotel during her cousin's wedding festivities this
weekend.

"Mr. Ryan, keep Mr. Townsend's daughter out of trouble—
and out of the papers," Townsend's attorney had requested,
"and you may keep this substantial bodyguarding bonus."

Bodyguarding, hell. This was baby-sitting. Plain and simple. But he'd made a promise. It was a promise not only to
Townsend but to his own boss. And she expected Château du
Coeur to be a haven for its guests, a place where privacy
would be upheld at all costs.

So, owing to that sense of duty, the better part of Neil
stretched out his weight-trained arms and made a catch that
would do a Red Sox outfielder proud. He knew in an instant
that he—and not this shell of bombed blonde—would be the
one to carry the next morning's aches. Miss Tiffany would
never thank him. Even if she did know what happened, she'd
barely trouble herself.

Cornelius Patrick Ryan may have guarded presidents and
princes in his day, but tonight he had no delusions that he
was on protection detail. Tonight he was merely another
"cushion" for the wealthy.

"Hey, Neil, I see you caught yourself a debutante. Maybe
we should wake up Chef Antonio and have her filleted for
tomorrow's wedding banquet?"

Neil turned to find his younger brother standing by the patio
doors and wiping his hands on a bar towel. Though they only
shared one parent—their mother, Maura—twenty-three-year-

old J. J. Ryan was a near carbon copy of Neil. Seven years apart, the brothers each had lantern-square jaws; tall, solid builds; and hair as dark as the midnight sea.

But where J. J. had green eyes and an easy smile with dimples betraying Irish mischief, his thirty-year-old half brother had a stare as hard as blue steel and an attitude to match.

Somewhere inside him, Neil recalled a time when he could stare into a mirror and see that very same ready smile and quick-witted mischief. But too many rough years had chipped away at his countenance until, like the cold, rigid guardian of this stone fountain, he was left with only the hard edges.

"J. J., do me a favor," said Neil as he carried Miss Tiffany across the marble patio, her red silk dress fluttering in the wind, "and help Master Von Pickled up to his room."

"Sure."

"And be quiet about it. The hotel's nearly full for the Townsend/Sumner wedding."

J. J. smiled as he made his way onto the chilly lawn and wrestled Clark from his blacked-out bed at the foot of the dry fountain. It wasn't hard. Both Ryans had been high school wrestling stars, brown belts in tae kwon do, and disciplined enough weight-trainers to fireman-carry the heftiest drunken preppies that the finest New England colleges had to offer.

"C'mon, Master Trashed," muttered J. J. "Time for beddie-bye."

With a dull thud, Hannah's small bag and tan briefcase hit the hotel lobby's marble floor. She felt strangely numb as she watched a familiar-looking, raven-haired form walk through the glass patio doors with something red in his arms.

"Oh, my God . . ." she breathed. *"Neil?"*

He didn't see her at first. He was tired, and frustrated, and wanted to get Miss Tiffany Townsend to her bedroom—and out of his arms *and* hair—as soon as humanly possible. But when the familiar voice finally registered and Neil looked up, he could barely believe his eyes.

"Hannah . . . Hannah Whitmore?"

She nodded, suffering through a few silent seconds until her stunned voice box could provide her with some other response. Neil Patrick Ryan wasn't off in the U.S. Army as she'd expected. He wasn't carrying out his duties on some foreign soil. He was here. *Now.*

Wearing a beautifully tailored blue suit, and apparently carrying a pretty woman off to bed. A very *young* pretty woman—not to mention unconscious.

Neil stared at Hannah, then he blinked and shifted a bit—because Miss Tiffany wasn't as light as she looked. "You got married," he blurted without thinking.

"I did—"

They both turned at the sound of a low singing. "Oh, what do ya do with a drunkin' sailor? What do ya do with a drunkin' sailor? What do ya do with a drunkin' sailor, early in the—"

"John James?" blurted Hannah to the younger version of Neil.

J. J. stared at the rumpled businesswoman standing in the middle of the grand hotel's main hall. Dressed more casually than his older brother, he wore a simple pair of navy dress slacks and a button-down shirt with sleeves rolled to the elbows. And he seemed to have an unconscious young man draped over his shoulders and back.

"Uh . . . guilty," he said. "But call me J. J."

"You don't recognize me, do you?" she asked.

Like his brother, J. J. shifted. "Should I?"

"It's Hannah," said Neil stiffly.

"Hannah?" J. J.'s green eyes searched her face. "You mean *Homemaking* Hannah on television? You know, you do look like that woman—"

"Don't be dense, J. J.," said Neil, his cool blue eyes remaining fixed on Hannah. "She *is* that woman—"

"Hey, you are!" exclaimed J. J. "Then you're the one who used to live here with your family, right? You're Hannah Whitmore—"

"*Mrs.* Hannah Whitmore *Peabody*," Neil corrected sharply. "Herbert married you, didn't he?"

And left me. Hannah didn't say it. Couldn't. Not while a grown-up Neil Ryan was holding what looked to be a beautiful piece of jailbait in his arms. *Control, control, control . . .*

"Neil," she quickly said, trying not to consider how well he'd matured, how ruggedly attractive he'd become since his late teens. "I can see you have your hands full . . . ah, rather literally—"

Suddenly, this entire scene struck Hannah as ludicrously embarrassing. Absurdly awful. The effect was a slight trembling in her voice that sounded like giggling. She took a deep breath, trying hard to keep her weary bewilderment from transforming into giddiness. She wasn't entirely successful.

"—so . . . ah . . . don't let me . . . hold you up—" *Even though you're obviously holding up that young woman well enough,* Hannah's caustic sense of irony added silently.

She's laughing at me. Neil swallowed uneasily as he felt a slow boiling anger enter his bloodstream. That wasn't like him. He never lost his cool when it came to his job—or women. *I don't need this.*

"Excuse me," he said shortly. "I'll be back to see that you're checked in." Then he turned on his heel and headed for the small guest elevator secluded behind an ornate grille in a corner of the room.

J. J. followed and the brothers were soon ascending up in the slow-moving box. "Did you know she was coming?" J. J. asked Neil.

"No."

"Boss didn't tell you?"

"No," snapped Neil. "Ma didn't tell me."

"I see." J. J. usually knew when to shut up. And yet, his mischievous Irish blood—and little-brother sense of goading— just couldn't stay quiet when it came to his older brother. "Wasn't there something between you two?"

"Zip it, J. J."

"I mean, that was over ten years ago, when you were still working for the Whitmores, and I was pretty young, but I seem to remember that you two—"

Neil's blue eyes blew an icy blast his brother's way. So J. J. finally zipped it and turned instead back to his favorite tune of the night. "Oh, what do ya do with a drunkin' sailor, early in the mornin' . . ."

The elevator doors opened on the second floor and Neil advised his brother to stop with the lullaby to the drunken Von Devon.

"You'll wake the other guests."

"Yeah, Bro. Sure thing. I'll cork it."

"And after you put the guy down, take the back stairs to the kitchen and make sure Antonio's staff has locked the back securely for the night."

"Check, Captain."

As J. J. headed toward Clark's room, Neil rode the elevator up one more flight, then carried Miss Tiffany to hers. At the carved white door of room 307, he gently set the girl down and reached into the breast pocket of his suit jacket, brushing the cold steel of his .38 as he retrieved a master passkey. He opened the door, reached down, and once again lifted the girl into his arms.

"Mmmm, nice and strong," she murmured, cuddling up to Neil. It immediately set him on edge.

The room was dimly lit by a small table lamp at the far end. He carried her over to the large queen-size bed and gently laid her down. He almost sighed in relief as he finally released her. He couldn't wait to get out of here. On the other hand, he didn't relish going back downstairs, back to *Mrs.* Hannah Whitmore Peabody.

Hannah was obviously disheveled from her long drive, but the disarray somehow made her all the more . . . touchable. Those big, luminous gray eyes, hidden behind a pair of trendy wire-rimmed glasses, were still bright with intelligence and humor. That generous, slightly smirking mouth still looked as if it was always on the verge of a quick-witted remark.

Neil sighed, for the first time contemplating the origin of the term "old flame." Even after ten years, a little pilot light leapt somewhere inside him. He'd never before realized it had been burning in there. Not until he'd seen her again. *She's plain,* he said harshly to himself, *and she's married.*

It wasn't surprising to Neil that the second thought influenced him a thousand times more than the first. Looks were never what had attracted Neil to Hannah. But it didn't matter either way. He wasn't about to give any notions toward the woman a chance in hell.

Sure, he was tired and, lately, sexually frustrated, but a good dousing of ice-cold water would likely do the trick to cure his sudden nostalgic feelings. He'd take care of it just as soon as he left the princess of prime mortgages here. . . .

Neil quickly set Tiffany down on the bed and began to straighten up. That was when he realized the girl was coming

up with him. She'd wrapped her arms around his neck and
wasn't letting go.

"Mmmm don't leave, Corny honey," she whispered. Then,
before he knew what was happening, she was pressing her
imported French lipstick against his neck.

Neil now wondered just how "unconscious" the girl had
been all along. As gently as he could, he tried to coax her
arms from him. But the girl seemed to have a grip as strong
as an anaconda.

"Ssssssstay with me tonight," slurred her woozy voice.
"C'mon, guard . . . here's my body . . . do what you do
best . . ."

"Uh, no, Miss Townsend," said Neil simply. "Just get
some rest."

"No?" she asked, clearly not believing her emerald-
studded ears.

"No," returned Neil patiently.

The anger came fast and harsh to Miss Tiffany's blue eyes,
and Neil recalled the lash of the Atlantic just ten minutes ago.

"You *can't* mean that," she barked. "*You* re-re-rejecting
me?"

"It happens."

"And—and—after what my daddy's *paying* you!"

This time, Neil's grip wasn't so gentle as he pulled at her
arms and in a second he was stepping back and turning for
the door.

"Sleep it off, Miss Townsend. Good night," he stated
evenly as he opened the door and closed it behind him.

He'd barely heard the click of the automatic lock when a
harsh *thump* sounded against the door's thick wood a moment
later. Neil deduced, by the height of the sound, that she'd
hurled a small object straight for his head. And, by the tone
of the thud, he presumed it was one of her expensive designer
pumps.

Hardly a mystery to be solved by Holmes, Marlowe, or
much closer to home, Dan and Daisy Doyle. It didn't matter
much, thought Neil, a small smile cracking the hard planes
of his perpetually stony expression. Whatever Miss Townsend
decided to throw, these hotel walls were thick, so they'd easily cushion the other exclusive guests from being disturbed
by her rantings.

And, if the "woman spurned" decided to start venting her rage with objects more breakable than her shoes, then at least Vincent Townsend had left that blank check to cushion the cost.

Chapter
Four

You are a grown woman. Get hold of yourself.

Hannah stood in the vast, deserted lobby, feeling a little more than stunned, a little less than faint.

Neil Ryan.

The man was here. Now. And in another few minutes he'd be back. "My God," she whispered. "After all these years, and I look like a refugee from hurricane season."

Hannah resisted the urge to tear open her handbag and put her face together. She'd never put on a show for Neil before. She certainly wasn't going to start now. And yet . . . *God, how could he still look so good? The man looked better at thirty than he had at twenty.*

But then the years were always better on men than women, thought Hannah with a sigh. A law of cruel nature—a stinking unfair one, too. She'd love to do a show on that topic when *Homemaking* went back into production.

"Sure," she murmured. "I'll call it 'How an Evening by Candlelight Can Hide Your Wrinkles.' Or maybe 'The Forgotten Romance of Hats with Veils.' "

Hannah rubbed her arms. A sharp coldness was suddenly

upon her. Strangely, though, the mansion itself was cozy and comfortable, not drafty in the least. The chill she felt seemed to be coming from right next to her skin, as if needle-thin shards of ice were rushing through her flesh.

Maybe I'm imagining it, thought Hannah. After all, the sound of the ocean's winds were really kicking up outside. And seeing Neil in this mansion again after all this time had stretched her nerves more than a tad tightly.

Hannah walked toward the immense white stone fireplace near the rosewood-and-mahogany bar. A nice fire was still blazing in the hearth, and a cozy, velvet love seat looked inviting. As she sat down near the crackling flames, reacquainting herself with the Gothic-style carvings of knights-errant in the tall mantle, she was sure she'd warm up again. And yet, Hannah continued to feel the harsh cold needles running through her.

She continued to rub her arms, but her skin was now freezing and the fine hairs on the back of her neck were standing on end. There was definitely something odd in the air. She closed her eyes a moment, feeling very tired, and that was when she heard it . . . the song. That same tinny Jazz Age ballad she'd heard out on the lawn.

"A dreamer can awaken to a Heaven on the Earth . . ."

Her eyes opened and her head throbbed at the strange echo. It was coming from across the room and behind the closed double doors that led to the mansion's ballroom.

Slowly she rose from her seat and walked, none too steadily, toward the doors. She heard a band suddenly strike up, the laughing noises of a big party. It did not make sense in an empty hotel, at two in the morning, when the only sounds present a moment before had been the outside ocean winds and the crackling flames of the fireplace.

As she neared the doors, she realized something else odd. She recalled the strange vision she'd seen out on the lawn. She'd assumed it had been a hallucination from her memories—one of her mother's theme parties coming back to haunt her.

But it couldn't have been from her memories, she realized now. *The cars.* None had been modern. *Every* one had been antiques, relics of the 1920s, yet all appeared brand-new.

Hannah's palms were damp as she reached for the handles

of the ballroom doors. She swallowed nervously, then gathered her courage, took a deep breath, and pulled.

Locked.

The doors wouldn't budge, yet she could still hear the party . . . and especially the haunting melody of a male singer.

"A dreamer can awaken to a Heaven on the Earth . . ."

She put her ear to the door and closed her eyes, trying to recognize voices or names. *". . . when the heart is finally taken by a love that knows its worth . . ."*

But, after a brief few seconds, the sounds of the party faded. The band's tinny music seemed to ascend upward through the vast lobby in a strangely ethereal cloud—like a residue from ages long over, a hollow echo from the mansion's past.

"It's gone . . ." whispered Hannah, confused.

"What's gone?"

The male voice so close to her ear made Hannah jump, a small shout bursting from her throat. Behind her wire-rimmed glasses, her gray eyes blinked open to find Neil Ryan's handsomely weathered face inches from hers.

"God, Neil, you're as quiet as a cat burglar."

"Sorry."

Hannah let out a shaky breath. "Did you hear it?" she asked, her expression a little wild-looking.

"Hear *what*?"

"The music."

Neil's cool blue gaze studied Hannah somberly for a long moment.

"The music!" she said again.

Slowly, he shook his head. "I don't know what—"

"Behind these doors." Agitated, Hannah pulled at the doors again.

"The ballroom is locked for the night."

"Can you open them, please?" Hannah begged.

"Why?"

"Please!"

Neil surveyed Hannah's tense expression. After a moment, he nodded. He reached into his pocket for the master passkey and unlocked the ballroom's dead bolt with a loud click. Then he stepped back and stared at Hannah as she stared at the closed doors.

"Well?" he asked.

"I heard music."

"The Townsend/Sumner wedding is scheduled for tomorrow evening," he said carefully. "No one's used the ballroom tonight."

Hannah took a deep breath and pushed at the doors. They gave way to a dark room. A dark, *empty* room.

She gasped when her eye caught an orange-red glimmer in the black room. The light flickered brightly off of one of the three great crystal chandeliers. But she realized an instant later that it was only a reflection from the dancing fireplace flames across the lobby.

"Do you feel all right, Mrs. Peabody?"

"Yes," said Hannah shortly. She closed her eyes, then turned and left the doorway. Neil closed the double doors and locked them securely again. When he turned, he found her standing a few feet away, staring at him with her arms crossed.

"I heard the music," she insisted.

"You must be tired, Mrs. Peabody."

Hannah sighed in frustration. "Neil, please don't call me that."

"What?"

"Mrs. Peabody."

"It's your name."

"Hannah's my name."

"Are you sure you're all right?" he asked again.

"Yes, I'm fine . . . just tired from the drive."

She waited for some kind of personal question. *How've you been? What brings you here after all this time?* She had already surmised, by the shock on his face when he first saw her, that his mother hadn't told him a thing about Holly's wedding, or her coming.

"If you're tired, then I should see you to your room. Just give me a moment to arrange things. Our night clerk went off duty unexpectedly. I haven't called in a replacement yet, so I'll take care of you for the moment."

"I see."

Neil crossed the room swiftly, trying to keep as much emotional distance as possible from the woman two steps behind him. He passed the Louis XVI reservation desk and disappeared into the anteroom office as she signed her name on the old-fashioned ledger.

When he came out again, he'd confirmed the reservation on the computer system. It had been entered and initialed by his mother. She'd reserved one of the most beautiful suites in the place, the Daisy Channing Doyle Suite, named after a former mistress of the mansion who'd married a Pinkerton detective then teamed up with him to open their own agency.

Dan and Daisy Doyle had become a legendary sleuthing team of the thirties and forties and had gone on to write some well-loved detective novels based on their cases. As legend had it, even after their deaths, the duo had been spotted around Newport and Providence, supposedly still sleuthing together even beyond the grave.

Neil knew their story well—as did everyone who worked on staff at the mansion. It was one of the "quaint" romantic tales that drew people to the exclusive hotel, and Maura Ryan insisted all of her employees memorize it well.

Looking at the glowing computer screen, Neil could see that his mother had clearly marked *No charge* on the reservation. *All services complimentary.* Technically, then, there was no need for Neil to run a credit-card check on Hannah; after all, she was well-known here. But something needled him into going by the book with her.

"May I have a credit card?" asked Neil after stepping out of the anteroom office.

Hannah fished in her purse and handed over the plastic rectangle. Neil was surprised to see the less than exclusive brand of card. It was the kind a typical Jane Doe might carry, not a daughter of wealth and privilege.

He ran the card through their system and was even more surprised to see that her credit limit was a dismal fraction of their average guest. It didn't make sense, and he wanted to question her about it, but he knew it would be crossing a line that he was trying to draw between them.

He presented the receipt for her to sign, assuring coverage of charges up to her card's paltry limit. Hannah said nothing, even though Maura had technically comped all of Hannah's charges anyway. Oddly, Neil was surprised—even a little disappointed—that she didn't pitch a fit about this.

"All checked in?" asked Hannah, trying to sound bright

and friendly when he returned from the office again.

Neil nodded silently, his brow betraying a crease of tension as he closed the office door behind him, then handed Hannah back her credit card.

"Are the rest of your bags in your car?" he asked, walking toward the small leather bag she'd left on the floor.

"Yes, but I won't need them tonight."

"Fine," he said, picking up the bag and her briefcase. "This way."

They rode the small elevator in silence. Then suddenly Neil spoke up. "Mrs. Peabody, if you leave me your car keys, I'll have a valet bring the rest of your bags in first thing in the morning. Just ring the desk as soon as you'd like them brought to your room."

Hannah nodded stiffly, her heart heavier than ever. It hurt her that Neil was so coldly demarcating boundaries.

So much for a warm welcome home.

She fished the car keys from her handbag, dismayed that she'd held out any hope of rekindling their friendship. But then why should she? Neil Patrick Ryan had been the one who'd lost interest in her all those years ago. *He'd* been the one to break it off.

Grasping the cold metal of the keys, Hannah pulled them free of her bag and held them out to Neil. His rough hands touched hers lightly as he took the car keys from her, and she was *sure* she'd noticed a slight break in his steely expression. The ice blue gaze had actually *looked* at her for the first time, and she was certain she'd noticed a glimmer of something . . . could it be a *feeling*?

As the elevator door slid open on the third floor, Hannah's eyebrows arched. Maybe, just maybe, there was a human being inside this stone carving of a man after all.

Chapter
Five

"Mmmm. It smells beautiful up here." A subtle floral scent enveloped Hannah as she followed Neil Ryan down the long carpeted hallway of the mansion's third floor. Every few yards, they passed a highly polished antique stand holding an exquisitely cut crystal vase filled with colorful blossoms.

"The staff checks the flowers for freshness every morning," Neil said briskly. "Maura sees to it."

"Yes," said Hannah absently. "She always did."

A small, unhappy grunt from Neil made Hannah puzzle for a moment, wondering if she'd said something wrong. Then, as she passed a particularly stunning arrangement of orchids, lilies, blue salvia, and baby's breath, she stopped.

That odd chill—the one she'd experienced in the lobby— was back. Cold sharp needles pricked at her arms and neck. And she felt something else this time. Very strongly—

"What's wrong?" Neil was ten feet beyond Hannah when he realized she was no longer following him. She'd stopped dead in the middle of the mansion's long hallway.

"Mrs. Peabody?"

"Neil, do you feel—"

"What?"

Hannah swallowed. Her tired gray eyes searched Neil's lantern-jawed face, his steel blue gaze holding anything but warmth.

"Nothing," she breathed after a moment. Her legs resumed their stiff motion forward and Neil followed.

"He'll think I'm cracking up," Hannah murmured to herself. "First hearing music in an empty ballroom and then feeling as though someone is watching us . . ."

"Did you say something, Mrs. Peabody?"

"No. Nothing . . ."

Neil stayed silent as he continued along, but not all entities present in the hallway remained that way. In the elegant sea air of Château du Coeur, on a plane invisible to the frailties of human vision, there existed an incarnate residue of energy.

Living humans sometimes called such manifestations *spirits, ghosts,* or *apparitions.* But those perfunctory labels were of no use to these particular entities. They simply called each other by the same names they'd used during their long, happy life together in this seaside mansion.

"Oh, Dan, she came!"

"Who came?"

"Hannah. The girl who used to live here during the summers."

"Who?"

"Last night, Maura Ryan was speaking with her over the phone, and I tried my best to influence her across the wire—to get her here as soon as possible. It worked, Dan. It worked! She came!"

"I still don't get it. Who came?"

"Hannah! Don't tell me you don't remember her?"

Dan considered the woman walking along the hallway below him. *"I suppose she looks familiar . . ."*

"You suppose!" cried Daisy. *"The family were relatives of mine. Do you remember my sister Ernesta's daughter Edith?"*

"Uh . . . yeah," said Dan, even though he barely did.

"She had a daughter named Lilian."

"Sure, if you say so."

"Dan! Lily married a man named Whitmore. This is one of their daughters, which makes her our great grandniece."

"Uh-huh."

"You must *recall her, Dan,"* Daisy exclaimed with enough force to ripple the petals of the flowers down the hall. *"She's the one you didn't catch!"*

"What?"

"At her coming-out party. She fell down the steps. Don't you remember? We tripped her. Unfortunate how she ended up falling on her—"

"Right, I remember now," said Dan. *"And, as I recall it, we didn't trip her. You tripped her. It was even your idea—"*

"The girl absolutely hated being there. And I couldn't stand her being presented like a plate of hors d'oeuvres to that arrogant little line of society blue-blood boys."

Dan laughed. *"Sounds more like what you told me was your coming out. That's where you met that rummy first husband of yours."*

"So it was."

"And so you tripped her," Dan reiterated.

"To give her an excuse to leave that horrid party. But you agreed to catch *her,"* pointed out Daisy. *"Which you didn't."*

"Excuse me, sweetie, but I did—"

"I remember she went to her room with a twisted ankle."

"Aw, she just faked that," pointed out Dan, *"which was part of the plan. And besides, our Ryan boy made her forget all about it by the end of the night."*

"Yes, he did . . . but that didn't end very well at all."

"No," said Dan after a long pause. *"It didn't."*

Daisy watched Neil open the door to the restored bedroom suite, which boasted the most spectacular view of the ocean in the entire mansion. Hannah hesitated a moment, looked up and down the hall, then tensely walked in. Neil followed with her bags.

"Dan . . ."

"Yes, Daisy."

"Do you know why I called Hannah here so urgently?"

"No, Daisy."

"I had an idea—"

Suddenly Dan realized what was coming. *"Oh, no, Dais. Absolutely not."*

"C'mon, sweetie, I need your help—"

"No! No more matchmaking schemes. You're just bored, that's all," warned Dan.

"I am not!" argued Daisy.

"Yes, you are. We haven't had a good theft, missing person, or attempted murder investigation in ages."

"I tell you, this case will be profound. You won't regret it . . . please, Danny."

Dan made a sound that amounted to a ghostly sigh. The air molecules in the hallway twirled. *"Okay, Daisy, all right,"* he finally said. *"I suppose you'd wear me down eventually anyway."*

"Goody!"

"So what's your first move?"

"Mmmm. Let me think . . ."

"Oh, Neil. It's beautiful. . . ."

For a long moment, Hannah forgot all about the cold chill on her skin and the feeling of being watched in the hallway. She was too busy taking in the most remarkable restoration job in the entire mansion.

The Daisy Channing Doyle Suite was an absolutely gorgeous example of Victorian Newport's love of the European. The walls were covered in a subtle pattern of hearts in blushing silk damask, the fancifully carved and gilded rococo desk, drawers, and dressing tables were all topped with dusty rose marble. Chubby, sweet-faced cherubs were set in relief in the swirls and curves of the white moldings along the high edges of the walls.

On the floor was a lushly loomed cream-and-burgundy Persian, on the ceiling an Italian-style fresco of pink-tinted white clouds in a blue sky at sunrise—a match for the mural in the vast ballroom two floors below, only those clouds held the red-orange tinted clouds of a sunset.

Near the corner, beside the marble-mantled fireplace, an interesting antique caught Hannah's eye—it was a large brass vase in the shape of a cat. Something about it unsettled her.

"Where did that piece come from?"

Neil was already occupied with starting a fire. "What piece?"

"That antique vase. The one shaped like a cat?"

Neil glanced quickly at the brass vase then went back to

his task of placing splits of wood into the hearth. "Maura found it in the mansion's attic," she said shortly. "Says it belongs here."

"Oh, really? Why is that?" Hannah stared at Neil's back and waited for him to answer. A small shake of his head was the only answer she got.

With a sigh, Hannah walked to one of the line of Palladian windows near the king-size bed. The cream silk drapes were all drawn closed upon the dark windy night, but she drew one open anyway, knowing that the morning would bring a panoramic view of the Atlantic Ocean.

Despite her earlier chill, Hannah unlatched one of the tall, paneled windows and cracked it enough to let in the clean salty briskness of the sea air. She inhaled deeply, her eyes closing as she drew in the familiar scents from her happy childhood.

In a flash of memory Hannah's father was teaching her to swim in the mansion's pool again, her mother was showing her how to clip a beautiful bouquet from the cutting garden, and her little sister was hollering with joy as they ran up and down the Cliff Walk, trying to launch their kites on the windy wings of the Atlantic.

When she opened her eyes again, she tried to make out, through the inky darkness, the ocean's treacherous white-capped waves. She gasped in surprise when the black sky was pierced suddenly by a bright light flashing in the distance.

"Easton Point Lighthouse," murmured Neil right behind her.

Hannah started, not realizing how close he'd been standing. She turned her head to speak to him, but he was already moving away, walking across the large room.

"The suite is remarkable," Hannah said to his stiff back. It was also going to be way too expensive.

Hannah had worked hard to build up her finances over the past few years. But she was nowhere even close to the two-million-dollar inheritance her parents had left her after their deaths five years ago.

Her sister's two-million share was still intact, thank Heaven, and would easily fund an extravagant wedding here, but Hannah didn't expect her sister to cover her own expenses. After all, it was her decision to come here two weeks early to get a little R&R.

Rest and relaxation? asked a little voice inside her. *Or to run away and hide from your nonexistent personal life until your workaholic schedule starts up again?*

Hannah silently told the voice to find another room.

Oh, well, thought Hannah, admiring the beauty around her, two weeks here would be okay. It was likely all the other rooms were taken anyway, and she'd only let Maura know of her intentions yesterday. Besides, she did have some pride left. If she had to make a request for a less expensive room, she did *not* want to make it to a former boyfriend who, at the moment, had jailbait in red warming his sheets.

"You've done an incredible restoration job here," said Hannah.

"Not me."

"Well, Maura, then, and the staff. The third floor wasn't even inhabitable when I was growing up. Certainly, this room wasn't. I think we used it for storage."

"I have no knowledge of the restorations. I came after the place was already up and running as a hotel." He crossed the room to a tall door. "Here's your bath," he said in a monotone, opening it, then turning to another door. "Your dressing room is through here. Your television and VCR are tucked away in this armoire. . . ."

Hannah shifted uneasily. He was obviously trying his hardest not to look at her as he went through his bellhop routine. The man was acting like a robot—as efficient and emotionless as that automated operator who'd connected her with her sister's long-distance call back in her company Mercedes.

"Neil—"

"And the bar is located—"

"Neil—"

"—in the cabinet beneath the—"

"Neil!"

He stopped, finally, and looked at her. "Yes, Mrs. Peabody? You have a question?"

Hannah stood there, studying his face, searching yet again for even a small sign of welcome, of friendship. But there was nothing. He looked at her as if she were a stranger . . . a complete stranger in her old home.

Across the room, Neil watched Hannah struggling, but he refused to make it easy for her. This may have been her home once, thought Neil coldly; it may have been her family's palace, and he their employee, but it wasn't so any longer. In fact, as head of security, he had more of a right to be here now than she did.

They stood like that, in silence, for a long moment until a banging jolted them both.

"The door," said Hannah, her eyes noting the suite's front door had slammed shut.

"The window you opened, Mrs. Peabody," said Neil, none too friendly as he turned from her to leave. "Close it or you'll feel a draft all night."

The crisp, borderline rude command was too much. A flash of hurt quickly flared to anger.

"I already feel a draft, *Mr.* Ryan," snapped Hannah, her nerves and patience snapping, too. "Because you're being an unconscionably cold bastard to me."

Neil tried to ignore the remark.

"Did you *hear* me?"

Neil stopped at the door. He flashed back on young Miss Tiffany Townsend throwing shoes at the other end of the hall. In the years he had known Hannah, she had never acted the part of the spoiled rich girl, but it was beginning to sound as though she'd learned the part well enough from Herbert Peabody in recent years—and in Neil's estimation, there was no better jerk to teach her.

"Frankly," said Neil, his voice completely controlled, "I don't—"

"Give a damn?" quipped Hannah. "Oh, please, Neil, haven't you got something a little more original rolling around in that concrete block head of yours?"

"*Frankly,* Mrs. Peabody," said Neil, turning slowly to face her, "I don't see where you have a right to speak to me that way."

"The last I checked, we lived in a free country—"

"And the last *I* checked, your family no longer owns this place *or* employs me."

"What is that supposed to mean?"

"I'm leaving—" He turned again to make his escape.

"Oh, no you don't!" exclaimed Hannah, the hurt still evident in her voice. "Answer me. Tell me to my face what's on your mind—'' But Neil was ignoring her. Instead he stepped toward the door again.

Hannah felt defeated. *Go then,* she thought to herself. *Who needs you . . .*

It was exactly that moment that she found something strange overcome her. That needling chill was back, pricking her skin. And suddenly her tongue and lips were loudly forming words that a low voice seemed to be whispering into her ear . . .

"STOP TRYING TO RUN AWAY!" she found herself announcing to Neil's back. *"BE A MAN ABOUT IT, AT LEAST."*

Oh, Heaven, thought Hannah in horror. Where had that come from? It certainly hadn't been from the little needling voice of her conscience—the one she usually told to butt out. This voice was deep and commanding, taking over her tongue like a mad passenger jerking her car's steering wheel.

Wherever those words *had* come from, something in them seemed to hit a very significant bull's-eye in the man across the room, because Neil Ryan had frozen in his tracks.

Chapter Six

For a long moment Neil was silent.

Stop trying to run away . . . The words echoed through his soul, chilling him to the bone. *Be a man about it, at least.*

There'd only been one other time he'd heard those words. It had been three years ago, on a hideous night he didn't care to remember ever again.

But how could Hannah know? he wondered.

He didn't like this at all. No, not at all. She had to be goading him, pushing him for some reason. The words *must* have been a stab in the dark.

Neil was still facing the door, his back ramrod straight, when he finally spoke again, his low voice under tight control. "I warn you, Hannah, be careful what line you cross with me tonight."

"I-I . . ." Hannah stammered, until she realized with astonishment that he was *finally* calling her something besides her cursed married name. Hannah blinked. She liked hearing Neil call her Hannah again. She liked it very much.

With a deep breath, she decided that perhaps her tongue had been wiser than her brain after all. "It's a free country," she stated, gaining back her composure. "And I intend to exercise my freedom of speech . . . in fact, I intend to do it *every* time I see you from now on, until you answer me."

Neil's tense body wheeled. "You want to cross lines, do you?" he threatened as he strode across the room. "Then you'd better be prepared to take on what lies across it."

As he closed in, she began to step back—

"Stand your ground, Hannah." Again Hannah heard a voice ring in her ears; and again, it wasn't her own. It was another's—this time higher, a woman's voice.

"Did you hear that?" Hannah's head spun, looking for who had spoken.

"Hear *what*?"

"I heard a woman's voice in my ear. Just now."

"What's the matter with you? Are you on medication?"

Hannah's eyes flashed sharper than the beam of the Easton Point Lighthouse. "I am *not* on medication, thank you very much!"

"You're acting strangely."

"*I'm* acting strangely! Me!"

"Yes, you."

"You're the one who's treating an old friend like a complete stranger."

Neil remained silent, her words echoing through his conscience. He surveyed Hannah Daisy Whitmore Peabody standing there in an agitated state. This little fit of anger brought a brilliant sheen to the gray eyes behind her wire-rimmed glasses, and an attractive flush to her cheeks.

While Hannah had never been beautiful in the conventional sense, the sum of her attributes had a certain impact on a man. Her hair, for instance, was in a prim bun tonight, as she usually wore it on her show, but a few tendrils had escaped their pins and brushed her blushing cheeks in a seductive caress. Her face itself was plain, her chin too pointy, her cheeks too round to be considered chic, yet her skin was a smooth ivory cream, and her lips were perfectly formed—full with a natural rose color that needed no makeup to make them inviting. And then there was the way she spoke, with a warmth and intelligence and a tone that sometimes became low and soft, reminding a man of smoke and velvet.

Neil didn't like this train of thought. He hadn't been with

a woman in months, and his current monklike existence had only been achievable through his constant reminders of where involvement with women, all women, *including* this one, had led him—on a path straight to hellish agony.

Still, he was a man. And his body's reaction to Hannah was hard to ignore. It prompted him to set aside his original "cold shoulder" plan, and try another strategy.

"So . . ." he began, stepping back into the room. "You want to be *friends* again, do you? Friends with me . . . to-night?"

Hannah watched his well-built form stride forward, the muscles moving fluidly under the expertly cut, dark blue suit. And his blue eyes were staring at her now, dark as his suit, direct and piercing—a marked change from his earlier efforts to keep them averted.

Hannah blinked, taken aback by the sudden change she felt in him. "I just meant that you . . . weren't being very friendly . . . and I just—"

"You just wanted me to be," he said, closing in.

"To be what?" asked Hannah, wanting to take a step back with his advance, and yet trying to stand her ground—as that disembodied female voice, that must have been her better judgment, had advised her.

"To be *friendly*." Neil's voice carried an edge that seemed to be taunting her—or warning her.

Hannah swallowed uneasily, her anger giving way to un-certainty. This was not the boy she remembered, she coun-seled herself. This was a *man*. A grown one. With a very potent and disturbing streak of something running just beneath that stone-cold surface.

Sexuality. Hannah realized it with the force of a hurricane wind. She felt it coming off him in waves. "Neil, don't mis-understand me—"

"Misunderstand?" asked Neil. He was toe-to-toe with her now, gazing down at her upturned face. His hand came up, his finger reaching out to touch a brownish-blond curl that had brushed her flushed cheek. It felt soft. Softer than he remembered.

Hannah looked at the man standing a good six inches over her. His sharp blue eyes seemed to blur into the sky mural painted above the bed.

"*Yes, the bed!*" coaxed some disembodied female voice in her ear.

"Oh, Heaven," breathed Hannah, "I think you'd better go."

"Go?" A small smile tipped the edge of Neil Ryan's sensuous mouth. As he continued to finger her wayward curl, his blue gaze caressed her face. "Why, *Mrs.* Peabody, I thought you were looking to rekindle our *friendship*," he murmured low. "For a night or two, anyway. After all, you are a married woman. And I am the hired help, right?"

Hannah's gray eyes narrowed at the harshness of his words. Her hand pushed his away.

"What's this?" asked Neil in sarcastic surprise. "Have you changed your mind? Too tired tonight? I can always come back tomorrow evening. Just ring the front desk for service—"

"You really have changed, haven't you?"

"What's the matter, Mrs. Peabody . . . disappointed?"

Hannah heard the sharp edge in Neil's voice. He wanted to cut her, she realized, to hurt her. But why? "You know I don't deserve this," she whispered.

The words pierced Neil Ryan's heart—because he knew she was right. She *didn't* deserve this; but then he didn't deserve to be in emotional conflict, recognizing an attraction to a woman he'd never have. If he were lucky, from now on, she'd turn tail and run the moment she saw him.

Without another word, Neil wheeled sharply on his heel and strode toward the door, forcing himself not to look back, nor to apologize. He reached the door and turned the knob, perhaps with more force than necessary. But the door wouldn't open.

He tried again.

Nothing.

"Neil?"

Her voice was soft, plaintive. She didn't want to fight. Didn't want to see him go like this. He heard it all in one wretched syllable.

Desperately, Neil tried the knob again. "Open. Open, damn you," he cursed.

From across the room, Hannah watched Neil struggling. What she couldn't figure out was whether he was truly struggling with the door or struggling with himself.

She slowly walked forward, watched him turn abruptly and stride to the room's ornate desk. He picked up the room key he'd deposited there just a few minutes ago. Without a word, or a glance at her, he returned to the front door.

Again he was struggling, and Hannah realized that there was no dilemma within Neil Ryan's heart. He had every intention of leaving, it was just the door that was stopping him.

And the room key didn't seem to be working.

"What's wrong?" Hannah asked.

Neil gritted his teeth with tension. "The door's locked," he said, turning to face her. "Something's wrong with the room key."

He handed her back the key, then reached a hand inside his suit jacket. Hannah noticed the glint of something metallic beneath his arm, and she realized with a start that Neil was carrying a gun.

"What are you going to do? Shoot the thing open?"

Neil produced a key, which he held up for her to see. "Master passkey." Then he turned and slipped it in the lock. "You watch too many television shows, Mrs. Peabody."

Hannah folded her arms. "I don't like the idea of your having a key to my room—"

"As the head of security here, I'm bonded, Mrs. Peabody, and *usually* trustworthy. But if you're worried I won't be able to *resist* you, just use the door chain . . . there," he finally said, hearing the click. The lock had felt jammed, but he'd been able to throw the bolt with the master key.

His hand went to the knob and turned. "I'll say good night, then."

But the knob would not budge. A click sounded, and it seemed as though the lock had slipped back into place. "What the—"

"Go, then, Ryan, what's stopping you?"

Neil struggled and struggled, but the door seemed to be dead set against letting him pass. It seemed ridiculous to him, yet he felt the thing was actually working against him, trying to keep him from leaving.

"What's the matter?" said Hannah, her arms still folded across her chest. "Are you waiting for a tip? Here's one: You're acting like a horse's ass."

"Gee, princess," said Neil, still struggling. "Are you this charming on your television show?"

"Don't call me princess," she snapped. Then she held out her hand. "Give the key here. I'll have a try."

But the results were the same for Hannah as they'd been for Neil. "This is crazy," whispered Hannah. She turned to find Neil's hands on his hips, his suit jacket spread open enough for her to again glimpse the pistol he carried. His gaze searched her face. It seemed as if Neil Ryan were about to say something.

"What?" prompted Hannah.

"Does it seem—"

Hannah waited, wondering if he'd felt it, too. Felt as though the door were somehow alive, and fighting to keep them from leaving. "What?"

He studied her for another moment and then dropped his eyes. "Forget it," he said, turning from her. He strode across the room. When he reached the desk, he picked up the phone and pressed 0. Then he put the phone to his ear, trying hard not to look at Hannah, though he knew she was staring at him.

"J. J. will be up in a minute and fix the problem," said Neil, his voice back to its cold bellhop monotone. Then he listened at the phone receiver.

Hannah expected a conversation to begin. But it didn't. Instead, an expression of confusion crossed his face. He put down the receiver with what looked like tightly controlled frustration. Then he put it to his ear again.

"What's wrong?" asked Hannah.

Neil glanced at her, but he didn't answer. Instead he checked the phone's cord and wire, following it until he'd found the phone jack in the wall. He stooped down to make a close examination.

"Neil?" she asked.

"Phone's out."

"Out?"

"I don't understand it. No dial tone. Nothing. And everything looks fine."

Hannah shook her head in disbelief. She walked to the phone, picking it up for herself. Neil watched her. Her gray eyes met his as she heard the silence for herself.

"What do we do? Bang on the door and holler?"

Neil was silent for a long moment. "That's your prerogative, of course, but it would likely disturb quite a number of our guests. High-paying guests. Many here for the first time."

Hannah understood. "I wouldn't want to do that."

"Thank you," managed Neil. A pained sigh came from somewhere deep inside of him. "I'm sorry," he said quietly, "for the inconvenience."

"Please don't apologize," said Hannah. "Not for *that* anyway."

Neil shifted uncomfortably. He walked to the open window. The winds were high tonight; the ocean's black waves struck the rocky Rhode Island cliffs with a kind of restless violence. He looked down, judging the height of the three floors.

"Neil?"

"Yes?" he answered absently.

"You're not thinking of jumping, are you?" she asked his stiff back. "You can't hate me that much."

A reactive smile came to Neil's lips. His eyes closed for a moment as he fought it. "I'll write a note," he said finally, turning back toward her with his usual stony expression.

"A note?"

Neil walked to the ornate desk and grabbed a sheet of stationery from the drawer. He scribbled on it and then strode back to the front door of the suite.

Hannah watched as he crouched down and slipped it underneath the door, shooting it hard so it would land in the middle of the hallway.

"For a staff member?" asked Hannah.

"J. J.'s bound to spot it," Neil explained. "He'll see that I'm missing and then he'll make the rounds on the floors, looking for me."

Hannah thought for a moment. "But what if he assumes . . ."

She felt awkward bringing the idea up, but it was a possibility. Maybe Neil would think of it, too. She looked up, into his blue eyes.

Neil appeared oblivious—and a tad impatient. He folded his arms across his chest. "Assumes?" he prompted.

She began to pace, a bit nervously. "He could assume . . . I mean . . ."

"What?"

"Well, did he know you were showing me to my room?"

"Yes."

"And did he know that you and I had been . . . that we'd been involved . . . at one time?" Hannah stopped her pacing and looked directly at Neil.

His eyes met hers. "I think he recalled that, yes," he said softly.

"Well, then," continued Hannah, dropping her gaze and starting to pace again. "If he doesn't see you come back down to the front desk again, he might just assume . . ."

The rest of the sentence hit Neil like a rifle butt to the head. He wanted to tell Hannah that she was wrong. That J. J. would never assume he'd gone to bed with his old flame—his *married* old flame—her first night in the hotel. But he knew his cavalier brother would assume *exactly* that.

Neil's response was not in words. Instead he strode back to the front door.

"Neil?"

Again, he brought out his passkey. With an uncharacteristic sense of panic, the head of hotel security jammed it hard into the lock and began to struggle. The door shook with his efforts, but the result was still the same.

The way out remained barred.

The lock—and Daisy's plan—were both firmly in place.

Chapter Seven

For the life of him, J. J. Ryan could not figure why his older brother had lost track of the time.

Neil Ryan was a walking log of details. Control and clockwork were his middle names. And the hotel time clock's present face had already rendered J. J. *off* duty for the night.

After stepping from the small elevator, J. J. sauntered down the third floor's hallway, listening for any sound of his brother's footsteps, looking for any sign of something out of the ordinary.

Just a few minutes ago, J. J. would have certainly seen such a thing in the immaculately kept hallway. But the note that Neil had slid under the door had disappeared, the result of a mysterious draft. Like an invisible hand, it had pushed the note along until it slipped beneath the door of a utility closet.

So, J. J., detecting nothing special—other than another of those bizarre cold spots that seemed to appear out of nowhere in the old hotel—continued to the end of the hall.

It wasn't until he actually returned down the hallway, passing by room 308 for a second time, that J. J. heard muffled voices seeping very faintly through the thick wood. He paused a moment and realized that one of the voices was Neil's. His brother was talking intimately with Mrs. Peabody.

"Well, son of a gun," mumbled J. J. "I'd never have pegged him for this."

Without more than a moment's hesitation, J. J. turned and headed straight for the elevator. He wasn't about to disturb his older brother. For one thing, the man usually worked like he was driven by demons. Neil deserved a break from routine, and it was nobody's damned business what the reason was.

When J. J. got to the office behind the front desk, he dialed a number to one of the nearby carriage house staff rooms. Most of the staff lived in their own homes around Newport and Middletown, but on busy wedding weekends, Maura had certain extra help standing by for on-call duty.

"Hey, Stokes, can you come on the desk tonight? Great, I'm due off, and Neil . . . well, something's come up."

Stokes sounded happy to get J. J.'s call. On the other end of the phone line, the older man told J. J. he'd be right over.

J. J. no sooner hung up than the front desk line rang. "Front desk, at your service—" began J. J. brightly.

"My head is throbbing and I can't sleep," snapped the voice of Tiffany Townsend. "Send aspirin and Perrier to room 307. And be quick about it."

"Certainly—" began J. J., but the caller had already disconnected. J. J. sighed. He'd no sooner prepared a silver tray when the door to the service staircase opened and a robust older man with bright brown eyes, ruddy cheeks, and a close-cropped beard stepped through.

"Evenin', Master Ryan, how goes it?"

"Hey, Joe, that was fast. You were already up when I called, weren't you?"

For a man of seventy, Joe Stokes looked darned good. His build was solid, suggesting that he must have had incredible strength in his prime; and, though the signs of age were there in the gray of his hair and beard, the retired sailor still had an attractive air about him—an observation especially evident in the admiring looks of the many female guests he could charm with a word and a wink. Even Maura Ryan referred to Stokes as the Sean Connery of the Yankee coast.

"Ahhh-yep," Stokes answered. "Been draftin' plans for

my next model. Almost through with the current master-piece.''

J. J. had heard that Stokes was building a replica of *Reliance*, an elegant defender of the America's Cup back in 1903. In fact, modeling supplies were supposedly the reason Joe'd come to the hotel a few months ago. He'd said he'd once worked as a gardener's helper on these very grounds, before he'd gone to sea. And now he was back, needing some part-time work to continue affording his hobby.

But J. J. suspected there was another reason he'd come back to Château du Coeur. The man seemed awfully lonely.

"Y'know, Joe," said J. J., regarding the older man, "I've never seen your models. Think I could get a look sometime?"

Stokes's eyebrows rose as he walked up to J. J. "Never knew you was int'rested.''

J. J. nodded. "I've been building models since I was a kid.''

"You don't say? Ships then?"

"Usually from kits. Sometimes I build from scratch. But I always paint them myself. And not just ships. Cars, planes, space stations—''

"Space stations?" Stokes scratched his head. "Well, don't know about that kind o' thing, but I'd be happy to show you my fleet sometime.''

"A whole fleet?" J. J.'s eyes widened.

"Ayyy-yep." Stokes's face flushed with pride. "How's Monday?"

"Oh, man, I've got class Monday nights . . ." J. J. sighed as he picked up his silver tray and balanced it over a shoulder. "I'm so busy with work here during the day then classes at night, it's tough to find any free time—''

"Where're you going with that?"

"Room 307 wants aspirin.''

"Let me take it.''

"It's okay," said J. J. "It'll only take a few minutes, then I'm sacking out at the carriage house.''

"I see," said Stokes, turning toward the front desk. "Well, good night then, Master Ryan.''

"Night." J. J. was turning the other way when he stopped and looked back at Stokes again. "You know, I've got classes

Mondays, Tuesdays, and Wednesdays. But a Thursday night—that would be good. What do you think?''

''How about this Thursday?'' Stokes said slowly, as if trying to keep his voice from betraying too much pleasure. ''And I could stir us up a bite to eat—if you have the time, that is.''

''That would be great,'' said J. J. with a nod.

''It's a plan then—''

J. J. was about to turn to leave once more when Stokes's voice stopped him. ''Those classes of yours—what is it you're studyin', if ya don't mind my asking?''

''I'm trying to get my advanced degree,'' said J. J. ''To become a teacher.''

Stokes nodded. ''Education is a wonderful thing. What is it you'll be wanting to teach once you graduate?''

J. J. looked down a moment then back up. ''Promise me you won't let it get around,'' he said in a low tone.

Stokes's eyes widened. ''Okeydoke, I'll bite.''

''Art.''

Stokes looked confused. ''I don't get it. What's so scandalous 'bout that?''

J. J. shrugged. ''Let's just say my old wrestling buddies wouldn't understand.''

''Gottya, Master Ryan. Mum's the word.''

Whistling softly to himself, J. J. strode to the elevator and rode to the third floor. When he stepped on the landing, he noticed that the odd chill he'd felt earlier seemed to have completely disappeared.

With the tray balanced over his shoulder, J. J. sauntered forward, his whistling becoming a low hum. *Oh, what do ya do with a drunken sailor, what do ya do with a drunken sailor* . . . He'd barely tapped on the door when it jerked open to reveal a sight that left J. J. feeling like the subject of his favorite ditty.

Tiffany Townsend, the little blond debutante who inhabited this guest room, had boldly stepped forward, showing off her skimpy red satin nightgown to the shameless glare of the bright hall lights.

J. J. was not used to this sort of behavior. Female guests of the Château du Coeur usually stayed demurely behind half-closed doors. And if they ever wore anything this provocative it was always carefully hidden under a thick layer of Ralph Lauren terry cloth.

Still, J. J. managed to keep his composure. He'd learned that much from his unemotional brother after working alongside him for the last two years. *See nothing. Hear nothing. Just do your job.*

And yet . . . it wasn't every day that a young man in his sexual prime was confronted with a barely clothed debutante, her expertly cut shoulder-length blond hair attractively mussed, as if she'd just arisen from a warm bed.

"At your service, miss," J. J. managed to choke out more or less steadily.

Tiffany Townsend surveyed the specimen in front of her. For the last forty minutes she'd been stewing furiously in her room. Neil Ryan had rejected her. Rejected *her*. She still could not fathom it, and the fact was she hadn't called for aspirin so much as the opportunity to take out her anger on whichever stupid valet decided to deliver it.

As she expected, the excuse for a good tongue-lashing was right there in front of her. The valet had brought her a bottle of sparkling water but the brand was wrong. She'd *expressly* asked for *Perrier*, hadn't she?

The opening words of her tirade were bubbling up in her throat; and yet, she stifled the release. Instead, Tiffany considered the prime male flesh that now stood at her door. Granted, this young valet was less sexy than Neil Ryan, but he was no less handsome. In fact, he looked a lot like the very guy who'd left her seething with rage. Midnight-black hair, lantern-square jaw, powerfully muscular build.

"What's your name?" asked Tiffany none too politely as she ran her gaze up and down his form.

"John James," he answered without hesitation. "Is there a problem, miss?"

"You were one of the bartenders tonight. Weren't you?"

J. J. nodded.

As Tiffany considered this, her half-pouting expression remained fixed. Slowly, she leaned her body back against the door, casually thrusting forward a surgically enhanced pair of gifts she'd received three years ago, for her eighteenth birthday. The cleavage was a magnet to J. J.'s young gaze.

Stay professional, J. J. lectured himself with clenched teeth.

He did everything in his power to keep looking the young woman straight in her bubbly blue eyes.

"What's your *last* name, John James?"

"Ryan."

"Ryan?" Tiffany's tilting head suddenly became erect, tendrils of fluffy blond hair moved across her cheek. "Your name is John James *Ryan?*"

"People call me J. J."

A slow smile stretched across Tiffany's collagen-injected lips—a present for her nineteenth birthday. "You must be Cornelius Ryan's younger brother?"

J. J. nodded.

"It's all in the family then, isn't it?" *Or it will be,* thought Tiffany, deciding then and there how she was going to get back at Neil Ryan for his ghastly treatment of her earlier in the evening.

"Excuse me?"

Tiffany crooked a finger. "Come in. You can place the tray beside my bed."

J. J. nodded efficiently and stepped inside Tiffany's beautiful cream-and-yellow accented ocean-view room. The fireplace was crackling with a cozy blaze, and the shaded bulb from her bedside lamp was the only other source of light.

The moment J. J. passed her, Tiffany shut and locked the room's front door. Barefoot, she followed him quietly, and, when he turned around, he was startled to find her nearly on top of him.

"Stay with me a little?" asked Tiffany, her blue eyes wide with little-girl pleading. "I'm feeling so . . . *alone* tonight."

J. J.'s brow creased. "I really shouldn't stay."

Tiffany thought of offering money. She'd had much luck before with that approach. Minimum wage—whatever the hell the pathetic amount was now—couldn't hold a candle to what she offered for an hour or two of a little *personal* manual labor. In fact, two or three crisp hundred dollar bills were always enough for the handsome service worker of her choice to jump up and say please.

Yet . . . something about J. J. told her not to offer money. If he was Neil Ryan's brother, then he'd probably be too proud or professional or something equally tiresome. Persuasion was the key with this one, reasoned Tiffany.

"I realize you shouldn't," said Tiffany, looking very seriously into the guileless green of J. J.'s eyes. "How about if you just talk to me for five minutes. I'll take my aspirin, and I'm sure I just need to calm down . . . I had a strange dream and I'm just feeling a little . . . strange . . ."

"Oh," said J. J. "Well, for five minutes then. I guess that can't do any harm."

"Good," said Tiffany, trying to hide her extreme pleasure. She knew from experience when there was one little crack in the male armor—that was all she needed to slip her crowbar in and lever it wide-open.

"Sit down," Tiffany instructed J. J., trying hard to keep her voice pleasant and friendly, a marked departure from the commanding impatience of her usual tone. She gestured to an overstuffed armchair next to the bed. "I'll tell you about my dream . . ."

As Tiffany took two aspirins and settled back on her bed, J. J. sank down into the armchair and immediately felt guilty. For one thing, he'd promised his brother over and over that he'd never, ever fraternize with the female guests—Neil had made this clear many times and in many ways to his younger brother.

J. J., you're a very handsome kid. I'm warning you to be careful. Don't get personal with female guests. Don't get physical. And for God's sake never get sentimental. When J. J. would ask him what he meant by sentimental, Neil usually shrugged. Once he'd muttered, "Don't fantasize . . . don't pretend . . ."

Neil Ryan seemed to be completely obsessed with this rule, and up to now, J. J. had been careful enough about following it, mainly because he didn't want any hassles from his big brother—but also because he'd never really been in much of a position *to* fraternize. Other than jokes and smiles at the bar with some of the female guests, which he could carefully control, J. J.'s life was relegated to being part of the conveniently unnoticed staff to most all of the guests most all of the time.

J. J. knew, however, that there was a second reason to feel guilty. Besides his promise to his brother. As Tiffany Townsend began to talk about her "strange dream," J. J. could *not* keep his gaze on her pretty, perky face. He was a healthy, red-blooded male, after all—a condition that's been known to create a kind of gravity on the eyesight.

In his own case, J. J. knew Tiffany was not his type. And yet, he felt that natural male pull on his vision, taking his gaze ever lower, over the shapely hills and valleys of revealing red satin that began just below Tiffany's slender, Palm Beach tanned neck.

Intense warmth overcame J. J. as he began to wonder where her tan lines were—or if, indeed, she had *any* tan lines at all. *Don't go there,* he lectured himself. And yet, it seemed he'd already gone too far.

". . . and then I was on the beach," Tiffany was saying. "I was all alone on all of this white sand, or at least I thought I was. I sat on a big fluffy towel, and I was wearing my silver bikini. I decided to take off my top to get an even tan, you know?"

J. J.'s throat muscles, not to mention some other muscles, had suddenly grown too tight to risk using. He simply nodded.

"I reached around and unhooked the bikini's bra strap, then this weird mist started rolling in, surrounding me completely. That's when I heard someone coming up out of the water. I looked up, just as I let my bikini top fall, and suddenly there was this strange man standing over me—"

J. J. felt the tension within him growing to a nearly impossible level. "Miss," he interrupted, beginning to rise, "I think I'd better—"

Tiffany was off the bed and on her feet, standing in front of him in the next moment. "Don't go," she insisted.

"But—"

Very carefully, very lightly, Tiffany brushed her fingers against the back of J. J.'s muscled forearm. He closed his eyes as a shiver of pure lust raced up his spine and tickled the hairs at the base of his neck.

"Don't you want to find out first . . ." whispered Tiffany, letting her words trail off as she gently pushed him back into the chair.

"Find out?" asked J. J., falling backward.

"Yes," whispered Tiffany, leaning over him as she rested one hand on each arm of the chair, effectively entrapping him.

"Ahhh . . . find out what?" managed J. J., feeling dazed by the heavy scent of Tiffany's imported orchid perfume and the tantalizing glimpse of cleavage as she bent toward him.

"Find out how my dream ends," said Tiffany.

J. J. blinked. As the point of Tiffany's pink tongue peeked out to slowly and thoroughly wet her bee-stung lips, he realized he probably had about ten seconds to decide. Otherwise she'd either change her mind and throw him out or figure he had an IQ of 12 and begin explaining her offer in plainer terms.

"Well?" prompted Tiffany. "Do you want to know?"

Eight seconds. J. J. considered his options: He had no girl-friend to speak of; and they were both consenting adults.

Then again, argued his conscience, there was his brother's rule about never fraternizing with the guests. He *had* promised Neil that he'd never do this.

But wasn't Neil himself doing it tonight? Wasn't Neil himself breaking his own rule?

Three seconds. J. J. glanced at his watch then back up into Tiffany Townsend's pretty but impatient young face. She'd begun to twist a lock of her bright blond hair around her finger, and J. J. let himself become mesmerized by it. The twisting, twisting, twisting seemed to echo itself in the building tension in his lower body until suddenly the solution to his dilemma presented itself like an inflatable raft to a drowning man.

J. J. smiled slowly. He slipped his expanding watchband from his wrist and tossed it onto the nearby silver tray that he'd brought up only a few minutes ago.

"It seems," he said, "that time is on our side."

"I don't understand," said Tiffany.

"I'm officially *off* duty."

"Oh, I see." Tiffany's eyebrows rose. "But you're still *at my service*, aren't you?"

J. J. didn't answer.

For a moment, Tiffany was startled by the confidence and power suddenly unleashed in the direct green gaze in front of her. John James Ryan had shed his banal, easy-to-control, "at your service" staff facade to reveal the nature of a potently aroused young man. The change threw Tiffany off balance for a moment, prompting an internal reaction of honest fascination inside of her. But she quickly squashed it, favoring instead her need for power and control.

She did her level best to take it back by making the next move. Before J. J. knew what was happening, Tiffany had lowered her satin-covered form onto his lap and begun brushing her lips across his. Quickly, her manicured fingers turned J. J.'s button-down into an un-buttoned-down and began fumbling with his belt buckle. *I'll show your brother,* thought Tiffany with glee that her plan was working. Then an idea occurred to her.

Carefully Tiffany pushed her mouth forward onto J. J.'s to distract him, and as her tongue slipped inside his mouth, she used one hand to reach behind her. Her fingers found the cold metal band of his wristwatch, and she dropped it onto the carpeted floor.

J. J. tried to accept Tiffany's ministrations, but something inside of him was holding back. He was no virgin, and, by the way she kissed and tempted, he knew Tiffany was a far cry from sexually inexperienced. Yet he could not make himself feel at ease with what was happening.

Tiffany seemed to feel his hesitation, and she responded by dipping a hand between his legs. J. J.'s body automatically responded to the touch of her experienced hand. His own hands began to gently touch what had been flaunted so shamelessly in front of him. But Tiffany now had little patience for gentleness. The line was crossed, the flag dropped, and she saw no reason to waste time.

She wanted what she wanted, when she wanted it.

Her free hand went to the neckline of her expensive French lingerie and ripped quickly. The bodice fell away, revealing the tanned smooth ovals of her surgically enhanced chest.

"Like what you see?" she asked.

J. J. gazed at her firm, perfect flesh. To J. J., it seemed somehow too firm, too perfect. It seemed unnatural. Artifice had its place, he knew, but he also knew, from his own studies of art history, that there was a kind of perfection in imperfection. Artists strove their whole lives to capture on canvas what was so beautifully and imperfectly created in nature.

He touched the tip of Tiffany's full, perfect breast and she moaned in appreciation. There were a lot of men, he supposed, who appreciated artifice, but for his own taste, J. J. knew that in a primal state of sexual passion he was the kind who preferred to feel as close as possible to nature . . . and all her natural imperfections.

"Harder," commanded Tiffany, her blue eyes flashing fiercely. "Tweak it harder."

J. J. obeyed without thinking. He watched her smile, enjoying the play of his fingers. Then he lowered his mouth, placing his lips where his fingers had been a moment before.

"Ahhhh . . . that's more like it . . ." murmured Tiffany, her head thrown back, her eyes closed in ecstasy. "Now touch me," she directed in a breathless voice. "You know where."

"Mmmm," murmured J. J. But he didn't obey her this time. Instead he rose from the chair, carefully cradling her in his arms, hoping to interject at least the semblance of tenderness, of feeling, into this exercise.

"What . . . what are you doing? I told you to touch me . . ."

"I know," said J. J.

"Then *do* it!" she insisted.

J. J. hesitated a moment, less than enthusiastic about the sharp, superior tone that had edged out the sweetly teasing voice she'd had earlier. The cold concern that he was making a terrible mistake began to slice into his lust-fogged mind. He let Tiffany's legs drop to the floor.

Suddenly, Tiffany realized her misstep. She quickly melted against him. Her naked breasts brushed across his arm and chest. "Oh, John James, I just want you so badly . . . please understand . . ."

Tiffany practically choked on the apologetic-sounding words, but she was so close to getting back at Neil Ryan. *So close.*

The thought reminded her of the wristwatch plan. Carefully, while staring up into J. J.'s eyes, Tiffany moved her toes around on the carpet until she felt the cold metal of the watch's band. She shoved J. J.'s timepiece hard, making sure it would end up hidden well beneath the bed.

J. J. didn't notice what was happening with Tiffany's feet. He was too distracted by her wide blue eyes, suddenly appearing so innocent, so apparently needy. He felt her hand begin to touch him again. She stroked and massaged, watching what effect her fingers had on the persuasion.

Plenty. J. J. felt a fever overtake him again, eclipsing the light of better judgment and leading him back into the dark heat of blind lust. He began to pull off his clothes. In turn, she allowed the ripped piece of satin nightie to pool at her bare feet.

Tiffany surveyed J. J.'s strong, muscular young body. He was fully aroused now, and ready to make love. Her lips curled into a satisfied smile, and she tamped down impatient orders. Her fists clenched as she forced herself to wait for him.

C'mon, you stupid bellhop, let's get going! she railed to herself but didn't dare voice. After all, there was no cash involved in this particular transaction. No tip to dangle in front of his nose to coerce him into following her every command.

Instead, a pseudo smile-of-love was firmly affixed to her perky, perfect features. *Sheesh,* she thought, *it is* so *much easier to just buy them.*

Slowly, J. J. bent down and gathered her into his arms. As he laid her back with gentleness, Tiffany actually felt something flutter deep inside her. She gazed up into his bright green eyes. His handsome expression was so full of intelligence, consideration, and masculine desire, that, for a moment, a *feeling* for him actually penetrated . . .

But then she reminded herself of her plan.

Quickly the girl crushed any and all feelings of sentimentality. After all, Neil Ryan had carried her up to her bedroom and laid her down just like this earlier tonight. But then he'd had the nerve to reject her with a condescending good night.

Tiffany's need for revenge was far more important to her than any other consideration. And it gave her a great deal of satisfaction to know that all she'd had to do was snap her fingers to have Neil Ryan's younger brother in the exact same position he'd been in. Only *this* Ryan wasn't leaving. Not until she was ready to throw him out . . . and she wouldn't be ready for that until he gave her what she wanted.

"Good," she barked. "*Finally* we're getting somewhere."

J. J. heard the bite in the girl's remark, saw the truth in her cold blue eyes, and his body stilled. For all of Tiffany Townsend's surgically enhanced perfection, it would make sense that any man would choose to feast his eyes on her body and make love to her.

But J. J. chose differently. Though he was bursting to feel

release, he abruptly turned away. *This is not what I want,* he realized. *This is not what I need.*

"I can't do this . . ." he rasped.

"What? Hey, what the hell are you doing—where are you going?!" came the outraged voice on the bed beside him as he quickly stood and jerked on his clothes.

"Sorry," he managed. "I can't. Sorry . . ."

J. J. stumbled out of the room and closed the door on a barrage of inventive curses. He hurried onto the back staircase, descended a flight, then sat down on a step to compose himself.

J. J. leaned against the wall in the lonely stairwell and closed his eyes, listening to his own labored breaths. "What the hell are you doing?" he whispered bitterly. "You know what it is you *don't* want, but what the hell is it you *do* want?"

Within his darkened vision, J. J.'s memory banks suddenly produced an image. It was the face of one particular young woman he'd known from his childhood.

He used to see the girl only on special occasions years ago, but he'd always remembered her. She'd been average-looking, not especially beautiful to look at. But when that girl had gazed at J. J., her smile—unlike the girl on the bed beside him just a few minutes ago—had been radiant with a joyful vivacity that had been honest.

And a warm affection that had been genuine.

Chapter Eight

"This is nuts."

"Neil?"

"We're trapped. . . ." Turning from the barred door, Neil Ryan considered the situation.

He needed to think rationally. Analytically. Being locked in a romantic hotel suite with an old flame did not logically compare to securing airfields in Saudi Arabia or guarding diplomats on international protection detail. And yet, standing at the inexplicably stuck front door to the Daisy Channing Doyle Memorial Suite, Neil felt his head automatically running through combat checklists.

Hannah observed Neil as he began to pace, his mind clearly occupied. "Has this ever happened here before?" she asked.

"No," he said.

"Well, then"—Hannah began unbuttoning her jacket—"I guess we'll just have to wait it out."

Neil observed Hannah slipping off her tailored gray pantsuit jacket and draping it over the back of a chair near the fireplace. The white silk blouse that had been revealed was elegant, demure, and simple. Yet something about it somehow seemed deceitfully sexy to him.

69

It was the sheerness, he decided, after a moment's assessment. The delicate material allowed for a conservative appearance while hinting at the white satin undergarment beneath . . . a nicely filled out satin undergarment.

The thin teenage figure of the girl he'd known was good and gone. As Hannah planted her hands on the feminine flare of her hips, her breasts pressed forward, molding themselves against the ivory buttons of her criminally deceptive conservative blouse. It felt to Neil as though he were being inexorably assaulted.

Fight or flight. There was another choice, but Neil ignored it. Instead he turned abruptly away. The window seemed the closest refuge. So he peered with focused concentration out into the dark cold night and down into the rear grounds three stories below.

Hannah realized at once that something was wrong, though for the hundredth time that night she had no idea what. "Neil," she called across the room. "*What* are you doing?"

"Problem solving," he muttered, rubbing his chin. It was very late and he hadn't shaved since morning. He could already feel a rough stubble forming on his skin.

"Excuse me?" she asked, striding closer to his broad shoulders. After a silent minute, she spoke again. "Neil?"

"Yes?"

Hannah exhaled heavily. "Would you mind turning around and talking to me?"

Reluctantly, Neil turned. He was instantly sorry that he had. She was standing much too close. He caught a scent of her. No perfume, just a touch of baby powder and a light peachy floral freshness—her shampoo? And something else . . . like fast-food French fries, but he could hardly believe the girl who'd grown up dining on foie gras, lobster, and white truffles would be eating something like that.

"Well?" asked Hannah.

"Well . . . what?"

Hannah was beginning to feel as though she were trying to sip a ten-pound olive through a tiny cocktail straw. She sighed. "Ryan, in case you haven't noticed, I'm trapped in this room, too. Will you please *talk* to me? Tell me what this 'problem-solving' thing is you're doing."

The brief, furtive blue of Neil's glances reminded Hannah

of the lighthouse in the distance: there and gone, there and gone, there and—

"R.G.D.A.S.," he suddenly said. "It's a process."

Hannah waited. Neil took in her patient stare a moment then began ticking off steps on his fingers. "Recognize and define the problem; gather facts and make assumptions; develop possible solutions; analyze and compare the possible solutions; select the best solution."

Hannah stared at him a moment, mouth agape. "Where did you pick up that little rap?"

"Army," muttered Neil. "It's standard leadership training."

"Leadership? What did you do? I mean—"

"I was a first sergeant during the Gulf War," he explained shortly. "Afterwards, I earned a degree and rose to the level of captain in the MPs."

"MPs?"

Neil's stiff jaw told her that he was extending her extreme patience. "Military Police."

"I see." Hannah studied Neil's tense form and her mind suddenly produced an image of a twenty-year-old Neil on the warm August day he'd abandoned her. She'd never understood it: One week they were laughing on the steep cliffs of glacial period rocks above Second Beach and the next he was quitting his job on the Whitmores's house staff and leaving for Fort Bragg.

With little more than an "I've got to get on with my life," Neil Ryan was out of her life. The only trouble was, Hannah had been planning for an "our" life. And she had naively assumed that Neil felt the same.

"I wrote you," said Hannah quietly. She'd meant to throw the comment out casually, without a care, but the vulnerability came through loud and clear. She almost cringed when she heard her own voice.

Neil studied her face but said nothing. He simply turned back to the window.

Hannah wanted to kick herself for letting her pathetic emotions show. What did she expect from him after all these years anyway? An apology? An explanation? She took a deep breath. Down deep, she had to admit to herself that from the moment she saw him tonight, she'd been expecting both.

God, she was *still* acting naive!

They'd just been kids then. It was long over now, dead. And dead things were supposed to remain buried. Or at least it was clear that Neil wanted it that way. No use trying to persuade him otherwise.

"Oh, really, dear? Why not?"

Hannah wheeled, her eyes wide. Not for the first time that night, she felt *certain* she'd heard a woman's voice in her ear.

Silently, Hannah let her gaze sweep the room.

Empty and still was how she found it. A fluttering of papers on the desk the only movement—a chilly breeze from the open window the obvious explanation for that.

Calling out to Neil might have been an option, but Hannah pressed her lips tight instead. "I've really got to get some rest . . ." she muttered to herself, rubbing her forehead.

"I know," Neil said, overhearing her. He hadn't turned. He was still looking out the window—at Heaven knew what.

Sighing, Hannah moved her hands up and down her arms. She liked the fresh air, but the night breeze was beginning to give the room a chill too intense for the fireplace to dispel.

"Listen, Ryan," said Hannah, stepping up to his back. "Is jumping *really* the best alternative 'solution' to talking with me? Or would you rather *I* be the one to take a flying leap?"

Despite himself, a small smile edged a corner of Neil's mouth northward. He tried his best to keep his face turned toward the open window, but the other half of the pane was pulled partially closed and Hannah caught sight of his half-smile reflected in the glass.

"Aha! You're found out. There *is* a sense of humor entombed in that undertaker expression after all."

Neil turned and surveyed her. The trace of smile was gone. "I do *not* have an undertaker expression."

Hannah smirked. "What do you call it then?"

"A *professional* expression."

"Nonemotional."

"That's right."

"And where did you pick that up? In the army, along with your problem-solving theories?"

"Soldiers learn to contain emotions. And so do good police officers, good detectives . . . and, while we're on the subject, good domestics."

Hannah's eyebrows rose. "Were we on the subject of domestics?"

She caught a glimmer in the blue of Neil's eye. "We were on the subject of containing emotions."

"I see. Well, I never considered that particular comparison."

"Emotions cloud judgment. Emotions distort facts. And, as for domestics, emotions are just plain messy—they imply to their employer that there's a human being and not simply a robot performing less than desirable tasks."

Hannah studied Neil's blue eyes. They were no longer evasive but were steady, the sparkle of challenge evident inside them. Behind her wire-rimmed glasses, Hannah met that challenge with a steady gaze of her own. "Is that how you feel my family treated its staff here? Like impersonal robots? Is that how you feel they treated you?"

Neil didn't answer. Instead he seemed to notice for the first time that Hannah was rubbing her arms. She was cold, he realized. Without hesitation, he turned back toward the open window. With one swift motion he shut and latched it.

"Neil, do you?"

"No," he said shortly but certainly. "I think your parents were kind and fair employers."

Hannah thanked Neil silently for that. In her own memories, Hannah had felt that her late mother and father were exceptionally good people. They knew every member of their staff by name and treated them with as much dignity and respect as any business owner would his or her workers.

"But," continued Neil, "your parents' guests didn't always share their good character."

Hannah sighed. Now it was her turn to cast her gaze out to sea. "Yes, that's true," she admitted. "I can't say that I liked every person who ever stepped under the roof of this house. It's too bad my parents couldn't see through some of them. . . ."

A sharp sound, half laugh, half grunt, came from Neil's throat. Hannah's words were miserably ironic to him.

"What's the laugh for?" asked Hannah.

Neil didn't dare say what was on his mind. In fact, he was still doing his level best to stay in control of this very odd situation.

"Neil?"

He shook his head. "Forget it."

"No," said Hannah, peeved. "Tell me." Without thinking her slender hand reached out, pushing his shoulder in agitation.

The intimate action, as if they were back above the cliffs of Second Beach again, jolted Neil into an automatic response. He captured her hand.

For a second, Neil wanted to be Hannah's friend again, the kind of friend who could share what was really on his mind. He wanted to tell her that she had no business discussing her parents' judgment of character when, within two years after their deaths, she herself had gone and married the very *worst* excuse for a man who'd ever entered the Whitmores's social circle. Neil had always thought Hannah had possessed a more level head than that. But he had obviously thought wrong.

"Neil?"

He looked away. Down at the hand he'd captured. It was her left hand and he had the urge to caress it. But the gold sparkle of her wedding band may as well have been the white-hot flash of a flaming torch. As if burned, he suddenly dropped it.

"Is your husband joining you here?" he asked in as neutral a voice as he could manage.

Hannah bit her tongue a moment at the shock of the question. She hadn't been ready for that. Her arms quickly folded across her stomach. "No," was all the answer she could muster before slowly adding, "not tonight . . ."

A heavy silence descended. Hannah wasn't about to tell Neil the pitiful truth of her personal life. She could take anger from him, even coldness, but she could never take pity.

There was no need for anyone at this hotel to assume anything more than her television audience: that she was Hannah the "happy homemaker." After all, it wasn't as if she were going to rekindle any kind of love affair with Neil Ryan. He had his own life now, didn't he? That piece of jailbait in his arms downstairs came to mind immediately.

"You remember Holly, my younger sister?" asked Hannah, directing the subject off her missing husband.

"Of course," said Neil.

"Then you know about the wedding?"

Neil shook his head. "No. Whose wedding? Holly's?"

"Yes, she'll be having a gala wedding here in two weeks. Maura knows about it. I spoke with her just two days ago—"

Neil gritted his teeth. If he'd had a clue two days ago that Hannah was coming, he certainly would have made himself scarce. He knew now why his mother had been careful not to say a word. Even the schedules had no *Whitmore* on them. Two weeks from now *Carraway* was the wedding registered.

"What's the name of the groom?"

"Reggie. Actually it's Sir Reginald Carraway. I haven't met him yet. He's a British businessman from a prominent family. Holly met him while she was studying in Europe. That's where she is now, finishing her exams in Florence."

"I see."

"It was a whirlwind courtship, and Holly asked me to finalize things for her here," continued Hannah, "which I'm glad to do. Actually, that's how I got the idea for my new *Homemaking* book. It will focus on weddings, and I'm looking forward to your mother coauthoring it with me."

Neil sighed. "I can't believe my mother never said a word to me about this. Not even the book."

"Well, I haven't asked her yet—about the book. But I will."

Neil nodded. "So hubby would get in the way, huh?"

Hannah's gaze turned down at once. She stepped away from Neil and walked toward the fireplace. "Something like that," she murmured, as she warmed her hands. "Herbert will be coming for the wedding," she added quietly.

A fist of frustration tensed in Neil's stomach as he watched Hannah obviously struggling so hard to make believe everything was peachy in homemaker land. *Her marriage is a disaster.* It was as clear as day. A blind man could see it.

Neil ran a hand through his short, thick, raven hair as he toyed for a moment with the idea of pressing her, making her break and tell him the truth. But he knew it would give neither one of them pleasure.

Dammit to hell. He may have harbored regrets over the past, but he wasn't a cruel man. And he disliked immensely seeing this woman in pain. He was a little surprised just how much he disliked it. But what could he do, really, besides give her a wide berth and allow her the privacy she plainly wanted? He almost laughed out loud with the irony. That was exactly what he was paid so highly to do, wasn't it? To ensure the privacy and security of this hotel's exclusive guests.

"I wonder what's keeping that kid brother of mine," stated Neil, his voice laced with tension. He walked to the phone and tried dialing the front desk again.

Hannah checked her watch, surprised at the time. They'd been trapped in here for well over an hour. It seemed like a fraction of that. Now she was really beginning to feel the effects of the long drive. The sight of the time alone made her collapse into the elaborately carved antique armchair near the fireplace. When she did, her eyes caught sight of that odd cat-shaped vase again. It was a strange antique, vaguely Egyptian in design, but it was brass, not bronze, and was likely fashioned sometime in the last few centuries.

"Neil?"

"Phone's still dead," muttered Neil at the desk.

"What's the story on this vase?"

"What story?" Neil looked up and took in the sight of the exhausted woman across the room as he replaced the receiver.

"You said Maura thought it belonged here," reminded Hannah, her gaze strangely drawn to the cat's brassy eyes, dark golden almonds that seemed almost to glow. "What did you mean by that? What did she mean?"

Neil walked slowly over to Hannah again. He glanced uneasily at the vase, then back to her. "Maura found a passage in Daisy Doyle's letters. She—Daisy—talked about a cat-shaped brass vase in her possession."

"And?" Hannah looked up at Neil, sensing strongly that he was holding something back.

Neil shrugged. "And Maura felt it belonged in Daisy's original bedroom."

"*And?*" goaded Hannah. "There's obviously more to it."

Neil stared unhappily at Hannah. "No," he stated, "there's really nothing more—" But Hannah's steadfast glare continued to needle him. He sighed, recalling how stubborn she used to be—how she liked to dig and dig until she got to the truth.

"Daisy Doyle believed that this vase was one of three in existence," Neil finally explained. "She traced its origin back over a century. Apparently a Yankee clipper had brought the three vases here from North Africa. The design is Egyptian."

Neil stopped yet again, hoping that was as far as he'd have to go. But Hannah's continued stare soon had him throwing up his hands and relinquishing the rest of the tale.

"Oh, all right! Apparently the cat symbolized eternal life to the Egyptians, and Daisy believed a legend that was attached to a vessel like this one described in some writings thought to be part of the Egyptian *Book of the Dead*. If fashioned correctly, the vessel is supposedly able to catch the willing souls of lovers who die under the same roof with it, uniting their spirits. Dan Doyle died of natural causes in this mansion, and Daisy believed the vase caught Dan's soul, allowing him to wait for her. When she became terminally ill a year later, Daisy arranged to pass away under the mansion's roof, too. She'd placed the cat vase near her bed to remind her that her soul would be united with Dan's for eternity."

Hannah blinked with surprise. "That's a wonderfully romantic story, Neil." She looked again at the vase. "Why didn't you want to tell me?"

Neil's arms folded across his chest. "It's just another part of the tourist ghost lore around here. I don't enjoy repeating it."

Hannah was taken aback. "Why in the world not?"

"It's just too ridiculous."

"Oh, I see. Not plausible enough for the hard-boiled hotel detective's hard-boiled reality?"

Neil's eyebrow rose at the bull's-eye, but he said nothing. Instead he watched as Hannah twisted and turned in the stiff-backed antique chair.

"Uncomfortable?" he asked her, thinking how ironic the idea was when she obviously seemed set on making him feel that way tonight.

"I think this thing was made for looking at rather than sitting in," complained Hannah. That was a major sin in her decorating creed. There were no "show" rooms in Homemaking Hannah's world. On her cozy set, she always gave decorating tips that exemplified, as she'd coined it, "livable elegance." She made a mental note to speak with Maura about the sense of it.

"Then maybe you shouldn't sit in it any longer," suggested Neil.

"Fine," she said, giving up on the chair and standing to face him. "What do you suggest?"

"Why don't you go to bed?" he said, then his voice softened. "You look dead tired."

Hannah glanced across the room at the king-size mattress with the down comforter and the elaborately carved head- and footboards. It did look inviting. With her thumb and forefinger she reached beneath her wire-rimmed glasses and rubbed her tired eyes.

Neil watched her. Then, in a gesture that came to him without his usual analytical thought, he stepped closer. Reaching out, he slipped the glasses from her nose and folded them gently in his hands.

Shocked, Hannah simply stared up at him.

Neil studied her wide gray eyes, sans the barrier between them. They were so luminously open with expectation, he felt almost drawn into them. For a moment, his attention strayed to her mouth. *Christ...*

Neil closed his eyes a moment to compose himself. As gently as he could, he took her hand, cradling it softly in his own. Then he placed the glasses in her palm. "You need to rest," he said. "I'll pull up a chair by the fire and wait for someone to answer that note. Why don't you turn off the lights and lie down?"

If there had been a star out on this cloudy night, Hannah knew, in that moment, what she would have wished on it. But the clouds were thick over the ocean, so she bit her tongue and silently nodded her agreement to Neil.

She turned and walked across the room, her legs less than steady as she picked up her bag and headed into the bathroom. Closing the door behind her, she barely noticed the beautiful restoration job that had been done on the large master bath. The Italian marble, the Jacuzzi in the double-size bathtub, the intricately patterned floor tiles.

She dropped her bag, then went to the wall to lean on the sink and stare into the mirror. An average-looking face with pale skin, round cheeks, pointy chin, and tired eyes stared back.

When Hannah had been sixteen, she'd fantasized about the idea of plastic surgery. But her face was so average—there was no *one* thing she felt was truly fixable with a few slices of even a gifted surgeon's scalpel. *Your spirit is beautiful,* her mother had told her back then. *It shines from your eyes . . . and there's no amount of collagen and stitches that can give a woman that.*

Still, on a painful exhale, she recalled the image of Neil holding that blonde in red. Suddenly, Hannah understood why Neil was acting so frustrated and angry at being trapped in this suite. He was probably livid about missing his chance with that gorgeous young woman.

Hannah couldn't really blame him. After all, look at what he was stuck with in here. She sighed. It wasn't like she felt sorry for herself; the truth was, she'd completely accepted her physical drawbacks. That acceptance was what protected her from further disappointments with men—a true waste of energy, in Hannah's opinion.

Sure, Neil seemed to be finally warming up to their friendship again, but she wasn't kidding herself. If Neil Ryan had ever really felt an attraction to her all those years ago, he'd probably felt that way out of pity—or some kind of misplaced loyalty to her parents. But that was a long time ago.

And, as for the only other man she'd had in her life, well, she and Herbert now had their relationship "arranged" to suit them both perfectly, didn't they? Percentages and everything.

Abruptly, Hannah looked away from the mirror and turned on the faucet. With quick, sharp motions she splashed cold water on her tired face, then scrubbed it again. But after only a minute, she found herself staring at the woman in the mirror again.

Your perfectly arranged life doesn't feel so perfect anymore, does it?

Hannah shut her eyes, not wanting to face the truth.

For the past few years, the happy homemaker and trustworthy tastemaker act had absorbed her more thoroughly than a child's view from a merry-go-round, blurring everything into a swirl of color and light.

Night after night she would fall into bed exhausted, then rise at the crack of dawn to start all over again, without a moment to consider what was reality—and what was illusion.

But Hannah's whirling schedule had stopped a few days ago, and her perfect *Homemaking* set was no longer waiting for her every morning. Suddenly, her real life had come into painfully sharp focus: Her actual home was a barren, too-silent, barely furnished apartment with a faintly smelly refrigerator, a few dying plants, and an empty bed. She had no family life, few friends, and no idea how to have fun.

It was no wonder she'd fled Chicago as fast as possible, trying somehow to find a real home again. But not even this beautiful place was the same anymore. Neil certainly wasn't.

Hannah opened her eyes and stared at the mirror. *It's all been a sham.*

Okay, maybe not all. Maybe her *work* wasn't—but that wasn't enough. Not anymore.

"Face it, Hannah," she mumbled. "Your life's a grand illusion. And you have no idea how to change it."

With a sluggish numbness, Hannah splashed more cold water on her face and scrubbed it again. Next she pulled the pins from her dull, dark blond hair, which fell limply past her shoulders, and began to brush out the tangles. She dug in her bag for her peach skin cream and smoothed it into her face and hands.

Back inside her small overnight bag, she decidedly reached past the white negligee and instead grabbed a pair of gray workout sweatpants and an oversized *Homemaking* T-shirt that the technicians on her show liked to wear. She quickly changed, then picked up her wire-rimmed glasses. She was ready to put them away for the night, into their case, when she hesitated.

Hannah didn't really need the glasses to see. Her vision was only slightly farsighted, so she mainly wore them for driving. Nevertheless, she felt the need to slip the frames back onto her nose.

Better to face him with her glasses on, thought Hannah resolutely, if only to keep herself from ever losing focus again.

Outside the bathroom door, in the main room of the suite, Neil Ryan was nervously pacing. At first he loosened his tie, then he gave up and impatiently whipped the strip of navy-and-red patterned silk off altogether. He didn't know what had happened to J. J., but his best theory at this point was that he'd simply gone off duty, calling in a front desk replacement. Which meant Neil was stuck here until morning.

After slipping out of his suit coat and hanging it over one of the chairs near the fireplace, Neil crossed the room and flipped off the lights. By the glow of the fireplace, he unbuttoned his shirt collar and began crisply rolling up his starched sleeves when Hannah reappeared.

As she clicked off the bathroom light and stepped out into the suite's main room, Neil felt as if he'd entered a Greek myth—the one about the human turning into a tree. With one look at her, he was transformed, rooted there mid-motion in the center of the room, unable to move, to breathe.

In her oversized T-shirt and sweatpants, her long hair cascading over her shoulders with a newly brushed sheen, Hannah looked like a teenager again. Neil blinked, but the vision was still there. He saw her in a field of yellow daisies, relaxing on the grass, then running along the Cliff Walk, her long sun-kissed ponytail flying out in the ocean's stiff breeze, her fluid movements as graceful and free as a deer in the forest, a seagull on the wind.

For a moment, it made him feel young again, too. Carefree and happy . . . when every dream seemed possible. When even love was pure and sweet, a thing that could not be sucked hollow by greed, rumor, and the souring blight of self-interest.

Hannah moved into the room a few steps before she realized that he was staring at her. Her gray eyes were shining in the firelight, the few golden highlights left in her hair shimmered like ripe wheat.

"Neil? Is everything all right?" Her voice was close to a whisper—a natural reaction to the suite's dimmed lighting.

Neil had lost his voice for a moment. "Yes," he finally managed, forcing himself to turn away. "I'm just settling in over here."

Hannah stepped toward the bed. It was so very big. She saw Neil had removed his tie and jacket. Beneath a starched, whiter-than-white Arrow shirt, she saw his muscles move as he positioned the chair to fully face the fireplace.

Then he turned, and she gasped. He was still wearing his dark brown leather shoulder holster. She saw the butt of his handgun under his left shoulder.

"Why do you have to wear . . . that . . . "

"What?"

"The . . . the . . ."

Neil's eyebrows rose. He was so accustomed to wearing a firearm, he'd long ago taken that fact for granted. "Does the gun bother you? I'm sorry."

Hannah was amazed at how quickly and gallantly he removed the offending item from her sight. After slipping out of the straps, he wrapped the leather upon itself then set it carefully on the rococo desk.

"Thank you. I'm sorry . . . I knew you were wearing one, I was just surprised. I mean, I forgot that you were wearing . . ." She stopped her awkward rambling and took a deep breath. "You didn't have to do that," she stated evenly.

Neil shook his head. "It's all right. I'm not expecting any kidnappers to break in on us tonight—especially since we can't seem to get out. But it *is* part of my job, Hannah, the hotel has had its share of . . . well, of difficulties."

"Really?" Hannah was intrigued now and a little surprised that Neil Ryan's earlier coldness had melted into a need to somehow explain himself to her. She stepped closer to the bed and climbed on, arranging some of the many pillows behind her. "Tell me."

The sight of Hannah settling onto the king-size bed was giving Neil a king-size ache—much lower than his head. "You don't want to hear about it," he said after clearing his suddenly dry throat. "Why don't you just get some rest?"

"I will." Hannah punched a pillow and propped it up behind her. "But I'm curious now. Tell me about *one* at least. Just one 'difficulty.' "

"No."

"Aw, c'mon," she prompted. "Just one and I'll let you off the hook for the night. I'll even let you sleep with your gun."

"Hannah," Neil responded, walking toward the bed, "I know you may find this hard to believe, but even I don't share my bed with a gun."

"Oh? Who do you share it with then?"

Hannah's eyes widened when she realized what she'd asked. She had meant the words as a joke. But they had come out much differently, like a hazardously teasing invitation.

The warmth of embarrassment slowly flooded Hannah's

cheeks, but she fought the urge to babble some kind of apology, or even look away. Instead, clenching her teeth in stoic silence, Hannah kept her eyes on Neil's paralyzed face.

She intended to hear his answer.

Chapter Nine

Who do you share your bed with?

Hannah's words echoed inside Neil's skull like the blare of reveille to a hungover soldier. *What a friggin' question!*

For a long moment, Neil stared blankly into Hannah's face, lit by the flickering fireplace across the room. He noticed a pink blush had dawned on her cheeks. It slowly blossomed to a rosy hue.

My God, she's refreshing. The women he usually got involved with couldn't blush for the life of them. The innocence of it sparked something warm and hopeful within Neil, as if he were seeing a tiny ray of brilliance after a night of freezing black.

Unfortunately, the blush also sparked something else. Something that had Neil closing his eyes a moment to regain his precious control. *Options, options, think of your options,* he silently commanded himself.

Solution Option Number One: Tell her the truth.

Sure, he could tell her that he hadn't shared his bed in over six months. And six months before that he'd had nothing more than a series of one-night stands. Safe sex every one—

more than physically, they'd been "safe" to Neil because every one had been without emotion.

He could tell her about his failed first marriage, too. But what would she think of him then?

A flash of masculine pride suddenly streaked through his gut. Why the hell should he give a rat's ass what Hannah Whitmore thought of him, anyway? She'd made her choice, hadn't she? Married the kind of man everyone expected her to.

Solution Option Number Two: Tell her off.

He could. But somehow he knew that exhuming long-buried anger would be a grave mistake. He had no desire to feel those teenage emotions again, to relive the accusations that had made him feel worthless. And yet their echoes were still there inside him, living and breathing despite the years of dormancy:

Why else would a handsome boy like that go for a little plain thing like Hannah? The itinerant housemaids had gossiped plenty all those years ago.

Maybe he's got a life of leisure planned for himself, eh? And all's the work he'll need to do will be in the sack, if you get me.

Even some of his townie friends couldn't be convinced. To them it was some kind of coup. *Nice goin', Neil.*

Yeah, you're settin' yourself up good, all right. Bangin' her yet?

He tried to ignore the gossip, punch out the wisecrackers, but then other voices began to say things. Voices that he couldn't ignore because their opinions had always meant something to him.

You got to admit, the money's an issue, Charlie Baxter, the head gardener, had said one day in the back kitchen area.

My son's a good boy, Maura Ryan had insisted to all present. *With a good heart.*

Of course he is, agreed her assistant housekeeper, Sally Ellen Grady, *but it may have nothing to do with a good heart. He is very young, after all. And the young don't know their own minds.*

That's true, chauffeur Benji had argued. *Could be he don't even realize all the things attractin' him to Hannah. Maybe he thinks it's the girl and claims it's the girl, but down deep the girl wouldn't hold half the appeal if she didn't have the money.*

Neil knew now that the pride of a young man is a fragile thing, a main artery to a still-forming identity. Back then all the gossip had lashed at his ego day in and day out. His own mother was gradually doubting his intentions. But the worst of it was that Neil Ryan himself had come to mistrust his own feelings.

After one terrible confrontation with Hannah's grandmother Edith, in which she called him an aspiring gigolo, Neil's solution was to put an end to the torture. To just cut all ties and leave.

He'd gone to the army, where merit and not money was supposed to be the measure of a man. But even there he'd had some hard lessons.

For a short time, in the back of his mind, Neil had hoped somehow that Hannah would know to wait for him. As irrational as it was, he'd wanted her to wait until he'd made a name for himself, wait until he'd gathered together his own fortune. *I'll show them all. They'll see. They'll all see,* he told himself.

But there was no name. No fortune. Only mistakes and missteps, and these days he had nothing more to show than a slowly growing investigations business. Sure, he was proud enough of it, but it was nothing spectacular. In his own way, to the rich and powerful, he was still the hired help. And she was married to Herbert Peabody, although it appeared to be an unhappy marriage.

Solution Option Number Three: Make love to her.

Neil could do it. He could make her happy—at least for one night. They'd never crossed that line all those years ago. They'd kissed, caressed, fooled around some, but he hadn't pushed her to consummate their affections, romantically hoping they could wait until their wedding night.

But there'd been no wedding night for them, and now he felt his sexual curiosity rising. Obviously so had she.

Still, a voice inside him asked where that would leave him. Tonight was the present, not the past, and this was a married woman looking for an affair.

Don't you want more?

The question unnerved him. He'd denied such thoughts for

so long. Yet . . . maybe, just maybe, he did want more. And deserved more, too.

Solution Option Number Four: Cut and run.

With a sigh, Neil dropped his gaze, knowing it was the right thing to do . . . *again.* She was silent, still waiting for his answer. Well, he'd run, but he had no desire to *cut.* Not Hannah. But he had to. He was out of options—

"No, you're not."

Neil's eyes widened with confusion. He could swear a male voice had actually whispered the thought into his ear.

"Remember what you used to do?"

There it was again . . . and Neil had to admit, no matter where it came from, the suggestion *did* seem the exact right solution for letting him off the hook and making Hannah feel good.

When she saw his outstretched hand before her, she could hardly believe her eyes. Hannah swallowed nervously, feeling like a girl again as she slid her fingers across his palm.

Neil closed his thumb over her knuckles and gently pulled her hand up as he bent his head down. His lips were warm and tender on the back of her hand. Just as they'd been the night they'd gone to the Cliff Walk after her coming-out party. Just as they'd been the last time he'd said good-bye to her.

When Neil looked up, into her eyes, he saw them glistening. *She remembers . . .*

"Good night, Hannah," he whispered, renewing that old feeling of gallantry—that one gesture that made him feel like he'd been born to money, to position, to privilege, just like her.

Hannah didn't trust her voice, so she just smiled and nodded as he released her hand. Neil turned and headed for the chair's by the fireplace. The brilliant glowing flames seemed to light him up inside as he realized that he'd never kissed another woman's hand. Not in his life—not since Hannah.

Before tonight, Neil would have bet his reputation that such sentimental gestures had been long dead inside of him. Carefree men, like his younger brother, may have been capable of such things, but not Neil Ryan. Not anymore.

It was fatigue, Neil decided. That's what had made him regress into his romantic teenage years for a moment . . . except that he didn't feel particularly tired.

After crossing the suite, Neil settled into one of the elaborately carved chairs by the hearth. His gaze caught sight of the antique brass cat vase in the corner, the fire's flickering flame making the cat's dark golden eyes appear to shimmer with life.

Staring at the odd vase, Neil considered the bizarre happenings tonight. He added that to the strange ghostly hallucination he himself had been trying to write off for three solid years; and, against his will, Neil found himself adding up the evidence toward some truly insane musings. Could Daisy's preposterous romantic belief have been right all along? Could this strange cat-shaped vase have *really* caught Dan and Daisy Doyle's souls?

Neil shook his head. It was just too irrational. Too unbelievable—

A muffled rustling across the room snagged Neil's attention. Hannah was settling in, he realized, under the luxurious bedcovers. *She's safe and warm.* The thought warmed him.

With a sigh, Neil turned his attention to his own bed. He tried to get comfortable by leaning his broad shoulders against the antique chair's stiff backing, but that didn't help. He tried shifting and stretching his long legs out in front of him—no good, either. This wasn't a chair, he decided, it was an antique torture device.

He sighed. It was going to be a long night.

"Neil?"

He didn't turn. "Yes, Hannah?"

"The bed . . ."

"Yes?"

"It's very big."

Neil remained focused on the flames of the fireplace and took a deep breath. *Control, control, control.*

"Neil? Did you hear me?"

"Yes," he whispered.

"There's no reason for you to sit in that chair all night."

Oh, yes there is, thought Neil, *there damn well is.*

"Neil?"

"Just go to sleep, Hannah," he said softly.

"But you could just lie on the other side—"

"Go to sleep," he said again, this time not so softly and far from sweetly.

He heard the sound of a frustrated *humph* and the dull *floof* of a thick down pillow being punched. That was when he sighed himself and pulled the second chair over. Then he untied his shoes, slipped them off, and propped his sock-covered feet onto the second chair.

In combat situations, he'd taught soldiers how to get sleep anytime and anywhere no matter the circumstance, or how long they were given for rest. Neil himself had been able to master the art of falling asleep at will, but he hadn't used it in years. He called upon that skill now, rusty as it was.

Forcing his eyes to close, he began to breathe deeply and concentrate on his breath. Soon he was drifting off. And, if he were lucky, he'd remain dead to the world until morning.

"What do you make of this?" asked Daisy, hovering above the lightly sleeping form of Neil Ryan.

Dan considered the situation. *"Disastrously bad plan, sweetie."*

"Dan, it's much too soon in the case to make such a concise summation. Besides, at least they're talking."

"Yes, well, not anymore. Now they're sleeping. And, I might add, far enough away from each other to employ telegraph service."

"Don't be negative."

"Don't be naive."

"Naive!" exclaimed Daisy, sending the fireplace into a momentarily violent flare.

"Daisy, they haven't seen each other for years, what did you expect?"

"How about love at second sight?"

Dan Doyle swirled over to where Hannah was lying on the bed. She was sleeping, but only lightly. Tossing and turning had put her bedcovers into a wretched twist.

"Should we wake her up?" Daisy asked. *"Or him?"*

"The woman looks a little like you, I think. When you were her age . . . and alive, of course."

"How rude."

"What's rude about that? You're not alive, are you?"

"Not that, the reference to my age."

Dan laughed, sending little ripples into the air molecules

around him. *"Your age, sweetie, should only be of consequence to literary critics at this point."*

Daisy huffed. *"You're older than me anyway . . ."*

"I would have been one hundred and five. If I'd lived. But beggars can't be choosers. Existence is existence. This form has its advantages. I guess you're right, Dais. Let's have some fun."

"What shall we do?"

"Well, I think I know where you got your plan. Remember back in the late thirties when Skipper Vandenburg hired us to track down his five missing yachting cups?"

"Dan, don't be ridiculous. Do you see any trophies in this room?"

"Daisy, don't you recall where we found them?"

"I recall the skipper thought his chief competitor had done the dirty deed."

"That's what the skipper thought, but the truth was his wife had taken them. To shake him up," recalled Dan. *"The skipper's obsession with winning the cups had taken up half a decade. She wanted a family and they had yet to start one."*

"Yes, that's right," agreed Daisy. *"Didn't we write about that case?"*

"It was only a short story."

"Now I remember! 'In His Cups,' wasn't it? But the skipper didn't drink, did he?"

"Nope, but he sure treated his yachting like an addiction."

"True." Daisy laughed. *"You were always the one to think of clever titles, but really, what does that have to do with these two?"*

"C'mon, Dais, don't you remember? During a routine search of the skipper's home we found the cups in the wife's dressing room—"

"Yes, yes!" Daisy broke in excitedly. *"I remember now. They were barely hidden. She'd obviously wanted us to find them."*

"Right," said Dan. *"She was at the end of her rope with trying to get her husband to understand how she felt. So we found a way to lock the skipper in her bedroom with her—"*

"And the cups!" exclaimed Daisy. *"Yes, I recall!"*

"They resolved their differences, and started a family that very night . . . yes, that was a splendid idea I had—"

"You *had!*" exclaimed Daisy. "*But it was my idea!*"

"*Mmmm, was it? Can't recall.*"

"*Oh, Danny, it was mine all right. In fact, I'm sure that's why I thought it up again tonight.*"

"Really?" groaned Dan skeptically. "Well, there ain't exactly any families being started tonight that I can see."

A loud snore issued from Neil Ryan. The sudden noise startled the deceased detectives into silence for a moment. Finally, Daisy released a ghostly sigh. "*I suppose this brings us to my original question.*"

"*Which was?*"

"*Whom do we awaken?*"

Dan considered this and so did Daisy. They flitted from Hannah to Neil and back again. Then they both reached the same conclusion at once.

A sharp jolt to his body abruptly startled Neil. For a split second he thought he'd fallen asleep on a protection detail back in D.C. He automatically shot to his feet and reached for his sidearm. But there was no sidearm. He turned one way, then another.

"Damn," he murmured, seeing the overturned chair at his feet. With a sigh he rubbed his eyes with the efficient use of one hand's thumb and forefinger. The room was very dark. The fire had just about died out and there was an odd chill in the air—sharper than you'd expect. His skin prickled with it.

He checked the illuminated face of his watch—4:15 A.M.

Peering into the darkness around him, Neil thought it was extremely odd that he would have toppled the chair on which he'd been soundly sleeping. He usually slept like a corpse, hardly disturbing a thing around him. The idea just didn't sit right, and yet that had to be the explanation.

Neil bent down and righted the chair, but he didn't sit down again. His back and neck were protesting too much. He stretched one way and then another. Then he went to the fire and dropped on a few new splits of wood. He grabbed a poker and began resuscitating the low flame when he heard a soft moan.

"Neil . . ."

It was Hannah, he realized. She was calling him. With care,

Neil set down the poker and lightly stepped across the Persian carpet until he reached her side of the king-size bed.

He would have liked to say that Hannah looked like an angel as she slept—but her expression wasn't serene enough. In fact, it appeared very troubled. A frown distorted her normally pleasant features and her slender body was violently tossing and turning. He touched his hand to her forehead to check for fever, but she felt fine. Was it just plain frustration that was unsettling her tonight? he wondered. Maybe even *sexual* frustration?

Neil wondered how bad her marriage really was. Maybe he could use a colleague in Chicago for a discreet investigation. Why not? At least to satisfy his own curiosity. A quick, quiet call was all it would take.

At the other end of the room, the fire was catching and the darkness was alleviated somewhat by the glow of rising flame. Hannah began kicking off the bedcovers. She twisted toward him and settled down a moment, her face relaxing. Tendrils of dark blond hair now framed her cheeks, long locks spread out on the pillow around her, looking more golden in the firelight, as if they'd caught fire, too.

Now, thought Neil, a slight smile touching him, *now she looks like an angel*.

Neil couldn't stop his gaze from drifting lower, taking in the braless form beneath the thin T-shirt with the word *Homemaking* printed across it in cookie-cutter letters. He tried to picture her as she might have been on their wedding night: sans shirt, sans sweatpants, just lounging there, naked and lovely, wanting him.

Neil swallowed uncomfortably.

"This is nuts," he murmured for the millionth time that night. Yet, as his eyes strayed back to her face, and, more specifically, her rose-colored mouth, Neil felt an overwhelming sexual curiosity rising in his veins. A voice seemed to coax him to do what he most wanted—at least at this moment.

"Go ahead, Neil . . . go ahead . . ."

He wanted to do it, to bend down low, lean his weight in. Just the thought brought him a little closer to her. His shadow covered Hannah's face. After all these years, a part of him wanted to know what it would feel like to kiss his girl again.

Would it be a cool whisper-light brushing of silk on velvet? Or a hot combination of softness and sensuality?

The idea of her sleeping made it all the more powerful a temptation for him, as if he'd entered a fairy tale and his kiss was what would wake Hannah to some kind of happily ever after for them both.

Neil closed his eyes tightly and forced himself to get control of his thoughts. This was crazy. She was married, and he was off romance for good. He was about to turn away when an invisible hand seemed to connect with his back. And shove.

"What the—"

In an instant he was on top of her.

"Ooooph!" Hannah had been sleeping lightly for the past few hours, but the sudden dropping of a one-hundred-ninety-pound man across her stomach would probably have woken a coma patient.

"—hell!" cursed Neil in shock. He felt like a half-suffocated fish, flopping around on an outboard deck—only there was no deck, just a king-size bed with a half-crazed, half-conscious woman squirming in alarm beneath him.

"Wha . . . wha . . . what the heck is happening?" demanded a still-groggy Hannah. Her limbs were thrashing in chaotic movements, twisting the bedcovers and preventing Neil from regaining his balance. For a few seconds, a tangle of arms and legs was all either of them could make out.

"Yow!" exclaimed Hannah as her long hair got snagged and pulled in the wrestling match. "Neil, what the heck are you doing!?"

"Sorry, sorry . . . I just tripped and—"

Neil tried to place his hand down on the mattress but failed. Too late he realized he'd ended up with a palm full of Hannah's right breast. The idea of it feeling nice registered about the same instant before the slap to his cheek. "Ouch!"

"Get off me!"

"Christ, Hannah, you don't understand. It was a mistake. Dammit! I am *not* attacking you—even though that's what it obviously looks like—"

"Are you crazy or something!?"

"You moaned—called my name. I just came over to check

on you . . . I tripped or something. Lost my balance. Believe me, Hannah, please. . . ."

Hannah watched Neil slide away from her on the mattress. He had a look on his handsome features that could only be described as contrite horror. She realized that he was telling the truth.

"God, Neil, you really are crazy," said Hannah as she struggled to bring herself into a sitting position. "But I do believe you."

Neil froze. "You do?"

Hannah nodded. She felt like she was crazy, too. She'd actually been dreaming of kissing Neil. Was *sure* it had been only a dream . . .

"Neil, just answer me this," asked Hannah. "Were you . . . I mean, were we . . . ?"

Neil rolled away and sat up, leaning his back against the headboard—a beautifully carved antique with a subtle cleave in the center that suggested, as so many other things did in this place, a heart.

"Were we *what*?" asked Neil, not sure how to handle this situation. For him it was definitely a first.

"Were we . . . kissing? I mean, were you kissing me just now? In my sleep?"

This was just about the most humiliated Neil had felt since basic training. "No, Hannah," he said softly, tipping a guilty glance her way, *I was merely fantasizing about it.* "Let's just forget this happened, okay?"

Hannah could agree to it, but she didn't think she wanted to. It was just too satisfying to see cool, collected Neil Ryan this uncomfortable. The thought of it made her smile—and then begin to laugh.

"Stop laughing," said Neil. But she didn't and before he could stop himself he added in frustration, "That's an order."

Hannah really did want to stop; but, when she looked at him sitting there so stiffly and seriously, giving orders in front of two delicately carved cupids in the bed's headboard, she only began to laugh harder.

"C'mon, Hannah—" he tried, but then realized it didn't matter. For one thing she wasn't listening anyway. And, for another, there was something about her laughter that was irresistibly infectious. The whole thing *was* kind of funny. In fact, so was this whole screwed-up night, ever since he'd had to greet Hannah after all these years with a spoiled, trashed debutante sprawled across his arms.

It took a full minute before the paroxysms that shook both their bodies dissipated into coughing chuckles. Finally, Neil's blue eyes risked a glance at Hannah. She was pulling back her long hair and still giggling to herself. When she caught him spying on her, he looked away.

"I saw you looking, Ryan," she accused.

"No way," he returned, trying not to begin laughing again.

"I *saw* you," she insisted, then playfully pushed him in the arm. Hannah remembered the teasing games they used to play, and, for just a moment, she felt like a teenager again, carefree and happy, and—

"Hannah, I'm sorry."

The bubble burst quickly. Neil had stopped the game, stopped the play. His voice had gone serious all of a sudden. His demeanor back to treating her like a stranger.

But we are strangers, aren't we? realized Hannah. Too much had happened over too many years to pretend they weren't—that's what Neil had been trying to tell her all night.

"Don't be sorry, Neil," she said after a moment. "It's okay . . . really."

Neil nodded and turned his face away. Hannah realized he was going to leave the bed, probably for those torturous antique chairs again. "Neil, you really don't have to spend the rest of the night on the rack."

"What?" He turned back.

"Why don't you just take one side of the bed? I don't mind."

"But—" Neil rubbed his stiff neck. He wasn't as young as he used to be, and he didn't like admitting his back ached.

"It's okay," assured Hannah. "For Heaven's sake, the bed's Olympic-sized. We'd have to hail a cab to get to each other."

"You trust me?"

Hannah laughed. "I always trusted you, Neil Ryan." Then she turned away from him and lay down on her side before adding softly, "It was you who never trusted me."

Neil's eyebrows rose and he sat there on the bed for a few long minutes. The crackle of the fire and the distant pounding of the ocean surf outside filled the quiet of the room. Without a word he turned to look at Hannah. He noticed that some of the covers were still twisted and he reached to smooth them out. In the process, he drew them up over her.

Reluctantly, he finally settled in on the other side of her, far enough away so that he wouldn't risk rolling into her—though he might just roll off his end, he was so close to it.

There were a thousand thoughts scrambling up Neil's usually orderly mind. *Just go to sleep,* he commanded himself, preferring not to make sense of any of them tonight. Instead, he concentrated once more on his breathing.

Across the mattress, Hannah had closed her eyes, but she could not yet fall asleep. She was listening to Neil's breathing, she realized. She wasn't used to a man breathing near her at night.

Her own deep breaths didn't do much to relax her. She'd dreamed that Neil was kissing her. It had seemed so real that now it completely unsettled her. In fact, it was likely to ruin her slumber for the next six months.

"Stupid," Hannah whispered to herself. "You're just plain stupid." She was supposed to be a *married* woman. Three years ago she'd had a choice, and she'd chosen to keep the ring on her finger. Back then she had known what sacrifices it would entail, and she'd made them. In fact, she'd been all too eager to make them.

Hannah Whitmore Peabody was a *Mrs.* happy homemaker. That's how she'd been able to get and keep the host position on the *Homemaking* show. That was the identity that had allowed her to enter the book publishing world, and now a major television network. *Mrs.* happy homemaker was supposed to be a wholesome role model for family life.

Face it, Hannah, having an affair with an old flame could get your ass fired. Sure, maybe some really big star could handle the assault on her image, but Hannah wasn't a really big star. She was just a rising one.

Chip Saunders, and the show's sponsors, and the network brass wanted a wholesome host. If those executives and money men and women thought she was doing anything to jeopardize that image, they'd dump her from *Homemaking* faster than a burned tin of banana nut muffins.

Anyway, reasoned Hannah, being a *Mrs.* had always had

its advantages socially. A *Mrs.* didn't have to risk her heart and dignity with fly-by-night Don Juans who'd laugh themselves silly if they knew the truth of her sexual experience.

A *Mrs.* didn't have well-meaning friends forcing blind dates down her throat and worrying that she was "lonely." A *Mrs.* was all taken care of, snug as a bug, thank you very much, and not missing a thing.

"Except maybe one thing," a disembodied voice whispered into Hannah's ear. But she ignored it, listening instead to the sound of Neil's breathing until she herself finally fell asleep.

Chapter
Ten

Tiffany Townsend had heard somewhere that sex kept people young. She examined her face as she stepped, dripping wet, from her morning shower and stood naked in front of the bathroom's full-length anti-fogging mirror.

"God, if that's true, I'm in trouble," she murmured.

Slight shadows were detectable under tired blue eyes, and her skin looked sallow. Then she paused and examined her mouth.

"What's this?"

She pulled out the small barbering mirror, attached by an extending arm to the wall, and flipped it around to the magnified side. The enlarged reflection of her skin showed a very tiny line around her mouth. *Shit.*

Like her mother, Tiffany didn't think she'd be needing her first face-lift until thirty-seven or thirty-eight, at least. But, if she wasn't careful, she'd have to start a decade sooner. Maybe she should cut back on the drinking. And switch to a domestic cigarette—one with a filter.

Or maybe, thought Tiffany, that saying about sex *was* true. After all, last night had been an unprecedented disaster.

Thanks to *both* Ryans, she was becoming old before her time.

"But nobody rejects Tiffany Ashton Townsend," she murmured with narrowed eyes. *"Nobody."* There'd have to be consequences, she decided. Yes, one way or another, she'd make the Ryan boys pay.

A knock at the door sounded, and Tiffany grabbed one of the hotel's thick terry bathrobes. She belted it around her tiny waist as she walked across the room.

"Room service," said a thin, very average-looking young man in a hotel uniform, holding a silver breakfast tray.

"You'd better have the aspirins or I'll be *very* annoyed."

The young man smiled brightly. "Got them, miss, don't worry."

Another Mr. At-Your-Service, thought Tiffany, *how tiresome.*

"Fine," said Tiffany as he stepped in to set up.

Tiffany was about to turn and follow when she heard a familiar voice down the hall. Carefully, she peeked around the slightly recessed doorway of her guest room and recognized Neil Ryan.

Now what the hell was he doing coming out of a guest room doorway at eight-forty in the morning?

"Morning, Tif."

Tiffany turned to see her drinking buddy from last night, her second cousin Clark Von Devon, standing there in J. Crew safari khakis and a Ralph Lauren knit shirt. He looked ever the chipper WASP, tanned and ready for a day of recreation. Hardly hungover, too—the bastard.

Since boarding school, Tiffany had learned how to hold her liquor better than anyone, but she could never wear it well when morning came.

"Shhhhh," she said quickly. "Come in."

Clark stepped inside the room as Tiffany again peeked around the corner of the slightly recessed doorway.

"What are we—"

"Shhhhh!" Tiffany emphasized again with irritation. "I want to see what's going on. Be quiet."

When she looked down the hall again, the lusciously hard body of Neil Ryan was standing by the door of the next room. His black hair was mussed, his shirt and slacks a wrinkled mess. As he chatted he slipped on his jacket, covering up his gun and leather shoulder holster.

Tiffany strained to hear the conversation Neil was having with the person inside the room. She definitely heard the words *last night* come from his mouth.

"Unbelievable," whispered Tiffany in shock. But the evidence was right in front of her. Neil Ryan, after having rejected her sexual invitation last evening, had obviously turned around and taken up with the woman in the very next room.

Her curiosity made her bolder, and she stepped forward a little to get a glimpse of this woman. *She has to be some kind of devastatingly beautiful goddess,* thought Tiffany. *How else could it be explained?*

But when Tiffany saw the woman, she was sure there had to be a mistake. Far from a goddess, Tiffany would have a hard time even calling her attractive. Mousy dark blond hair hung limply around a plain face. She even wore *glasses,* for God's sake, thought Tiffany, appalled.

"Clark," whispered Tiffany, turning her head back to her cousin. "Who is that woman?"

Clark sighed with boredom at Tiffany's little game, but he made the effort nonetheless. "Hmmm," he murmured low after leaning forward for a peek. "She looks vaguely familiar."

"Have a good morning, then, Hannah," Neil Ryan stated clearly to the woman in farewell. Then he turned toward the elevator, beyond Tiffany's room.

"Get back, get back," Tiffany frantically whispered to Clark. The last thing she wanted was for Neil Ryan to see Clark in her room.

"All set up," said the room service valet as he passed by Clark on his way to the door.

"Fine, fine," said Tiffany, holding the door open.

The valet nodded as he moved quickly into the hallway, nearly colliding with Neil.

"Morning, Billy," said Neil.

"Morning, Mr. Ryan," said the valet, who continued heading down the hall to the stairway.

"Hello, Ryan," spoke up Tiffany, leaning her back against the doorway in a blatantly seductive pose. "*Sleep* well, did you?"

Neil looked at the young woman standing barefoot in her bathrobe, her hair soaking wet. "Good morning, Ms. Townsend. Yes, and you?"

"Well enough, considering the mattresses in this place," sniffed Tiffany. "Of course, *you'd* know better than I would."

Neil Ryan eyed Tiffany a long moment, saying nothing. Tiffany was annoyed at his silence. Nevertheless, she smiled slowly, licked her lips, and tilted her head toward the doorway from which he'd just emerged. "You know what I mean, don't you?"

"No, I don't."

"Well, your *brother* certainly does. Oh, that reminds me, would you wait just a sec?" Tiffany tried to contain her glee as she ducked back into her room a moment and dove onto her stomach, shoving her arm underneath the bed.

"What's going on?" asked Clark, who'd already discovered the breakfast tray. He was nibbling a butter croissant from the overflowing pastry basket.

"It's too delicious," whispered Tiffany.

"Mmmm, so's your breakfast."

Tiffany ignored Clark and felt around underneath the bed until she felt the cold metal of J. J's wristwatch. Tiffany's heart was beating quickly as she raced back to the front door.

"Here, Ryan," she said, dangling the metal band on the end of a manicured finger.

"What's this?" asked Neil warily.

"Why, it's your brother J. J's watch, of course. He left it in my room *last night*."

Tiffany took pleasure in seeing the color rise in Neil Ryan's face. She waited for him to respond, to question, to do something, but he simply stared at the watch, his jaw clenched so tightly a vein began pulsing in his neck.

"I guess," continued Tiffany, "he was too...um... caught up in the moment to notice. I suppose we both were—"

"Thank you, Ms. Townsend," Neil bit out, cutting her off. "I'll see that he gets it. Good day."

A satisfied smile curled Tiffany's lips as she watched Neil Ryan stride angrily down the hallway. "Got you," she whispered, closing the door and walking back into the main part of the room.

"What was that all about?" asked Clark, pouring cream into a steaming cup of French roast coffee.

"Just a little fun," said Tiffany.

"Tell."

"Guess."

"Well . . . I overheard the little watch gambit, and I take it you had a little fling with the help?"

"Little is right. Our bartender from last night."

"Not up to snuff?"

"Ryan the younger may be a master of mixing martinis, but he's stinko in the sack. I gave him a chance but kicked him out when it was obvious he wouldn't please," lied Tiffany, who was still too horrified by what had truly happened to ever admit it.

"Really?" Clark's eyebrows rose as he selected another croissant and surveyed an array of tiny gourmet jars of fruit preserves.

"He can kiss okay and everything, but that's all."

"No repeat performances scheduled, I take it?" asked Clark, spreading apricot preserves on yet another pastry.

"Definitely not. The 'at your service' part of the routine here is complete hype. I should have Daddy sue the hotel for false advertising."

"Maybe you should have just ordered toast."

"Very funny."

"Or maybe . . ." Clark paused to chew and swallow.

"What?"

"Maybe girls just aren't his cup of java. It happens, you know. The guy may not even realize it himself."

Tiffany thought for a moment. She remembered the look in his eyes when she'd begun to tease him. "No. It's not that. Actually, I think he's hung up on all that romantic garbage."

"Too bad you wasted your time. You are definitely not the romantic type."

Tiffany uncapped the aspirins and swallowed two with a swig of orange juice. "J. J. Ryan may have been a disappointment, but he was hardly a waste of time."

Clark leaned back in the chair with his cup of coffee and raised a blond eyebrow. "Tell."

"Let's just say it's not the younger but the older Ryan who I want jumping through hoops for me."

"Oh, really? And how do you know all Ryans aren't duds in the sack?"

Tiffany smiled. "I just know."

Sexual prowess was something Tiffany could smell on a man. And Neil's seemed to flow from him in waves. Just the way he looked around a room, the way he talked, the way he held himself. He fairly oozed masculinity.

Neil Ryan was a cynical, hard-edged, worldly man. Clearly, he was a womanizer in his spare time—full grown and fully developed. His younger brother was obviously handsome but way too naive. A boy. Neil Ryan, on the other hand, was mature, jaded, and sizzlingly hot. He was a man, one who *had* to be a stud between the sheets.

Tiffany was well aware that most things came easily to her. Too easily. Neil was a fascinating diversion, a wild, strong thing with a steely will, whose rejection of her last night was, in its own way, even more of a sexual turn-on. It was a game to her, and Tiffany relished the challenge. If only for one night, she would find a way to bridle all that masculine power. She *would* get Neil Ryan into her bed. Or finally slip into his herself.

"What are you planning to do?" asked Clark curiously as he leaned forward to pilfer another pastry from the quickly depleting breakfast basket.

"You'll see soon enough. Just do me one favor. Find out all you can about that woman in the next room. I think he called her 'Hannah.' "

Clark tore his chocolate croissant in two. "Hannah, huh?" He paused for a moment, then his eyes widened. "Hey, I know where I saw her before."

"Where?"

"Television."

"What do you mean? Is she some blue blood? She's homely enough to be royalty," reasoned Tiffany. "She must at least be loaded or else why would Neil sleep with her?"

"She's Hannah Peabody. *Mrs.* Hannah Peabody. Sis watches her *Homemaking* show religiously. It's absolutely tacky to me, Bourgeois Boulevard, but Sis says it makes her feel nostalgic."

"Nostalgic?"

"Old-fashioned, you know, like making holiday wreaths out of fall leaves, flower arranging, and cookie baking, and all that waste of time."

Tiffany rolled her tired blue eyes. "How corny!"

"I know."

After a moment's pause, Tiffany's eyes widened with a realization. "Oh, my God, Clark!" she shrieked. "Neil just banged the happy homemaker. The *married* happy homemaker?"

"Irony City."

"Oh, this is too delicious!"

"So are these croissants." Clark took another bite. "You really should try one before they're gone."

But Tiffany was too busy pacing, her mind's gears spinning.

"This has to be some kind of game," mumbled Tiffany.

"What does?"

"It makes no sense for Neil Ryan to reject me then turn around and sleep with plain Hannah Homemaker."

"He rejected you, huh? There's a first. Better be careful it doesn't turn into a trend."

"Shut up, Clark," snapped Tiffany, stung anew. Her mind was working furiously again and she began pacing. "You know," she said after a few minutes. "I think it was a *tad* coincidental that Ryan chose the woman in the room right next to mine."

"What do you mean?" asked Clark, his mouth half full.

"Don't you see? Neil Ryan wanted me all along. Why else would he have made sure I saw his little departure this morning? Yes, that has to be it. The whole thing was for my benefit."

"Your benefit?"

"Clark, you're so dense! He's playing a sexual game with me. Don't you see?"

"What? To get you jealous or something?"

"To heighten the tension between us." And it had worked, too, because Tiffany now wanted Neil more than ever.

"Oh, I see now . . ."

"He's supposed to be bodyguarding me, you know. But half the time he has some stiff in a suit and a military crew cut trailing me instead. I bet he's doing that to make me want him even more.''

"You're really twisted, Cuz, you know? By the way, can you loan me some ciggys?''

"Sure, they're on the dresser, next to my bag.'' Tiffany sucked on her bottom lip. "Now, let's see, I've got to think of some way to pay back my little Homemaking neighbor . . . and get her out of the picture.''

"Whatever.'' Clark walked to the dresser and grabbed a pack of imported French cigarettes. "How can you smoke unfiltered?''

"I'm switching. As soon as I run through the imports. I've got it!'' announced Tiffany.

"Got what?''

"A way to get back at that little scarecrow next door. And get her out of the picture.''

Clark's eyebrows rose with interest. "Tell.''

"I'll get her *in* the picture!''

"What?''

"Listen, wouldn't it be funny if the whole world knew what we knew? It's like those delicious royal scandals in Limey Land. What if everyone knew that Mrs. Happy Homemaker was banging the help at Château du Coeur?''

"Hmmm . . . how would they?''

"Simple. I'll have to find a way to get news of Happy Hannah's little affair to some of those supermarket tabloids.''

"Pretty low, Tif. Even for you.''

"It's deliciously low. Now . . . I understand these papers need a source for the story and a photo for evidence. I'm obviously an eyewitness source, but I'll need a photo. Or a few photos. That shouldn't be too hard.''

Clark laughed in her face. "Are you crazy? There's a reason celebs get married here, Tiffany. No cracks in security. And no unauthorized photography. People can't just roam around the hotel snapping photos without the staff supervising other guests' privacy. Didn't you know that?''

"No,'' said Tiffany, her lips forming an unhappy pout.

"By the way,'' continued Clark with a forced nonchalance, "can you loan me a few bills? Mum and Dad have been boating so much I can never hook up.''

"You're bound to see them today at the wedding—'' Suddenly Tiffany stopped. "The wedding. That's it! Every wedding has a professional *photographer*, right? A photographer who's going to be *allowed* to roam the grounds for photos."

Clark studied Tiffany. "So?"

"So what photographer wouldn't want to get a tip that could make him six figures overnight?"

"One who'd never get hired again."

Tiffany sighed. "I'm sure I can persuade *somebody* to do it. Maybe there'll be a photographer's assistant who'll risk it for the money. I can always try a bribe, too . . ."

"Whatever. Listen, I wanted to duck into town for a few things, you know, before the ceremony."

"So?"

"So, like I said, can I borrow a few bills?"

Tiffany didn't care about money. She had a seemingly endless supply. Still, Clark was getting tiresome with his constant borrowing. And she wanted to figure out how to persuade the wedding photographer's assistant to do some dirty work today.

"Just get it from my bag," she snapped. "I've got some planning to do."

Chapter
Eleven

It was just after one o'clock and Maura Ryan was almost finished giving Hannah the VIP tour of the hotel and grounds.

The day had the kind of exhilarating spring wind that blew away every cloud from the sky, leaving behind a stunning backdrop of powder blue that seemed to go on forever.

In the distance, beyond the Cliff Walk at the rear of the mansion's grounds, the sun drenched the ocean waves with brilliance, while closer to shore a rush of white foam washed the jagged edges of the cliffside rocks.

Hannah breathed in the scene along with the fresh salty sea air, and a part of her realized just how much she'd missed this view. A gentle touch to her shoulder coaxed Hannah to turn back toward the mansion. Once again, the purity of Château du Coeur's white stones renewed her spirit.

"We should be going in," said Maura.

"Yes," agreed Hannah, and they started for the rear of the hotel, passing the cupid fountain on their way. "Thank you for the tour. The place has never looked better that I can recall. And neither have you, by the way."

"Oh, my dear, one thing about relics, treat us right and we do preserve well."

In her sixties now, Maura Ryan still possessed the energy of a twenty-year-old. Her raven hair still had little gray in it, due, she said, to expert coloring at the hotel's salon. She wore it efficiently but attractively up in a French twist.

Unlike her usual dark gray housekeeper jumper and apron, which Hannah was so used to seeing Maura clothed in, the woman now wore a conservative but much more stylish Anne Klein suit, a shade of green that perfectly set off her eyes. A small name tag declared to the world this was *Maura Ryan, Executive Manager.*

"Hannah, you'll have to come by my private rooms. I've had a section of the attic converted, and I'd love to show you some of the things we've found stored there. I don't think your parents knew about them."

"Really . . ." said Hannah, her attention caught by the festive white tent being erected on the rear grounds, off the ballroom. "Perhaps I'll find some time after Holly's wedding. Who's getting married today, by the way?"

"Townsend/Sumner," answered Maura, a slight brogue adding a barely detectable lilt to her speech. "About fifty are guests in the hotel and two hundred are coming for the ceremony and dinner later this afternoon."

"Townsend . . . Townsend . . . sounds familiar. I think I saw that name on Grandmother Edith's guest list for Holly."

"Why don't you come to the wedding, Hannah? You can stick by me to see how we throw our little parties."

"Thanks." Hannah smiled, knowing from the articles she'd seen on Maura's gala affairs that nothing was ever "little" about them. "I do love weddings—I think they might just be the last true expression of the romantic tradition in our modern culture."

"Sounds to me like you're writing the opening of your book already."

"Sorry," said Hannah with a laugh. "But since my show began I'm always taking notes in one way or another. What are you serving today?"

Maura smiled. "You haven't seen Antonio since you've arrived, have you?"

Hannah shook her head.

"C'mon, then."

Hannah followed Maura through one of the hotel's rear

doors, then across the large lobby. When they passed the entrance to the dining room for a door marked *Staff Only*, a warm rush of nostalgia engulfed Hannah. Even if Maura hadn't been leading the way, she could have easily recalled the maze of service areas, the passage to the pantry and scullery, by the doors to the china room and subcellars. And, of course, she could have followed the smells.

"Cream of sorrel soup," she guessed. "And fresh baked brioche."

The heavenly aromas from the mansion's kitchen were what first lured Hannah down these narrow passages years ago. She was barely ten when Chef Tony had allowed her to prop herself on a stool and just watch all the kitchen activity before meals and parties.

By the time she'd reached her teens she was trying recipes herself. Chef Tony and his European-trained assistants often amused themselves by giving Hannah an education that rivaled any culinary institute's.

Now Hannah moved behind Maura into the bright, busy, and very modern kitchen—much more so than when she'd been a little girl. Immediately she recognized the master of this room for the last two decades, Executive Chef Antonio Jean-Paul Capagio.

He had at least a dozen white-jacketed assistants diligently preparing that evening's wedding feast. Executive Chef Antonio moved among them, murmuring orders as he tasted stocks and sauces. Every one of his staff seemed ready to jump to the moon at his slightest nod.

"Who's the chef here?" called Hannah loudly, her hands planted on her hips for dramatic effect. "I'm sure he's added too much pea puree to his chicken stock!"

A communal gasp ascended with the kitchen aromas. Every one of the white-jackets froze dumbly in place. Who had dared voice such an outrage? Who had dared question last year's winner of the James Beard award, one of the country's most prestigious culinary prizes?

The man himself turned slowly. He was the shortest among the white-jackets. But what he lacked in stature, he made up for in sheer force of personality. Half-Italian and half-French, it had been written in a gourmet magazine recently that Chef Antonio of Château du Coeur ran his kitchen like a cross between Napoleon Bonaparte and Benito Mussolini.

No one had ever questioned Chef Antonio in his own kitchen. No one, that is, except—

"Hannah?"

As her acquaintances had known for years, Hannah had a nondescript, rather plain face . . . until she smiled. She did so now and her large gray eyes became luminous, casting her face in a remarkable radiance that instantly dazzled the room. The answering pleasure in Chef Antonio's expression considerably stunned his tense staff.

"Chef Tony," called Hannah. "*Bonjour!*"

Another small gasp ascended with the kitchen aromas. *Tony?* No one but Maura Ryan had dared called Chef Antonio such a name.

"*Bonjour* Hannah!" returned Chef Antonio boisterously. "*Bonjour* and *buon giorno*! Welcome home!"

The staff watched dumbfounded as Chef Antonio raced to Hannah and embraced her in an unrestrained bear hug. As she held on tightly, every person in the room was certain that the resulting glow of happiness could have lit every lighthouse on Aquidneck Island.

For most of the morning, Neil Ryan had tried his damnedest to accomplish one thing above all others—avoid Hannah Whitmore Peabody.

After finding her mysteriously jammed guest-room door just as mysteriously *un*jammed, Neil Ryan went straight to his small apartment in the mansion's carriage house, a two-room suite conveniently set up next to the private office he'd opened two years ago for Ryan Investigations.

He'd barely stepped out of the shower when his mother was knocking on his door, asking him to join her in giving Hannah a VIP tour of the hotel grounds. Neil had carefully declined, using the excuse of a business meeting.

Maura's usual buoyant energy had not faltered at his refusal, yet the slightest disappointment seemed to register in her green eyes. It made him feel like a heel, which in turn made him angry, and he cursed the coming of Hannah yet again.

I'm doomed to look like the villain all over again.

For the next few hours, Neil focused his turmoil on the

unfinished paperwork in his files. He didn't look up again until his clients entered the outer office door.

Sitting behind his large, polished oak desk, Neil reached for the case file on the bride of today's scheduled wedding. It was the groom himself, at the prompting of his family, who'd ordered the investigation.

Conner Sumner and his father greeted Neil, then took their seats, crossing their perfectly tailored and pressed gray slacks in unison.

"I assure you both," began Neil, "that there is no foundation for the charges you've asked me to confirm."

"But . . . the rumors?" asked Hanson Sumner, the groom's father.

"That's all they were," explained Neil, "rumors. I've found no evidence whatever that the bride has been unfaithful to your son, who, I might remind you, is due to say 'I do' in less than three hours."

Neil watched the older Sumner shift a bit in his leather chair across from Neil. Both father and son had curly brown hair and bright dark eyes. But the son wasn't as calm as the father. While Hanson uncrossed then recrossed his legs, Conner Sumner restlessly rose from his seat to stare out the window at the crash of the ocean twenty yards away.

The rear rooms of the carriage house were located much closer to the turbulent surf than the main building of the hotel, where Neil maintained his small office as head of security. Most days, he preferred the distance.

A sigh came from the groom's father, a man with a pained, faraway look on his handsome, tanned face. The Sumner son was an only child, destined to inherit a vast fortune along with the family's canning factories on the east and west coasts. Naturally he was worried about any legal union that would affect the family's financial legacy.

Hanson Sumner's face was no different than the others Neil had seen over the past two years—fearful, worried, borderline angry that money couldn't solve every problem.

"You see, Mr. Ryan," said the father, "the bride won't sign a prenuptial agreement."

The man had addressed Neil, but Neil knew the statement was directed straight for his son.

"I understand," answered Neil, which was absolutely no answer at all.

"Tell us about her finances again," requested the father.

Neil recalled the report from memory, but he cued up the computer file anyway and briefed himself with the facts on the screen.

"As I told you last month, Sarah Blaine Townsend is niece to Vincent Townsend, owner of one of the most successful real estate companies in America. However, Vincent Townsend's immediate family is where the vast fortune will fall. Your son's intended is due to inherit only a token amount. Her father's position within the family firm is salaried."

"You see, son," said Hanson Sumner, "you see why she won't sign the prenuptial agreement?"

"I don't care," said the son tightly. "You heard what the man said. There's no evidence of infidelity. Let's just drop all this."

Hanson Sumner didn't care for his son's angry tone. "You'll have enough when I say so, Conner. Remember the family's affairs are my responsibility. Someday they'll be yours and you'll understand what a great burden they are, but for now it is up to me to decide."

"Mr. Ryan, what do you think?" asked Conner, suddenly wheeling to face Neil. "Put yourself in my shoes. I love this girl. What would you do?"

Sumner glared at his son but said nothing. A long terrible tension hung in the room, the angry crash of ocean the only sound.

Neil's more vulnerable clients often tried to extract personal opinions from him, even ask him to make their decisions for them. But Neil had vowed from the start never to counsel clients beyond the results of his investigations. He wasn't a shrink, and he was out of his depth in such things—especially where love and marriage were concerned.

"Mr. Sumner," said Neil finally, addressing the young groom, "no man can walk in another's shoes. This is a highly personal decision. I cannot help you beyond informing you of the plain facts—which I've already done."

Conner's gaze faltered and he dared a glance at his enraged father. Both seemed embarrassed to realize they were airing dirty laundry in front of a hired man.

"Conner, I think we should take a walk," said Hanson stiffly, then through a tight-lipped smile turned to Neil. "Excuse us, won't you?"

Neil nodded and returned to his screen as the two men left. He sighed as he drummed his fingers. The whole thing really didn't matter to Neil. It wasn't as if he hadn't heard it a dozen times before.

Ryan Investigations had built itself organically from hotel guests asking Neil and his staff to perform extra services, from private security and recovery of heirlooms, to protection and investigations. Naturally, many of his cases stemmed from the bride's family wanting to run a background check on the groom, or the groom's family wanting to investigate the bride. Today's case happened to be the latter.

At one point, Neil may have felt sorry for these people, but no more. This was their world, not his. And the world of problems and decisions it came with was their responsibility to bear, not his. Turning to his computer's keyboard, Neil pressed a single button. The name of Sarah Blaine Townsend was made to instantly vanish.

And yet, for some reason, the echo of Conner's plaintive words seemed to resound in his ears. *Mr. Ryan . . . put yourself in my shoes. I love this girl. What would you do?*

Hannah's face suddenly came to him and Neil shut his eyes, as if he could blot the image from his subconscious as easily as he'd made Sarah Blaine Townsend vanish from his computer screen.

What would you do? Rubbing his throbbing temples, Neil dropped his head into his hands.

"Neil?"

Looking up, Neil found his younger brother staring at him from the doorway. He sighed as he studied J. J.'s expression. He looked about as sheepish as the time he'd scratched Neil's treasured first pressing of Elvis's *Heartbreak Hotel*. Well, the mishap was much worse this time, thought Neil, because it was much less innocent. Today Neil wasn't just angry with his younger brother, he was disappointed. Seriously disappointed.

"Are you okay?" asked J. J. "I heard you wanted to see me."

"Yes," said Neil, taking a deep breath. Just thinking about

it made his blood begin to boil again. "Come in. Sit down."

"Uh-oh, single syllable words, huh?" J. J. managed to tease weakly. "Guess I'm in deep."

"You. Sure. Are."

Neil waited for J. J. to sit down in the leather chair Conner Sumner had just vacated. The kid was nearly dressed for serving at today's wedding. His bow tie was not yet tied and he'd thrown his tuxedo jacket over the second chair. Still, even half put together his little brother looked like a heartbreaker. It was no wonder Tiffany Townsend threw herself at him.

Neil knew that his brother had been seduced—used. Still, it had been J. J.'s choice to make such a decision, and Neil was seriously disappointed that his brother hadn't exercised better sense.

It was *time*, thought Neil. Time the kid smartened up.

"So, Bro? What's the problem?"

Neil's blue eyes became chips of ice as he reached into his inside jacket pocket for J. J.'s wristwatch. He slapped it on the desk between them and, in the ensuing silence, heard his brother swallow sickly.

"Found a watch, huh?"

"Not *a* watch. *Your* watch. And it wasn't found, it was *given* to me. I think you know by whom."

J. J. had learned years ago that Neil only hated one thing more than a liar: a coward. Instinctively, J. J. knew that now was not the time to test any change in his brother's philosophy.

"Okay, Neil. What do you want me to say?"

Neil's jaw worked a moment. "Tell me what happened."

J. J. ran a hand through his short black hair. "Look, I'm not going through the blow-by-blow. I screwed up, okay. It was on my own time."

"On your own time!" Neil roared. "Of all the—" Suddenly, Neil stopped himself, clearly trying with all his strength to control his emotions. A vein in his neck pulsed as he sat in silence, teeth clenched.

J. J. squirmed unhappily for a full minute until his brother spoke again.

"J. J., whatever goes on *inside* this hotel, regardless of the *time*," Neil stated tightly, "has the potential to impact its reputation. Last night, you risked the good name of your employer's business, and I will not stand for it.''

J. J.'s guilt weighed on him like a ten-ton anchor. He knew in his heart and his head that he'd made a terrible mistake, not only in almost sleeping with a hotel guest, but in almost sleeping with a woman like Tiffany.

Earlier today, J. J. had tried to speak with her, apologize. But she'd given him nothing more than a condescending sneer, treating him like dirt. Not for a second did she acknowledge that they'd shared more than a handshake the night before. The whole encounter had made J. J. sick to his stomach, and the fact that his brother knew was making him feel even sicker.

''I admit it was a mistake, okay. A bad one,'' offered J. J. ''Look, it won't happen again. I've learned my lesson. So let's drop it, Neil. Please?''

''We can't drop it. You're going to have to suffer as much as any employee that pulled a stunt like this. I'm sorry, J. J., you're fired.''

''What?'' J. J. paused a moment because he simply could not believe his ears. ''You can't . . . you can't do that!''

''Yes, J. J., I can. And I'd advise you to be quiet about it or else Mother's going to find out her son's aspiring to be a gigolo.''

''Screw you, Neil!'' cried J. J., leaping to his feet. ''It wasn't like that and you know it. The fact is, I *didn't* sleep with her.''

''What?''

J. J. felt mortified having to reveal the specifics, but he had no choice now. ''We started, but . . . she wasn't . . . I mean, I didn't . . .''

''You *didn't*?''

''No. I didn't. I knew it was wrong. We started, but I left. Before we . . .'' His voice trailed off.

Neil felt a little less angry, but only a little. ''You still crossed the line,'' he said evenly. ''I can't condone that, even if you are my brother.''

''Look, Neil, I'm sorry, okay. I screwed up, but I'm in the middle of night school. I *need* this job.''

''You should have thought of that before.''

J. J. began to pace the room, feeling ill used and misjudged.

"What about you, then?" he snapped unhappily. "Are you going to fire yourself?"

"Me?"

"You spent the night with Hannah Peabody, Neil. *Mrs.* Hannah Peabody, as you pointed out to me last night. What about that, huh?! That's one of the reasons I decided your little rule could be bent a little. But I guess I was wrong. Only the boss gets to screw around?"

Neil felt as if he'd been frozen to the black leather of his office chair. A pale chalk took over the color of his face. "How did you know . . . that I spent the night with her?"

"Who do you think took care of things last night?"

"But—"

"I went looking for you when you disappeared. I heard your voice inside her room. Then I went back down and called Joe Stokes on."

"J. J., I did spend the night with . . . with Mrs. Peabody, but I was trapped in there. Nothing happened between us."

"What do you mean you were *trapped*?"

"The door's lock jammed. And the phone went dead. We were trapped—"

"C'mon, Neil, who's the kidder now?"

"You'll see that I filed a report with maintenance."

"Yeah, of course you did, it's a great cover-up for her, too. But I don't know anyone who'd believe it."

Neil stared blindly at his brother. That was twice in two days that Neil had been caught completely off balance—first with Hannah and now with J. J. Twice in two days that his usual certainty, his usual control, had completely escaped him and he was left not knowing what in hell to do next.

"Listen, Neil, like I said, I need this job, so let's talk about this," said J. J., sitting back down.

"Talk?"

"Yeah, why don't we make some kind of agreement . . . a deal?"

Neil studied his brother's face. "What kind of 'deal'?"

J. J. thought for a moment, his gaze glued to the watch between them. "If I ever, *ever* pull a stunt like that again, which I swear to you I won't, you can fire me on the spot." J. J.'s green eyes met his brother's. "Just let me off the hook this time, and we can call it even. I promise not to say a thing about you and Mrs. Peabody—not to Mom, not to anyone.''

Neil drew a deep painful breath. His brother. His naive, guileless, carefree little brother had finally smartened up, all right. And, in the process, he'd discovered the realm of mistrust and suspicion, deals and coercion that existed beyond innocence. He'd finally passed through the gate that said you were now an official citizen in the lousy land of adulthood.

''Okay,'' said Neil hoarsely, his only thought now of Hannah's reputation. ''You're not fired. Keep your mouth shut.''

''Good,'' said J. J. shortly.

''But you are suspended from the main hotel for one month.'' Neil figured Tiffany Townsend would be long gone by then. J. J. probably didn't know it yet, but Neil was doing him a favor. That girl was nothing but trouble, and J. J. would be better off out of her path.

''What the hell am I supposed to do for money then?''

''You'll work. On the grounds. Under Charlie Baxter.''

J. J. stared at his brother angrily. ''Fine,'' was all he said before standing up and grabbing his tuxedo jacket. ''Do I work today's wedding?''

''No,'' said Neil. ''But don't get bent out of shape; there may not even be one.''

J. J. released an agitated breath and turned to go.

''Don't forget your watch,'' called Neil.

For a long moment, J. J. stared at the timepiece, then he picked it up and without another word headed for the door. The ring of metal on metal told Neil all he needed to know. The wristwatch hit the bottom of the anteroom's trash can just before the outer door slammed shut.

Neil sighed and ran a hand through his hair. Glancing out the wall of windows on the right side of his office, he took in the ocean view. The two Sumner men were walking briskly in the direction of his office.

Well, it looked like he'd soon know whether or not to tell his mother to march two hundred and seventy lobsters back into the Atlantic. He turned to his computer screen to cue up Sarah Blaine Townsend and realized there was a terrible chill in the room.

It was just like last night, thought Neil. That same strange feeling as if cold shards of ice were penetrating the surface of his skin. Neil rubbed his hands together, then poised his finger over the keyboard when something utterly unexplainable began to happen.

There, on the screen, letters began to appear.

H . . . E . . . R . . .

"What in hell?"

Neil hadn't typed so much as a letter. He drew his hands away and examined the keyboard. He couldn't believe his eyes, but the keys were depressing—by themselves.

B . . . E . . . R . . . T . . .

Dumbfounded, Neil watched as the screen finally spelled out a full name: HERBERT THEOPHILUS PEABODY.

"What the hell?" Neil had considered investigating Hannah's husband last night, just to get some answers about her marriage. But by this morning, Neil had discarded the idea, hoping to discard any residual feelings for Hannah in the process.

Neil read the screen again with disbelief.

Other than last night, there'd been only one other time in his life that he'd felt the indisputable presence of a ghostly entity. It was that hideous night three years ago. The one in which he almost decided to cash in his chips for good. Instead, Dan Doyle had appeared to Neil with a message that had changed his life.

Neil tried to believe he'd been saved by his own drunken hallucination. Sure, he was even grateful to it, but he'd never wanted to acknowledge that the strange visitation had been a *real* ghost.

"My God . . ." Neil knew he was stone-cold sober now. Yet there was no doubt that the keyboard was typing by itself.

The outer office door opened and closed, and Neil heard the voices of Hanson Sumner and his son coming toward his inner office. Before they knocked, Neil found himself whispering into the chilly air, "Dan Doyle, is that you?"

When he saw the answer, Neil immediately picked up the phone to call his colleague in Chicago. If he was lucky, he'd have a report on Herbert Peabody faxed to him by this evening. What else could he do? Especially now that Dan Doyle's spirit was involved—that fact was as clear as the three letters that appeared on the glowing computer screen.

Y . . . E . . . S.

Chapter Twelve

Fifteen minutes later, Neil Ryan was walking purposefully toward one of the back staff entrances to the mansion, in urgent search of his mother.

As he entered the large kitchen, something seemed odd to Neil. Most of the white-jacketed staff was crowded in a circle in the center of the room, and every few moments, the forest of tall white chefs' hats bobbed in amusement as the group chuckled happily. Levity was a sight seldom seen in the little general's tensely run kitchen.

"Tell them!" Chef Antonio's happy voice boomed from the center of the circle.

"Yes," answered a female voice that Neil assumed to be his mother's, "you see, I was so excited to help, I ran to the fresh herbs and grabbed them much too quickly—"

"She bring me cilantro instead of parsley," rang out Chef Antonio's voice again.

"Ah . . ." murmured the crowd of sous-chefs.

"And so," continued the executive chef, "I try it, and I *love* it. My Frog Legs Forestier never be the same again!"

The crowd was laughing again as Neil nudged a tall shoulder and peered inside the group, expecting to find his mother. What he saw instead sent a variety of very unwelcome emotions screaming through his system.

The woman laughing with Chef Antonio was not Maura Ryan. It was Hannah.

His Hannah.

The Hannah he'd spent the night with.

The Hannah he'd been trying to avoid all day.

He blinked, unable to comprehend why she was sitting here, in the kitchen of all places. He had been absolutely certain that by now she would have grown bored with the mansion. After all, she had lived here almost every summer of her childhood. Why wasn't she off shopping in Newport, visiting old society friends, or on some other diversion?

The sound of Hannah's warm, low laughter seemed to send a new ripple of delight through the gaggle of admiring males surrounding her. The very notion made Neil's entire body go rigid.

Suddenly, a large, surly-looking chef stepped up to Hannah and bowed gallantly. "For you, Madame," he said in a basso voice, then took off his hat and placed it on her head. The crowd of admiring males applauded as Hannah laughed again.

Her gray eyes were shining with pure joy behind her wire-framed glasses. The casual dress she wore was very plain, but the soft gray color set off her eyes and the cling of the knit subtly outlined her attractive figure. Too late, Neil realized he was staring—gawking really—and before he could make a quick exit, Chef Antonio recognized him.

"Ah, look who we have. Neil Ryan!"

Despite himself, Neil looked with curiosity to Hannah's expression. For a split second he felt a kind of thrill at her happy surprise. But after her quick observation of his own guarded expression, she seemed to recast her own. The carefree smile became a pensive line, the laughter in her eyes now a hooded apprehension.

"Do you see, Neil Ryan, that our Hannah has come home?" asked the executive chef, his voice bubbling with joy.

"Yes," answered Neil stiffly after a moment's thought. "But it's not her home anymore."

The terse remark left scowls on the chefs' faces, including

Chef Antonio, who set his small dark eyes on Neil. "That is not a very welcome thing to say."

"It's the truth," Neil returned, his blue eyes blowing a gale so sharp and cold it seemed to chill the entire room.

Neil saw the hurt on Hannah's face. He didn't like knowing he was the cause, but he had to make certain that any rumors started about them were put to rest at once.

For his own punishment, Neil forced himself to endure watching the pain he'd caused. He lasted a full five seconds before he had to look away—and right into the very angry face of Minnow, the surly chef who'd given Hannah his chef's hat.

The large man took a threatening step forward, and Neil's body subtly dropped into an automatic hand-to-hand stance, one foot in front of the other, weight perfectly balanced.

"Minnow, *non*," whispered Antonio Capagio to his underling.

The two words were all it took to restrain the enraged bull of a man, leaving Neil with the uneasy feeling that the executive chef had his own small army at his beck and call.

A terrible tension hung heavily in the room until Neil tipped his head to Hannah. "No offense meant, Mrs. Peabody."

"None taken, Mr. Ryan," said Hannah before he turned to leave the kitchen. The atmosphere returned to jovial again as Chef Antonio began telling another story of "little Hannah's" escapades in his kitchen.

But Hannah's heart was no longer in it.

"Here you are . . ." grumbled Neil. He'd left the kitchen quickly and went straight to the next likely place he'd find Maura—the ballroom. She was standing in the center of the floor, chatting with Mrs. Sally Ellen Grady, the former assistant housekeeper turned hotel banquet manager.

"Excuse me," said Neil, touching his mother's shoulder.

Maura nodded to Neil as she finished her instructions to Mrs. Grady. But before the older woman could see to her banquet staff, she turned to Neil.

"Oh, Neil! Have you heard who's here?" asked Mrs. Grady with a bubbling high-pitched voice.

Neil took a deep breath. "*Who*, Mrs. Grady?"

"Why, you *must* have heard!" Sally Ellen Grady looked to Maura Ryan. "Your boy's just teasing me, isn't he?"

Maura Ryan's arms folded across her chest, but she said nothing.

Mrs. Grady turned back to the head of security. "You just *have* to know that our little Hannah is back home!"

Neil's jaw tightened. "I know about every guest who checks into this hotel, Mrs. Grady."

"And?" prompted Mrs. Grady, her hazel eyes flashing.

"And . . . *what*?" Neil glanced at his mother and had the distinct impression that she was enjoying this immensely.

"And . . ." Mrs. Grady looked from Maura to Neil and back again. "And are you and little Hannah . . . um . . . getting acquainted again?"

Neil stared at Mrs. Grady with a fairly ferocious sternness, but it didn't seem to phase the busybody.

"Sally," said Maura at last, "I think Neil hasn't had much time to visit with her yet."

"Oh," said Sally Grady, her eyebrows rising in disbelief. "I understand. Well," she concluded, patting Neil sympathetically on his shoulder, "I'm sure she'll find the time to say hello soon."

"Off you go, now," said Maura quickly, spotting the volcano bubbling under her son's surface. Neil's mother always seemed to know just when he was ready to blow.

When Sally Ellen Grady was finally off fussing with her staff, Neil turned to his mother. "Well?"

"Well, what?" asked Maura.

"Aren't *you* going to say something about Hannah?"

"No," said Maura shortly. "You haven't asked me about her, and she certainly hasn't asked me about you."

"She hasn't?" Neil didn't want to acknowledge it, but, for just the slightest moment, he felt as though the wind had dropped from his sail.

"Not a word," assured Maura. "Of course, we've been busy talking business, you know. After we finalize Holly's wedding, we'll be working on a book together, and then she's wanting to tape some of her television shows here."

"What?"

"You heard me."

"Why wasn't I told about this?"

"What? About the tapings?" Maura stared down her son. "We *just* talked about it this morning. On the tour of the grounds that *you* were too busy to attend."

Neil blinked, trying to get a line on his suddenly rudderless emotions. "That reminds me," he said shortly, "the reason I was busy—and the reason I have to speak to you now. I just had a meeting with the Sumner groom and his father."

Maura's expression turned concerned at once. "Yes?"

"The wedding may be off."

"Off?" asked Maura.

Neil watched his mother's routinely unflappable posture droop ever so slightly. They'd all been through this before, and it was never pleasant.

"Yes, it seems—" Neil paused when two bustling waiters brushed by them. Glancing around, Neil quickly touched his mother's elbow and guided her to an empty section of the ballroom before speaking again.

"It seems the groom now agrees with his father that unless his bride signs the prenuptial agreement, he won't go through with the wedding."

"When did this come up?" asked Maura.

"It's been in the air for a few weeks. But a few days ago the father of the groom heard a rumor that the bride was sleeping around. She wasn't, but it's shaken the faith of the family."

"And what's to happen?" asked Maura.

"Up to me, I suppose. They've asked me to handle it." Neil opened his coat slightly and pointed out the folded legal papers in his inside jacket pocket.

"You're going to speak to the bride *now*?" Maura checked her watch. "The ceremony is due to begin in two hours. The guests will be arriving in one."

"What the hell. I get paid no matter what she says," said Neil with a shrug.

"That's rather cold," chided Maura.

Neil stared at his mother a moment in silence. "See you later."

Maura sighed. "I'd really prefer *sooner*," she called to her son's retreating back.

"What would you prefer sooner?" Hannah stepped up to Maura a few moments after Neil stepped away.

"Oh," said Maura, a bit startled by Hannah's abrupt entrance. "I'd prefer that Neil return sooner. And successfully. You see, he's off to save a marriage."

The two women watched the man's tall, strong form quickly cross the ballroom and disappear through the ballroom's large polished wooden doors.

"Really?" asked Hannah, a forced cheerfulness in her voice. "Is that like being off to see the wizard?"

"Now that you mention it," murmured Maura, staring at the ballroom door that Neil had just closed, "that wouldn't be a bad idea . . ."

"What wouldn't?"

Maura turned to face Hannah. "My son's become a lot like the tin man."

"I don't understand?"

Maura eyed Hannah carefully. "Do you really care, my dear? I mean about Neil. You are happily married, aren't you?"

Hannah's gaze left Maura's and searched the floor. Hannah had told herself she'd come up to the ballroom to see the final preparations in progress, but the truth was, after that little scene with Neil in the kitchen, she had felt driven somehow to find him again, perhaps even to provoke him.

"Maura, the truth is—" Hannah began, then stopped herself.

"Yes?" prompted Maura, her intelligent green eyes pensive for an answer.

"The truth is . . . I do still care about him . . . I mean, I wish I could be a friend to him again, but he's become so—" This was harder than she'd anticipated. "Maura, I don't understand why he's so . . . why he's—"

"Changed?"

"Yes," said Hannah on an exhaled breath.

Maura linked her arm through Hannah's and prompted her into a little walk about the large elegant ballroom.

Charlie Baxter, the head gardener, who also served as the hotel's floral designer, waved a hello at them as he supervised the final assembly of twenty-five magnificent table centerpieces. Elaborate bouquets of white now sat atop crystal pedestals throughout the ballroom, filling the air with a heavenly fragrance.

"Hannah," Maura began to explain, "Neil joined us here at the hotel after he had some . . . disappointments in his life."

"What sort of disappoint—"

"His military career fell apart, and his marriage quickly followed."

"What happened?"

"He really should be the one to tell you more, my dear, but let's just say he was left very unhappy and disillusioned. When he finally came to work here at the hotel, he worked like the devil. Still does. He takes on extra duties anytime he can. You see, many of the exclusive guests here wanted to hire him for private services."

"What? You mean like investigating?"

"Yes, security, too. He formed his own company and runs it out of the carriage house. He's terribly good at his job, proud of it, you know. Even had a number of offers from corporate presidents and such to work exclusively for them. But he's declined every one."

"Why? Because of you?"

"Oh, no. He knows I can live without him. I think it's because he's proud of having his own business, answering only to himself. I mean, here, at the hotel, I'm technically his superior, but he runs his security staff with a completely free hand. I think he stays here because he really is his own boss, you see?"

"Yes. I can't tell you how many times I wish I were my own boss."

"You're not?"

"Heavens no. I'm an employee of *Homemaking* as much as anyone on its production staff. The entire show is owned by the executive producer, a man named Chip Saunders."

"I understand."

"But you were saying? About why Neil has changed?"

Maura sighed. "It's a combination of things, I think, but part of it is his work. Brides investigating grooms. Grooms investigating brides. It's affected his outlook. Do you see what I mean?"

Hannah shook her head. "I'm not sure—"

Maura suddenly stopped to look Hannah in the eye. "I mean there are consequences for a man who works in a profession that operates on the premise of basic mistrust."

Hannah thought this over a long moment and considered Maura's earlier comment about the tin man. "You're saying he's lost his heart?"

"You've nailed it, my dear. Precisely."

Lost his heart. Hannah's gaze dropped as the idea echoed through her insides again and again as if her own organs were gone and she'd been left completely hollow. And then she realized why the words had penetrated so deeply.

Most days, Hannah felt as if she'd lost her heart, too.

Chapter Thirteen

"Don't you just love a wedding?"

It was sunset, and the ghost of Daisy Channing Doyle floated near the top of the snow-white wedding tent. The happy couple stood far below, exchanging vows in front of a white-robed minister.

"Yeah, sure . . . very romantic," said her ghostly husband, hovering beside her. *"But I could live without the pink cupid ornaments hung on every blasted chair."*

"Except you can't technically 'live' with or without anything now, my darling," pointed out Daisy. *"Besides, I like them."*

"Dames," Dan grumbled, making part of the tent flutter. *"Wasn't there a case we worked on . . . some peeping perp who kept leaving pink cupid cards on ladies' windowsills?"*

"Oh, Dan, you have a curious memory. The cards were pink, but they didn't have cupids on them, they had a certain pink-colored male organ, which is why half the town was in a fury over it."

"Hey, that's right," realized Dan with a chuckle. *"That was pretty funny."*

"The ladies didn't think so. And neither did the members of the Newport Police Department—"

"Well, to be perfectly accurate, sweetie, some of them did."

"Anyway! I think the little cupids are charming. They were the bride's idea, after all, and when it comes to weddings, the bride is always right."

"Not true, Dais. You're forgetting what happened a few hours ago—when the bride herself decided she'd been wrong."

"Yes, I guess so." Daisy had to agree with her eternal partner. After all, they were both there to witness the scene in which the bride finally agreed to sign the prenuptial agreement.

"There'd be no wedding now if our boy Ryan hadn't gotten the dame to see the light," pointed out Dan.

"Yes, he performed admirably."

"And, of course, your scaring the bejesus out of the girl helped, too."

"Oh, Dan, all I did was show her a little something in the mirror," explained Daisy.

The other day, the ghosts had overheard the bride's father and her attorney sanctioning the prenuptial agreement as abundantly fair, and recommending the girl sign. But then the bride's cousin Tiffany and two other girlfriends in the wedding party had declared the bride "a fool" to do so.

Daisy was certain that pride alone would have kept Sarah Blaine Townsend off the altar today if Neil Ryan hadn't shown up to persuade her otherwise.

"What exactly did you show her, Dais?"

"Just herself—as an old woman. Very little teeth, very little hair, an awful lot of money, but very much alone."

"Dan," said Daisy after they watched the bridegroom slip a ring on the bride's finger, *"do you suppose I did the right thing?"*

"They love each other, don't they?"

"Yes."

"Then, honey, I'm surprised you asked."

Daisy swooped lower then, silently moving about the tent, between and sometimes through the well-dressed crowd. She spotted Hannah standing in the back, Maura Ryan beside her, and floated over to get a closer look.

Hannah had changed her clothes for the wedding. Her plain gray knit dress was gone now and a conservative maroon suit took its place. Daisy let out a drafty sigh. What in Heaven's name possessed this girl to wear nothing but drab colors all the time? For goodness sake, it was springtime! And the cut of the suit—it was terribly boxy, failing to show off her figure in the least. Why, the girl was only twenty-seven, yet she looked almost matronly.

Suddenly, Daisy took note of something very interesting. Every few minutes, Hannah seemed to be embarrassingly brushing her fingers across her cheeks.

"Dan, come here a moment," called Daisy. *"Our girl here seems to be moved by the ceremony. I think she's crying."*

"Yes, looks that way, all right . . . and look who's watching her bawl—besides us, I mean."

Daisy floated upward to get a better view. *"Ahhhh, I see! I see!"*

Neil Ryan, dressed gorgeously in a tailored black tuxedo with a black vest and bow tie, had approached the back of the tent from the side. He stood far enough away for Hannah not to notice his blue eyes staring directly at her.

"This is splendid!" exclaimed Daisy.

"Splendid?" asked Dan. *"Can you please explain why?"*

"Dan, you're usually not this dense. There's nothing that melts a man's defenses like a female crying."

"Hmmm . . . normally I'd agree. But you're forgetting that Neil's a private dick. Female tears have little effect on them. I can tell you they never worked on me."

Daisy circled around her eternal mate, stirring up a ticklish draft. *"Mine did."*

"Only because you were the one female that I loved."

"Exactly!" Daisy exclaimed.

Dan thought this over a moment. He observed Neil Ryan's sad internal condition. Quite troubling to observe in any fellow male, not to mention a fellow PI.

"Do you suppose we can try another one of my little plans tonight?" asked Daisy.

"Yeah, sweetie," answered Dan at once. *"I think we'd better."*

*   *   *

It was late evening, and the Townsend/Sumner wedding was quickly drawing to a close. Hannah was still amazed at the dance of well-timed steps she'd witnessed earlier in the evening.

The moment the wedding ceremony had concluded in the tent and the two hundred and fifty guests stepped into the ballroom for a sit-down dinner, a crack white-gloved hotel battalion instantly went to work transforming the big top.

Aisles of three hundred chairs had been broken down to reveal a sturdy wooden dance floor, where members of a seven-piece band moved in to set up. Pedestals of flowers and white tulle had been relocated to the tent's perimeter, where cozy tables had been assembled. White linen and glowing lanterns had flashed magically in the air then settled into their proper places.

When the swirl of activity was through, the tent that had served as outdoor church had become a stunning extension of the interior ballroom, complete with three freestanding bars and a champagne fountain to match the one inside. All the flaps were even lowered to keep the warmth in and the cold Atlantic wind out.

"It was a remarkable transformation," Hannah commented to Maura as the crowd began to thin markedly for the night.

The groom had long ago swept the bride into his arms and up to the luxurious bridal suite. Now the ballroom's orchestra was packing up for the evening, though the band in the tent would continue to play for another hour or so.

"Neil tells me that our weddings are a lot like military operations. Timing and teamwork, and a very good plan of action."

"I suppose he ought to know."

"Good evening to you, ladies."

"Joe, hello," greeted Maura.

Hannah turned to see a handsome man probably in his late sixties. She had noticed him among the guests before and wondered who he was. With his trimmed gray beard and sparkling brown eyes, the man could give Sean Connery a run for his money. He was dressed smartly for the wedding in a finely tailored black tuxedo. A red plaid vest and matching bow tie added stylish color.

With one glance at his rugged, ruddy complexion, strong hands, and sturdy physique, Hannah guessed him a Newport yachtsman for sure, possibly even an America's Cup contender.

"You're looking very nice tonight, Joe, very nice indeed."

"Thank you, Mrs. Ryan."

"Hannah, this is Joe Stokes. Joe, Mrs. Hannah Whitmore Peabody—"

"Please, just call me Hannah." She extended her hand, and Joe took it with a happy smile, bowing over it gallantly.

"Hannah, it's my pleasure to meet you."

Hannah smiled warmly. "Are you here for the bride, Mr. Stokes? Or the groom?"

Joe looked up with an amused expression on his handsome, rugged face. "Both, my dear," he said with a wink. "And neither."

"I'm sorry," said Hannah, perplexed. "I don't understand."

Joe tipped a glance at Maura. "Shall you answer, Mrs. Ryan?"

"Hannah's a friend, Joe. In fact, she used to live here at the mansion."

Joe's expression changed suddenly to one of extreme interest. "That so? Well, now, I hope to get a chance to converse with you on the subject sometime. I've always had a *sentimental* interest in Château du Coeur."

"Really?" said Hannah. "Did you know my parents? Lilian and Lawrence Whitmore?"

"Not at all, not at all," said Joe, "but—"

"Excuse me, Mr. Stokes," interrupted a young woman in a blue crepe gown. "My grandmother was wondering if you were free for that dance she promised you?"

Joe's thousand-watt smile seemed to reflect off the girl's face as he consented. Then he turned back to Hannah and Maura, and bowed slightly. "Until another time, Mrs. Peabody—"

"Hannah. Please."

"Hannah. At your service."

After he'd gone, Hannah turned to Maura. "Who is he, Maura? Which of the families is he here for?"

"As he said, Hannah. Both. And neither. He works for the

hotel," she explained. "You see, Joe normally helps out behind the scenes. But during parties and banquets and receptions, he acts as a host."

"You mean, as a kind of maître d'?"

Maura smiled. "No. As a kind of escort."

Hannah's eyes widened. "Really?"

"There are always single older women at these affairs, brought by sons, grandchildren, nephews. I like to see that each of our guests is taken care of, that they're engaged in happy conversation, that they get the chance to dance if they wish. Joe acts as a distant friend of the families—and, you see, in his own way, he is. It's all quite discreet. Nothing beyond the dance floor or a stroll around the grounds."

"What a wonderful notion."

"Not everyone thinks so. Neil, for instance, loathes the idea. But Joe loves doing it."

"He's quite an impressive figure."

"The truth is," said Maura low, "I think he's lonely. Lost his wife a year ago in a boating accident. He has one child, but she married and moved to the West Coast. Now he lives alone near the harbor and builds model ships. If you ask me, he came to work here more for the companionship than the money."

"He certainly looks like a million in that tuxedo."

Maura smiled knowingly. "That's the idea."

"What did he mean about always having an interest in the mansion?"

"Oh, he once worked here, ages ago. Before you were born."

"I wonder if my grandmother remembers him. Edith used to visit the house when Daisy and Dan Doyle lived here. She's coming down in two weeks for Holly's wedding. God, I dread that."

Maura smiled. "Will she be coming *alone*?"

Hannah studied Maura a moment, then a devilish smile crept across her face. "Now that I think of it, I believe she will."

"Excuse me, are you Mrs. Peabody?"

Hannah turned at the firm tapping on her shoulder. A stoic-faced young man stood before her, and she knew at one glance who he belonged to.

The black tuxedo helped the boy blend into the formal crowd, but he looked far from comfortable in the monkey suit, and his brown crew cut seemed to be standing at attention as much as his stiff muscular posture—making Hannah want to bet a million dollars that he'd come fresh from graduation ceremonies at the police academy.

The dead giveaway, however, came with the crackle of the walkie-talkie in his inside breast pocket. Yep, thought Hannah, he *had* to be one of Neil's.

"Just got a call, ma'am," said the young man.

God, how she hated to be called *ma'am*. It made her feel as though her entire youth had passed her by for good.

"Mr. Ryan would like you to speak with him."

"Oh?" Hannah looked questioningly to Maura, who shook her head and showed her palms to the sky. *Hmmm,* thought Hannah. *I guess he's finally ready to act civil to me. Maybe he wants to apologize.* "Okay, where is he?"

"You should probably grab a coat," suggested the young man. "Then I'll show you."

"Ryan! They told me I'd find you out here."

Neil had been striding around the cold dark grounds for the last hour of the reception. He told himself he was simply checking on his guards, placed at every hotel entrance and at different points of the hotel's perimeters. But the truth was he'd needed to walk off his frustrations, unable to take seeing one more happy couple dancing in each other's arms.

What the hell is the matter with me? Neil had been to a hundred weddings at this hotel. He'd never felt this way before.

"Ryan?"

The head of security turned to find himself approached by a well-built middle-aged man with a receding hairline. Vincent Townsend wore a tailored tuxedo; in one hand was a lit cigar, in the other a martini glass. "Hard of hearing out here, Ryan?"

"Excuse me?"

"I was calling you for two minutes."

"Yes, Mr. Townsend, anything the matter?"

"No, no, not at all. Just wanted a word." Vincent Townsend didn't bother emptying either hand to offer it, but he did offer a compliment. "Very nice place here, Ryan. Very nice."

"Thank you."

"No, it's you I'd like to thank, for watching over my most precious commodity."

"Your daughter Tiffany has had a pleasant stay, I trust?"

"Yes, of course. She's enjoying the wedding. My brother tells me he has you to thank for that, as well."

"No, sir. My mother is in charge of the reception and banquet—"

"No, no, not that. It's all very nice, I'm sure, but I'm talking about your convincing my niece Sarah to sign the Sumner prenup. Very fair document. Very fair. For God's sake, once she said, 'I do,' her net worth became six times its present value, no questions asked—even if her new hubby walks out on her tomorrow. Gets plenty more if children come into the picture. Girl would be a fool to let that go—"

"It was her decision, sir," broke in Neil uneasily. "I did little more than convey the facts." *And revive her after she looked in the mirror and fainted.* Neil was still perplexed about that one.

"No need to be humble, Ryan," continued Townsend. "I know my brother is grateful—he'd had no luck convincing her. And I am, too: another family member off the ol' Vince Townsend dole, you know. I tell you it can be a great pain in the ass having money. A great pain. Anyway, I'll be showing my own appreciation with a little added bonus on top of the bonus already coming for taking care of my daughter."

"Thank you, Mr. Townsend. I know my staff will appreciate it. And I'm sure we'll all miss her."

"Right, Ryan, right," said Townsend, turning to go. Then he stopped. "Oh, almost forgot. You all won't be missing her right away."

"What's that you say?" Neil prayed the chill of the Atlantic had damaged his hearing.

"Tiffany wants to stay on another two weeks, along with her cousin Clark. My wife tells me we'll be attending another wedding here. Family of the bride is Whit- something or other—"

"Whit*more*, Mr. Townsend?"

"Yes, that's right, groom's an English lord or knight or something or other—can't keep those damn Limey titles straight. Anyway, my little Tiffany says she wants to 'hang out' at the hotel. Says her acting classes don't start until summer, so just go ahead and continue our little guarding arrangement until she checks out. Pleasant night then, Ryan.''

"Yes, good night." Neil sighed heavily and closed his eyes. Two more weeks of Tiffany. Thank God he'd removed J. J. from the hotel's inside staff and put him to work on the grounds.

"Neil?"

That voice. Neil knew it, but could think of no reason on Earth how it could have found him here in the shadows of the cold dark lawn. Hoping for the second time that he was hearing things, Neil opened his eyes. *Damn.*

"Hannah? What are you doing out here?"

"What do you mean?" asked Hannah, stunned by the question. "You called for me."

"No, I didn't."

Hannah's brow wrinkled in consternation. "Yes, you did. You called for me over your walkie-talkie. That young man said so."

"What young man?"

Hannah turned to confront the young man who'd just pointed out Neil on the vast lawn, but he was already rushing back to his post at the party. His tuxedo jacket quickly blended with a group of others and then disappeared into the tent.

"Is this some kind of prank?" asked Hannah, hands on hips. She felt ridiculous enough in the oversized bright yellow rain slicker, but it was the only coat she could easily grab from the banquet manager's office. A hotel staff member had apparently left it behind—obviously a very tall staff member.

"I don't know," said Neil. "You tell me. The past twenty-four hours have had more strange things happen than I can remember."

"Oh, I'm just another 'strange' thing, am I?" She certainly felt that way in this slicker. *My God, I must look like a deranged Donald Duck.*

"I didn't say that. I only meant—Oh, forget it. Look, I didn't summon you, so you can go back to the party."

"*Summon* me! See here, Neil Ryan, I am not a poodle. I do not jump at your command."

"I don't know," goaded Neil, his arms crossing his chest in obvious amusement. "You came when you thought I called, didn't you?"

Hannah tried her best glare, though she suspected the effect was lost coming out of a mountain of yellow vinyl. "Of all the arrogant, egotistical, tyrannical—"

"Hannah—"

"I only came out here because I've been waiting all day to give you a piece of my mind!"

"Well, then?" prompted Neil, the sharp blue of his eyes harshly defined by the glow of crystal lanterns strung nearby. "Give it."

Hannah blinked, hands still on hips, stance still ready for war. Yet, in the face of Neil's cold hard gaze, her well of roiling emotions seemed to go suddenly dry.

"Hannah? I'm waiting."

The uncivil tone was all Hannah needed to light a fire under her tempered resolve. "Fine, let's start with the fact that you owe me an apology. In fact, *that's* the reason I came out here, I thought you were ready to apologize."

"For what?"

"Your behavior."

"What about my behavior?" asked Neil.

"It stinks, that's what. What do you mean treating me like a traitor to king and country? What the heck is your problem anyway?"

"I've got no problem." Neil tried to turn from her and walk away, but Hannah was just getting started.

"Yes, you do!" she exclaimed, yanking his arm until he was either forced to turn and face her again or risk having his fine black overcoat's sleeve ripped off. "Everyone around here is happy to see me except you!"

Neil dredged up his best junkyard dog glare, the steady, evil one that scared all the bad guys. It failed to move Hannah one inch.

"Hello!" she spouted instead. "Anybody *in* there?"

"Pipe down," he commanded as he grabbed her elbow and guided her roughly down the lawn, toward the cutting garden.

"Where are we going?"

"Away from the tent."

"Why? Are you planning something sinister? Trying to avoid any witnesses?"

Neil sighed in exasperation as he walked her far enough away to risk rounding on her. "I'm trying to avoid prying eyes, Hannah, and so should you."

"What?"

"*Mrs.* Peabody, your reputation, as I understand it, has been established on television as a happy homemaker. A *married* happy homemaker."

"So?"

"So, my reputation has been established as a *reputable* officer of this hotel. Respectable, scrupulous, and honorable. That's why people trust me with such items as their precious valuables and their unpredictable daughters. I'm a *trustworthy* investigator at an *esteemed* hotel."

"Yes!" snapped Hannah. "Tell me something I don't know. What the heck is your point?!"

"Are you deaf, dumb, *and* blind, Hannah? People around here know that we were involved once. What will they think if we start chumming around again?"

"My God, Neil, you're crazy."

"I'm realistic."

Hannah couldn't believe Neil Ryan had become such a paranoid stuffed shirt. She felt like walking away for good, but wanted first to get rid of the boiling rage that had been scalding her insides for most of the day—and she planned to dump it directly on Neil Ryan's head.

"Well, then, Mr. Reputable, Respectable, and Honorable," she spat, pounding her index finger into his chest with each new adjective, "explain to me why you were taking that jailbait off to bed last night before I so rudely interrupted you!"

Neil blinked. "What the hell are you talking about?"

"When I walked into the hotel last night, you were holding a drunken debutante in your arms. And obviously carrying her off to bed."

"So?"

"So!" Hannah gave up. Shaking her head, she turned to leave. But this time it was Neil stopping her. Hannah would have let his jerking tug rip her shiny, yellow, Donald Duck coat sleeve to pieces, except that it didn't belong to her and she felt guilty letting it get damaged. So instead she yielded to Neil's pull and wheeled toward him again.

"You don't mean to suggest," stated Neil tensely, "that I was going to have sex with that girl?"

"No. I mean to *say* that's what you were going to do."

"Hannah, I was taking her off to bed because she was *drunk*. The girl is my client's daughter. I was hired to bodyguard her."

Hannah's jaw dropped open but nothing came out for a few moments. "Bodyguard her?"

"Yes, and most of the time it's one of my staff who does the guarding. Last night happened to be an exception. She'd gotten drunk and out of control, not to mention verbally abusive. I didn't want to subject my staff to that."

"But . . . I don't understand. Why would you subject *yourself* to it instead?"

"Tiffany's just a spoiled brat, that's all. And I'm in a position of authority here. I know I can chuck the entire protection contract if she's more trouble than she's worth—she knows it, too. That's how I control her."

"But if she's so much trouble . . ."

"She's just a little girl who makes a game of twisting people around her finger. I've handled worse. Besides, Tiffany's father is paying me a very generous fee, and I plan to use it to give my men bonuses. God knows they deserve it."

"Oh," was all Hannah could think to say.

The evening was dark but the lights from the grounds were enough for Neil to watch a red flush of embarrassment bloom on Hannah's cheeks. He tried not to enjoy it as much as he had last night. Just the reminder of last night, of being so close to her again, sent a warmth through his veins.

"So you see," he said softly, "my concern is valid. Looks can be deceiving, and I don't want anyone making the wrong assumptions. About us, I mean."

"Us?" echoed Hannah. "But that was a long time ago. We were kids then. We're adults now."

"Exactly my point."

"Neil, are you telling me that's why you're avoiding me and being so cold to me? Because you're afraid what people will *think* if we enjoy a friendly conversation?"

"Hannah—" Neil stopped, wanting to tell her, yet not wanting to tell her.

"What, Neil? Please tell me what's on your mind."

"Hannah . . . people know that we spent last night together in your suite."

Neil watched the blush instantly vanish from Hannah's face. His words had made her visibly pale.

"But we didn't *do* anything," argued Hannah, her voice suddenly weak in the chilly ocean wind. "It was perfectly innocent."

"It didn't *look* innocent. And I'm sorry to say that these days the truth matters less than the *appearance* of truth."

"Oh, Neil, don't say that."

"Hannah, look what you assumed after seeing me with the girl I was hired to bodyguard."

Hannah's legs felt unnaturally unsteady. She glanced around quickly for a place to sit down.

"Hannah?" Neil watched with concern as Hannah began to wobble around the garden. He realized that she was heading for a sculpted stone bench when he strode up behind her. "Hannah, are you all right?"

Hannah turned a little too quickly and lost her footing in the damp grass. Neil caught her before she fell completely. In the process, she was enveloped completely in his arms for a few seconds.

Neil was so concerned with helping Hannah that he barely noticed a strange fluttering sound coming from the nearby bushes.

"I don't want any mess," Hannah kept murmuring, oblivious to Neil's catch. "Not now. I've worked too hard to endure another mess. I can't have people starting rumors. I can't have it, Neil."

"Yes, Hannah, I know that. I agree."

Hannah gazed up into Neil's blue eyes. They no longer looked like chips of ice—chilly hard gems with no feeling. Now they seemed warmer, softer . . . more human.

Carefully, Neil lowered Hannah to the flat stone surface of the bench, then he sat down beside her. His body blocked some of the ocean wind, but the seat was freezing beneath them.

"Are you okay?" he asked. "You must be cold—do you want to go in?"

When Hannah didn't answer, she felt his arm go around her shoulders. She liked the effect on her senses. It didn't really make her feel any warmer, but it made her feel protected—something she hadn't enjoyed in a long time. Not since her parents had been alive.

"Hannah, did you hear me? Do you want to go in?" asked Neil again, the concern evident in his voice.

Hannah shook her head.

So they sat like that, silently, for a long time: Hannah thinking, Neil with his arm around her shoulders, and the ocean beating an endless rhythm on the jagged rocks beyond the edge of the grounds.

Occasionally Neil noticed again that a quiet fluttering sound was sporadically coming from the bushes. *What the hell is that?* A part of him was bothered by it, yet he was too focused on Hannah at the moment to be more than momentarily distracted.

"Did you enjoy the wedding?" asked Neil finally, trying to assess whether Hannah was all right.

"Yes," Hannah answered absently. "It was very romantic."

Neil remembered seeing Hannah crying at the ceremony. Something about the sight had glued him to his spot.

"Were you thinking about your own wedding?" asked Neil softly.

"Heavens no!" blurted Hannah without thinking.

"Oh."

"I mean, I wasn't thinking of anything in particular, you know, just about how nice the ceremony was, and the decorations, and the music, that sort of thing," Hannah babbled quickly.

"So you think marriage is a fine institution, then?"

Hannah glanced at Neil. "What kind of a question is that?"

Neil sighed. "I don't know, a stupid one, I guess. Look, maybe we should go in."

Hannah sat, waiting for Neil to make a move to rise. But he just continued to sit beside her. Finally she made a soft suggestion. "I'll answer if you will."

A short, sharp grunt escaped Neil's throat. Hannah wondered if maybe the noise had been a laugh. "Okay," said Neil. "You go first."

"Me? No. No way."

"Hey, I thought of the question," pointed out Neil.

"And I thought of the rules."

"You're just being difficult."

"Not as difficult as you."

Hannah noticed a kind of smile had touched the edge of Neil's normally tightly closed lips. "Look at that," she said.

"What?"

"On your face."

"What?"

"It's the Neil Ryan almost-smile."

"Stop it, Hannah."

"You know, that thing might just be on the endangered species list."

"Hannah—"

"Maybe if we filed the right papers with the government, we could get your face declared a federally protected habitat. Oh, my God, now you're laughing—now that has got to be a practically extinct commodity. Maybe we should record it for posterity."

"Okay, Hannah, I give up. I'll answer."

Hannah folded her arms across her chest and waited.

"I think marriage is fine for *some* people. And you? What do you think?"

"Oh, well . . ." Hannah chewed on her bottom lip a moment. "I suppose I agree with you. But the people involved really should love each other. . . ."

Neil stared out into the vast darkness of the ocean, a body of blue that had become a lonely black vastness with the descent of night. "Hannah?"

"Yes, Neil?"

"Do you love your husband?"

Hannah swallowed uneasily, not prepared for the question in the least. "That's a silly question. Brides love their grooms, don't they? What do you think of today's couple? Will they end in the divorce courts, do you suppose?"

Neil was silent a long moment, and Hannah felt that he was considering her evasion of his question more than the answer to hers. Finally, after a full minute of silence, he spoke softly. "I think they'll be fine."

"What makes you so sure? I heard the bride was forced to sign the prenuptial agreement."

"She wasn't forced," said Neil. "In fact, it was something the bride said after she asked to sign the papers that made me certain she really did love the groom."

"What did she say?"

"She said that life was too short to risk losing someone she loved."

"Really? She really said that?"

"Yes, sounds wise beyond her years, doesn't it? It did to me . . . almost oddly so."

"What about the groom?"

"Oh, the groom loves her. No doubt about it. I saw it in his eyes."

"You can *see* something like that, huh?"

"Yes. If you know how to look. You know, Hannah, it is part of my job to know how to read people."

"I see. So what do you read in me?"

Neil let out an uneasy breath. "You don't want to know."

"Oh, no, Neil Ryan, you're not getting away with a statement like that."

Neil looked down at her. *Your marriage is a disaster. And you don't want to admit it,* thought Neil, but he refused to say it. Why state something she would just deny?

"C'mon, Ryan," teased Hannah, "look at me. Tell me what you see."

Neil gazed down into Hannah's face. A flash of light in the distance reflected itself off her glasses and he realized the Easton Point Lighthouse had been with them all along.

She's smiling, he noticed, and as always, the bright warmth of Hannah's smile transformed her plain face into a thing of radiance, changing her gray eyes into shimmering pools, defining her cheekbones, and generally gleaming with more goodness than Christmas.

"You know, you're beautiful," he breathed without thinking.

"What?" Her eyes instantly widened, as if in shock.

"You heard me," said Neil softly.

"Why did you say that?"

Neil took a deep breath. "Because it's true."

"It's the dark," said Hannah, trying her best to turn the whole moment into a wisecrack. Hannah had learned long ago the best technique for avoiding hurt was to laugh at herself before anyone else could.

"Dim lighting always blots out my best features," joked Hannah. "You should see me during an eclipse of the sun."

"I mean it," assured Neil softly.

"Please don't tease me," she managed on what felt like the last breath of air in her lungs.

"I'm not teasing. You are a very beautiful woman," he said, and then, despite his clear concerns for his reputation— and hers—Neil Ryan found himself, for once in his adult life, acting against all logic and sense.

Slowly he bent forward, never hesitating once as he moved toward the face he found so appealing, toward the lips he found so inviting, toward the woman he'd always found so much to his liking.

"Neil?" whispered Hannah, trying to take a breath and failing. She was certain her lungs had frozen solid. She watched as Neil's strong, square jaw came toward her. It all seemed real enough, yet a part of her was unable to believe what was happening.

And then it did happen.

Neil Ryan's lips brushed across hers.

The kiss was as pure a feeling of affection as Hannah could ever remember experiencing. And as pure a moment of longing that had ever come to pass.

And yet, as the heat of his lips seemed to warm every molecule of her body, Hannah couldn't help but feel deep inside that Neil was simply being her friend, taking pity on a plain-looking woman whose life had gone to pieces, and whose heart was forever lost.

She never even heard the fluttering sound coming loudly from the bushes nearby.

Chapter Fourteen

"Damn it!"

In the space of a millisecond, Hannah watched, completely stunned, as Neil Ryan tore himself from their tender kiss. In one fluid movement, he launched himself headfirst into the rosebushes a few yards away.

Neil cursed loudly at the necessity of wrenching himself away from Hannah's warm mouth, but he had no choice. He'd finally recognized that fluttering sound that had been gnawing at his consciousness for the last fifteen minutes. It was the sound of a 35-millimeter camera's motorized advance—the kind that allowed the shutter to take two or three incriminating photos with every blink of the eye.

"Neil!" shrieked Hannah a moment later when a blood-curdling squawk came out of the bushes. "What the hell is going on?!"

She watched in horror as a red-haired young man, dressed in dark clothing, fell backward out of the bushes, then began frantically scrambling away.

Like a swamp alligator on the heels of his prey, Neil pulled himself forward low on the ground, oblivious to the scratches of bared branches and sharp thorns. In his soul he cursed a blue streak, ready to kill whoever was on the other end of that shutter. On elbows and knees, he issued a guttural yell of frustration until his arm was able to jerk straight and capture one of the young man's ankles.

"Lemme go, lemme go!" shrieked the kid, frantically kicking at Neil's head.

"Code Two. Location Eight. Now!" Neil shouted into his walkie-talkie, which he'd somehow managed to pull from his inside jacket pocket, and within fifteen seconds a small army of security guards was at Neil's side as he subdued the errant photographer.

"I was just taking pictures! For the wedding album!" he shouted in a panic. "Impromptu shots of guests! What the hell's wrong with you, man?!"

"Cut the crap," said Neil in a dangerously low voice. "Give me the camera."

With a shaking hand the young man held it out to Neil. "There are no unauthorized photos on these grounds," said Neil evenly as he flipped open the back of the Nikon and ripped out the film.

"Hey, don't do that! Oh, man! I'm authorized, I work for the wedding photographer, you jerk!"

"Watch your mouth," snapped Neil.

The kid immediately backed down. "Sorry, man, but you ruined my whole roll!"

Taking a step closer, Neil examined the boy's face to confirm his ID. Neil *did* recognize the kid from the ceremony. But he'd replaced his tuxedo jacket with a pitch-black turtleneck pullover and had covered his head with a black knit cap.

"Empty your pockets," commanded Neil.

The kid stared angrily at Neil, ready to protest, but he thought better of it and did as he was ordered. Nothing but loose change, a pocketknife, a wallet, and some scraps of paper.

"Satisfied?" sassed the kid.

"Yes, as a matter of fact," said Neil evenly. "If you're here for the wedding photos, then take them in the tent and the ballroom, as warranted. Some of my staff here will see you report back to your boss, and they will stay with you until you leave the premises."

"Oh, man!"

"Johnny Houston, Martin Wilson, see to it. The rest of you, back to your posts."

As the small army of crew-cut security guards broke up, Hannah watched two members break off and flank the hapless photographer's assistant. Linking one arm in each of his, the guards escorted the kid directly back to the tent, just as Neil had ordered.

Neil turned to Hannah, a look of indescribable distress on his handsome face. "I'm sorry, Hannah," he said awkwardly.

"I don't understand," said Hannah. "The boy was just taking photos for the couple's album, wasn't he?"

"Hannah, you know and I know that innocent wedding photographers don't hide in rosebushes at night wearing black camouflage, trying to take photos of famous ladies in compromising positions."

"Oh, God, Neil." Hannah suddenly felt sick to her stomach.

"Hannah, haven't you had this problem before?"

Hannah shook her head. "My life in Chicago is pretty much . . . well, reclusive. I work all the time. I don't have any time left over to worry about . . . well, about compromising positions."

Neil studied Hannah a long moment. "Are you and your husband separated?" he whispered. "Is that what you're trying to keep quiet? For the sake of your career?"

Hannah's hand went to her pounding head; she suddenly felt as if an entire construction company was jackhammering concrete in the center of her skull.

"Hannah?"

"Yes," she said finally. "You're right, okay. Please don't say anything."

"No, of course not." Neil placed his hands on her arms and drew her closer. He wanted to make certain she heard his next words. "Hannah, the last thing I want to do is put you in a position that will hurt you."

Hannah studied Neil's wrinkled brow. She saw something in his eyes, but couldn't tell if it was vulnerability or pity. With as much gentleness as she could, Hannah touched her hand to his cheek.

"Thank you," she whispered. "I see now what you were

trying to tell me earlier, about what people might think. I guess you were right. It's best if we steer clear of each other from now on."

Neil should have been relieved to hear Hannah's words. But he wasn't relieved. For some reason, now that he'd finally persuaded Hannah of the certain sense in safeguarding appearances, he himself felt an illogical sense of uncertainty.

For one thing, Neil wanted to hear more about Hannah's failed marriage. Was she in mourning for it? Did she want to reconcile with Peabody? Or did she intend to end it soon?

The crackle of Neil's radio cut off his quiz before he even got started. Neil moved to turn it lower when a voice leapt out of the walkie-talkie's small receiver.

"Mr. Ryan, a problem. Your presence is requested. Location Two."

Neil sighed in frustration after confirming the transmission, then he turned to Hannah. "Come with me. I want us to finish this conversation."

But Hannah shook her head. "Do you think that's wise?"

"It'll be fine. Just follow me, okay. Wait by the fireplace in the lobby. When I'm through with this, I'll take us to a private place to talk."

Hannah nodded her head. "You go ahead. I'll follow. I don't think we should be seen together."

Neil's fists were clenched as he made his way to the main building of the hotel. Hannah was obviously as scared as a cornered rabbit. For a second time he cursed that lousy photographer. He could wring that snot-nosed kid's neck for this. What did he think he was going to do, anyway? Sell the photos to some supermarket rag?

The lobby was sparsely populated. Most of the wedding guests had gone up to their rooms or, if they were still lingering for final drinks and conversations, had remained in the tent and ballroom. Neil easily found his way to the front door of the mansion, where one of his security guards stood with the "problem."

Why was he not surprised to see Miss Tiffany Townsend?

It figures, thought Neil. The way his night had been going, who else could it be?

"Sorry to bother you, Mr. Ryan," said the guard named Kresky in a low voice as he stepped forward. "But you asked to be notified if Miss Townsend intended to leave the premises, and she—''

''And I do intend to, Corny, honey,'' broke in Tiffany, making sure to elbow the guard as she stepped forward. ''I can speak for myself, jughead.''

Neil eyed her with extreme patience. She had changed from the strappy evening gown she'd worn at the wedding. In its place was a short tight brown leather skirt and matching vest. A belted leather jacket, of the exact shade as the skirt and vest, hung open to reveal a generous helping of cleavage, which she seemed to enjoy flaunting directly under Neil's gaze.

''Don't abuse my staff, Miss Townsend,'' said Neil stiffly.

''Oh, don't go getting that handsome nose out of joint.''

''Apologize,'' demanded Neil.

Tiffany's hands planted themselves directly on her hips. She glared at Neil, her lips pouting. ''Sorry,'' she bit out, her gaze deigning, ever so briefly, to flicker to the guard she'd insulted.

''Okay, Miss Manners,'' said Neil. ''Where do you *intend* to go this evening?''

Tiffany took her time answering. She stepped even closer to Neil and slowly licked her lips invitingly. ''Out.''

''Out *where*?''

''Newport. By the wharf. I want to pick up a few sailors.''

Neil sighed, not entirely sure whether the girl was teasing him. He wouldn't put it past her to try bringing a few swabbies back to her bedroom—though Neil knew they'd never make it past the guard at the hotel's front gate.

Neil turned to Kresky, the guard who'd been looking after her for the last shift. ''Tap Samuels for me, will you? He's in the tent.''

''Who's Samuels?'' asked Tiffany after the other guard trotted swiftly off. ''Is he cute?''

''He's a moonlighting Newport cop. Newly married. Happily so, Miss Townsend, so you'll find him, as well as all of my guards, seduce-proof. That's *why* they're my guards.''

''And what about you, Corny? I'd say the rules don't have to apply to the rule-maker.''

''Of course they do.''

Tiffany smiled shrewdly. ''Sure, honey, whatever you

say . . . but listen—'' Tiffany's voice became soft, seductive. "Between you and me, why don't *you* guard me tonight? I know you want to."

Neil's eyebrow quirked. "Too busy."

"C'mon, we'll have some fun. Hit a few bars. You'll like it. I promise."

"I see Samuels coming. Try not to be too hard on him, Miss Townsend."

Tiffany turned to see the young cop coming toward them. She also saw the reason Neil wasn't joining her tonight. It was that *homemaker* person, realized Tiffany with a perverted sense of outraged betrayal. Hannah Peabody was standing across the lobby, by the large hotel fireplace, staring directly at her and Neil.

Tiffany looked back at Neil; his gaze had strayed to connect with the little scarecrow. The sight sent Tiffany's blood into a molten center-of-the-earth boil. *Fine, Ryan,* thought Tiffany angrily. *Keep teasing me. I know you can't be attracted to . . . to . . . that.* Tiffany was certain that Neil was simply playing another of his teasing games. *Well, go ahead, then.* She wouldn't hesitate to play her game, too.

"Good evening, Samuels," greeted Neil. "You're up."

"Right, Mr. Ryan. Are you having a pleasant evening, Miss Townsend?"

Tiffany twirled a blond curl around a finger as her blue gaze looked the handsome young police officer up and down in a haughty evaluation. Finally, she let out a smirking sound that resembled a high-pitched grunt.

"Like I said," reiterated Neil, "Mr. Samuels is a Newport police officer by day, so you'll find he'll know *just* how to keep you out of trouble. Won't you, Mr. Samuels?"

"You can count on me, Mr. Ryan."

Tiffany grunted again. "Well, I'd better find my cousin. Unless you want to drink with me?" she said with a pointed stare at the guard.

"I don't drink on duty, miss."

"How tiresome." With a roll of her eyes, Tiffany was about to turn away from Neil when she stopped herself. "Oh, one more thing, Corny."

"Yes, Miss Townsend?"

With a quick glance to make certain the little scarecrow

was watching, Tiffany stepped up close to Neil and crooked her finger. "Come closer," she whispered, "it's a private matter."

Warily, Neil bent closer, turning his head slightly for Tiffany to whisper her "private matter" into his ear. But her lips didn't move toward his ear, instead they zeroed in on another part of his face like an M1A1 tank on a moving target.

Before he could stop her, Tiffany's arms were tight around his neck, her lips pressed against his own—and her generous chest brushing shamelessly against him.

As quickly as he could manage, Neil pried her away from him, his eyes glaring with extreme anger. "Knock it off, Tiffany," he bit out low, "or I'll see that you're checked out of this hotel for good."

"Why don't you just spank me?" she teased with a laugh. "I'm sure it would be much more enjoyable for us both."

Neil looked to Samuels. "Get her out of here."

Samuels stepped up, but Tiffany was already moving away. "C'mon, Sammy, I have to find a friend."

Neil reached into his jacket for a handkerchief. He could taste some of Tiffany's lipstick on him and he couldn't wipe it off fast enough. He sighed as he turned back toward the fireplace, still very anxious to talk to Hannah.

But when he looked up to find her, she was gone.

Tiffany was careful as she stepped through the ballroom and into the attached tent. She made very sure that Samuels stayed at enough of a distance that she could converse without his overhearing a word.

The band was about to finish its last number, and she spotted her cousin Clark at the bar. She'd start toward him in a moment, but first she had some unfinished business.

As casually as she could manage, Tiffany sauntered by the wedding photographer, who was packing up the last of his equipment. She stopped near the red-haired assistant helping him.

"So," she asked sweetly, "did you get some good pictures?"

"Man, you should o' seen how close I came to—"

"Keep your voice down," whispered Tiffany. "There's a bodyguard about six feet in back of me."

"So what? I got two guards of my own watching," said the kid. "Look over there."

Tiffany saw two more stiffs in suits standing across the tent, watching them.

"Why are they watching *you*?" asked Tiffany with alarm.

"They're supposed to make sure I don't leave the tent or ballroom."

Tiffany's teeth clenched in frustration. *"Why?"*

"While I was out by the garden, lover boy nabbed the roll in my camera."

Tiffany stared in disbelief. "Tell me you're kidding."

"Nope."

"God," whispered Tiffany angrily. "Are you telling me you screwed this up, you little—"

"Calm down. The suit and his goons took the roll in the camera, and meanwhile I'm thinkin', hey, I need the money on this gig, you know. If I pull it off, it's New York City, here I come."

"What are you babbling about?"

"Just this. Look—"

"Look at what?"

Tiffany watched as the kid dragged something out of his pants pocket. When she saw what it was, a slow smile turned her slightly smeared lipstick into an upturned crescent of crimson.

In the kid's hand were two tiny canisters of used 35-millimeter film.

"I shot two full rolls more before the guy jumped me. They made me empty my pockets, but they never checked my socks."

Chapter Fifteen

So they kissed.

So what?

Slamming shut the door to the Daisy Channing Doyle Memorial Suite, Hannah told herself she didn't give a fig what Neil Ryan did with his lips. So one moment they were on Hannah's and the next they were on a young woman wearing tight leather. Really, what business was it of Hannah's?

None.

Whatsoever.

That was precisely why, the moment she saw that honey-haired debutante affix her mouth suction-style to Neil's, Hannah had fled the scene. She hadn't even waited for the elevator. Instead, she'd launched herself toward the staircase, rising three flights more swiftly than a frantic seagull.

With her heart pounding painfully, Hannah leaned back against the door to her suite. Reaching up, she slipped the dead bolt into place with a wince—less from the effects of the three-story sprint than the memory of the lock's peculiar behavior the night before.

''Why couldn't that stupid, moronic lock have worked last

night?'' Hannah muttered to herself as she began to pace the room. Then no one would have seen him spend the night with her.

Hannah sighed as she recalled what she had told Neil tonight—that she lived a separate life from Herbert Peabody. It was the truth, though not the whole of it. No one knew the entire story, except her sister Holly and her best friend Greta Green.

For a fleeting moment, Hannah wondered if she could trust Neil to keep her secret, too. Herbert would be making an appearance for Holly's wedding, just as they'd planned. Any wedding pictures would show her and Herbert to be a happy couple—exactly the facade she'd maintained for the last three years.

Why now, with a major network about to pick up *Homemaking*, did she have to endure this threat of bad publicity?

Wringing her hands as she continued to pace, Hannah wondered what she could do to settle her mind before she went insane with worry. She glanced at the hidden bar, but knew that alcohol, a tempting mind-eraser, never appealed to her. Then she spied her laptop, sitting invitingly on the ornate rococo desk.

Work.

Hannah sighed at the thought and immediately felt calmer. She stepped into the small dressing room, hung her boxy maroon suit on a padded, perfumed hanger, and pulled on jeans and a sweatshirt.

She strode to the desk, sat down, and flipped open her laptop. In no time, she was furiously typing away, utilizing the mental notes she'd made during the course of the day to begin sketching ideas for her latest book.

HOMEMAKING HANNAH'S WEDDINGS OLD AND NEW, she typed at the top of the screen, then continued:

"Weddings are like military operations," remarked Maura Ryan, Executive Manager of one of America's most exclusive wedding venues, Château du Coeur. "Timing and teamwork and a very good plan of action . . ."

In the back of Hannah's mind, she knew that it was Neil and not Maura who'd made this comparison. Maura had merely been quoting her son, but Hannah wasn't in the mood to even think of Neil's name right now, let alone type it.

"Literary license," she muttered, her fingers continuing to tap out letters.

After a good two hours of trying to outline her wedding book, Hannah leaned back in her chair with a sigh. Work used to be her escape—but tonight her concentration fell off quickly, her mind distracted. Without thinking, she found herself rising to cross the room, passing the watchful brass eyes of the cat vase in the corner.

Despite the slight chill that had already descended in the suite, Hannah's fingers felt an unexplainable urge to unlatch the tall window and push the heavy pane out against the whipping Atlantic wind.

Chaos was in the air. The black surf crashed against the jagged cliffside with a savage fury, yet the sound seemed to comfort Hannah, calling to her like an old song. She leaned her forearms against the sill, letting the stiff salty wind tear through her hair and batter her face.

"I wonder if Daisy and Dan liked the sea..." Hannah murmured to herself. Staring off into the inky blackness, she found herself considering whether they really were still around: Could two people really feel a love so strong that it would last beyond the grave?

Hannah couldn't help but wonder whether she herself would ever experience such a love. She closed her eyes, feeling a pain in what was left of her heart, yet feeling the need in some small part of it to make a wish for just that.

Suddenly, a white specter flashed before Hannah's eyes. She gasped, recoiling, until she realized it was merely the stark beam of the Easton Point Lighthouse. With an exhaled breath, she leaned back on the sill and began watching the light turn rhythmically in the distance, as it did every evening, warning sailors of the danger they could not see.

Hannah wondered why there had been no lighthouse for her in the year after her parents' deaths. But, perhaps, even if there had been, she would have ignored its warning. Perhaps, in her sadness and despair, she would have felt it necessary to wreck herself on some jutting piece of rock whether its name had been Herbert Peabody or John Doe.

Still, if she could choose all over again, Hannah wished she had wrecked herself on a boy named Neil Ryan. At least then she would have seen her silly girlish fantasies to their crashing end for once and for all, instead of wrestling with her feelings now in one ridiculously frustrating round after another.

Hannah took a deep breath to clear her head. Then, with a firm hand, she pulled the window shut on all her childhood dreams, frustrating feelings, and useless wishes. She turned on her heel and started again for the desk, ready to resume work, when a sound—like music—made her stop cold.

"A dreamer can awaken to a Heaven on the Earth..."

"What in the world?" whispered Hannah. It was music, all right, and it was coming from outside.

"... when the heart is finally taken by a love that knows its worth..."

Returning to the window, Hannah quickly looked down on the rear grounds. The wedding tent was dark, the lawn empty. The party had ended long ago. The bands *had* to have packed it in for the night.

So why was she still hearing music?

Hannah opened the window again. The music grew louder. Strangely, it sounded like an old tinny twenties ballad—the kind a singer would warble through a megaphone. It sounded familiar, too, but neither the ballroom orchestra nor the tent's rock band had played anything like it during the entire reception.

Then, as she searched the grounds, something caught her eye. It was the figure of a woman in a powder-blue gown. Something about it seemed particularly odd ... the blue of the gown seemed to glow brightly, as if one of the mansion's ground lights were reflecting off of it.

"She must be cold," murmured Hannah. The woman wore no coat, and the gown's material looked light and filmy, like a crepe de chine. The chilly ocean wind lifted and dropped the skirt as she walked, giving the impression of gentle blue waves rolling along the dark lawn.

Hannah herself was growing cold by the open window, but something compelled her to stand there and keep watching. That same strange song continued to play as the woman walked toward the rear wall, then strode right through the archway, as if no gate stood there at all.

"And a heart in love can last beyond the sun, beyond the sea . . ."

It was too dark to see, but Hannah was *sure* there had been a black iron gate standing closed in that archway. On the tour Maura had given Hannah, she'd said that Neil's staff made certain it was supervised during the day and locked securely at night.

Hannah didn't like the look of this all of a sudden. Beyond that archway, Hannah knew that a set of stone steps led to the Cliff Walk and the rocky shore. Why was this woman taking a walk toward the shore at this hour—all alone, and with no coat?

Hannah tried to shake off the troubling feeling, but she couldn't. The music, she realized, seemed to grow fainter, and she was certain something seemed disturbingly familiar about it.

She'd heard it before, hadn't she? But where?

". . . when the song of love it sings is meant for all eternity . . ."

Blinking in alarm, Hannah realized it was the same tune that had haunted her the night before on the front lawn. And then again in the empty ballroom.

"Maybe I'll just have a look," she murmured as she shut the window and strode across the room. After slipping on her sneakers and grabbing a red windbreaker, Hannah quickly left her suite and headed for the hotel's rear grounds.

Sitting in a deep leather easy chair, his long legs stretched out in front of him, Neil Ryan shut the book he was reading and sighed. The Dan and Daisy Doyle collection of short stories held a *very* interesting piece of information he couldn't wait to share with Hannah.

He stared at the phone on the table beside him. He could call her now, he thought, glancing at his watch. It wasn't *that* late.

His hand reached out toward the phone. But, at the last moment, instead of grasping the receiver, Neil's long fingers went for a tumbler half-filled with deep violet liquid.

"Chicken," he muttered to himself as he took a drink.

He supposed grape soda was not the sort of thing grown men drank, let alone private detectives. But he'd been off alcohol for the last few years and, for some reason, Welch's own seemed to calm his nerves, though he only drank it at night. Nothing less professional than a grown man with a purple tongue.

Sighing, he took another sip, but it failed to calm his nerves tonight. They'd been on edge ever since that scene in the lobby.

He'd told himself that Hannah's disappearance had nothing to do with Tiffany's kiss. Still, maybe he should have gone after her—stopped by her suite. But at the time it felt ridiculous to chase a woman who'd just told him it was better if they kept their distance.

And maybe it was. Maybe he shouldn't call her after all. Maybe he should just let them drift away from each other—as he had years ago.

Neil pulled at his already loosened bow tie, letting its ends hang freely around his neck. After going off duty an hour ago, he'd returned to his carriage house apartment, flung his tuxedo jacket over the sofa, then grabbed the Dan and Daisy short story collection he had just put down. He had hoped the stories would help him lose his frustrations, but one particular story had only heightened them—reminding him all too vividly of his time with Hannah the night before.

The sudden ring of the phone startled Neil into a momentary hope that Hannah had decided to call him. Then he realized it was the office fax line. He stood up, recalling that he'd asked his colleague to fax him any information he could dig up on Herbert Peabody.

After setting down his grape soda, Neil left his small apartment's living room and stepped into the hallway that led to his Ryan Investigations office. He wanted to read that fax as soon as possible.

Outside, behind the main building of the mansion, Hannah crossed the dark lawn, bypassing the stone statue of cupid and the white wedding tent. The night was chilly and damp, but the wind had kept the clouds at bay, creating the kind of crystal clear night that could only be seen near the ocean.

Hercules was clearly visible, Draco, Virgo, and the Little

Dipper. But the Earth hadn't moved far enough around its orbit yet for Pegasus to appear. He was still beneath the horizon, waiting for summer before he galloped onto the sky's dark canvas.

Hannah continued striding across the lawn. She listened for further sounds of music. But there were none. And, when she finally reached the stone archway at the edge of Château du Coeur's grounds, she saw that the black iron gate stood closed beneath it.

"That's really odd," she whispered into the strengthening sea breeze. Hannah knew for certain the woman had simply walked *right through* the archway. She hadn't paused at all; certainly she'd made no movement to open or close the gate.

Hannah's hand reached out, her fingers closing around one of the black gate's cold iron bars. She pushed. But the gate didn't budge. She tried pulling instead. But, again, the gate didn't move.

With more force, Hannah tried again. The heavy gate shook slightly this time but still would not open.

But it can't be locked, thought Hannah in agitation. She'd just watched the woman pass through.

"I'm here . . ."

It was the woman's voice Hannah heard, she was sure of it. The sound was weak, as if the ageless roar of the pounding surf had swallowed any real force that had been there. Hannah peered through the bars of the black gate, her cheeks pressing hard against the icy metal, but she could see nothing, just the shadowy stone steps leading downward.

With a feeling of growing urgency, she moved away from the archway to the low wall that stretched the length of the grounds. A significant drop greeted her, then the dirt-covered stone path of the Cliff Walk. But not a soul could be seen taking a stroll on this chilly spring night.

"I'm here. . . . Here I am . . ."

A bubbly laugh followed the words, and Hannah looked beyond the Walk and searched the shoreline. The sound of the woman's laughter was louder than her voice. It continued long enough for Hannah to trace its direction until, with a sharp gasp, she finally spotted the woman in blue.

For some crazy reason the woman had climbed out on a natural jetty of sharp rocks. She stood there now on what had to be a terribly slippery surface, her powder-blue dress billowing in the stiff breeze, her arms extended for balance as if it were a game.

Hannah's eyes widened in shock as she watched the woman's white leather heels toddle even farther out on the jetty. Below her, the cold, black waves of the ocean were pounding against the boulders, whipping themselves into a foamy froth.

As inviting as the concoction may have looked in a soda glass, Hannah knew how dangerous the rough surf was—not just because the cold could cause hypothermia to set in very quickly, but because the power of the churning waves could bash a person's skull into the jagged rocks like an egg against a skillet.

"Hey, you!" shouted Hannah, her arm waving frantically. "Come back!"

Hannah watched, her breath labored, as the woman turned. Her right arm bobbled a bit as her palm turned up in a little greeting to Hannah.

"You!" shouted Hannah again. "Please, come back!"

Hannah let out a little sigh of relief as the woman smiled at her. *She* must *hear me,* thought Hannah. *She'll come back now.*

But, in the next moment, Hannah realized there was something about the smile that was unsettling. It was strangely amused. As if she were about to share some kind of inside joke with Hannah.

"Hey! Can you hear me?!" Hannah tried shouting to her again.

But the woman didn't answer. She simply kept smiling, even as she turned back toward the churning ocean waves and jumped toward them.

Hannah blinked in shock.

Without taking a second to think, she simply reacted. Placing both palms on the cold stone surface of the low wall, Hannah pushed hard, throwing herself over the wall and into thin air.

She fell hard on the Cliff Walk's stone ten feet below, grunting as a sharp pain shot through her ankle. In her panic, she didn't hesitate, but launched herself down the rocky slope beyond the Walk until she'd reached the water.

"Hey! Can you hear me?!" she shouted as she limped along toward the jetty.

She searched frantically for any sign of the woman. The short blond hair, the billowing blue gown. But there was no sign. No sign at all.

"No!" screamed Hannah, as she realized there was only one thing she could do. And so she did it.

She jumped in after her.

Chapter
Sixteen

"Mr. Ryan, this is Houston."

"Yes?"

"We have a problem."

"What is it, Johnny?" Neil had just finished reading over the fax from Chicago when the phone rang again; this time it was the special line set up for the exclusive use of his security staff.

"It's not far from your door, sir, just meet the guards heading for Location Nine."

"What's going on?"

"Some woman's trying to commit suicide."

Neil slammed down the phone and raced for the door, grabbing his raincoat on the way. It took only a few steps beyond the door before he saw two guards racing down the lawn with bright searchlights glaring. Three more guards were twenty yards behind them.

"Damn." Neil had seen this twice before. Some guest must have gotten drunk and maudlin, deciding a life of luxury wasn't enough to salve a broken heart or a wrecked marriage.

"Wilson, what's going on?" he called as he jogged up to

one of the first guards, who'd just reached the rear archway in the center of the low wall that edged the back grounds.

"Security camera caught a woman shouting then leaping over the wall. She must be really nuts—"

"Or really drunk," put in the second guard.

"That's enough on the speculation," said Neil sharply. "Get the gate open so we can help her out."

Wilson took no longer than ten seconds to unlock the black iron gate, but Neil became impatient, even in that short a time. Grabbing the light of the second guard, he moved to the low wall and panned the area. Almost immediately he spotted a head bobbing in the water, near the natural jetty.

"Christ!" Without waiting another moment, Neil leapt over the low wall.

"Mr. Ryan!" shouted one of the guards. But it was too late, Neil was already shedding his raincoat and diving into frigid waves.

Neil steeled himself against the icy cold, concentrating instead on the movement of his limbs and the woman who could easily be dashed against the jagged rocks ahead.

"Hey!" he shouted as he moved closer to the head bobbing just above the violent waves.

"Help!" shrieked the woman when she realized that someone was nearby. "Help!"

And then he was upon her and when she turned her face to him, he nearly had a heart attack. "My God! Hannah?!"

"Neil! Oh, Heaven, Neil, help me! Help me!"

"Christ, Hannah! Grab on to me! I'll swim you back in!" he called over the pounding wash of the ocean surf against the nearby jetty.

"No! There's a woman out here . . . drowning! Help me find her!"

Neil didn't know whether Hannah was delusional from the cold or truly crazy, but he did know he couldn't risk allowing her to stay out here another second.

"Hannah! For God's sake, grab on!" he shouted even more forcefully. When she shook her head, he reached out to take her arms. But she pushed him away.

"No!" she shrieked. "I've got to find her!"

The cold was bitter, stinging him, scorching his skin like flames of ice. Hannah had to be even colder, and Neil's instinct took over. Lifeguard training for part-time work on Newport beaches didn't go to total waste as an adult. With a swift, strong motion, he pulled Hannah toward his body, disarming her flailing limbs with a deft hold.

"You're coming in, *now*, Hannah. Don't fight me!"

"No!"

But Neil was stronger and in a manner of seconds he was pulling her in, and she could do little about it. By the time they reached the shore, she was letting him help her to her feet. With his arm firmly around her waist, she limped onto the narrow rocky beach, where she stood, too stunned and cold to do much more than point weakly at the jetty.

"A woman," she whispered. "A woman in a blue dress jumped from the jetty."

Neil grabbed his raincoat from one of the security guards and, oblivious to his own chill in the stiff salty wind, wrapped it closely around Hannah. Then his hands began to briskly rub her arms to keep the blood flowing.

"Throw those lights out there!" Neil instructed his staff.

The guards did as Neil said, two of them searching the shoreline around the jetty, another two carefully stepping out on the jetty itself. But no one found any sign of Hannah's woman in blue.

"Wilson," Neil finally called, "come here."

Hannah's breathing was labored, her body weakened from the shock of the cold. Her glasses were lost in the water, but her eyes were bright and alert, continuing their own futile search for any sign of blue in the inky black waves.

"Yes, Mr. Ryan?"

"Were you watching the security camera?"

"Yes."

"What did you see?"

"Uh . . . the lady here crossed the lawn, then tried to get through the archway gate, but it was locked. She moved to the wall and began shouting and waving her arm. Then she jumped over the wall."

"I see."

Hannah blinked at the guard impatiently. "I was following the woman. Tell him about the woman!"

Neil studied Hannah. Her features were tense, her tone earnest. He turned back to the guard with a questioning gaze, but the guard just shook his head. "Sorry, ma'am."

"There *was* a woman," insisted Hannah, her voice almost desperate now. "She crossed the lawn before me. Went right through the archway. There was no gate . . . or it was unlocked or something . . . I don't know how she did it, but she did . . ."

"I'm sorry, Mr. Ryan," said the guard softly, his eyes downcast. "But our cameras show the lady here was the only one to cross the lawn."

"But . . ." Hannah's voice suddenly grew weak, her wet skin and hair finally making her shiver uncontrollably. "I saw her."

As Hannah continued to gaze toward the jetty, Neil gestured for the guard to lean closer. "Wilson," he said low, "tell Houston to pop that videotape and send it to my apartment."

"Neil?"

Using as gentle a tone as he could muster, Neil turned back to speak to Hannah. "Let's get inside, Hannah. Please don't argue with me. You're shivering. We have to get you warm."

"But . . ." Hannah's gray eyes met Neil's wet face and she realized that he was standing in the chill with not even a coat. For his sake more than her own, she nodded her head.

"Good," said Neil. "Come on."

With his arm around her waist, Neil quickly led Hannah back up the embankment to the Cliff Walk, then up the stone steps, through the hotel's archway and toward the nearby carriage house.

"I d-don't th-think I've ever b-been th-this c-cold."

Hannah's teeth were actually chattering as Neil guided her up the main staircase of the carriage house.

"I have," he told her.

"R-really?"

"Yes," he answered as he guided her down the carpeted hallway and toward a highly polished wooden door. "I had this all-night protection detail at a houseboat party on the Chesapeake Bay. Foreign ambassadors, State Department suits, that sort of thing."

"Y-yes?"

"It was November. Terrible storm came out of nowhere,

and the thing capsized before we made it back to shore.''

"Oh, H-heaven.''

"Yeah, I thought I was going to see it that night. Or maybe the place south of there.'' Neil turned the doorknob and pushed.

"W-what happened?'' she asked, watching him walk through the doorway and hold the door for her.

"Coast Guard came. Dragged us all out.''

"Th-thank G-god,'' said Hannah as she hesitantly stepped across the threshold.

"Thank the life jackets, too,'' said Neil as he shut and locked the door, then led her inside. "I'll never forget that ride back. There wasn't enough room in the Coast Guard cabin for us all. Me and the other two guards in the detail stayed on deck till we got back to shore. I was definitely colder then.''

Hannah glanced around the room. It was a tastefully appointed place with subtle masculine touches. A cozy leather chair sat in the corner near a small fireplace with an oak mantle. There was a serviceable sofa upholstered in plain forest green, two bookcases, an armoire, and small end tables of the same dark oak. The floor was covered with a thick area rug that blended nicely with the green of the sofa and the dark woods in the room.

Beyond the room was another doorway, which Hannah assumed led to the bedroom. At the other end was a small open kitchen, separated from the living area by a breakfast bar.

"Wh-where are w-we?'' asked Hannah, dreading the answer.

"My apartment.''

Hannah closed her eyes. "Why are w-we—''

"Because it's closer than the hotel,'' stated Neil flatly. "And if we don't warm you up immediately, you're going to the hospital.''

"Oh, I d-don't w-want t-to g-go t-to the h-hospi—''

"You won't, if you listen to me. C'mon.'' Guiding her firmly by the shoulders, Neil directed Hannah through the doorway at the end of the room.

Hannah cursed silently as she entered what was obviously Neil Ryan's bedroom.

"Get out of those clothes at once," he ordered as he stepped past her.

Hannah heard Neil. His instructions were perfectly clear. But she failed to move a muscle. Instead, her gaze followed Neil as he walked into the bathroom, bent over the tub, and worked the faucet. Hannah could hear the burbling sound of a bath being run, watched as Neil tested the water with care, obviously making sure it was the exact right temperature.

"I'll put on some tea," he said when he finally came out. He stopped dead as soon as he saw her standing there, still dripping on his bedroom carpeting.

"What in hell are you doing?!" he exclaimed with outrage. "I *told* you to get out of those wet clothes."

Hannah merely blinked. Like a drowned rat she stood there staring at him, her hair sopping wet, Neil's oversized raincoat draped around her slender shoulders like an orphan blanket.

"C'mon, Hannah." Neil sounded like he was at the end of his patience. Immediately, he reached for the raincoat, pulling it from her. Next he pulled off her red windbreaker.

"Neil—wh-what are y-you—"

"Getting you out of these wet things, what do you think?"

With an abrupt but gentle push, he had her falling backward onto the forest-green bedding. Hannah felt the backs of her knees connect with the mattress a second before her backside did. She had no sooner floofed onto the goose down comforter than she felt Neil's hands pulling off her sneakers and socks and reaching for the button of her jeans.

"N-Neil—" she called, trying to stop him.

But he wasn't listening. The button was undone, the zipper down before she could say his name a second time. Then, with three hard tugs, he was stripping her soaked blue jeans from her long chilled legs.

"Neil!"

Half-lying, half-sitting in nothing but her panties and a sopping sweatshirt, Hannah felt her face flushing with a combination of alarm and fury as Neil threw down the wet jeans, then scooped her up in his arms and carried her into the bathroom.

"Like I said," stated Neil. "I'll make some tea. Get in that tub at once or I'll be back to finish what I started."

And then he was gone, the bathroom door shut firmly behind him. Still shivering, Hannah didn't waste a moment pulling off the sweatshirt and stepping out of her panties. She had no doubt he meant what he said and she wasn't about to invite further examples of it.

Quickly, she sank her body into the water, steeling herself against the discomfort. The lukewarm bath felt like boiling water to her frigid skin, but she knew she had no choice.

Closing her eyes, Hannah felt both grateful and angry, excited and horrified, as one question alone pounded through her cold-numbed mind.

How the heck did I end up here?

Chapter
Seventeen

After Neil was satisfied that Hannah had gotten into the tub, he pulled his ear away from the bathroom door and began stripping off his own wet clothes.

Grabbing a thick terry towel from the closet, he dried off his naked body and sopping hair. From his drawer, he pulled a pair of fleece sweatpants and an old sweatshirt; it was worn, the top of the *A* in *Army* nearly faded out completely, but it was still warm and comfortable.

Within a minute he was dressed and standing by the bathroom door again, listening to Hannah sloshing around in the tub. *God, she's cute.* He could almost picture her long legs and gentle curves beneath the bathwater. All that ivory skin. How he'd enjoy seeing it blush . . . all he'd have to do was turn the knob, step inside, and suggest joining her.

"Control yourself, Ryan," Neil muttered to himself. Then, after clearing his unnaturally dry throat, he tapped lightly on the door.

"Hannah?"

"You don't have to come in!" she shouted. "I'm in the tub! I'm in the tub!"

"I know," he called through the door, biting his lip to keep from laughing. "I just wanted to tell you that I'm laying out a robe for you on the bed."

"Oh," she said in a tone he could swear sounded disappointed.

As he walked to the kitchen to put on a kettle for tea, Neil considered the implications of her disappointed tone. Had she been looking forward to his forcing the issue? Had she really *wanted* him to come in?

A light feeling buoyed him, especially when he considered what had been in that fax from his colleague in Chicago. Maybe, once Hannah had warmed up thoroughly in the bath, he'd try testing his theory.

Hannah sighed, her eyes were closed, her head resting comfortably against the tiled wall of Neil's bathroom, when she heard the teakettle whistling.

She'd spent fifteen minutes soaking in the lukewarm bath and it had pretty much thawed her. With a yawn, she opened her eyes and stretched, deciding she was ready to climb out.

"Hannah?"

Neil's voice seemed to freeze her all over again. "Yes?"

"Are you okay?"

"Perfectly fine. Now I know how Frosty the Snowman would feel in Palm Beach."

"Need help?"

"No."

"I'd like to see for myself."

"Stay *out*."

Hannah could have sworn she heard a grumbling grizzly bear on the other side of the bathroom door, possibly waking up from hibernation.

"How about if I keep my eyes shut?" came Neil's voice again.

Hannah rose from the bathwater and stepped onto the little round rug affixed to the floor. Quickly she searched the small, neat bathroom for a nice big towel to wrap around herself. But there was not a scrap of terry cloth to be found. Not even a hand towel.

"Neil?"

"Yes?"

"There are no *towels* in here!"

"Yes, I know. Wash day. I just realized. They're all in the closet."

Hannah's arms wrapped around herself, more for modesty than warmth. "Can you please hand me one, then!"

"I'll do better than that."

Too late, Hannah realized that Neil was coming through the bathroom door, a fluffy oversized bath towel held out in front of him. Even if his eyes had been open, which they weren't, he had wrapped her in the towel before she'd even had a moment to protest.

"Neil! What are you doing?"

"Taking care of you," he said softly as he rubbed her arms in what felt more like a gentle caress than a handmaid's duties. "Dry off and get into that robe."

And then he was gone, seemingly unaware of the chain reaction he'd started inside of her.

Once again Hannah stood alone in the bathroom, trembling like a leaf. This time, however, it wasn't caused by the cold. But the heat.

A warm, smoldering smoke seemed to be floating through her limbs and settling somewhere in the center of her body. It made her want more contact from this man.

"Control yourself," she commanded. Then, with a deep breath, Hannah returned to the task at hand. Drying off.

Once that was done she stepped back into the bedroom, another subtly masculine room, also decorated with a scheme of forest green and dark woods. More fluffy white towels were piled on the bed, and Hannah used one like a turban to wrap up her long, tangled hair.

She picked up the dark green robe Neil had laid out on the bed. It was obviously his own, a large masculine thing of thick velour. Hannah wrapped the garment around her and closed her eyes a moment. The robe was so warm, so comforting, and it smelled of him, making her feel as if he were enveloping her in his arms once again.

"Coming," called Neil.

Hannah was about to answer when she realized that Neil wasn't speaking to her. Someone was knocking lightly on the front door.

Standing perfectly still, Hannah cocked an ear.

"Thanks, Wilson . . . yes . . . no, she's all right."

"Night, sir."

"Good night."

Hannah nearly jumped when she heard Neil speak again.

"Hannah!" he called from the living room.

"Ah—" She cleared her throat. "Yes?"

"Are you ready for some tea?"

No. I am not ready, she thought with closed eyes. *Not for tea. Not for you . . .* "Ah . . . yes."

Tightening the belt of Neil's robe, she forced one foot to move and then the other. The physics of movement alone were what carried her from the bedroom to the living room. It certainly had nothing to do with nerve.

As she entered Neil's living area again—unhampered this time by the annoying distraction of possibly freezing to death—she decided to take a moment to look around.

Hannah truly believed that for a house to become a home, it had to reflect the personality of the person residing there.

The room seemed very much like Neil. Masculine, orderly, and, once you got used to the solemn, somber color scheme, it felt rather secure and cozy . . . perhaps even comforting.

Maybe it could use a few plants, she thought, and more personal items, but she knew she was in no position to critique his place. It was already a thousand times more inviting than the bare box she went back to after leaving her cozy *Homemaking* set.

Neil stood rather awkwardly in the middle of his dwelling, watching her take in his world. He looked as if he were awaiting comments on her inspection, she thought, slightly amused.

She could see he'd already placed an empty mug on the side table with a box of tea bags, a few sugar packets, and a small thermos of hot water. When she caught Neil's suddenly sheepish expression, she realized with a start that he was embarrassed.

It wasn't the first time she'd felt a host's or hostess's strain at entertaining "Homemaking Hannah." But it was the first time for Neil, and the idea of it touched her heart.

"Uh," he murmured. "Sorry it's not silver service—"

Hannah quickly cut off his apology. "It'll warm me up just the same." Then she smiled, unable to resist teasing him a little. "At ease, Captain Ryan."

Neil studied Hannah a moment before allowing a slight smile of his own. "Sit down, Hannah . . . please."

Hannah moved to the forest-green sofa as Neil uncapped the thermos and poured hot water into her mug. *Something is different about him,* she thought. Her gray eyes studied his face. It was much more at ease than she'd seen it since she'd arrived last night. Relaxed . . . almost *happy* she realized.

It must be this place, she thought. Here, inside his own private walls, Neil finally felt safe enough to let down the constant guard that his job required. That was definitely a feeling she could understand well.

After capping the thermos again, Neil stepped to the cold fireplace to start a blaze. Hannah picked up a tea bag from the half-empty box on the table—no fancy herbal concoctions, just a plain and simple orange pekoe, which was exactly what she preferred anyway.

As she dipped the bag into the steaming water, she watched Neil's muscular form move about the small room, bending and reaching, stoking the hearth with splits of wood from a nearby metal basket.

His back was broad and strong, tapering down to a trim waist and muscular legs. His thick midnight-black hair was neatly trimmed, the back barely brushing the collar of his army sweatshirt. When he turned unexpectedly to say something, he abruptly stopped. She had been staring directly at him, and he'd obviously caught her in the act.

Hannah was about to look away, but changed her mind. Instead her gray eyes remained there, fixed on his blue ones. They were no longer steel-blue, she realized, but had melted to a warmer color, like the ocean on a summer afternoon.

The ocean.

The reminder suddenly did force Hannah to look away unhappily. Down at her tea. The bag was staining her hot water well enough and she picked up her spoon to wring out whatever life was left in the little thing. Her spirits felt as if they were in an identical state.

"Are you okay?" asked Neil softly.

"Yes."

"You look as though something upset you all of a sudden."

Hannah shook her head, swallowing down her frustration.

"You must think I'm crazy," she whispered. "Maybe I am. . . ."

"Why?"

"No reason, really. I just happened to take a flying leap into the freezing cold Atlantic, chasing a woman who apparently vanished into thin air. Your staff must think I'm suicidal. And you must think I'm—"

"What my staff thinks doesn't matter," said Neil, sitting down beside her on the sofa. "I trust them to secure the privacy of the hotel's guests."

"And what about you? Do you think I'm so distraught over my marriage or something that I just flung myself into the sea?"

Neil rubbed his chin, contemplating his next words. "Why don't you tell me about your marriage?"

"What's to tell?" asked Hannah defensively. "I told you enough already."

"That you're separated."

"Well . . ." Hannah took a deep breath. *Fix it,* she told herself. *Fix it, now.*

Hannah knew that no matter how nice it felt sitting in Neil Ryan's apartment, no matter how much she still felt for him, she wasn't about to risk jeopardizing her career on a few pleasant moments with an old boyfriend. She had to protect the image she'd built.

"Well?" prompted Neil.

"*Well* . . . what I told you earlier this evening. About being separated. That wasn't entirely true."

Neil allowed a small smile to touch his lips. Ever since he'd received that fax from Chicago, his spirit had felt lighter, happier. If there was one thing Neil hated, it was to be lied to. He was relieved and happy that Hannah trusted him enough to tell him the real state of her marriage.

"Herbert and I have had our marital troubles, but we've . . . uh . . . we've worked things out now to both our satisfaction." *There,* thought Hannah, *that sounded perfectly fine, and it was all perfectly true.*

"You know, Herbert will be coming for Holly's wedding," she added for good measure. "Everything will be all right again between us very soon. At least, I hope it will."

Neil stared at Hannah for a long moment. He couldn't believe it. Didn't want to. *She lied. Right to my face.*

"Hannah," he began, his jaw working in slowly simmering anger, "answer me a question. And answer it straight."

"Yes?"

"Are you, right this moment, *legally* married to Herbert Peabody?"

"Herbert Peabody and I were legally married." *That's a good answer,* thought Hannah. *It was true, wasn't it?*

"I see," said Neil, rubbing his chin again. She was tougher to crack than she looked.

After another moment's thought, Neil met her eyes. "One more question."

"Yes?"

"Do you love him?"

Hannah's gray eyes registered stark panic as she studied Neil's rigid face. She realized that his guard had gone up again, and the steel was most definitely back in his blue eyes.

"What kind of a question is that!?" she exclaimed with mock outrage, hoping an emotional response would embarrass him off the subject.

"Just answer it."

Damn, didn't work. "No! You have no right to give me the third degree."

"And you have no right to expect me to swallow a load of evasive garbage."

"What?"

"You're not legally married to Herbert Peabody," said Neil calmly. "You haven't been for three years. You're simply using his name and posing as his wife—"

Hannah leapt to her feet, this time with *real* outrage. "How *dare* you accuse me of—"

"Sweetheart, I never *accuse* without cold, hard evidence."

"What evidence?" she demanded, hands on hips.

"Official annulment papers."

Hannah stared dumbly at Neil as he crossed the room to the kitchen counter and picked up a stack of fax paper. He handed it to her for her examination, and she couldn't believe what she was reading. It was a private investigator's report—on her and Herbert!

It was all here: The marriage certificate. The annulment papers—dated barely seven months later. With it were newspaper clippings over the past three years showing them together, posing as a "happy couple" at various public functions around Chicago.

When she got to the last page, she read the notes from the investigator. It seemed Herbert, though he now resided in London, had left some unsavory baggage in his wake. Two ladies of the evening had confirmed to Neil's investigator that they'd often slept with Herbert Peabody when he came through town in the last few years—usually at the same time.

The investigator's report said he had paid for this information, but the ladies had snapshots as proof. Thank Heaven, the investigator hadn't faxed the pictures. Hannah had no desire to see Herbert Peabody naked again as long as she lived.

"Where did you get this?" she finally rasped to Neil.

"I have a colleague in Chicago."

Hannah collapsed back onto the couch like a discarded rag doll. "Why, Neil? I don't understand. Why would you invade my privacy like this?"

There was such hurt in Hannah's voice that Neil almost couldn't stand it. "Hannah, I'm sorry. I didn't do it to hurt you. I did it to help you."

"*Help* me?"

"If you had told me the truth, I would have spared you the gory details, but you obviously needed to be woken up to reality."

"Go to hell."

"You don't understand—"

"I understand, all right. I understand that you've invaded my privacy to prove something about your *fine* detection services and put me down in the process—"

"No, Hannah —"

"Well, you can just stuff it, Neil Ryan!" shouted Hannah, getting her second wind. "I'm out of here—"

"Hannah!" Neil got to his feet a second after Hannah. "Just hear me out!" he pleaded, holding her back from racing away. "I was trying to protect you. I understand you, Hannah. I know what you were trying to do—"

"Protect me?! What are you talking about, protect me? I was the one protecting myself—and doing just fine, thank you very much. How on Earth could you pretend to understand the first thing about me?!"

"Because I do understand you, Hannah Whitmore. I understand you all too well. You've spent three years constructing a perfect little world for yourself. You've got everyone believing that you're Homemaking Hannah, the perfectly happy, perfectly married woman. But don't you understand? This home of yours is flimsy, transparent as glass, and the pressure of fame is going to smash it."

"You're wrong. It's been fine so far—"

"Because you've just been a rising star, small potatoes. But Maura tells me you're moving to a network now."

"That's right."

"Hannah, the bigger you get, the more the reporters are going to start sniffing around."

"I can handle it—"

"They'll see right through your little transparent home, and then crush it—and you—to bits. Not because you're imperfect, but because you're *pretending* not to be. People don't like to be lied to."

"But . . ."

"Hannah, my own man found all of this out in one day's work. Don't you see? You've got to come clean. You've got to stop pretending—"

Hannah's mouth grew slack as she watched the array of feelings cross Neil's usually stone face. His strong fingers were wrapped around her upper arm as if he never wanted to let her go again.

"But, Neil," she whispered, "you yourself said that these days appearances matter more than the truth."

"I was wrong," he stated softly. "The truth matters. It matters to me. It matters to anyone worth a damn."

Hannah's gray eyes were glistening with emotion. Pick one, any one, and she was feeling it.

"I just can't stop now," she murmured, as she crumbled back to the couch. "It's gone too far. . . ."

Neil sat down beside her and put his arm around her shoulder. There was such hurt, such pain in her voice that he wanted to do nothing more than stroke it all away. It was an overwhelming feeling of tenderness he couldn't recall experiencing in many years.

Hannah felt Neil's coaxing touch around her shoulders. It was all the encouragement she needed to lean her cheek against his broad, strong chest. She closed her eyes a moment. It felt safe and warm, like a place she didn't want to leave.

Neil held her close, his chin nestling against the towel turban on her head. He liked the feeling of her clinging to him for support. He wanted to be there for her, he realized, and to be needed by her.

"It's true. All of it," she admitted. "Herbert and I worked out a deal. I use his name, he shows up when I give him sufficient notice."

"What does he get?" asked Neil.

"Twenty-five percent."

Neil's teeth clenched. "Twenty-five percent? Of your hard-earned income?"

"Yes," said Hannah. "It's fair, Neil. He pays his own airfare, comes when I ask him, as long as I give him enough notice, and—"

"Hannah, why? Why in hell did you do this?"

"I was a newlywed when my friend Greta Green persuaded me to interview with Chip Saunders—the executive producer. I thought I was going to be a staff writer on *Homemaking* but Chip decided I was exactly the type he wanted to host. He said he'd been interviewing actresses, but what he really wanted was a *real* wife and homemaker."

Neil sighed. "What happened when your marriage began to go sour? Did you try to work things out with your boss?"

"Yes, I tried to explain things to him, but Chip wouldn't hear of it. He said that his contract was with Mrs. Hannah Peabody and he'd invested in that name and image. If I changed it, I'd be fired."

Neil sighed in frustration. "Why didn't you just walk away?"

"Couldn't." Hannah looked down and shrugged. "I needed the money."

"What do you mean?" asked Neil, his brow furrowing in confusion. He knew very well that the Whitmore girls were heiresses to small fortunes. "What happened to your inheritance?"

"It's gone."

Neil stared into the fireplace for a long moment. *That's why,* he realized with a numbing jolt. *That's why her credit card's limit was so low.*

"How?" he whispered softly.

Hannah shook her head. "You'll think I was a fool . . . you must think that already."

"I don't," he said simply. "Please tell me."

"It's just . . . gone. Lost. Wrecked on the shoals of the stock market. My marriage drowned in the aftermath, and the sharks were in the water waiting. I had creditors lined up ready to eat me alive."

Neil closed his eyes, silently kicking himself for putting Hannah, even for a second, in the same class as that spoiled Townsend brat. Clearly, the woman in his arms had worked herself to the bone for the last three years to build up a thriving career out of nothing—and with a bloodsucking leech of an ex-husband attached to her the entire time.

"Neil, you have to understand. Herbert was confident and kind when he started dating me at college. He was working at the Chicago exchange, and I thought he wanted to settle down, that marriage was the right thing . . . he said he wanted to use my inheritance and his trust fund to start his own firm. It was a way to prove to prospective clients that he could double their money in no time at all. So, of course, I trusted him with the inheritance. He was my husband. And he sounded so sure of what he was doing . . ."

"Oh, Hannah—"

"When he lost the money—his and mine—he was a broken man. He was so embarrassed. He drank and cried night after night. He was so sorry, Neil, what could I do? I know it sounds like I was a fool to trust him, and maybe I was. Maybe I should have tried harder to protect him from himself. The truth is, I was selfish and stupid. A child. I didn't want to think about the money. I just wanted to hand it over to someone—and there Herbert was with his hand out."

"Your parents had just died," said Neil softly.

"You don't understand, Neil, I was a coward. Even after he lost the money, I couldn't watch his suffering night after night. I couldn't stick it out. When he suggested separating, I was all too happy to see him go, even if it meant taking on the financial problems he'd left behind."

Neil listened to Hannah as he stared into the hearth. The red-orange flames were hot, but the blaze inside Neil was burning even hotter. Neil knew very well who the coward was in this little story, and it wasn't Hannah.

"I didn't know anything about Herbert's extracurricular activities in Chicago," said Hannah at last. "Do you think anyone will find out?"

After a long moment of silence, in which Neil tried his damndest to contain his fury, he answered. "I can have my contact arrange things with the ladies. We'll have to pay them off."

"Not 'we,' " said Hannah. "*Me.* This is my mess. Just advise me what I should do."

"We'll talk about it later," said Neil, knowing well and good that he'd begin tracking Peabody's financial records by the crack of dawn the next morning. The guy was extremely sloppy, and Neil would bet Hannah's full two-million-dollar inheritance that there was more to this country-club scum's story than Hannah's point of view.

"Neil?" asked Hannah, staring into the fireplace, her cheek finding its place against his broad chest once more.

"Yes, Hannah?"

"What made you start to investigate Herbert?"

Neil smiled. He could still see those letters slowly being typed onto his computer screen. "A hunch."

Hannah thought that over a moment. "What sort of hunch?"

Neil shifted and sighed. "I could tell that you weren't happy, Hannah. When I mentioned your husband, I could see the deadness enter your eyes, and I was concerned. That was what gave me my primary motivation. But the real reason I went ahead with the investigation . . ." Neil paused, suddenly self conscious.

"Yes?"

"Now you'll think *I'm* crazy."

Hannah pulled away from him to examine his face. "Tell me."

"The ghost of Dan Doyle," said Neil simply. "He typed Herbert's name on my computer screen."

Hannah's gray eyes widened. "You're not kidding, are you?"

"No."

"I don't understand, Neil. How do you know it was Dan Doyle? I mean, his ghost?"

"I *asked* him."

Hannah stared at Neil, openly astounded.

With a sigh, he rose from the sofa and crossed the room. "I'm not crazy, Hannah."

"I—I didn't say you were—what's that?"

Neil picked up a rectangular object and came back to the oak armoire against the wall. When he opened the doors, Hannah could see a small entertainment center—television, VCR, CD player, and radio.

"This is a videotape from one of our security cameras."

"What's it for?"

"You'll see."

Hannah watched Neil cue up the picture.

"The hotel's rear grounds?"

"Yes, since I came to work here, I made sure everything about the hotel was secure," he explained as he fast-forwarded the tape through the last six hours of the evening.

"We've put up decorative walls and erected fencing—all camouflaged with statues, vines, and topiary. Can't have the guests feel they're inside a prison compound—but the truth is, the effect is the same. Getting into or out of the hotel without detection is no mean feat. Cameras are used around the outer perimeters for added security."

"Is that all really necessary?" asked Hannah.

"We get celebrities and CEOs staying here at the hotel, members of Congress, politicians, and international royalty. I've had more than a few crazies try to gain entrance."

"Crazies?"

"Fans of stars, desperate paparazzi, a few kidnapping attempts, and even an assassination attempt last year."

"Really?" Hannah was amazed, but she knew she shouldn't be. The evening news was full of far worse things surrounding the rich and famous. "There!" exclaimed Hannah when she saw herself racing across the television screen. "Rewind it."

Neil did and reran the tape at normal speed.

"No. Go back a little farther," said Hannah.

When he reran the tape again, both Hannah and Neil leaned forward in disbelief.

"Do you see what I see?" whispered Hannah.

"Yes," rasped Neil.

There was no woman in a blue gown walking across the lawn. But there was something in the picture—an amorphous form that glowed and flickered like a candle flame. It flittered around on the lawn and then slowly moved toward the rear wall.

In another few minutes, Hannah was in the picture, striding across the lawn after the light.

Neil rose from the sofa and pushed the stop button on the VCR. Then he turned to look at Hannah. Her gray eyes were bright with a strange combination of excitement and fear.

"Neil . . ." she said softly. "Do you really believe that the mansion is haunted?"

Neil's brow furrowed. He hated to admit believing in something so outrageous, so seemingly illogical. But evidence was evidence.

"Yes, Hannah. I suppose I do."

Chapter Eighteen

"So you *do* believe I actually saw a woman in blue jump from the jetty?"

"Yes." Neil turned off the television and VCR and walked to the table beside his leather easy chair. After throwing another log onto the fire, he returned to the sofa with a hardcover bound collection of mystery stories.

"I want you to look at this," said Neil. He thumbed through the pages, holding it open on a short story near the end.

" 'In His Cups' by Dan and Daisy Doyle," read Hannah as she took it from him. "What's it about?"

"Dan and Daisy are on a case and decide to solve an estranged romance along with the crime. They throw the couple together in a room and lock them in for the night."

Hannah's face grew pale. "Oh, no. Neil, you don't think—"

"Yes," he said. "I do."

Hannah couldn't believe it. But what else could it be? The evidence was piling up like a snowdrift against a backwoods cabin.

"It's Dan and Daisy Doyle," concluded Neil. "I think

they're trying to . . .'' He paused, suddenly feeling self-conscious.

"Trying to what?'' prompted Hannah.

"Trying to . . . well, to . . .''

"To get us together?'' guessed Hannah.

"Again,'' finished Neil, looking into Hannah's eyes.

"Well, they do seem to be succeeding.''

Hannah saw the hope clearly stirring in Neil's face and she did her best to swallow her misgivings. Maybe it was finally time to take a chance again, thought Hannah. A chance at not being unhappy.

"What I mean is,'' she continued softly, "I was beginning to hope they were . . . getting us together. What about you?''

"Me?'' Neil's blue eyes looked away for a moment, but when they returned to her face, they seemed to smolder in a way that had nothing to do with the reflected heat of the fire in front of them. "The truth is . . . I was hoping that, too.''

"Really?''

"Really.'' Neil's hand seemed to find its own way to the ivory skin of Hannah's cheek, slightly flushed from the warmth of the fire, or perhaps their nearness. He hoped it was their nearness.

Gently, his fingers caressed her jawline, coaxing her mouth to tilt ever so slightly, until it was in just the perfect position.

"Hannah,'' he whispered, admiring the shining pools of her gray eyes, luminous in the firelight.

"Yes?''

"Do you think the ghosts would mind if I kissed you?''

Hannah smiled, her face lighting up into a thing of beauty. "You know, I bet they're counting on it.''

His lips were soft and full as they brushed across hers, lightly at first and then with more force, clearly wanting more.

She returned his kiss in earnest, her arms wrapping themselves around his neck, her fingers tangling in his thick black hair. She felt his own hands touching her, pulling the towel from her head and releasing her long damp hair. It fell down her back and he softly stroked it.

"I always liked the way you kissed,'' he murmured against her mouth. "You have a way of giving yourself over to it. As if you were a seabird, letting the wind take you where it wished. . . .''

Hannah smiled at the image, touched that he thought of her this way. She looked up at him, admiring him, too. Her fingers traced his soft mouth. How she liked the uneven shape of it. His crooked lips, the slight dimple at the edge of one upturned corner.

How she adored his face, the strong chin, and square jaw, the heavy beard that roughened his clean-shaven cheeks by evening. And his eyes. She supposed she admired his blue eyes more than anything. In them she saw the soul of a man who saw more than most, and tried so hard to live up to a standard so many men of today would merely scoff at.

She noticed the new scars on his face now, the small crevice in his cheek, the line in his chin, and the slightly crooked nose, a bump in the place where a straight line had been in their youth—had he broken it in the army?

She prized every flaw and blemish, every sign of the rough road he'd traveled to get here tonight. Every mark that told her he'd suffered as much pain as she had.

Hannah felt Neil's tongue slip between her lips and dip into her mouth. The sweet invasion set the core of her on fire, and her own tongue caressed him in return, pushing forward for more of him.

He tasted warm and rich and masculine, and she could feel his hands becoming bolder in their caress of her body. With exquisite care he slipped the robe from her shoulder, and pulled his mouth from hers to taste her bared skin.

The sensuous moistness of his mouth on her body made her tremble slightly. Her response made Neil still and slightly pull away. "Are you cold, Hannah?" he whispered with concern.

Hannah nearly laughed out loud. "Just the opposite. Heaven, Neil, I think I'm burning up with wanting you."

It was all he needed to hear. Perhaps all he'd been wanting to hear . . . for far too long. A ravenous smile of anticipation captured his mouth and he slipped from the couch, kneeling in front of her on the soft, thick rug.

In a swift, sharp movement he'd pulled off his sweatshirt, and Hannah's eyes widened with admiration. *This is no boy,* she breathed to herself as she took in the thick muscles before her. When they'd been together years ago, Neil hadn't fully filled out. He'd been nice-looking, of course, but not yet a full-grown man.

He was that tonight.

Hannah's limbs grew weak at just the sight of him. In the radiant reflection of the firelight, his hard muscles appeared almost bronzed. Kneeling before her, he waited, watching her admire him. Enjoying the look of pleasure on her face. When she finally returned her gaze to his face, he smiled, but said nothing.

He's waiting for me to touch him, realized Hannah. She felt so awkward, so inexperienced . . . still, she wanted to try.

She decided to pretend that she was an art dealer, like her parents, inspecting a fine piece. Slowly, hesitantly, she reached out her hand. Her palm lightly brushed across one broad shoulder and in alarm she drew it back.

Her slightest touch had made him quiver, she realized. She glanced into his face and was surprised to find his eyes closed, his lips slightly parted in abandon.

She reached out again to caress him, and heard a low moan of desire issue from his throat. He quivered again as she continued to touch him, and she realized with a start that *she* was doing this to him. She held the power to move him . . . to incite his passion.

With renewed purpose, Hannah began to touch him more boldly, letting her instincts take over. Her palms brushed across one broad shoulder then flowed downward into a chest of sculpted power.

The pads of her fingers followed the river of dark hair that swirled around his masculine nipples then snaked downward, toward a rock-hard abdomen. She caressed the ridges there then followed the flow of dusted hair, stopping at the spot where it disappeared in the waistline of his sweatpants.

Suddenly shy, she began to pull away.

Neil's blue eyes opened as he felt her draw back. His hands reached out, gently grasped her elbows, and pulled her forward again. With his hand, he took one of her own and brought it low again, to the spot she'd just left. Unashamed, she let him guide her until her fingers felt the long rigid hardness beneath the soft cloth of his sweatpants, clear evidence of his arousal.

"Do you see what you've done to me?" he asked with a smile, pulling her gently toward him until she was kneeling with him on the soft carpet.

"Yes," she whispered with an impish smile.

"And what do you propose to do about it?"

Hannah shivered as his warm, moist mouth found its way from the back of her ear to the edge of her jawline.

"Hmmm?" he prompted.

But she had no voice. As he tasted the length of her neck, the hollow of her throat, and then her bared shoulder, she could do nothing but close her eyes and give herself up to the thousand sensations he was causing to ripple through her.

Finally, she was breathless with anticipation and longing. He stopped his kisses and waited until she had opened her eyes again. Slowly, with his blue eyes burning into her expectant gaze, he pulled at the belt of his own forest-green robe.

His hands were large and strong and a bit calloused. She felt their slight roughness as he pushed back the soft material around her. The contrast of his strength against her softness felt exquisitely right to her. And then she was bare, naked before him; the forest-green fell away to reveal her completely to his roaming eyes.

Despite the teasing hints he'd seen the previous evening, Neil wasn't ready for what he found beneath his oversized garment. The Hannah he remembered had been a thin little thing, nearly flat as a pancake in her swimsuit. But the unveiled form before him now was that of a fully developed woman. In the golden sheen of the evening firelight, Hannah became a gilded wonder with skin as soft as rose petals and curves as enticingly sweet as a dewy peach.

Yes, he had seen naked women before, many of them quite attractive. But none had been Hannah. And, to Neil, none had ever been this beautiful.

His slightly calloused hands seemed to lift of their own accord, unable to keep from gently cupping and caressing the full, tempting breasts tipped with blushing pink buds.

"They're begging to be tasted," he murmured low, and in the next moment, he was bending his head, and coaxing Hannah to lean the small of her back into his calloused hands. He bowed her back with ease, arching her enough to give him easy access to her beautiful full breasts.

With the soft, moist point of his tongue, he relentlessly teased one erect nipple and then the other, arousing them into tiny hard jewels. Hannah didn't think she could stand the pleasure. Neil's mouth was a wizard's spell, casting her into a blissful oblivion.

Sensations, hot and hungry, rolled through every fiber of her form. As one of his hands continued to hold her steady, the other moved forward to explore her body. Neil's lips continued to suckle, his teeth nipping gently at the tip of her breasts as his fingers moved to the full flesh of them, to caress and tease, cup and fondle.

Soon, he was moving lower, his hands feeling the softness of her curves, the silkiness of the tight triangle of dark blond curls at the apex of her thighs.

Finally, with gentle care, he coaxed her to lie back, spreading the soft velour of the discarded robe like a warm blanket beneath her.

Hannah closed her eyes at the touch of Neil's hands. He treated her body with such affection and such gentle passion that light tears slipped from the edges of her eyes.

Neil found them, his tongue tasting the salty drops, kissing her cheeks clean again. Before long, he was fully naked, too, and highly aroused. When he moved over her and touched his mouth to hers again, she opened her eyes.

"Tell me that you want me," whispered Neil. "Tell me again."

Hannah was surprised to hear the longing beneath the words. The need. It was a need for *her*, she realized in slight amazement.

She looked up into the blue of Neil's eyes and, for a moment, felt completely lost. The crackle of the fire seemed to wrap them in a tight, warm cocoon, a world away from any outside interference.

"I want you, Neil Ryan," whispered Hannah. "I've always wanted you."

With extreme satisfaction, Hannah saw the happiness break across Neil's pensive expression, and then came the heat. *It will happen now,* she thought with awe. *Finally, after all these years . . .*

Hannah could hardly believe her senses. This was the fulfilling of a forgotten dream, one she'd long ago discarded in despair of it ever coming to pass.

She felt his knee nudging her legs apart, and she obliged him. Breathing deeply, she closed her eyes, automatically bracing herself for the pain.

Neil felt Hannah stiffen and stopped his movements toward their coupling. *Something's wrong,* he realized.

With concern, he dropped a kiss on her lips, his tongue dipping inside her mouth once more, coaxing her to relax. He'd thought she was ready, but perhaps he'd been mistaken. With care, he moved off her slightly and slid his hand back along her curves once more.

Hannah felt Neil's palm brush her hip and then the side of her thigh. Slowly, his fingertips explored until he found the warm sweet entrance he desired. In the next moment, a soft sound of surprise escaped her throat as he pushed two fingers inside of her.

Neil found her very wet, but also very tight. As his mouth continued to tease hers, he used his fingers to caress and massage, making certain she was ready for his hard length.

Finally, he was satisfied. Her writhing and twisting and little gasping cries made him certain that she was more than ready for him this time.

Again he moved over her, and she opened her eyes.

He was smiling as he looked down at her. "Touch me," he whispered.

Hannah licked her lips. She wanted to please him, and her hand moved to find him there, poised just above her thighs. Her soft slender fingers closed around him and he growled in response. His eyes closed as she softly stroked him. She felt awed by his size—and just a little worried. But she trusted him now, knowing how much she wanted him.

"I'm ready," she whispered. "I'm ready for you."

"Good," said Neil, his blue eyes taking her in again.

She felt him surge forward, his hard length finding its natural path between her soft thighs and then inside of her.

With eyes closed, Hannah tried to remain relaxed, but she couldn't help her body's automatic response. She stiffened, bracing for the discomfort, the pain.

But there was none.

This is Neil, she realized. *Not Herbert.* And the sensations were nothing like she'd ever felt before. Herbert had been rough and quick, finishing seconds after he'd begun. He'd never *fully* entered her, barely even looked at her the few times they did go to bed together during their short-lived marriage, and Hannah had been too naive, too self-conscious to expect anything more.

Neil was nothing like Herbert. He was so controlled, so tender. He *was* a wizard, she realized, for he had made his rock hardness into something softer than she'd ever felt.

"Hannah?"

Her eyes were still closed when she realized that Neil was calling. "Hannah?"

She opened her eyes to find Neil looking with concern into her face. "What's wrong?" he asked tensely. "Am I hurting you?"

"No," she whispered, then softly smiled. "Not at all. Not even close."

"Good," Neil breathed, then brushed his lips across hers, admiring the flecks of brightness in her liquid gray eyes. "Because you feel so good."

She was the velvet night, thought Neil, a mixture of shadow and light, darkness and shimmering bits of silver. A part of him wanted to claim her quickly, take her as high as he could, but he forced himself to stay in control as long as possible.

Through the misty veil of pleasure, Neil recognized just how hard it was to control himself with Hannah. In fact, he couldn't recall feeling such urgency to possess any other woman—not even his ex-wife. The realization stunned him.

Hannah felt as if the world were spinning off its axis. Neil hadn't pushed fully inside her yet. Instead, he was toying with her in a very controlled half-thrusting motion, first offering what she desired and then withdrawing it, teasing her terribly, making her want him so desperately that she felt as if she were being driven over the edge.

And then, like a star going supernova, she was there. In a burst of dazzling sensation, Hannah felt as though she were flying free as sunlight, free as the wind and waves, and the hopeful white clouds.

She was only halfway back to Earth when Neil dropped another kiss on her lips and thrust fully into her.

The feeling was wonderful, and she welcomed him, reveling in his filling her completely, after only a small sharp discomfort deep inside of her as he broke through the natural barrier. It was quickly replaced with a feeling of hunger again, a need for more of him.

But suddenly, she realized Neil had stilled.

When she looked into his face, he was staring at her, a strange expression on his face—like one of confusion or disbelief.

"Hannah?" he breathed.

He knows, she realized, trying not to feel ashamed or embarrassed. "Yes, Neil?" She swallowed, bracing herself emotionally, awaiting his questions, his criticism, possibly even his ridicule.

But there was none.

After a moment's silence, Neil simply smiled.

Then he looked deep into her eyes. With a renewed purpose, he began to move again, taking her once more to the wind and the sky.

Chapter Nineteen

The next morning, Hannah rose very early, as she usually did. The shower was running and a pot of coffee was brewing in the kitchen—a nice robust African blend from the smell of it.

Yawning, Hannah swung her legs off the edge of the large, comfortable mattress. She was naked, she realized, and immediately sighed with relief.

For a terrible moment there, she wondered whether the night of extraordinarily wonderful sex had been some kind of elaborate fantasy—like maybe she'd been watching an erotic video and dreamed she'd entered the thing, her mind conveniently replacing some hunky actor with her old boyfriend.

But it wasn't a *dream* dream, she realized. It was a *real* dream. As real as her swollen lips and slightly sore limbs; as real as the utterly masculine voice singing in the shower about a drunken sailor, and the heaven-sent scent of liquid caffeine, tempting her to follow wherever it led.

Stretching contentedly, Hannah descended from the bed, stark naked and not concerned in the least—except for the slight chill in the air, and the premature question of whether she'd be seeing Neil again tonight.

191

Peeking around the corner to the living room, she spied the green velour robe. It was still there on the floor, where they'd made love. Neil had left it there after gathering her up in his arms and carrying her to the bed—where they'd nuzzled and kissed and eventually made love once more before drifting off.

She picked up the heavy garment and slipped into its cozy warmth. Pulling the belt tight, she glanced around, curious with what the grown-up Neil Ryan kept inside his private walls.

On the wall there were framed photos of his mother, half brother, and deceased stepfather. No pictures of any women or other older men. No *father,* realized Hannah.

Hannah wasn't surprised at this. When she was growing up, she'd often heard the rumors about Neil's biological father—that he was a well-off married man in the Newport area, someone Maura had worked for when she was young. But Hannah had developed an early distaste for gossip, and seldom gave any of it much attention.

Her gaze brushed along a snapshot in a heavy brass frame. It was Neil with his men, posing in camouflage gear on what looked to be a Middle Eastern sand dune. Hannah realized it was a photo from his duty in Desert Storm.

She stepped closer and saw that some of the young men were looking at the camera but most were looking toward Neil, respect and admiration clearly shining from their expressions.

Hannah prowled around a bit more, looking specifically for one particular item: a certain stargazing telescope.

After she'd begun dating him, her parents and sister had grown to know Neil as more than just an employee. Her mother and father had made a wonderful gesture in giving Neil the beautiful telescope as a gift.

But the telescope was nowhere to be found, not even in the small closet near the kitchen, which she couldn't stop herself from snooping inside. Maybe it was in storage somewhere, she thought, but in her heart she felt an acute sense of disappointment and wondered if maybe Neil had given it away. Perhaps he hadn't wanted it to remind him of his time with her.

Moving back to the living area, Hannah glanced over the

many books he'd collected. He still had his astronomy books, she noticed, along with poetry, science fiction, and plenty of mysteries—including Dan and Daisy Doyle's work and a number of Dashiell Hammett's books, too, another writer who'd once worked as a real detective.

Curiously, Hannah touched a well-worn copy of Malory's *Morte d'Arthur*. For some reason Neil had placed it amid his collection of detective novels . . . though it actually looked right at home between Chandler's *The Little Sister* and *Farewell, My Lovely*.

"Good morning."

Neil stood a few feet behind her. His hair was damp, finger-combed straight back off his brow, and he wore a white terry cloth robe, *Château du Coeur* embroidered in a flamboyant script on the left breast pocket.

"Nice robe," remarked Hannah with a smile.

Neil took in her own hastily thrown on garment with a hedonistic sort of gaze. "You, too," he murmured, his gravelly voice betraying the general naughty direction of his thoughts.

"Oh, this old thing. I just picked it up somewhere."

"Mmmmm. Right off my floor, I'll bet."

"You'd win that bed—I mean *bet*."

Neil's low chuckle seemed to dance along her skin. "You meant *bed*. I know a Freudian slip when I hear it."

"I did enjoy being there."

"Yes," said Neil. His hands found her shoulders and he drew her close, placing a light kiss on her lips. "I did, too."

"Thanks, by the way."

Neil's chin rose a fraction. "For?"

"For my first orgasm," she said simply, congratulating herself silently for saying it with such cool composure. "Not that you only gave me one last night, there were quite a few, as I recall. I . . . I actually lost count."

Neil studied Hannah's jerky hand gestures, her darting eyes. "You're blushing," he whispered, trying not to smile.

For a horrified second, Hannah stared directly at Neil, then turned abruptly away. "That coffee smells wonderful! Is it an African blend? I enjoy a nice strong jolt in the morning—"

"Hannah?"

"Wakes you up, you know—?"

"Hannah!"

She turned. He hadn't budged from the spot where she'd left him. "Yes, Neil? Something the matter?"

Neil wanted to know why she'd been so sexually inexperienced. Not that their lovemaking suffered because of it. Neil couldn't recall ever feeling so much pleasure.

Like everything she seemed to do, Hannah threw herself into their lovemaking with abandon. It was as if every touch, every breath was pure magic to her. She didn't hold back, didn't try to calculate or control. She simply gave herself to the moment and to him with as much innocent excitement as she held in her soul.

It was a pure kind of passion he'd never experienced before—joy without restraint. For Neil it made everything new again, as if, like Hannah, he were making love for the first time, too.

His only concern this morning was the reason why, as a *married* woman, Hannah had been a *virgin*.

He'd felt the barrier the first time he'd fully entered her and knew at once the reason she'd been so exquisitely tight. It was a wonderful surprise. An incredible gift for them both, after all these years. What he didn't know was *why* it had happened. He wanted to ask her, but, looking at her blush, he held his tongue, realizing just how much of a failure her marriage to Herbert Peabody had been after all.

"Nothing's the matter, Hannah," he finally said, his words washing her pensive expression clear again. "Nothing at all."

The heavy green drapes had been shut the night before, and Neil stepped up to them now, pulling them back to reveal a breathtaking view of the ocean.

It was a glorious morning, and Hannah's eyes widened as she took in the dawning sky. A brilliant semicircle of golden light was announcing itself over the watery horizon as streaks of pink and violet blended into the lightening blue above it. A few die-hard stars were still winking their slowly weakening challenge to the one so much closer to Earth.

"It's wonderful," she whispered.

"Isn't it? Sunrises are the greatest asset to living close to the Atlantic. No alarm clock needed. It's a pleasure to get up early enough to see this."

"I remember," agreed Hannah, still mesmerized by the

view. "I remember it well." When she turned, she found Neil staring intently. Not at the view, but at her.

"So, Captain," she said, trying to keep her voice light, "what's on your agenda today?"

"I have a little business to get out of the way, and then I'll take some time off."

Hannah held her breath. "Oh, you have plans for the day."

"Yes, of course. I plan to spend it with you."

"Well, Dan, what have you got to say now?" Fluttering up and down the carriage house hallways with glee, the ghost of Daisy Doyle was beside herself with pride. Her matchmaking efforts on these two wayward souls had worked! It had finally worked!

"Don't gloat, sweetheart," returned Dan, his ethereal form hovering patiently near the door of Ryan Investigations. *"It's not professional."*

"Professional! Ha! I'll tell you what's professional, getting the job done. That's professional!"

"You were lucky. That little jetty stunt of yours last night could have gotten her killed. It almost got you killed back in the forties when you tried it."

"Don't remind me." It had been a foolhardy stunt, even for Daisy. She'd been having a grand time at her niece Edith's seventeenth birthday party.

In light of her sister Ernesta's snobby influence over her daughter, Edith, Daisy felt it was her obligation to foster the girl's free spirit. So, near the end of the party, when Edith had confided something outrageous to Daisy—that she harbored a secret crush on one of that summer's gardener's helpers at Château du Coeur—Daisy was overjoyed.

"You must follow your heart, little Edith!" Daisy had exclaimed. "You must dance and sing, and embrace life while you can!" They laughed together and Daisy danced her way onto the rock jetty, betting Dan that she could dance out and back without slipping.

She hadn't made it. Dan was forced to take a dip to make sure she got back to shore. But they'd all laughed about it in the end, and Edith whispered to Daisy that she'd think about talking to that boy before the summer's end.

"I wonder what ever happened to that gardener's helper?"

murmured Daisy distractedly. *"What was his name? Do you recall, Dan?"*

"I don't recall things like that, Daisy, you know that."

"It'll come back to me. I know it will. . . ."

At the moment, Dan was vastly more interested in the present than the past. He noted that Neil Ryan had gotten up at the crack of dawn to begin some financial investigating of Herbert Peabody. Faxes, e-mails, and calls went out in quick order.

After Neil had gone off to have breakfast with Hannah, Dan decided to wait right here in the carriage house until the man came back to his office for the answers to his inquiries.

Dan really didn't care how long he'd have to wait. These days, Dan Doyle had all the time in the world.

If a beating heart existed in the center of "America's first resort town," it could be found along the bustling street called Thames. Zipping up and down the restored waterfront area, the wide thoroughfare nicely connected the rebuilt wharves and Newport Yachting Center with a host of bars, restaurants, hotels, and stores.

Thames was the colorful street from which to enjoy the contrasts of Newport's choppy harbor, where white sails of world-class racing yachts fluttered precariously near rust-stained freighters and luxury cruise ships. It was also the place to watch the contrasts of people. Tourists and locals, summer people and year-rounders alike packed the area to overflowing during "the season" and actively peppered the area the rest of the year.

It was in this very area, on a rebuilt wharf, that Tiffany Townsend first spotted the couple. She'd been sitting in the window seat of a popular restaurant, part of a building originally erected in the 1700s, when Newport had been the most active port on the East Coast.

Tiffany, however, never gave a thought to the historical integrity of her environments. She was much too concerned with the shifting winds of the present—one of which had blown the pair of lovers her way.

The man and woman were walking hand in hand along Bowen's Wharf like a pair of carefree newlyweds. Tiffany found the very idea of it galling; and, as her blue eyes followed their every move and expression, a cool kind of rage began to overtake her, building into contained fury when she saw what the man was doing.

This ruggedly handsome specimen, whose tight blue jeans and black cable knit sweater did everything to accent his muscular build, was nuzzling the woman's neck. *Nuzzling* her neck!

"Clark," Tiffany snapped at her preppie cousin, immaculately dressed in Calvin Klein khakis and a pale blue button-down shirt, "will you *look* at that."

"Wha—?" asked Clark, his mouth still chewing a jumbo shrimp.

Tiffany pointed a French-manicured fingernail. "It's Ryan. And he's with that little scarecrow. Obviously she thinks she's fooling people."

Before leaving the hotel grounds with Neil, "Homemaking" Hannah Peabody had evidently slipped on a pair of over-sized sunglasses and stuffed a long, mousy blond ponytail through the back of a baseball cap in a blatant attempt to disguise herself.

Well, thought Tiffany, it hadn't fooled her. The moment she'd spotted Neil Ryan on the wharf, she'd recognized exactly who was on his arm.

"What are you talking about?" asked Clark, looking directly at Hannah.

"It's that Homemaking person. You remember, the one that Ryan's getting it on with." It irritated her that Clark didn't recognize Hannah right away. Come to think of it, no one around the woman seemed to notice her in the least.

"I recognize Ryan," said Clark, craning his neck, "but I don't see—Oh, is *that* her, in the jeans and red windbreaker?"

"*Yes*, that's her! God, Clark, are you *blind*!?"

Clark shrugged. "Tif, she's nobody to get your panties in a twist over. I barely even noticed her."

Tiffany let out a groan of supreme annoyance that only increased when she glanced back at the happy, laughing couple. Laughing? She couldn't believe it. Neil Ryan was actually *laughing*!

What was this? thought Tiffany in outrage. The man was a jaded womanizer, she was *sure* of it. He never laughed—he never even smiled, as far as Tiffany could see. She had yet to get him to break his stone-cold expression—and here the scarecrow had him so loose, they had even danced a few steps to some street musician's guitar.

"This is a disaster," said Tiffany, self-consciously smoothing out the invisible wrinkles in her lime-green Betsy Johnson Lycra dress, a garment that fit tighter than a surgical glove. "I've got to think of something more extreme than getting even with those photos—"

"What's going on with that anyway?" asked Clark, his attention back on his food.

"Oh, you'll see, Clark, dear. Before the end of the week, everyone who checks out of a supermarket will see. Our little assistant photographer made a quick sale to *The National Tattler*. They stopped the presses to rush it right into this week's issue. Homemaking Hannah's little fling will soon be all the buzz."

Clark nodded as he leaned back in his chair and motioned for the waitress to bring another shrimp cocktail. "You've got the check today, Tif, haven't you? I'm short again."

Tiffany dug into her bag for a cigarette. "When *aren't* you?"

"Thanks, cuz."

"You can *thank* me by helping me come up with something to get Ryan's attention. Once those photos hit, I want to be ready." Tiffany glanced over her shoulder to make sure Samuels was still sitting at the bar—far enough away that he couldn't overhear her.

Yes, there he was, all right, as usual. The moonlighting cop's beady little eyes were still on her. God, he'd been *such* a killjoy the night before, tailing her everywhere she went and pretty much drowning her chances for a good lay. As a last resort, Tiffany had tried halfheartedly to get the bodyguard himself into bed, but Ryan wasn't kidding when he said his guards were seduce-proof. It was enough to give Tiffany a complex.

God, she wished her New York therapist had a satellite office in Newport. Oh, well, she really wasn't interested in Ryan's *second*-string anyway. She'd set her sights on Ryan himself. And she meant to have him.

"Well, it shouldn't be too hard to get Ryan to come running,'' remarked Clark in passing. "Just stage something dangerous.''

Tiffany stopped digging in her bag and stared openmouthed at Clark. "That's an idea. Like what?''

Clark shrugged. "Attempted murder, maybe? Kidnapping? Burglary?''

"Hmmmm . . . that all sounds delicious. But complicated. How do we do it?''

"*We?*''

"Yes, Clark, *I* didn't think of it. *You* did.'' Finally finding her golden cigarette case, Tiffany snapped it open and placed one of the thin white cylinders between her deep crimson lips. Pointedly, she waited until Clark jumped to light it for her.

"In fact, dear cousin,'' she continued, "now that I think about it, I figure you owe me a nice fat favor for all the bills I've been shelling out for you lately. So *you're* going arrange something that will get Ryan's attention—all by yourself.''

"You're kidding? Right?''

"Not in the least,'' she said, taking a long drag from her cigarette. "And you'd better make it work,'' she threatened sweetly as she pointed the lit end right at him, "or from this day forward, the bank is closed.''

Chapter Twenty

Purgatory Chasm.

"I know where we're driving," Hannah told Neil as he turned his black Volvo south on Paradise Avenue. "I remember this road like an old song."

Neil said nothing, just smiled with an ease and quickness that, for the hundredth time that day, completely disarmed and delighted her. Silently, he moved a hand from the steering wheel and took one of hers. He fixed it flat on the seat between them, so his fingertip could trace a feathery spiderweb onto her palm.

She sighed as the teasing sensation worked a kind of sorcery on her, sending waves of heat on a trip through her entire being. Making her desire him more than ever.

The bright May sun was sinking low now on what Hannah felt was the most perfect day she'd ever had. She and Neil had spent every moment together, acting more like wide-eyed newlywed tourists than jaded old flames in their own hometown.

They window-shopped along Thames Street, took a harbor cruise on a public charter, and ate lunch at a little bistro on

Ocean Avenue. In the afternoon, they took Preservation Society tours of some of the great mansions. On a whim they even took a private tour of eerie Belcourt Castle—a mansion, like Château du Coeur, that was said to be haunted.

After stopping by a seafood shack for a dinner of fried quahogs—a huge hard-shell clam that was a local favorite—they'd returned to Neil's car, and he'd steered it toward Purgatory Chasm.

It was a breathtaking spot high on the rocky cliffs that overlooked the blue Atlantic, secluded nicely in the brush and trees of Middletown, a few miles from Newport's city limits.

Ten years ago, they used to go there regularly to watch the summer sunsets and gaze at the stars. It was incredibly liberating, a place where she and Neil had no names, identities, or backgrounds. Like the real Purgatory, such things mattered little there. All of it evaporated beside the dwarfing power of the ocean and the vast reaches of the starlit heavens above it.

"I think I could have found my way here blindfolded," said Neil as he neared the turnoff.

"Well, don't try it on my account," teased Hannah. "Volvos may be safe cars, but never once in all of their television commercials did I see a driver with a rag around his eyes."

Neil laughed as he pulled the car into a little dirt area near a patch of woods. As Neil pulled his heavy, black, cable knit sweater back over his T-shirt, Hannah took off her sunglasses and baseball cap. They were in relative seclusion now and there was no need for the incognito act any longer.

She stepped from the car, ready to start down the narrow dirt path, when she saw Neil had stopped by the car's trunk.

"I want to get a few things," he said with a secretive smile.

"What things?"

Hannah watched as Neil pulled out a thick blanket, two Styrofoam cups, and a bottle of champagne, which had been chilling inside a small cooler. With happy surprise, Hannah realized that Neil had been planning this stop well before they'd left the hotel that morning.

The last item Neil pulled from the trunk looked incongruous at first. A long, black case.

"What's—?" Hannah began to ask, then stopped herself cold. "It's the telescope, isn't it? The one my parents gave you."

"Yes," said Neil.

"Then you didn't get rid of it, after all?" asked Hannah in amazement. She was sure he hadn't wanted it around, hadn't wanted to be reminded of the past.

"Of course I didn't get rid of it," said Neil, slamming the trunk. "I've treasured this for years."

Neil took her hand and led her through the brush. In a few minutes, they were stepping into the clearing and onto the rocky cliffs, where they met with a spectacular view of sapphire waves below a scarlet-streaked sky. The ocean surf pounded below and sent a cool wind blowing through their hair.

"Heaven, it's beautiful," said Hannah on a sigh. She closed her eyes and inhaled the open sea air. It was salty fresh. Brisk and clean. Life-affirming.

"It is Heaven," returned Neil, then he reached his arm around her. "Always was for me."

Hannah turned her face toward Neil's and he bent his head, touching his lips to hers.

"Me, too," whispered Hannah, thrilled by Neil's admission—and yet a part of her questioned, deep in her soul, whether Heaven on Earth was ever meant to last.

It hadn't lasted before, she reminded herself, then promptly told herself to shove off.

"Do you want to see the Chasm?" asked Neil.

Hannah nodded, and he led her along the cliff to a spot where a cleft in the glacial-period rock had created a long natural fissure.

The split itself wasn't wide, ten feet or so across, but it was very long, at least one hundred feet, and the opening presented a bizarre and perilously steep drop of nearly fifty feet directly into the rushing surf below.

In the past, Hannah had heard that foolhardy people sometimes tried to leap across the chasm. One of the legends long attached to the place was of a Native American brave who, to prove his love for a favored maiden, jumped across the chasm, saying later that his jump had been from Purgatory to Paradise.

There was no need for such great leaps these days. Rhode Island's state park system maintained a wooden footbridge across the cleft. Now modern tourists could stand upon the bridge and look down into a dark abyss, from a secure observation platform.

"Do you believe that legend?" asked Hannah as they walked onto the little footbridge.

"Which one, the brave who leapt across to prove his love?"

"Yes."

"Why do you ask?" Neil smiled. "Do you want me to make that leap for you?"

"It's a modern world now," said Hannah, staring down into the darkness of the Chasm. "Maybe you should ask *me* to make it."

Neil turned to her. "In case you haven't noticed, this 'modern' world has provided a perfectly safe footbridge, which makes such grand gestures unnecessary."

"Unnecessary?"

"Obsolete."

"You know, Neil, that's the exact word that inspires me to do my television show," returned Hannah, a hand on her hip. "And inspires people to watch it."

"I don't follow—"

"People are fed up with the modern way of life—a philosophy of speed and progress that has no use for the very gestures and customs that made life worthwhile."

"Hannah, you can't compare baking cookies with making a dangerous leap over an abyss like this one."

"Can't I?" Hannah looked into the abyss again, leaning over the footbridge rail, her feet on tiptoe. "Seems to me it's only dangerous if whoever makes the jump doesn't put enough effort into completing it."

"Hannah! Don't lean so far over!"

"No kidding, Neil, what if I wanted to make a gesture like that?"

"You're being ridiculous." He tugged at her arm. But she refused to give up her precarious position.

"And what if . . ." Hannah felt mesmerized by the rushing seawaters below, powerful currents that would carry away anyone who might be foolish enough to try such a jump without having the strength of will to complete it.

"Hannah?" Neil prompted.

Hannah finally turned to look at the man standing beside her. "What if that's what true love is?"

Neil stared into Hannah's wide gray eyes a long moment, then he shook his head and turned away, back toward the dark drop that yawned before them both. "Risking a fall is plain foolishness."

"Is that really how you feel?" whispered Hannah, somehow bothered by Neil's response.

"Yes. Case closed," he said abruptly. "C'mon, let's go back to the cliff's edge before the sun sets completely."

Then he took Hannah's hand and led her away.

"Tell me again," urged Hannah thirty minutes later.

She and Neil, cozily settled on the thick blanket, were enjoying the bottle of champagne and the seaside sunset. They sat on a wide ledge beneath a shallow overhang, about ten feet below the top of the cliff.

It was an easy climb down, though not an obvious, or even legal one. A sign warning to stay off the cliffs had been prominently posted. But lovesick teenagers—not to mention lovesick adults—rarely paid heed to warning signs.

"I told you," said Neil as he poured more wine into Hannah's glass. "There's a suit of armor in Belcourt Castle that's haunted. It lifts its arm."

"By itself?"

"Yes, of course, by itself. What do you think, they have an invisible crane set up?"

"That place does give me the creeps. It's in the air or something."

"It's the negative energy. In the artifacts."

"*Negative* energy?" asked Hannah.

"Yes. Think about what we saw in the collection housed there. The place has got Napoleon's tea set, which he abandoned on his bloody retreat from the Russian front. It's got part of a slashed portrait saved from a riot in France where dozens were slaughtered. It's got suits of armor with dented helmets—which probably means the knights were killed inside of them—"

"Oh, I see what you mean. Bad luck." Hannah *had* felt a kind of unsettling roll in her stomach in certain rooms, and a strange sense of singed electricity in the air. Funny, she never felt such things in Château du Coeur. Just strange drafts from time to time, and odd cold spots that seemed to appear and disappear with no apparent explanation.

"What about *our* mansion, Neil?"

"What? You mean our ghosts?"

Hannah nodded.

"Our ghosts don't come from negative energy. They mean no harm," said Neil quietly.

Hannah stared at Neil. "You sound so . . . certain."

"Yes."

"Why?"

"I just . . . am."

"What about last night? The jetty. I could have gotten hurt."

"But you didn't."

"What are you saying? That the ghosts were protecting me?"

Neil shrugged. "I think they made sure that I got to you."

"But why are you so sure?"

Neil took a sip of the champagne. It was the first alcohol he'd had in almost three years. He well remembered the night he'd last had it. The visitation he'd had that had shocked him back into a state of sobriety.

"Hannah . . . I feel funny telling you about this, but . . ."

Hannah waited for Neil, but he seemed to lose his nerve all of a sudden. He had looked away from her and was just staring out toward the darkening sea.

"Neil?" she finally prompted.

"Dan Doyle's ghost," he said abruptly. "It appeared to me."

"When?!" blurted Hannah, nearly choking on the champagne bubbles. "Today?"

"No. About three years ago, just before I started working at the hotel. It's a strange story, I guess . . . it happened before I took the job as security director. My mother had offered the position to me, but I'd turned it down at first. You see, the only reason I had come back to Rhode Island was because I had nowhere else to go." Neil paused a moment to take another sip of champagne. Then he stared down at his drink. Without lifting his eyes, he began to speak again. "I'd left the army, I'd left my marriage, and I was planning to leave everything else for good.''

"Leave what else?" asked Hannah softly. "Newport?"

"No," said Neil, meeting her eyes. "Life."

Hannah blinked a moment. "What do you mean, *life*?"

"I mean I had a .45's barrel pointed at my skull. I was drunk, for about the sixtieth night in a row, and I didn't see any point in going on."

"My God, Neil," rasped Hannah. "I wish I'd known."

A tiny, cynical smile touched the corner of Neil's mouth. "It wouldn't have mattered. No one on Earth could have helped me then . . . literally, as it turned out."

Hannah could see the pain in Neil's expression. Clearly, this wasn't easy for him. He was a private, contained man. Yet a part of Hannah couldn't help but feel a sense of hope that he was beginning to see her again as one of his closest and truest friends. The kind of friend you trusted with your deepest secrets.

"When I was in the military police, I was promoted for breaking a drug ring inside the army. Unfortunately, though I was warned by a superior to stop the investigation at a certain point, I didn't. I kept at it until I found that a prominent officer with a very wealthy family and powerful political connections was involved."

"What did you do?"

"I played by the rules. I brought him up on charges. But it ruined me. The evidence I had gathered 'mysteriously' disappeared after I formally accused the officer. Then, when the officer was off the hook, I found myself framed for petty criminal violations. I was devastated. As it happened, I was able to work things out so I could resign before they could give me a court martial."

"Oh, God, Neil, I'm so sorry."

"Not half as sorry as I was."

"What about your marriage?"

Neil shook his head. "I married for a stupid reason. I simply thought it was time. She was the daughter of another military man. She married me for a stupid reason, too. She thought my star was rising. When it fell like a lead brick, our marriage fell with it. She's remarried now, to another officer.

In retrospect, I think she may have had her eye on him, even while we were married.''

Hannah sighed. ''It sounds like you've had about as much bad luck as I have.''

Neil's fingers brushed along Hannah's face. ''But I'll bet *you* always managed to keep that chin up.''

Hannah shook her head, looking down into her half empty cup. ''Not always.''

''Well, the truth is . . .'' As Neil's words trailed off, his fingers trailed down Hannah's shoulder and arm to find her hand. The way he'd done in the car, Neil turned her hand palm up and began to trace a featherlight web across her skin. A web in which she was happily becoming entangled.

''The truth?'' she asked.

''Yes. The truth is, I owe my life to a ghost.''

Neil's touches were making Hannah shiver in a way that had nothing to do with the ocean breeze—or his strange revelation. Nevertheless, she was more than a little intrigued by his story.

''Tell me how it happened,'' she whispered.

''Well, let's see . . . there I was, sitting on my bunk in the drafty carriage house—it hadn't been renovated yet and Maura was letting me stay there because I really had no place else to go at the time. Anyway, there I was and then all of a sudden, there he was, Dan Doyle, materializing out of thin air.''

''Did he . . . talk to you?''

''Yes, and I'll never forget what he said. He told me that life sometimes requires that you start over. He said he himself wasn't in that particular position at the moment, but I was. He told me something else, too . . .''

''What?''

Neil stopped his teasing touches a moment. He looked out to sea again and took a deep breath. ''He used the words you used the other night,'' said Neil, looking back into Hannah's eyes.

''What words?'' asked Hannah, swallowing uneasily.

'' 'Stop trying to run away,' he said. 'Be a man about it, at least.' ''

''Neil, you should know something . . . about those words. I thought I'd sound crazy repeating this to anyone, but . . .

you see, I had the weirdest feeling that those words weren't my own. It was as though someone were whispering to me.''

Neil's eyebrows rose and he leaned in, his lips close to her ear. "Like this?"

Neil's breath tickled and the warmth of his nearness suddenly had Hannah feeling less interest in spiritual matters than corporal ones. "Yes," she answered softly.

"Well, I'm not running anywhere tonight," he whispered. "I'm all yours."

Hannah turned her head to speak, but Neil's mouth was so close, she found a much more pleasant use for her lips than forming words.

The kiss Neil imparted was petal soft, yet she sensed a very strong need behind it. He began to embrace her, his hands reaching inside her open windbreaker. And, as his kiss became more passionate, his hands became more bold. With a sense of masculine possession, he began to take liberties with her body, slipping his fingers beneath her T-shirt to unclasp the front of her bra.

She didn't object in the least. In fact, she was thrilled that he wanted to tempt her again. Her hands followed his lead, reaching beneath his black cable-knit sweater, jerking his T-shirt from his jeans to gain access to his bare flesh. The muscles of his back were hard and well-formed. She caressed him there then let her fingers trail a path downward, toward the front of his pants.

When she found the length of him hard beneath the thick denim, she stroked and teased until his breath, too, came fast and harsh.

Her eyes widened the moment she realized his hands had moved to the button of her jeans. The night before, he'd disrobed her in record time; and now, tonight, before she could say *boo*, he was doing it again.

"Neil!" she exclaimed in surprise when he pulled down her zipper and reached a brazen hand inside her panties. "We're out-outside . . ."

"Yes," he rasped with a devilish smile.

"B-but we never went farther than necking out here before."

"We were teenagers then," said Neil, clearly amused as he dropped kisses on her jaw, her neck, her throat. "Now we're old enough to drink, vote, and do *all sorts* of wonderful things.''

"But we're . . . we're *outside*!"

"Yes, isn't it wonderful?" he growled, his fingers exploring her. "Last night you had your first orgasm, and tonight you'll have your first on a cliff by the ocean."

"Oh, you're a bad boy, Neil Ryan. A very bad boy."

Neil's laugh was low and lustful as he stopped his kisses long enough to finish removing her jeans and panties. The cool wind of the ocean on her hot skin sent a shocking thrill through her, and a sudden wild desire to hurry their coupling. But Neil pushed her back first so he could continue touching her.

The blue of twilight had already deepened to the black of night. It settled in around them like a darkening theater stage, the stars appearing as brilliant performers. Hannah admired their radiance as she lay back on the blanket. With abandon, she let herself enjoy it all—the night sky, the salty sea breeze, and the feel of her lover's strong fingers over her body.

Neil thought he was in control. Then he saw the play of silvery celestial light on Hannah's sweet face, her long hair spread out around her, and it nearly undid him. He'd barely begun to touch her when he felt an overwhelming need engulf him. He needed her so badly.

In the space of a few seconds, he'd quickly stretched his body over hers and released himself from his jeans.

"I'm sorry, I can't . . . wait," he murmured low into her ear, as he settled between her legs, and then, before he could say another word, he entered her. His sudden hard thrust had her crying out softly with pleasurable surprise. He filled her so completely, and she'd been so hungry for him—not just for this entire day; it felt as though she'd been waiting for Neil her entire life.

As he began to move, Hannah knew at once that their love-making would be more urgent than the leisurely pace they'd taken the previous night. Neil's movements were fast and hungry, almost desperate, as if he couldn't wait to possess her. Hannah reveled in the very idea, welcoming the rush of sensations, the passionate burst that sent her careening over the edge like an out-of-control thing that finds itself flying over a bottomless cliff.

In less than five minutes after he'd entered her, Neil was crying out her name and gasping for air, his body finally releasing itself from the dire tension. The fierce need. And yet, deep in his soul, Neil knew he didn't want to be released from this need for Hannah. Not ever again.

She did more than touch some ethereal part of him, she nurtured and cultivated something he seemed to desperately want, yet couldn't even name. Something that felt like coming home.

Is this another of your second chances, Dan Doyle? Neil Ryan silently asked. With eyes closed, Neil tasted the sweet flesh of Hannah's neck and prayed that it was, because finally, after all he'd been through, he was beginning to feel that maybe, just maybe, he was ready to take it.

Chapter
Twenty-one

ELEVEN DAYS LATER

"Get Mrs. Peabody on the phone. *Now.*"

Sitting at his desk in his downtown Chicago office, Chip
Saunders, businessman, venture capitalist, and executive producer of the hit cable television show *Homemaking*, clutched
and released the small Iso-flex ball in the palm of his right
hand.

Some days the little ball was a tension reliever, other days
it was simply a way for him to continue to work on his body.
If he bent his elbow just right, he could build up his biceps
while he talked on the phone.

Today it was *definitely* a tension reliever.

He glanced at his watch. It was close to eleven o'clock in
Chicago, which meant it was high noon on the East Coast.
Chip suspected he'd be interrupting Hannah's lunch at that
posh hotel where she was staying. He didn't give a damn.

"Greta Green on line one," sang his secretary's voice on
the intercom, *much* too cheerfully.

He pressed the intercom. "Tone it down a notch, Diane, I'm not in the mood."

"Yes, Mr. Saunders. Oh, there're about ten new messages from the network—"

Chip Saunders groaned and squeezed his Iso-flex. He'd been ducking them all morning.

"—and twelve more calls from reporters."

Chip groaned again. "Keep taking messages. I'm *not* available." At least until he thought of some way to explain why Happy Homemaker Hannah Peabody, the *married* star of his soon-to-be *network* show, was making out with some bohunk security guard in a moonlit garden. And how the hell it had become the cover story of a supermarket tabloid!

"Oh, before I forget," added Chip, "find me about ten more copies of *The National Tattler*."

"But, Mr. Saunders, I already told you. They're sold out almost everywhere."

"*Almost*, Diane, is the key word here. It's the reason I want you to get your butt out the door and *look*. I don't care if you have to dig the last ten copies out of the trash bins, just *get* them—*after* you get Hannah Peabody on the line."

"I've been trying, Mr. Saunders."

"*Trying* isn't good enough. *Do* it!" Chip let go of the intercom button and picked the phone up to talk to *Homemaking*'s staff writer. "Greta, have you seen it?"

"Yes, Chip."

"I swear to God, Greta, I'm not even forty-five yet, and this thing is going to put me on blood pressure pills for sure."

"Calm down, Chip. Squeeze your Iso-flex or something."

"I *am* squeezing it. I've *been* squeezing it."

"Fine. What else are you going to do?"

"Well, *first*, I'm going to tell Hannah about the story. *Then*, I'm going to calmly, patiently listen to what she has to say."

"That's very good, Chip."

"And *finally* I'm going to pretend my Iso-flex ball is really her scrawny little neck."

"Oh. That's not so good, Chip. Not so good at all."

Neil Ryan happened to be near the hotel's front desk when the fax for Hannah came in from Chicago. For the past week and a half, they'd both been busy during the day—Neil with his job and Hannah with her book, not to mention Holly's final wedding arrangements. But every evening they'd shared dinner and Neil's bed.

Last night they'd nearly made love right on the Cliff Walk. He smiled with the memory, realizing he'd begun to act—and feel—as carefree and happy as a teenager again.

After getting to sleep around two A.M., he'd barely managed to rouse himself for work at nine. He'd kissed a sleeping Hannah on the lips and planned to catch her for lunch. But when he saw the fax coming over the wire, all of his plans were put on hold.

He knew he shouldn't have been reading a fax addressed to Hannah. Still, he was a PI, which meant he was unreasonably nosy, especially when it involved people he cared about.

The fax had the logo of her television show on the letterhead. *Homemaking.* Neil glanced down the page:

> *To: Mrs. Hannah Peabody*
> *From: Chip Saunders, Executive Producer*
> *Re: What the hell's going on?*
>
> *Get back to me at once. Explain. Your job, not to mention my ass, is on the line. Newspapers and the network are calling. If they find you, DO NOT talk to them! CALL ME FIRST! We've got to figure out how to play this one out.*

Neil read the note with confusion and mild alarm. Obviously, something was upsetting this guy Chip—also, obviously, it was an urgent matter.

Neil picked up the house phone and dialed his carriage house apartment. The phone rang and rang, but no one was picking up. Maybe Hannah had already left.

"Hey, Neil."

Neil looked up to find his younger brother J. J. punching in for the day. He was dressed in the navy blue work pants and light blue shirt of the gardening staff.

"How's it going, J. J.?"

"Okay. Actually better than okay."

"Hmmmm?" asked Neil, distractedly looking back at Hannah's fax.

"Guess I should be steamed at you for putting me to work

on the grounds, but, you know, Charlie's great. I actually like working outside."

"What's that?" asked Neil, looking up.

J. J. slapped Neil on the back. "I said I'd like to stay on the gardening staff. I prefer it to working inside the hotel. It's actually giving me some ideas for projects at the community center. I think the kids would get a kick out of planting their own little garden for the summer."

"Right . . ."

"Hey? Earth to Neil," teased J. J., leaning over to look at the paper in Neil's hand. "What's got you so distracted?"

Neil shielded the paper from J. J. "It's Hannah's fax. I was just—" Suddenly, the fax line began to ring again, and Neil had a thought. He glanced at the top of the paper he held and saw that it was one of *two* pages. Clearly, the transmission had been interrupted.

When the second page finally came through, Neil found himself wishing to Heaven that faxes had never been invented.

Not to mention phones.

Newspapers and cameras also made Neil's short list of modern conveniences he'd like to see roughed up in an alley—because the second fax contained the lead story on the front page of this week's *National Tattler*.

HOMEMAKING HANNAH A HUSSY? read the headline with a large accompanying photo of Hannah kissing Neil at the Townsend/Sumner wedding, and a story that said two eye-witnesses at the Château du Coeur confirmed that Hannah had entertained a male guest "all night" in her bedroom.

"Christ," breathed Neil, staring numbly at the fax.

"Oh, no," whispered J. J., looking over Neil's shoulder.

Immediately, Neil jerked the page away from J. J.'s gaze. "Do you know anything about this?" he asked his brother sharply.

"God, no, Neil." J. J. looked hurt at the mere suggestion. "I swear I don't."

Neil exhaled heavily. He loved his half brother—and he couldn't really believe he'd have it in him to be a part of anything this low. The guy's heart was just too good. "Okay, J. J. Please don't mention it to anyone."

"No," said J. J. "Of course not . . . but, Neil, it *is* in the paper."

"Our guests don't read these kinds of papers."

J. J. nodded. "Yeah. I understand. Come to think of it, they don't go to supermarkets, either. Cooks and help do it for them."

"That's right, J. J., so pretend you didn't see this."

J. J. nodded, going back to his time card. But his concerned green eyes remained on his older brother. Neil Ryan was obviously taking this news very hard.

Neil's fist clenched tightly at his side as he reread the awful article in his hand. He didn't want to believe this was happening, but there it was. The evidence was right in front of him in black-and-white. Plain as day.

With all his training and expertise, he had been able to protect senators and princes, superstar athletes and movie-screen celebrities. But he hadn't been able to protect the one human being he'd most wanted to on this Earth.

"I've failed you, Hannah," he whispered in agony. "Again."

"Hol? Holly? Is that you?"

Neil heard what sounded like Hannah's voice calling someone out in the lobby. With a deep breath, he turned from the office and headed for the door.

"Holly! It *is* you!" Hannah cried across the hotel lobby, making more than a few wide-brimmed hats turn and plucked eyebrows raise.

"Han!" Holly Whitmore dropped her leather bag and ran the length of the large marble floor, embracing her beloved older sister with enthusiastic affection.

The two women spun around together, laughing like little girls, the way they used to in this very mansion.

"You're here at last!" Hannah couldn't stop smiling. "And you look absolutely gorgeous! What happened?!"

Hannah's little sister had always been as unexceptional in her looks as Hannah—not exactly homely, just nothing special. An average face on an average figure. But now, after only eight months in Europe, Holly looked more than just all grown-up. Her trip seemed to have re-feathered this common duckling with some very pretty plumage.

Her mousy brown pixie cut had grown out into a full shoulder-length mane of chestnut hair, the new auburn highlights and soft wave giving it a lustrous richness.

Her tortoiseshell glasses were gone, replaced with contacts that made it possible to admire her robin's-egg-blue eyes, and a tasteful application of makeup accented cheekbones that weren't there, evened out a mottled complexion, and filled out lips that were a bit too thin.

But the most striking change was her clothing. Her usual oversized flannel shirts and jeans were replaced with tailored designer couture. A red-and-white silk bolero jacket topped a formfitting little red dress.

In short, Holly's attractive form had become an object that made more than one male head peek above an open *Wall Street Journal* as she and Hannah strolled back to the front desk.

"Remember when I first got to Italy? I told you about a classmate whose mother owned a sort of beauty spa?"

"Yes?"

"Well, what I didn't tell you was that they decided to make me over. It was like some kind of little project for them. Like knitting a sweater or something. They seemed to love doing it. So I went along. And it really worked, don't you think?"

"And how, Holly."

"I could do the same for you, anytime," she whispered to her older sister, who looked exactly the same: Her dull, dark blond hair was still pinned back in its bun, her gray wire-rimmed glasses on her nose, and her figure disguised in a boxy brown pantsuit.

Hannah smiled but shook her head. "Homemaking Hannah's got a set image, kid. And this is it. But thanks for the offer."

"No problem. I'm just excited. The new me made quite an impression on the world. I doubt a man like Reggie would have flipped for the old me."

Holly laughed, but Hannah didn't think the remark was all that funny. She liked her sister just fine in jeans and flannel shirts—and she expected any husband of hers should, too.

"Reggie," said Hannah, looking around. "Now that you mention him—"

"Are you settled in okay?" asked Holly quickly. "How is it to be back at the old place?"

Hannah beamed, thinking of Neil. "Everything's going very well—the wedding plans included. Of course, Grandmother Edith's calling every day—"

"Of course."

"She's supposed to be here by tomorrow's rehearsal dinner," said Hannah. "But you know her."

"I know."

"So where is the bridegroom, anyway?"

"Reggie?"

"No, Prince Charles. Of course, Reggie! I've been looking forward to finally meeting him."

"He's . . . uh, gone into Newport."

Hannah studied her sister's fallen face. She didn't have to ask if anything was the matter. She knew her sister too well. "Did you have a disagreement?" asked Hannah softly.

"No, no. Everything's fine. He just . . ."

Hannah's concerned stare remained.

"I was tired," Holly said, the weak cheer in her voice doing its best to mask the strain. "He wanted to look around, and—and I wanted to check in right away."

"Yes, of course. It was a long trip for you," said Hannah quickly, not wanting to add to her sister's stress by putting her on the spot. "And you've both got a lot in front of you."

"That's right," agreed Holly. "Maybe, later, you and I can talk."

"Anytime," said Hannah, embracing her sister again. "Oh, it's so good to see you. And I have some news, too—"

"Hannah?"

Hannah turned to see Neil Ryan stepping out of the hotel's back offices. He looked wonderful, as usual, in tailored gray slacks and a black blazer. But his brow was furrowed, his face clouded with concern. "I just tried to call you. We've got to talk—"

"Neil," interrupted Hannah. "Look who's just arrived."

Hannah watched Neil turn his attention to the younger woman standing beside her. The furrowed brow on Neil's face remained, but he was at least polite enough to offer his hand to the girl.

"Holly. Hello. Congratulations on your wedding," said Neil stiffly.

"Thanks." Holly looked from Neil to Hannah and back again, very aware of the renewed familiarity between them. "How've you been, Neil? It's good to see you."

"You, too," said Neil, doing his best to lift his mouth into a smile and say something that sounded somewhat friendly. "I think you were still jumping rope and climbing trees the last time I saw you."

Holly nodded. "I don't suppose my swing is still on that old oak in the back?"

"No," cut in another male voice before Neil could answer. "But the oak's still there." J. J. Ryan had followed his brother out to the lobby. He quickly stepped up to the two women, his killer grin flashing brightly. "Isn't that right, Hannah?"

Hannah nodded as Holly's robin's-egg-blue eyes widened at the sight of the handsome young man before her. "Who are—?"

"I'm J. J., Neil's—"

"Brother," finished Holly. "You'd have to be. Look at you two. You've got the same features."

"Oh, no, don't start comparing us," teased J. J., putting his hands up. "Neil here is a workaholic, stick-in-the-mud, ten-hut kind of guy."

Hannah laughed and Neil raised his eyes to the ceiling, more than used to J. J.'s repertoire of wisecracks.

"And you're not?" asked Holly with a raised eyebrow.

"Ah, my good woman, let me enlighten you. *I'm* the brother with the Irish charm and flamboyant artistic streak— not to mention my newly discovered back-to-nature side."

"Back to nature?" asked Holly, clearly amused.

"He's working with Charlie the gardener," Neil informed flatly.

"Which means," added Hannah quickly, "that he'd be the perfect person to show you around the mansion's grounds. They're beautiful, Holly. They've never looked better."

"And everything's in bloom." J. J. flashed his brilliant grin. "At your service, Miss Whitmore," he said, bowing slightly.

Hannah was pleased to see Holly's face brighten so much.

If anyone could lift her spirits, it would be J. J. Ryan. "Go on, Hol. I'll make sure your bags get to your room. I need to talk to Neil anyway. I'll see you later."

Holly paused a moment, then turned to J. J. "You don't mind?"

"Sure and begorra, lass, 'twill be me pleasure." J. J. bent his elbow and offered Holly his arm.

"Oooooh," cooed Holly, laughing lightly as she took it. "I'm a sucker for an Irish accent."

"Ah, ye've come to the right man fur that, colleen."

Holly laughed again as J. J. led her across the lobby and toward the door to the rear grounds. "What does *begorra* mean, anyway?" Holly asked.

"Beats me."

Hannah was smiling when Neil stepped up to her. But her smile didn't last long.

"Hannah, I'm sorry. But I've got some disturbing news for you."

Hannah's gray eyes looked questioningly at Neil, but he knew better than to tell her in a place as public as the hotel lobby. Taking Hannah by the elbow, Neil guided her into a small glass room in the back offices near the hotel's front desk.

Hannah realized it was Neil's security office. She could see, through the glass partition, a side room where a guard was monitoring various security screens from cameras placed around the hotel's outside grounds.

She saw J. J. and Holly on one of the screens. He was pointing at some of the topiary and talking animatedly. It looked like both he and Holly were having a good time, even though, Hannah was sure, the two had practically no memory of each other. After all, a decade ago, while Neil was a teenager working at the mansion, J. J. was at the Ryan home in Middletown, busy being a rough-and-tumble kid.

"Hannah," said Neil, bringing her back to the present. "Sit down."

Hannah's palms had begun to sweat the moment she'd heard the words *disturbing news*. It reminded her too much of hearing about her parents' death five years ago.

She'd been at college then. Ill-prepared for the emotional turmoil that would follow—the sense of helplessness and loss that had left her feeling so confused and alone she'd consented to marry Herbert Peabody. God, she never wanted to go through that again—ever.

"Hannah?"

She wrung her hands and forced herself to calm down. "What is it, Neil?" she asked, finally sitting in a utilitarian chair opposite a very neatly kept metal desk. "A problem with the catering, maybe? We can't get enough white truffle oil for the grilled asparagus confit?"

"No," said Neil soberly, setting the fax down on the desk. "This came for you a few minutes ago."

He watched her as she picked up the papers. Her face paled as she read the damaging article. Neil thought surely she would break down, but she didn't. In fact she regained her color very quickly, and then some. A goodly amount of outraged anger accompanied the flush on her face.

"Damn it," she bit out, gray fire in her eyes. "I'm going to fight this."

"How?" asked Neil, more than a little surprised by Hannah's reaction. She'd seemed so vulnerable a moment before. He thought for sure she'd be crumbling into his arms by now. After all, he was standing there, ready to hold her, to comfort her.

"I don't know yet," she said, her angry fingers crushing the fax paper's delicate edges as she stood up to go. "But I'm going to think of a way."

"Can I help?"

"I'll need to call Chip right away," she murmured, "and Her—" Hannah stopped herself and stiffened. She glanced at Neil. He looked so miserable, so guilt-stricken.

"Hannah?"

She looked down at the fax again. A cold fist took hold of her spine. As much as she cared for Neil, she couldn't burden him with this. After all, it wasn't his fault. Or his lie.

"I'll have to talk to you later," she managed stiffly. Then she rose from her chair and walked away.

Chapter
Twenty-two

Herbert Theophilus Peabody picked up a chilled pitcher of martinis and filled two frosted glasses. It was late evening and streaks of water began to slash across the nearby window, obscuring the penthouse view of a fashionable street on London's West Side.

"Raining *again*." he said with a sigh he'd perfected to sound completely world-weary.

"Dis English weather. It is . . . how do you say it? For de birds, *sí*?" remarked the beautiful raven-haired Spanish model he'd met at an all-night private club the evening before.

"*Sí*," affirmed Herbert. "And the birdbrains."

"*¿Qué?*"

Herbert simply smiled, presenting the glass to the young woman as his hungry gaze took in her long legs. She crossed them, presenting him with more flesh than a Brooklyn butcher.

"Harry . . . I t'ink you will like Barcelona."

"I already do, my dear. It's on the water, and it's warm. I make it a point to spend most of my time in such places."

"Den, why are you here in London?"

"Same as you. Business. But only for a few days. Then I'm off again."

"Ohhh . . . don't be in such a hurry. Wait a week and my photo shoot will be *finito*. I will take you back to my Spain with me."

Herbert sipped his martini with satisfaction. Dry, dry, dry. How he loved things dry—his martinis, his wine, his weather.

"We'll see," he said, knowing it was what she wanted to hear. Herbert prided himself on his expertise in such things. Women were so very easy to manipulate.

The ring of the phone cut off the model before she could press him. "Ah, that must be our limo," said Herbert, glancing at the face of his $3,000 Patek Philipe. But when he picked up the phone, a long-distance operator's voice greeted him.

"Person-to-person from Hannah Whitmore Peabody for Herbert Peabody."

For God's sake, what could she *want?* "Yes, you've reached him," he said, very careful not to repeat the name the operator had used. He didn't want the model to hear it— then he'd just have to invent a story to explain it, and that would be more than a bit of a bother.

"Thank you," said the operator. "Go ahead, please—"

"Hannah? Love, what a pleasant surprise."

"Herbert, I've got to talk to you."

"Yes, well, here I am."

Herbert tried to keep the irritation out of his voice as he listened to Hannah go on and on about some sort of newspaper story. He noticed the model on his sofa was squinting suspiciously at him, so he made sure to cover the mouthpiece and whisper, "My sister."

That seemed to calm the girl and she went back to sucking down her martini, a rather noisy endeavor whose effects would no doubt prove worthwhile as the night progressed.

"Herbert? Herbert, are you there?"

"Yes, Hannah. You were saying?"

"Saying? I *said* it. And I'll say it *again*. I need you to come back to the States at once!"

Herbert sighed. "I *am* coming back. For Holly's wedding. My flight takes off tomorrow night. I already confirmed it with you." He absolutely hated the inconvenience, vastly preferring Monte Carlo at this time of year, but Hannah's sister's marriage was now his priority.

Ever since she'd told him about her sister's studies in Florence, Herbert had been hatching a promising little plan. The wedding announcement in the *Boston Herald* had made him glow like a proud parent.

"But the story, Herbert!" reiterated Hannah. "The story hit the tabloid newspapers today. There's a picture of me and . . . and . . . a friend. We were kissing at the mansion. It'll ruin my reputation, Herbert. It'll ruin the show. Don't you understand? If I'm fired, then you can say *good-bye* to your twenty-five percent."

Suddenly Herbert's attention span increased tenfold. "Ruin the show? What's going on there? Can't you fix it without me?"

"No . . . I need you to come back a day early. My boss, Chip Saunders, has set up an interview with one of those television magazine shows. It's the same network that's picking up *Homemaking*, so they're more than willing to do it. They're coming tomorrow, after the rehearsal dinner, to tape a *live* interview with us. You can't let me down now. You *agreed* to this arrangement—"

"I know," said Herbert. "I'll be there."

With a sigh, Herbert hung up the phone and cast a forlorn little glance to the promising prospect showing even more leg on his couch. Too bad, he thought, now that he'd have to catch a red-eye flight to the States tonight.

"Dat was your *sister*?"

"No, love," said Herbert after a long sip of his martini. With a profane little smile, he added two little words that, like a magician's incantation, could usually be counted on to make naive young women instantly disappear. "My wife."

Hannah hung up the phone and wrung her hands, abundantly aware that since her "humble," "broken" ex-husband had moved to London, his New England accent had taken a decidedly pompous turn—in the direction of Buckingham Palace.

"Heaven above! What a mess!" she exclaimed, pacing her suite. "A rotten, stinking mess!"

A knock at the door sounded, and Hannah found Neil on

the other side. "How are you?" he asked, after shutting the door behind him.

"Oh, Neil, I'm in a state."

"I know, Hannah . . ." Neil hated feeling so helpless, and so guilty. He had tried to protect her, but he'd failed—miserably, which was exactly how he'd been feeling for the last six hours since she'd walked away from him, like a teenager again, a hideous failure. "I'm so sorry this happened."

"You shouldn't apologize, Neil. You were right all along. I was stupid. Careless. I should have thought all this through—"

"We all make mistakes," interrupted Neil, his own words sharply stinging him. He, of all people, knew that. "In fact, I've done a lot of thinking for the last few hours. Maybe this thing is for the best."

"The best! How can you say that?"

"I know you've been dealing with a lot today, but I'd like you to calm down and realize that this incident gives you the opportunity to stop this whole masquerade of yours now."

"What do you mean, *stop*?"

"I mean come clean. Tell TV land that you're divorced. That your husband lives in London. That you're single and available, and—" Neil's eyes searched Hannah's expectantly, "perfectly within your rights to kiss an old boyfriend . . . or a new lover."

"Oh, Neil." Hannah just shook her head.

"What?"

"I'm giving an interview all right, but it's going to be with Herbert by my side, affirming that we're perfectly happy together." The moment she'd said the words, Hannah realized her fate. Neil looked as if she'd struck him with a bolt of lightning. He stared at her with such shock and confusion, she had to look away.

"Neil, please try to understand—" she rasped, though she knew in her heart that Neil Ryan was not the kind of man who'd be a party to a game of deception.

"I don't understand," he said, just as she'd expected. "How can you do this?"

"Because I can't give it up now . . . I don't want to . . . not like this. Maybe, after this all blows over, and I've established myself on the network . . . maybe then I can risk announcing that I've separated from Herbert. But I can't do it now. It would ruin me for good. I'd be a laughingstock, don't you see?''

"No, Hannah, I don't see," said Neil grimly, the mention of Herbert's name turning his blue eyes colder than she'd ever seen them before. "I'll never see any good come out of living a lie."

"Neil, I know how you feel. And I understand. But I have a point of view, too. And I've worked harder at building this career than I have at anything else in my life—"

"Of course you have, princess," Neil cut in, harshly turning on her. "You've had an easy ride otherwise. Your parents made sure of it."

"You know *nothing*, Ryan," returned Hannah, refusing to shrink away. "My life has been anything but easy."

A short laugh escaped Neil's lips. "Money always makes things easier. I know you haven't had it lately, but you sure had the benefits for most of your life."

"So what? Money can't buy happiness. Or fulfillment."

Neil stared her down. "Can't it?"

"No! And if it could, then you'd never see a rich person drink themselves into the hospital—or the grave. I've seen it enough times, Neil, and so have you."

"I've also seen it attract friends and spouses."

"My God, Neil, *what kind* of friends and spouses!? Money doesn't make life worth living. You *know* that!"

"And your career does?"

Hannah put a hand to her forehead as she nodded. She was getting a terrible headache. "It's . . . made me happy, given me purpose . . . a way to express myself." *And a career will never abandon me, like you did years ago; it can never throw me over for something "better"—another woman, another life.* Her gray eyes met his unyielding gaze. "It means everything to me."

"And us?" he asked simply, his voice a notch weaker than it had been before. "If you continue this false life, where does that leave us?"

"That depends on you," said Hannah softly.

Neil shook his head. "You want us to slink around in the dark? Keep our relationship secret?"

"For a little while . . ." *Maybe he'll bend,* thought Hannah. *Maybe, if he really loves me—*

But Neil's glare would not soften. "I can't do that."

"Then it's you alone and not my career that will keep us apart," snapped Hannah. "Just like the first time."

"What are you talking about?"

"The gossip, Neil. You couldn't take it." She hugged herself, hating to go on, yet unable to stop herself. *"Hannah's dating the hired help.* That's all I ever heard. *Poor girl's so plain she can't get anything better than a gold digger."*

"Hannah—"

The pointed gossip all those years ago still haunted her. Overnight, she'd gone from "poor lonely Hannah" to "poor *blind* Hannah," the girl who didn't know she was being played like a fiddle. Yet it hadn't been the rumors that had pricked her romantic bubble back then. Hannah knew that all along—Neil Ryan had done that all by himself.

"I knew all the gossip was wrong," she asserted. "I knew in my heart that you cared for me. And, naively, I thought that our true feelings were all that mattered . . . but something else mattered more to you, didn't it? Just like it does now."

"What?"

"Your pride."

Neil stared at Hannah in silence. Then he turned on his heel and headed for the door. She felt a last spark of hope inside of her as he stopped, his hand on the knob; but it was killed the moment he spoke again.

"You may be able to live a lie," he said before turning the knob and yanking the door open, "but I can't."

Then he was gone.

Hannah stared numbly at the closed door before her. She didn't want to believe he'd walked out of her life. Not again. And yet, she had to face reality. The molecules of space were cold and still where he'd been standing a moment before.

"Why didn't you lock him in?" Hannah rasped to the thin air.

But the ghosts gave her no response—unless she could count the gust of chilling sea air that came in suddenly through the open window.

On a disgusted sigh, Hannah crossed toward it. Glancing at the bright revolving warning of the lighthouse in the distance, she angrily shut and latched the window for the evening.

With any luck, she would soon shut the flood of unsettling feelings just as easily. Because, the fact was, though she may have been willing to wreck herself once on that confident, handsome Irish rock named Neil Ryan, Hannah was no longer so willing.

She'd worked much too hard for far too long to run aground now. She simply did not want to risk it.

Not for Neil Ryan.

Not for any man.

Chapter Twenty-three

"*Well, Daisy?*"

"*Well, what?*"

"*Look at this mess!*"

Dan and Daisy Doyle had witnessed the pitiful scene between Neil and Hannah, but the ghosts were both at a loss to stop the pair's renewed relationship from careening off track. Daisy hadn't bothered to lock Neil in again because she knew it simply wouldn't have worked. Hannah and Neil had reached a real impasse.

"*Dan,*" responded Daisy as they flew out the suite's window and out into the evening sky, "*don't you remember what you said yesterday?*"

"*What?*"

"*It's not professional to gloat.*"

"*I'm not gloating, Daisy. But Ryan did make some good points.*"

"*So did Hannah.*"

"*So what do we do?*" Dan watched from a high vantage point as Neil's stiff stride quickly ate up the ground between the back of the mansion and the carriage house.

"Oh, so now it's we!"

"It was always we."

"I didn't think you cared for matchmaking," pointed out Daisy as she trailed Dan's fluid movement across the lawn.

"I don't," affirmed Dan. *"But I care for our boy here."*

The two spirits tailed Neil through the front door—literally—of the carriage house and up to the second floor. They paused in the hallway when Neil neared his apartment, but the living man quickly bypassed that door and headed farther down the hall.

Ryan Investigations was closed for the day, but Neil unlocked the door anyway and walked in.

"I can't stand to see him like this," said Dan as he watched Neil move to his leather chair and sit down heavily. *"So damn pathetic. Look at the poor bastard. For Heaven's sake, I think there are actually tears in his eyes."*

"Not for Heaven's sake, Danny . . . for Hannah's."

The ghosts watched in bewilderment for fifteen silent minutes as Neil Ryan simply sat there in the shadows, morosely staring out at the darkening sea under a twilight sky.

"God." Dan sighed so dejectedly that he lightly ruffled the papers on Neil's desk. *"I hope he doesn't turn to the sauce again."*

Daisy regarded Neil. *"No. He's got more sense than that."*

"Fine," said Dan, skeptical. *"So what are you going to do now?"*

"Me?" asked Daisy, appalled.

"Yes," affirmed Dan.

"What happened to we?"

"Daisy, it was your idea to push them together again."

"You know, Danny, you were much less aggravating in your life than you are in your afterlife."

"Ditto, sweetie."

Daisy couldn't believe Dan was being so difficult! In a huff she rose to the ceiling, circling around and around the light fixture until she was sure she could control her temper.

"Well?" prompted Dan, who was getting impatient with Daisy's little transcendental display.

"I'm fresh out of ideas," snapped Daisy, swooping down.

"Fine!" Now Dan was getting angry. *"Just let our boy here suffer."*

"And what about our girl?"

"She seems altogether too cool about the whole thing if you ask me."

"You don't know women's hearts. Wait till she's alone on her pillow at midnight, thinking of him. You'll see her cry, too."

"I doubt it."

"She'll weep big fat tears."

"Ha!"

"You're making me very angry, Dan Doyle!"

"And you're a broad who doesn't know when to keep her mouth shut!"

"I don't even have a mouth anymore, you lummox!"

"Don't call me that, Daisy, you know I hate that word."

"Lummox, lummox, LUMMOX!"

"That's it. I'm outta here!"

"No!" returned Daisy. *"You stay with Ryan. I'm going to Hannah. I can see that we girls need to stick together."*

"Fine, you do that, missy."

Men, thought Daisy angrily as her spirit flew through the evening air back toward Hannah's suite. *Even having no form couldn't reform them!*

Back in Neil's office, the ghost of Dan Doyle hovered low. Neil rose slowly and moved to the fax machine, where a few pages had recently come in. As Neil picked them up, Dan read over his shoulder.

FACSIMILE

TO: Neil Ryan, Ryan Investigations
FROM: Trevor White, Continental & Standard
Per your submitted subject information:
NAME: Herbert Theophilus Peabody
BIRTH YEAR: 1963
CITIZENSHIP: U.S.
PREVIOUS RESIDENCES: Chicago, Illinois; Newport, Rhode Island
CURRENT RESIDENCE: London, England
Search Results:
EMPLOYMENT: Chambers Brokerage, Chicago. One

year. Terminated. No London employment records.
RESIDENCE: No confirmation of London residency.
BANK ACCOUNTS: Chicago & Newport. Closed. No London Bank accounts.
CREDIT RECORD: Delinquencies; high credit risk. No record of credit applications in London.
LICENSES: No London record of professional or personal licenses applied for.

"Nothing." With an ashen look on his face, Neil went back to his chair. In the air above, Dan Doyle watched as the living man sat for several silent minutes looking defeated.

Finally, Neil sighed. With a reluctant hand, he reached over to his computer and turned it on. A slight hum sounded in the room as the computer booted up and the monitor's screen glowed to life.

For another few minutes Neil simply sat there, his arms folded across his chest, his eyes staring at the blank screen.

Above him, Dan waited.

But Neil didn't type a thing.

That's when it occurred to Dan Doyle that Neil Ryan wasn't *going* to type a thing. Because he was waiting for Dan to!

A thrill shot through the ghost, sending a charge into the air. Even dead, that old PI electricity began to hum through Dan's essence as he gleefully approached the keyboard.

"I must be crazy," muttered Neil as he leaned forward to switch off the computer. "What kind of nutcase thinks he can contact a gho—"

But suddenly he stopped. The glowing computer screen began to flicker wildly—as if some kind of a power surge was shooting through it.

"What the—" Neil leaned forward with interest, vaguely aware that the room was quite chilly and the air seemed to be crackling with electricity. That's when he saw it . . .

Words were beginning to appear on the screen.

By themselves!

"Dan Doyle," whispered Neil, a shiver crossing his skin. Even though he'd been waiting for exactly this, Neil still

couldn't get used to the idea of communicating with a ghost.
READY FOR SOME HELP?
Neil swallowed uneasily, then leaned back and exhaled.
"Yeah," he finally said. "What do you propose?"
SEND ME TO LONDON.
"What?!"
I'VE GOT CONTACTS THERE.
"Contacts! What the hell do you mean, contacts? Other *ghosts* or something?"
YES. FROM THE GREAT WAR.
Neil scratched his head. "But . . . I don't get it . . . I mean . . . how the hell can I send you there?"
BY FAX.
Neil stared dumbfounded at the computer screen. Then he began to mumble to himself. "Okay, Neil, you're talking to the ghost of a dead detective through your computer. And now the ghost is telling you that he wants to be *faxed* to London, presumably to investigate Herbert Theophilus Peabody. And he's going to do it by using dead operatives, who he apparently met when they were alive, during World War One."
THAT ABOUT COVERS IT!
"Good God!" cried Neil. "I can't fax a ghost!"
WHY NOT? IF THE SPIRIT IS WILLING . . .
Neil sat for a long moment, considering.
"Well," he murmured, "I've got nothing to lose."
He rose from his chair and went to the fax machine. Then he dialed the number for Continental & Standard's offices in London. The fax line on the other end whistled in a loud, irritating tone. Neil put a piece of blank paper into the machine, and in the next few seconds, the transmission was done.
"Dan?" called Neil softly in the middle of the empty room. "Dan Doyle?"
But there was no answer on the computer screen.
The ghost of Dan Doyle had disappeared.

"Hannah?" called Holly's voice. "It's me."
It was after nine the next morning when Hannah opened her suite's front door to her little sister. Holly's soft pink sweater and white linen skirt looked like a cheerful combination, but her expression failed to reflect it.

The evening before, Hannah and Holly had joined Maura for dinner in the hotel's elegant restaurant. The meal had been a pleasant one, focusing mainly on the final details of the wedding. But Reggie had been glaringly absent from Holly's side the entire night.

Hannah said nothing about this. She simply nodded when Holly remarked he hadn't yet come back to the hotel. "He must have really gotten caught up in the sightseeing," she chirped lightly, then quickly changed the subject.

This morning, Hannah could see her sister wasn't so ready to change the subject.

"Can we talk?" Holly asked before Hannah had fully closed the front door.

"Sure, come in," said Hannah as she finished buttoning the jacket of her conservative gray pantsuit. "Are you ready for your final fitting in town?"

"I . . . I guess so. The dress fits fine, really, but since I brought it from Italy, I want to make absolutely sure it hangs perfectly."

"Of course." They'd barely stepped inside the room when the phone rang.

Hannah answered, listening silently to the caller while Holly sat down in one of the ornate antique chairs by the fireplace. "No. I'm sorry, but I have no comment on that article," said Hannah coolly.

Holly turned to find her sister hanging up—rather forcefully. "Who was that?"

"Nobody." But before she could step away again, the phone rang once more.

Hannah picked it up to find yet another reporter had tracked her down to ask a barrage of questions.

"He's just a friend," Hannah found herself saying. "That article was a terrible—" Suddenly she stopped herself, trying to remember what Chip had advised her. "No comment," she said firmly then hung up.

Immediately, she called the front desk. "No calls from outside the hotel, please."

"Certainly, Mrs. Peabody," said the front desk clerk. "We'll be happy to take your messages until further notice."

"Thank you."

"Hannah? What's that all about?"

"I've got a bit of a publicity glitch, Holly. I'm trying to straighten it out. Nothing to worry about—just the show."

"Are you sure—"

"Everything's fine. Now tell me what's on your mind," urged Hannah, crossing the room and settling into a chair beside her sister. The chairs were as uncomfortable as ever, and her mind couldn't help but recall Neil trying to spend the night on one of them. The memory dug painfully at her heart.

With a deep breath, Hannah tried hard to keep from thinking about Neil. She'd done just fine sleeping alone, after the tears finally stopped. Other than one long night on a soggy pillowcase, Hannah expected to have no more weak moments.

"Reggie didn't check into his room until very late last night," Holly finally confessed.

"I see," said Hannah.

"He stopped by my room this morning, but now he's off again, playing golf with some men he met this morning," she said, then rose from her chair and began to pace in a tight little circle.

"Why didn't you go with him?" asked Hannah.

"He didn't ask. He just made the plans and left!"

"And you're angry."

"Yes. And confused. It seems as though the closer we get to the wedding, the less . . . interested he is in being with me."

Hannah's blood turned cold. "Has this been going on very long?"

"For the last two weeks or so. He's just been disappearing on me. Usually in the evenings. And when I ask about it, he gets aloof. If I press, he gets miffed, says he doesn't want a nag for a wife."

"He actually *said* that to you?"

"Yes."

Hannah swallowed with extreme patience. "Holly. Tell me again how long you've known Reggie?"

Holly thought for a moment. "Six months . . . and twelve days. Don't you remember when I told you about meeting him?"

"I remember you said he was vacationing in Italy for the winter—at his family's villa, right? And you met him at a gallery opening."

"That's right. Our relationship had been so wonderful. Dinners and sightseeing, trips to the countryside.''

"And he's just started acting this way?''

"Yes.''

"Oh, Holly,'' said Hannah, rubbing her forehead. "Don't you think you should stop and consider this commitment you're about to make? I know there are some wonderful plans in place already, but maybe a longer engagement would be a good thing to—''

"No, Hannah, I'm not about to call off the wedding. It's too late, and I intend to go through with it.''

"It's *not* too late—''

"I want to do this, Hannah. Look, Reggie told me he's never been married before. I'll bet he's just nervous, don't you think?''

Hannah wrung her hands. "Holly, how much do you really know about Reggie?''

"Please don't start jumping to conclusions.''

Hannah rose to her feet. "You didn't answer my question.''

"I *know* him. I know he's handsome and romantic, and that his family is titled aristocracy—''

"Those things don't impress me. Does he love you?''

"God, I shouldn't have told you about this.''

"No, Holly, don't say that. I just don't want to see you make the same mistake I did.''

"I'm *not*,'' she insisted. "Nobody ever romanced me like Reggie has. He must love me, Hannah, he says it all the time. Everything will be just fine. In fact, now that I've talked it out, I feel much better about the whole thing.''

"Holly, don't try to bulldoze me—''

"I'm not,'' she insisted, but Hannah wasn't so certain.

"Hannah,'' continued Holly, "remember Dad's stories of how nervous he was before he married Mom? Once Reg and I are married, things'll be back to the way they were. I'm sure this is just cold feet.''

Hannah sighed and walked to the window, unable to trust her sister's judgment. Holly no longer had parents to protect and advise her, and Hannah felt it was now her duty to see to her sister's well-being. But what could she do, really? Her sister was a grown woman.

As Hannah gazed out the window, considering the situation, she noticed two men on the lawn. One was J. J. Ryan.

He was speaking with an older man who looked very familiar.

It was Joe Stokes, realized Hannah, that charming older man who Maura had introduced her to at the Townsend/Sumner wedding. She watched them talking and laughing. Then she saw J. J. pointing to the big oak tree on the edge of the grounds, the one where Holly used to have her swing.

"Holly," said Hannah, slowly getting an idea, "about your final fitting . . ."

"Yes? When is it exactly?" Holly checked her watch.

"Ah . . . ten o'clock," Hannah fibbed.

"Oh! I guess we'd better get going."

"The thing is . . . would you mind terribly if I had someone else drive you? I've got some last-minute business to see to."

"No problem," said Holly. "Who?"

Hannah looked down at the mansion's lawn again. "That Ryan boy," she said as casually as possible.

"J. J.?" asked Holly, her face brightening. "The one I met yesterday?"

"Yes," affirmed Hannah, turning from the window. "After all, you heard what he said. He's *at your service*."

Holly laughed. "J. J.'s a very nice guy. Did you know he's studying to be a teacher?"

"Yes," said Hannah. "Neil told me about it."

They were interrupted by a knock at the door. Holly headed for it. "I'll just grab my bag," she said. "Tell J. J. to buzz me when he's ready to go."

"Okay," said Hannah, following Holly to the front door. She was surprised to find Neil Ryan standing on the other side of it.

"Good morning, Holly," he said crisply.

"Morning, Neil," she called before leaving.

Hannah stood awkwardly in the doorway, her throat suddenly closing up on her. Neil looked terrible, she realized. His sapphire-blue eyes were bloodshot and his expression looked haggard. Could it be that he'd had as little sleep as she had?

She found it hard to believe. The man had turned on his heel so fast the day before, he could have given himself whiplash. Clearly, he had wanted out of her life—again. And that's where she intended to keep him.

No more heartache, she told herself. *And no more falling into dark chasms that sweep you into oblivion.*

"Yes, Mr. Ryan?" she finally asked, as flatly and emotionlessly as she could manage.

Neil's eyes seemed to flash at the use of his surname. "Sorry to bother you," he began, his voice and manner back to its stiff, just-the-facts-ma'am routine. "But I felt I should warn you about the paparazzi."

Hannah closed her eyes and sighed. "Come in, please," she whispered. "I don't want people overhearing."

Neil stepped inside, clearly uneasy to be back in her suite.

Hannah didn't expect him to make himself comfortable— nor did she want him to. With arms crossed, she simply stood in the middle of the room, facing him as he explained the situation.

"There are about a dozen reporters and photographers camped out at the entrance of the hotel," said Neil. "They're asking our guests about you."

Hannah groaned, her posture losing a bit of its defiance.

"My staff and I will do what we can, of course, to discourage them," said Neil. "But if they're on public property, there's not a lot we can do. I've spoken with the authorities in town. They may be able to break them up on a disturbing the peace charge, but they can't promise anything."

"I'm sorry, Neil."

Neil stared at Hannah, doing his damnedest to harden his heart. The woman had been nothing but a pain in his neck from Day One, he tried to tell himself over and over. The sooner she was off the premises, the better off he'd be. And yet, as he looked into her troubled gray eyes, he couldn't help but feel for her.

Even though she'd brought this on herself. And even though she refused to budge from her position. Neil's heart was still open to her.

Perhaps a part of him admired Hannah for her courage— and her steadfastness. But he knew he had to stop the admiring and the caring. She was clearly charting out a life he couldn't be a part of—and it was time to let her go.

"No apologies necessary," he said stiffly. "We've had celebrities here before, as I've told you. You're not the first to bring photographers to our gate."

Hannah nodded, only partly relieved. "Neil . . . I need your help with something."

Neil waited.

"I'd rather not drive my sister into Newport for her final fitting. With those photographers, you can see what a circus that would be."

Neil continued to wait.

"Well, do you think you could ask J. J. to take her? She enjoyed seeing the grounds with him yesterday, and—"

"Of course," said Neil briskly. "I'll see to it at once."

"Thanks," said Hannah softly.

"Anything else?"

Hannah hesitated to continue, but forced herself. "Yes," she finally said. "I believe I'll need the services of Ryan Investigations."

For the first time since he'd entered the suite, Neil Ryan's stone-cold expression actually broke, his eyebrows rising in surprise. "You would?"

"Yes," said Hannah, swallowing uncomfortably. "I'd like you to run a background check on Sir Reginald Carraway."

"Your future brother-in-law?"

"Yes. As soon as humanly possible."

Neil nearly laughed. With Dan Doyle still in London, he had yet to discover what was *in*humanly possible.

"I'll do what I can," said Neil as steadily as he could manage. "But you've got to fill me in." He pulled out a small notebook and pen. "Let's start with what you know . . ."

Chapter
Twenty-four

J. J. Ryan sat in the little dress boutique, his muscular wrestler's body among the delicate frills making him feel like a prizefighter at a flower show.

"Are you ready, J. J.?" called Holly from the dressing room.

"Ready and willing," J. J. said with a laugh.

Holly Whitmore was a real kick to be with, thought J. J. She was so funny and kind, honest and sweet. And she even laughed at all of his corny jokes.

When he and Holly had first arrived at the dress boutique, they'd found they were an hour early. Holly said her sister must have gotten the appointment time wrong. So, for the next sixty minutes, he and Holly had just bummed around Newport's quaint shopping district, sipping hot take-out coffee and talking.

"I used to love it here," Holly confessed, gazing toward the busy blue water of the nearby harbor.

"Aren't you moving back?" asked J. J. "After the wedding?"

"No," said Holly, a slight note of melancholy in her voice. "Reggie wants us to live in England."

"Perk up, kid," said J. J. at once. "The U.K.'s not so bad. You've got your fish and chips, your Shakespeare, and, of course, your Benny Hill memorials."

"Not to mention that shrine to the Beatles," put in Holly.

"Top of pop to the Brits, I suppose. On the other hand, if you're *really* talking shrines, you can't beat Graceland. My brother would definitely agree. He's got some oldies stashed away in a vault somewhere—far away from me."

"Uh-oh, what did you do?"

"Scratched one of his first pressings of an Elvis record."

"You didn't!"

"I was a young, drooling fool, trying to create a ballpoint pen masterpiece on black vinyl. On the other hand, I was also ahead of my time; you notice they picked up my idea for CDs. A lot of them have illustrations right on the compact disc."

"True, J. J., but they don't render them in ballpoint pen."

J. J. laughed. "Can't argue there."

As they strolled down one of the many little side streets of Newport, they passed by the back of a community building. Holly smiled when she saw a half dozen first-floor windows covered with colorful children's drawings.

"Look," said Holly, stepping off the sidewalk to get a closer view of them.

J. J. followed her, secretly pleased. "So, Holly, how do you like these? Guess it doesn't compare to those Renaissance dudes at the Uffizi in Florence."

Holly's gaze skimmed the children's visions of big ocean ships, stars and planets, far-off lands, and dinosaur monsters. "I think, in their own way, they're more beautiful."

"Really?" J. J. was taken aback. "You surprise me."

"Why?" Holly hadn't realized that J. J. had stepped right behind her. When she turned, she found herself closer than she expected. It unsettled her a little, as if she were going to lose her balance. Yet both feet were firmly planted, she thought. Or were they?

J. J.'s gaze observed Holly's open, vibrant expression. "You just spent a year studying in Europe. I just thought . . . you know, that you'd be—"

"A snob?" asked Holly bluntly, a tiny teasing smile tugging at the edge of her mouth.

J. J. saw the little smile and it seemed to tug at something inside of him. He knew he could step back, give her more space, but frankly he didn't want to. "What do you plan to do with your art history degree?" he asked instead, his green eyes meeting her blue ones.

Holly's tiny smile suddenly vanished, her eyes darting away. "I hadn't planned anything. I mean, before I met Reggie, I was thinking about working in a museum, or going further into academics, but none of that really inspires me."

"Did you know," said J. J. softly, "that John Lennon was an art student?"

"Really?"

"Yeah, I sometimes wonder what it would have been like to be one of his teachers. How would he have expressed his vision back when he was ten years old?" J. J.'s arm moved to point to one of the children's drawings. As it did, it seemed to partially entrap Holly. He leaned even closer. "This drawing of ships at sea, for instance. You see the child's natural sense of perspective. The way the ships get smaller as—"

"Yes, I see it," said Holly abruptly. She found herself swallowing nervously. She couldn't understand the nervousness. Or why her mouth was suddenly dry—her heartbeat suddenly quicker.

"Mr. Ryan! Mr. Ryan!"

Holly and J. J. turned to find two boys running toward them.

"Hi, Mr. Ryan," said the boys together. They looked like brothers, one about eight, the other a little younger, and both with curly brown hair and dimples in their cheeks.

"Hey, Sean, Ricky," said J. J. "What's up, guys?"

"Our uncle's taking us to buy kites," said the older boy as the younger pointed to a man in jeans and a baseball jacket. He was fumbling for change by a parking meter down the street.

"Well, I think kites are great," said J. J., hunkering down. "There are all kinds, too. Box kites and butterfly kites and airplane kites. Some people even design their own. Like this man I know named Joe. He even designs his own model ships."

"Really?" said the boys, their eyes wide.

Holly watched J. J. as he talked with the kids. It charmed

her. It also reminded her of the time she'd spent with some American schoolchildren who'd been touring through Florence. Come to think of it, realized Holly, those days she'd spent sharing her love of art had been some of her happiest.

A tug at her sleeve brought Holly's attention to the younger of the two boys. He was looking up at her with big expectant green eyes.

"Yes?" asked Holly, crouching down.

"Do you like my picture?" asked the boy.

Holly smiled. "Which one's yours?" she asked, and the little boy took Holly's hand and walked her a few feet away. He pointed to a lovely little drawing, full of color and life.

"That's my garden," he said. "See my footpath and my fountain. And here's my apple tree, and here's my flowers. And here's a little bench."

"This is very pretty," she said to him. "Is this the garden at the back of your house?"

"Oh, no. We don't have a big backyard, just a little square of grass. But Mr. Ryan told us that sometimes kids can see things that grown-ups can't see. And when we see them, he said we should try to keep seeing them, and sometimes draw them so that others can see them, too. I thought it would be nice to have a garden. So I drew myself one."

Holly stared at the little boy. "And Mr. Ryan told you that?"

"Sure."

"Sean, Ricky!" called the man down the street.

"We gotta go," said the older boy. "Bye!"

"See ya, miss," said the younger boy, and then the two boys scampered off.

J. J. was standing a few feet away when Holly turned back toward him. As she turned, he saw a strange look in her eyes.

"You teach here?" she asked him.

"A few times a week. It's a latchkey program—you know, after school." J. J. shrugged. "It doesn't pay much, but it's good teaching experience. One of my professors set me up with it."

"It sounds nice," said Holly. "You know, when I was in Europe, I was a guide for some American schoolchildren for a few weeks."

"No kidding. Did they drive you nuts?"

"Not at all. I actually loved it. Very much."

J. J. walked toward her. Her blue gaze was so intense, almost expectant. *But what is she expecting?* wondered J. J. *And who is she expecting it from?*

"Holly," began J. J. softly as he stepped very close to her, "maybe you should think about what's in your future a little more?"

"My . . . future?"

"Maybe you should think about doing what makes you happy."

Suddenly, a spring breeze blew through the side street and Holly's chestnut hair whipped across her face. Without thinking, J. J. reached out to brush it out of her eyes.

The intimate gesture surprised Holly. She looked up, into J. J.'s warm green gaze.

"Thanks," she whispered.

They stood like that, just studying each other's faces, for what seemed to them a very long time; each trying to guess what the other was thinking . . . and feeling.

"Holly—" J. J. finally began softly, his fingers reaching to brush back her hair again. But the chiming of a nearby clock sent a streak of realization flashing across Holly's face.

"The time!" she said, abruptly stepping back. "We'd better get back."

"Sure," said J. J. at once, looking away to recover his composure. "No problem."

Now he sat in the dress boutique, trying his best to remain aloof and cheerful. This woman was going to be another man's wife, he reminded himself. For God's sake, she was trying on her *bridal* gown!

So why did he feel this overwhelming urge to take her on a moonlit stroll along the Cliff Walk? Why did he want so badly to hold her in his arms and kiss her? And why did he feel, in the depths of his heart, that a beautiful chance for happiness was about to pass him by?

"I feel like I'm Hugh Grant in *Four Weddings and a Funeral*," joked J. J. loudly as Holly stepped out of the dressing room.

"You do?" laughed Holly, a radiant vision of cherub pink cheeks and Italian lace.

"Yes," said J. J. with a nod, "and you look more stunning than the stars in the sky."

"Really?"

"Cross my heart," said J. J., his bright smile beginning to fade, "and hope to die."

Chapter
Twenty-five

Neil had been working in his Ryan Investigations office for most of the morning, looking into the background of one Sir Reginald Carraway. When the phone began to vibrate, he snatched it up before it even finished its first ring.

"Mr. Ryan?"

"Yes?"

"Mr. Peabody has checked in."

Neil had asked the front desk to notify him the moment the jerk stepped foot inside his hotel.

"Where's he sleeping?" Neil asked the front desk clerk.

"Room 309."

He *wasn't* sleeping in the same room with Hannah, realized Neil. Extreme relief coursed through his system.

"Thanks," said Neil before hanging up and quickly ringing security. "Houston?"

"Yes, Mr. Ryan?"

"Keep an eye on Herbert Peabody. Room—"

"Three Zero Nine, yes, sir. I understand he just checked in."

"Very good, Houston." Neil was pleased as he replaced

the receiver. His staff was getting to be quicker than he was.

The call to Houston was simply a precautionary measure.

Dan Doyle—Neil's man, or rather his *ghost*, in London—had yet to report in, at least as far as Neil could figure it. There'd been no mysterious messages on his computer, and no faxed reports on Herbert Peabody. So, until Neil knew what the score really was on this joker, he wasn't taking any chances.

Neil turned back to his desk, and the routine background check on Carraway.

The quick clicking of laptop keys had been the only sound in Hannah's suite for the last few hours. But her fingers stilled on the keyboard the moment she caught a whiff of an all-too-familiar Paris cologne. Instantly she knew who was tapping lightly at her door.

"Hannah!" her ex-husband exclaimed when she opened it.

As usual, Herbert Peabody looked ever the responsible businessman—Saville Row pinstripes and a smart bow tie beneath a thick head of blond hair and a set of perfect teeth, which were now smiling beneficently at her. Herbert had always possessed the kind of Yale-man image with whom any upper-crust debutante would instantly trust her trust fund.

"Come in, Herbert. How are you?"

"Famished," he announced pleasantly as he waltzed into Hannah's suite. "But I've ordered up some lobster salad. On your tab, love, you don't mind? I'm still having money troubles. You know how it is."

Hannah sighed heavily as she shut the door. "Are you all settled in?"

"Yes, right next door. Now, tell me, really, love, are you all right?" Herbert's face and voice were suddenly full of concern as he put an arm around Hannah's shoulders.

"I don't know," said Hannah. "I just want to get through this. Do you think it will work, Herbert? Do you think we can pull off a 'happy couple' interview with a network news magazine?"

"Of course, Hannah. Nothing to it! Keep your chin up."

Herbert touched her just under her jawline—exactly where Neil had two days before. It pained her to recall Neil's touch.

Especially in this moment. God, she hoped she could get through the next few days.

"So where is this notorious article?" asked Herbert.

Hannah presented him with the fax.

"Thanks," he said, glancing around. "Got a bar in this place?"

"Sure. What would you like?"

"Scotch. Good Lord, what a ghastly invasion of privacy," he exclaimed as he glanced at the article.

"Yes, I know," said Hannah, opening the bar and pouring three fingers into a tumbler.

"By the way, who exactly *is* this bloke you're kissing?"

"Bloke?" Hannah stopped pouring and looked up.

"Man."

"I know what bloke means, Herbert. But don't you think you ought to tone down the British thing? After all, we're supposed to be a happy couple who live together in Chicago. That reminds me," she continued, walking toward him and handing him the tumbler of wheat-colored liquid, "I've discovered you left behind some *very* unsavory baggage in that city. Two women—"

"*You've* discovered?" interrupted Herbert after a good stiff swallow. "Listen, let's not get into the past. Not now." Suddenly his voice calmed tremendously—back into the soothing singsong that usually did the trick with her. "Why don't we concentrate on our strategy for the interview. Now tell me, when is it scheduled?"

"It'll be live. The crew will set up in a corner of the lobby tonight," said Hannah, trying her best to control her temper and just get through this. "But first we're expected at the rehearsal party with my sister and her fiancé. There's no real rehearsal since the vows will simply take place on the lawn, but the wedding party will be there. And possibly Grandmother Edith."

"Grandmother Edith? That would be Edith Channing Williamson, wouldn't it? Have I met her?"

"No," said Hannah, walking back to the bar to grab a mineral water. "For the past eight years, the woman's gone a little eccentric. She's claimed to be so worried about kidnappers that she refuses to leave her Boston town house. I still can't believe she'll make the trip."

"You don't say? She's worth that much money?"

"Quite a bit." Hannah bypassed a glass and twisted the top from the water's glass bottle. "Married into most of it. Her late husband made some sort of killing with a new kind of kitty litter."

"So you might say she's the queen of kitty litter, then?" said Herbert with a little laugh as Hannah took a long drink from the water bottle.

"*You* might say it," she remarked, licking her lips. "But I wouldn't call her that to her face."

"Of course, of course. Now, about the interview. Here's how I think we should play it . . ."

Play it, thought Hannah. She took a deep breath, recalling Neil's words in this very suite.

You may be able to live a lie, he'd said.

". . . and when they ask us about our home, we can say . . ."

But I can't.

Hannah tried her best to listen to Herbert's voice, but her mind, not to mention her gaze, kept drifting beyond the suite's windows and down to the carriage house—a poignant reminder of Neil Ryan's haunting words, not to mention his kisses, and touches, and—

With a miserable sigh, Hannah lifted the water bottle to her lips again and took another long swig, but she knew that no amount of any liquid would wash away her memories.

"Hannah? Hannah!"

Hannah realized Herbert was talking to her.

"Weren't you paying attention?"

"Oh . . . sorry, Herbert. Let's try again."

With a distasteful look on his face, Herbert began to look around the room. "Is there a *draft* in here?"

Hannah's eyebrows rose. She glanced to the windows. They were all shut.

"Must be the ghosts," she said matter-of-factly.

"What in hell are you talking about?"

"Cold spots are routinely associated with the supernatural," she informed him. "And the hotel is haunted."

"You're crazy."

"I'm not. The ghosts of the previous owners are still here. My great-great-aunt Daisy Doyle, and her husband Dan."

"Those *gumshoes*!" exclaimed Herbert with a laugh. "Why, I doubt those two were effective in life—let alone death. That's very droll, Hannah, but really, let's get back to business. And, oh, by the way, do you mind if I check over the wedding's guest list—who's coming and who's not, just to refresh my memory on the families?"

"Certainly," said Hannah, her fingers tightening around the water bottle as she wondered if that ghostly pair had overheard.

"Why that little pompous weasel!" exclaimed Daisy, who'd been flitting around Hannah's room by herself. *"I'll give him a draft!"*

"Daisy!" Dan Doyle disliked going through solid objects, but all of the windows in Hannah's suite were closed, so he really had no choice.

"Dan Doyle!" cried Daisy in shock as she watched him enter the room through the outside wall. *"I've looked all over this mansion for you! Where have you been hiding?"*

"London."

"Oh, no. Don't tell me."

"Yep."

"You accidentally faxed yourself again!"

"Well, actually, Neil faxed me. At my request."

"You went on purpose?"

"On business. I went sniffing around for background on Hannah's ex-husband, Herbert Peabody."

"Herbert Peabody!" asked Daisy. *"You mean this little no-account? You know he just called us ineffective gumshoes!"*

"Ineffective gumshoes?" Dan had been in such a hurry to see Daisy again that he hadn't noticed what was going on with the living beings in the room below him. Swooping downward, Dan circled them both until he was satisfied.

"That's the man, all right," said Dan as he returned to hover with Daisy by the cloud mural on the suite's ceiling. *"Only he doesn't go by Herbert Peabody in London. He has some aliases set up under a corporation."*

"Have you reported all this back to Neil?"

"This and plenty more. I typed what I found on his com-

puter. He seemed quite fascinated. Brother, this guy's a piece of work.''

"Tell me more.''

"It may take a while.''

"We're ghosts, Danny—we always have time!''

"I don't know, sweetie. With the way this guy works, that's debatable.''

Maura Ryan crossed the rear grounds, waving to Joe Stokes. He seemed to be working with Charlie on something by the old oak tree. She would have stopped, but she really didn't have the time.

After heading inside the carriage house, Maura went straight to her son's offices. She watched him working a moment, noticing the drained look to his face, the sadness in his blue eyes. Finally, with a light tap on the glass door, she stepped inside.

"Yes, Ma?"

"Son, I'll get right to the point. What's going on between you and Hannah?"

Neil's haggard face looked up. "Don't worry about that tabloid story. It'll blow over."

"I know it will. What I'm worried about is you—and Hannah. So please, answer my question. What's going on between you?"

"Nothing. Absolutely nothing."

"Don't stonewall me, Neil," scolded Maura, sitting down opposite his desk. "Remember, I'm your mother."

Neil shook his head. "There was something going on, okay, but there isn't any longer, and I don't want to discuss it beyond that."

"All right, Neil," said Maura with an annoyed sigh. "I can see you have work to do. I just stopped by to ask you to come to Holly's rehearsal party this evening. She specifically asked me to attend as a guest, and she's extended the invitations to you and J. J., as well. She considers us all family—those were her very words."

Neil's jaw worked a moment. "Yes, of course," he said finally. "I'll be there."

"Good." Maura rose and crossed the room. "I guess you know Herbert Peabody has checked in."

"I know."

"And you're not going to do anything about it?"

Neil spun his chair to face his mother. "What would you have me do? It's her life. Her choice."

"Neil, what would you do if one of your clients was about to walk into gunfire? Would you let her?"

"Of course not. I'd stop her. Or take the hit myself."

"You wouldn't abandon her out of fear that you'd get hurt in the process?"

Neil glared at Maura. "That's not a fair comparison."

"Son, you and I both know what kind of man Herbert Peabody is. You're abandoning Hannah when she needs you the most."

Neil shook his head as he spun his chair back to the desk. "I don't want to discuss it."

Maura sighed and turned toward the door. "See you at the party?" she asked.

Neil's only answer was a low irritated growl—as sure a sign as any, thought Maura, that she'd gotten through to him.

"One more thing. There's a registered letter for you at the front desk."

"Really? Who from?"

Maura seemed uneasy, then she finally met Neil's questioning eyes. "The law firm that represents Cornelius Vandenburg's estate."

"What?" Neil's eyes narrowed. "What would they want with me?"

"I don't know, son," said Maura, quickly turning on her heel. "The letter's addressed to you. Not me. It's not my . . ."

Neil couldn't quite hear Maura's last hesitant word as she shut the door to his office. But he guessed it was "affair."

Chapter Twenty-six

It was just two hours before the dinner party and the network interview, and Hannah was feeling like a caged animal in her suite. She'd paced the length of the room so many times, she was sure she'd owe Maura for the cost of relooming the rugs.

When the sharp, solid knock came at her door, she nearly jumped out of her own skin.

"Who is it?" she called softly.

"Ryan."

Heaven help me, Hannah prayed as she opened the door.

"I have some new information," said Neil, striding in. He'd obviously been working hard. His jacket was gone and his tie loosened, the top button of his dress shirt undone. The man had even rolled his sleeves to the elbows.

Hannah shut the door, feeling as though she'd entered a James Bond picture. "Neil, I don't want to invade the man's privacy. I just want to know if he's telling her the truth."

"Who?" Neil turned abruptly. A distraught Hannah hadn't noticed, and she plowed straight into a wall of muscle.

"Oh!"

"Hannah, are you all right?" asked Neil, grasping her arms to steady her as her palms went to his chest.

"Yes, of course." She'd also forgotten how solidly built this man was—a minor point in her present situation, yet one which unfortunately flashed an image of Neil Ryan's naked chest through her mind.

"Like hell you are. Look at you. You're shaking like a twig in the wind. And your face—"

"What about it?"

"It's flushed."

Hannah struggled to leave Neil's grasp, but he was holding firm. "Let me go, Neil," she whispered.

"No."

Behind her glasses. Hannah's gray eyes flashed in frustration. "I'm fine. Everything's under control." *Except my heart . . . and apparently my complexion.*

Neil studied Hannah. He tried to keep his mind on business, but the sight of her blushing cheeks and the scent of her soft peach skin lotion was unwillingly making his body tighten.

"I want you to be calm before I tell you the disturbing things I've found—"

"About Carraway?"

"Carraway?" Neil's grip on Hannah loosened, but she didn't step from his arms.

"Has he been lying to my sister? Has he been married before? Maybe his family's disowned him? He's after Holly for her inheritance?"

Neil shook his head. "Sir Reginald Carraway checks out in every way, Hannah. He's an English businessman whose deceased parents left him a fortune. He's got homes in London, Monte Carlo, and L.A., a villa near Florence, and an Innsbruck ski chalet. Never been married. Service in the royal navy—distinguished. Knighted by the Crown. His main interest now is apparently cigars."

"Cigars?"

Neil nodded. "His parents owned a cigar plantation and factory in the Dominican Republic. Now he's taken it over. Apparently, the thirty-year ban on Cuban cigars has made the business quite profitable."

Hannah felt weak. "Then he can't be after Holly for her money."

"No. Not Carraway," said Neil. Without considering it, his hands began to move slowly up and down Hannah's arms—a comforting gesture that came naturally to him.

"I suppose I should be happy," conceded Hannah, "but I'm still worried about her."

"She's your younger sister. You feel responsible. I know the feeling of wanting to protect someone you care a great deal about." Neil's blue eyes were shining as he looked at her.

"You mean J. J. and Maura?" rasped Hannah.

"I mean you," said Neil.

"Oh, Neil . . ." Hannah's hand lifted to touch his cheek and he turned his lips to kiss her palm.

"I know you have to do what you have to do," he said. "But I've been thinking. And I want you to know that I'll be here for you. If you need me."

I do need you, thought Hannah. God, why couldn't she just say it? Because she knew it wouldn't solve her problems, that's why. Neil still wasn't willing to live a lie. And he wasn't talking about love. He was just telling her that he wanted to be her friend.

"Neil, I'll always treasure your friendship."

"My *friendship*."

"Yes." assured Hannah. "And I hope you'll consider me someone you can count on, too."

Neil nodded, but from the chilly look that crossed his face, Hannah got the distinct impression he wasn't used to counting on, let alone needing, anyone but himself.

"So," she said, finally turning away from him. "Was that all you came to tell me, then? That my sister is marrying Prince Charming? That's hardly what I'd call disturbing—"

"Herbert Peabody is an extortionist."

"What?" Hannah stepped back. "Neil, what are you talking about? Herbert's a financial adviser. Living in London."

"Herbert Peabody uses two aliases in his work. Harry Princeton and Heathcliff Parkinson—"

"Heathcliff?!"

"All of them are conveniently utilized under his corporation, H. P. Ventures, Limited."

"H. P. Ventures is his company, Neil. That's who I make my checks out to when I pay him his twenty-five percent."

"And you say he *lost* your inheritance, as well as his, in some bad investments?"

"Yes, I have all the proof, the paperwork—"

"It's falsified. I'm certain of it. Herbert Peabody was cut off financially from his family the year he went after your hand. He'd spent his inheritance and was in grave debt. Hannah, I'm sorry to tell you all this, but it looks like you were an easy mark for Peabody. He took your money and ran—"

"No . . . it can't be. I mean, I'm the one who wanted him to go, I told him to—"

"That's the beauty of his manipulations. He makes people believe they're doing *exactly* what they want to."

"How did you find out all of this?" asked Hannah, suddenly feeling nauseated. She stepped back to the desk chair and sat down.

"I got some of the background from—a colleague, who has some . . . well . . . old acquaintances, you might say, at Scotland Yard. But I've done a lot of the tracking myself—debts and dates, bank records and credit companies. And I made a few calls to his family members, the ones to whom he appears to owe a great deal of money.

"It seems he's got a little trail of wealthy women, and a number of investment schemes, which always look legitimate—especially when the investments fail. And they always do."

Neil rubbed his chin, concerned with how Hannah would take all of this; but he knew she was a strong woman. And she'd want to know everything. "Hannah, I'm also sorry to say that your money really is gone at this point. Peabody's left a messy little trail of very high living and bad debts. Right now, he hasn't got more than thirty thousand to his name—or, I should say, his *names*. And I'm sure that's chump change to him."

"But how could he get away with it?" Hannah shook her head, bewildered. "Do the authorities know?"

"There's a file on him in Scotland Yard—under the Parkinson name. It's only a matter of time before evidence will sink him. So far, though, he's been careful in choosing marks in different countries—targets that are vulnerable and unlikely to sick the legal profession on him."

"Like stupid, foolish me, you mean?"

"You were alone, Hannah. You trusted him."

"My parents trusted his family. I thought that was enough.

But then Mom and Dad died before anyone had a clue the youngest Peabody would turn out to be such a bad seed—''

''I had a clue, Hannah. I always did. I wish I could have warned you. Protected you.''

Hannah lifted her gaze to Neil's eyes. ''How did you know?''

''When Peabody used to visit here with his family, he'd change his little nice-guy act the moment anyone of his 'class' stepped out of earshot. He was a bastard to the staff, nearly struck one of the housemaids.''

A look of horror crossed Hannah's face. ''God, Neil, this is awful. But I still don't understand why he'd want to continue this relationship with me—''

''You're *paying* him to, for one thing. And I'm sure he's already benefited from his connection to your family. Your parents were known as respected art dealers all over Europe. Your grandmother is one of the wealthiest widows in America.''

''Grandmother Edith.'' Hannah sighed, rubbing her forehead in dismay. ''She urged me to marry him. Said he was from a good family. Had good prospects. Oh, God.''

''Ironic, isn't it?'' said Neil, folding his arms across his chest. ''I remember when Edith called *me* a gold-digging gigolo.''

Hannah's head shot up in outrage, her eyes meeting Neil's. ''When? When did she say such a thing?!''

''I didn't want to tell you, Hannah. But it was a decade ago. It's what made me finally decide to leave, enlist in the army. I knew if that's what people really believed was happening between us, that I couldn't let your reputation be destroyed and your family lose respect for you. I loved you too much.''

Hannah's face turned ashen. ''You really did then? Love me, I mean?''

''Yes,'' said Neil, his voice slightly shaky—because all of a sudden, he was back at Purgatory Chasm, staring at the dark cold emptiness in front of him.

Make the leap, Neil, the voice whispered in his ear.

Neil blinked. He wasn't sure exactly what came over him in that moment. Maybe it was the voice. Or the look in Hannah's eyes. Or maybe Neil finally realized that *not* risking the leap would be an even greater tragedy than falling in.

"I still do, Hannah," Neil finally confessed, his voice no longer shaky, but rock steady, his blue eyes open and direct. "Love you, I mean."

Hannah couldn't believe her ears. She stared slack-jawed at Neil in a kind of numb shock.

Neil waited for Hannah to express what was in her heart. But she simply stared at him, as though he'd said something she couldn't—or wouldn't—reciprocate.

"Well," said Neil, finally looking away. "I guess love doesn't actually change anything, does it?"

Then he was turning quickly from her. "I'll drop the Carraway paperwork off later. But I wanted you to know about Peabody. I wanted you to be careful. Let me know if you want to pursue prosecution. I'll do what I can to help."

"I—I'll think about it, Neil," Hannah managed. "All of it."

"Okay."

"And, Neil—" Hannah's mind felt like chaos. Everything Neil had told her, from Peabody and Carraway to his own feelings, amounted to the force of a hurricane blowing through her head. She wanted to think it all through, yet she felt the need to say something to him—

"Yes?"

"Thank you," she whispered.

Neil nodded, a flash of pained disappointment crossing his face—as if he'd expected her to say something else. But she hadn't. And, in the next moment, he was gone, the suite's door shutting firmly behind him.

For twenty minutes, Hannah walked aimlessly about the Daisy Channing Doyle Memorial Suite, finally ending up in the small dressing room. She knew she had to get ready for the dinner party and the interview, yet she couldn't seem to focus.

There was a small antique vanity in the room, and she sat down in front of its mirror. For many minutes she simply sat numbly, staring into the glass.

"My entire life is a lie," she whispered to her reflection. "I don't think I've ever felt this lost."

"You're not lost, Hannah."

Hannah closed her eyes and took a breath. "I must be hearing things."

"You're not hearing things, my dear. You're hearing me."

Hannah opened her eyes and looked around the room, but she saw no one. The room had grown colder, she realized, and an elusive feeling of electricity seemed to be buzzing in the air.

"Who . . ." whispered Hannah, her heartbeat quickening. "Who are you?"

"I think you know," came the woman's voice, loud and clear in the small dressing room.

Hannah's limbs stiffened and her skin prickled as she recalled Neil's story of seeing the ghost of Dan Doyle. Could this be . . . no, it couldn't—

"Oh, Heaven, this can't be happening . . ."

"What, my dear?"

"Are you . . . Daisy? My great-great-aunt Daisy Doyle?"

"I was. Now I'm her ghost."

Hannah's eyes rolled back in her head, and she felt about as steady as a rocking chair on an ocean liner. After all, knowing that two ghosts haunted your mansion was one thing. Having one *converse* with you was quite another.

"No need to faint, my dear, I don't plan to materialize."

"B-but Neil *s-saw* D-Dan Doyle," stuttered Hannah, her white-knuckled hand gripping the edge of the vanity.

"Yes, that's true," said the ghost. *"Then again the boy had been so plastered it took some of the shock out of the visitation. I won't risk much more than talking to you."*

"*Much* more?"

"Now, as I see it, the problem you have is in your head."

"My head?" echoed Hannah. "That's it, I'm going crazy! Schizophrenic, or something. I've got to be. After all, I'm hearing voices *and* talking to myself—"

"You're not crazy, my dear. Just take a look—"

Hannah watched with wide-eyed shock as Daisy made a bottle of her peach skin lotion levitate off the vanity.

"You see."

"*And* I'm hallucinating!" cried Hannah, leaping to her feet.

"Calm down, dear! I have a message for you."

Hannah felt dizzy again so she sat back down and put her head between her knees. She also tried to breathe through her nose. That was right, wasn't it? Didn't it prevent fainting, or calm hysteria, or something like that?

"Are you paying attention?"

"Yes!" cried Hannah, back to being petrified.

"Good. Now listen, I've got a solution to your problem."

A solution? Hannah lifted her head. If this was a delusion, or a hysterical episode or whatever, maybe, at least, it would be an enlightening one. She could certainly use a little wisdom right about now.

"Hannah, I want you to close your eyes."

"Close my—?"

"Go on . . ."

"Okay." Hopefully she'd figure out later that she'd actually left the radio on in the next room, and the voice was really some FM New Age guru, practicing visualization therapy.

"Now, my dear, I'd like you to concentrate on your life."

"What about it?"

"Your existence."

"I don't understand."

"You living seldom do."

"What?"

"Listen, carefully. I want you to envision your life. Not the way it is. But the way it could be."

"I don't under—"

"What is it that you really want, Hannah? Ask yourself that question. Then answer it. Answer it honestly, my dear. Answer it from the depths of your soul."

"My soul?"

"Answer it," the ghost instructed, *"from the bottom of your heart."*

"My heart . . ." Hannah whispered softly. Then she sat silently for a very long time. She thought and thought and thought some more. She really didn't know how long she sat there with her eyes closed, but when she felt ready, Hannah opened her eyes.

The cold air and faint electrical charge were gone. But something had been left in its place. . . .

"What's different?" whispered Hannah to the empty air.

She was still in the dressing room. Still sitting at the antique vanity. But, remarkably, one thing had changed. She gasped when she saw it right there in front of her.

Putting out her hand, Hannah touched the smooth glass of the vanity's mirror. The mirror felt real enough. She pinched her skin. That felt real enough, too. Yet the image she now saw reflected in front of her was completely changed from just a moment ago.

It was a *brand-new* image, realized Hannah. An image snatched from the eye of her mind and placed right up there on the mirror. And in that moment, she understood, finally, what the ghost was trying to tell her.

"Love *can* change things," whispered Hannah, her fingers touching the image in the glass. And if she found the courage to make this vision real—if she really tried to take the leap . . .

It would change everything, whispered the girl in the looking glass.

"Yes, of course!" cried Hannah a moment later, leaping up from the vanity and running from the mirror, the elusive image leaving with her. "That's it!"

Grabbing the phone in the bedroom, Hannah quickly dialed her sister's room number. "Hello, Holly? Remember that offer you made to me yesterday? Well, I'm going to take you up on it. Right this second! . . . Okay, okay, I'm willing. Give Maura Ryan a call and ask for her help. If any woman can move a mountain, it's her!"

Chapter
Twenty-seven

The rehearsal party was getting into full swing now with a fashionable, wealthy crowd buzzing with laughter and conversation. A cozy fire was blazing in the carved stone hearth, a grand piano was playing Chopin, and a staff of white-gloved waiters were making the rounds among the group, offering silver trays full of rich and tempting canapés.

Dressed in his finely tailored black-tie tuxedo, Neil Ryan stopped by the lobby's busy bar. Two dozen flutes of champagne stood ready on the bar for guests to help themselves, but Neil bypassed them, asking for a club soda instead.

"Don't tell me you're drinking?"

Neil glanced over to find his brother J. J. sidling up next to him at the bar.

"Club soda," said Neil, taking a sip from the crystal flute and scanning the room full of people. "I'm still on the job."

"You're always on the job," pointed out J. J. "I thought this was a social thing."

"It is," he said. "But I'm worried about Hannah."

"Yeah, well, join the club. I'm worried about Holly."

"Holly?" Neil's eyebrows rose. "What's to worry about?

That's her fiancé over there, glad-handing the troops.''

Since the start of the party twenty minutes before, Reginald Carraway had been the perfect host, moving fluidly among his guests with his bride-to-be by his side. Neil thought the man looked the picture of wealth: a tailed tuxedo on a lean build; brownish-blond hair and a handsome face that sported a neatly trimmed beard.

''He doesn't deserve Holly,'' complained J. J.

''He's handsome, witty, titled, and very, very rich,'' pointed out Neil.

''So the hell what? Since when is that a recipe for happiness?''

Neil regarded his brother. J. J. looked like an aristocrat himself tonight. His tuxedo was freshly pressed, his dimpled jaw closely shaved, his midnight-black hair brushed to shine like the moon. But the carefree sparkle was gone from his warm green eyes—replaced with something a tad fiercer.

''What's up, J. J.?''

''I don't like this guy Carraway. Have you met him yet?''

''Not face-to-face. I've just heard a lot about him.''

''Well, I don't like the way he's been treating Holly. And I don't like his rich-boy pomposity, and there's something else I can't quite put my finger on. It's in his eyes. I don't like his eyes.''

''They're hazel,'' retorted Neil. ''What's not to like?''

''Stow it, will ya, Neil.''

Neil sighed as he spun the bubbly liquid in his crystal flute. It was obvious to him where J. J.'s gaze was completely focused—and it wasn't on Carraway.

''J. J., are you sure it's your *dis*like of Carraway that's really the issue—and not your *liking* of the woman beside him? The one you can't take your eyes off of.''

''What's the difference?''

''The difference is your judgment can be impaired by your feelings.''

''So?''

''So, you should always rely on the facts.''

''You don't,'' snapped J. J.

''No, you're right. Not solely.''

''You have hunches.''

''But a hunch is just an educated guess,'' explained Neil.

"Gut feelings that emerge from a preponderance of elusive information and not necessarily hard evidence."

"A leap of faith."

Neil glanced back at J. J. "In a manner of speaking. What are you getting at?"

"Nothing. I just have a *hunch* that Holly doesn't really love Carraway. Oh, maybe she's impressed by him, at the moment, but that won't last."

"I see," said Neil, intrigued by J. J.'s obvious devotion to the subject. "And Carraway?"

"Mark my words, under all the man's British bravado beats the heart of a creep."

Neil took a second look at Carraway and another sip of soda.

"Mr. Ryan?"

Neil turned to find one of his staff at his side. "Yes, Jackson?"

"You asked to be informed when the network crew arrived."

"They're here?" asked Neil.

"They've just been waved through the front gate."

"Fine." Neil nodded. "Take care of them when they come in. Don't let the party guests be disturbed. Have the crew set up in the library."

"Right, sir."

"What was that all about?" asked J. J. after Jackson departed.

"Hannah's giving a live interview tonight on one of those prime-time news magazine shows."

"Which one? Every network has one now."

"*Prime Insight*, I think it's called. And it's on the same national network her own show's moving to in a few weeks."

"And she's giving the interview tonight?" remarked J. J., surprised. "The day before her sister's wedding?"

"Couldn't be helped," said Neil, taking another sip of club soda and wishing for something stronger. "Her boss set it up to clear the air after that article hit the stands. The one I showed you yesterday."

"Yeah, I get it," said J. J.

After a few silent moments, Neil noticed his brother was

still casting long, forlorn looks Holly's way. "Hey, J. J., don't get involved."

"But—"

"Holly's taken. Take my advice, accept it and get over her."

"Nothing personal, bro," said J. J., lightly punching his shoulder before shoving off, "but tonight you can keep your advice. I don't want it."

"Hello, Neil," greeted Maura as she picked up a glass of champagne. "What was all that intense talk between you and J. J.?"

"Oh, nothing much," said Neil. "Let's just call it the folly of youth."

Maura shook her head. "You know, son, you're not so old that you can afford to count yourself above such things."

Neil smiled at his mother. "I didn't say that I did."

"Good," she said, touching her champagne flute to the edge of his with a tiny clink. "There may just be hope for you yet."

Neil laughed, but he didn't drink, not quite believing there *was* any hope left in the world, especially with the arrival of a certain guest. Herbert Peabody descended the heart-shaped staircase and strode across the room. Neil's blue eyes tracked him like night sentries on patrol.

"Well, well," murmured Maura, noticing her son's gaze. "Look who slithered in."

Eternally tan and perpetually pompous, Herbert Peabody made his way quickly across the room. His destination was exacting—a beeline straight for Holly and Reginald Carraway.

"He looks about the same," remarked Maura, watching him as closely as Neil. "A little older, of course, but just as—"

"Weasely."

"Mmmm," murmured Maura. "I remember him well. He used to visit the house with his parents when Lilian and Lawrence were alive."

"What was it you used to say about him?" asked Neil.

"Oh," said Maura, after taking a fortifying sip of champagne. "You mean about him having an Eddie Haskel kind of charm?"

A sharp laugh escaped Neil's throat. "That was it."

Ingratiating to the "right" set, Herbert Peabody had always been ready to impress, even dazzle, while on stage. But both Neil and Maura knew there was a Mr. Hyde waiting in the wings—they'd witnessed the transformation themselves many a time under this very roof.

"I think I'll take a stroll in his general direction," said Neil, setting down his drink. "See what I might overhear."

"You do that, son," said Maura. "I for one am staying as far away from that SOB as I possibly can."

"Good idea, Ma. You do that."

"Why, Holly Whitmore," cooed Herbert Peabody, "look at you! You're a vision!"

Neil Ryan stood at a careful but close distance, observing Peabody. He had to agree with Peabody on his opening remark. Holly did look very nice tonight. Her white tuxedo dress with satin lapels and cuffs dipped attractively to reveal a hint of cleavage. The dress was both conservative and daring, chaste and alluring. And, as Neil affirmed with a glance back at poor J. J., it was driving his little brother into an abyss of frustrated regret.

"Hello, Herbert," said Holly politely. "Have you met my fiancé, Sir Reginald Carraway?"

"No, I don't believe I have," said Herbert, extending a hand.

Carraway's right hand was holding one of the couple's gold-rimmed "bride and groom" champagne flutes—a special touch that Hannah had arranged. Carraway switched hands and finally took Herbert's with a slight nod. "You're Holly's—"

"Brother-in-law," informed Herbert. "And I've heard so very much about you, Sir Reginald."

"Oh, my good man, we're in the States. Revolution and all, in case you haven't heard! Please, call me Reggie."

"Reggie, then!" exclaimed Herbert with a laugh. "You have such a wonderful sense of humor. I expect you're settling in all right? Have you any hobbies you're especially interested in? Yachting? Crew? Golf?"

"I enjoyed a good eighteen holes earlier today," said Reggie, putting an arm around Holly. "The little one here was a bit miffed at me for disappearing, but I just couldn't resist grabbing some new friends for the outing—''

"New friends?" asked Herbert. "And who might they be?"

"Why, they're right over here—George, Hank, John! Come join us."

Neil listened as the group made the introductions and glad-handed. It wasn't long before the men were laughing and talking. Neil recognized the three gentlemen. They were wealthy businessmen, in from Boston, New York, and Pittsburgh as guests of the Whitmores.

"Reggie, I understand you have an interest in cigars?" asked Herbert after a few minutes of small talk.

Neil's ears immediately perked up. He took a careful step closer to the group.

"Yes, in the Dominican Republic. It's turned quite a profit, and I've actually been thinking of taking on some investors, maybe expanding."

"Investors?" asked Herbert, interested. "You know, my firm in London is always looking for a good investment."

The other men nodded with interest, and in another few minutes the group was agreeing how lucky it was that they'd discussed the idea.

"I'll call my man down there and have him fax some information on the plantation," said Reggie. "Should have it by the end of the night."

Neil noticed that Holly had already wandered away. In fact, she'd disappeared. Concerned, he stepped away from Peabody's group to make sure she wasn't with J. J. when he suddenly spotted her. She was coming down the heart-shaped steps behind a beautiful woman.

A *very* beautiful woman.

"Who the heck is that?" whispered Neil, stopping dead in his tracks to gape—an expression that more than a few men around him seemed to be wearing, too.

"Neil? Do you know that girl?" asked J. J., stepping up to him.

"Great stars in Heaven," breathed Neil in complete disbelief. "It's *Hannah*."

The homemaking bun was gone and so was her long mousy hair. In its place was a short, jaunty veil of shimmering gold, the color of sun-washed honey. It had been expertly colored and cut to fall, like a twenties flapper, across her jawline, exquisitely framing her face.

Makeup had been applied with precision, creating an airbrushed cover-girl perfection to her skin. Blush created the illusion of high cheekbones, and a deep red lipstick only brought out what Neil knew was a wonderfully natural redness to her already full, soft lips.

And then there were her eyes—no longer hidden behind glasses, those wide gray eyes were now accented with shadows and liners to make them even more luminous and radiant than they'd been before.

Like a swan's, her slender neck curved seductively, leading down to a strappy little black dress that could only be described as barely legal. Low in some places and high in others, it hugged Hannah's curves, revealing a tantalizing glimpse of cleavage and a luscious length of stocking-clad leg.

The vision took Neil's breath away. And he just knew that every man in the room was thinking the same thing: This alluring creature was *not* going to be baking cookies tonight.

"Everyone!" called Holly loudly. Then she clapped her hands together and waved to the pianist to stop for a moment.

The room grew silent and every pair of eyes was now on the bride, who was standing on the staircase beside a mysteriously beautiful woman in black.

"Reggie and I certainly thank you all for coming. But I just wanted to publicly thank the woman responsible for arranging this wonderful weekend ahead of us." Holly's arm went around Hannah and she kissed her cheek. "My sister, Miss Hannah Whitmore."

Neil was certain he heard a few champagne glasses crash to the floor in the ensuing silence. And then the whispers began.

"Hannah?" murmured voices in the crowd around Neil. "*That's* Hannah?"

"Miss?" whispered someone behind him. "Did she say *Miss* Whitmore? I thought Hannah was married?"

"Divorced," Neil said loudly enough for a good crowd of guests to hear. "Hannah's divorced now."

That should start the rumor mill rolling, he thought with a satisfied smile. After all, it was pretty darn clear that was what Holly and Hannah wanted.

Neil sincerely hoped the whole mansion would know Hannah's marital status—and lack thereof—by the end of the evening. And if he were *really* lucky, he joked to himself, the news would reach the rest of the country by then, too.

Suddenly, Neil blinked. *The rest of the country.* Good God, realized Neil, this was no joke. Hannah's big interview was scheduled for later tonight.

The reality of it hit him like a condemned New York skyscraper. Hannah Whitmore was actually going to risk changing her television image. No matter the consequences, she was coming clean tonight.

Well, I'll be damned, thought Neil.

"Hey," snapped a man's voice behind him with a sharp tap to his shoulder. "What makes you think she's divorced?"

Neil turned to find Herbert Peabody staring him in the nose. "I don't *think* she is, Peabody. I *know* she is."

Still up on the steps, Holly was waving to the pianist to start playing again. "It's a party, everyone! Have fun!"

"Excuse me," Neil said to a gaping Herbert, "but I believe Hannah is in need of a glass of champagne."

Neil's eyes were shining with renewed hope as he began to move through the crowd toward Hannah. He wasn't entirely certain of her feelings, but he sure as hell knew one thing: If this woman was going to try a leap across the Chasm, he'd be damned if he'd let her do it alone.

Watching from high above the festivities, a ghostly pair smiled at Neil Ryan's strong, sure strides across the room.

"Isn't it wonderful, Dan?"

"It'll be wonderful when she's back in our boy's arms."

"Oh, Danny! How romantic."

"I can think of something even more romantic."

"What?"

"Well, you remember ten years ago? When Hannah was coming down this very staircase?"

"Her coming-out party?"

"Yes."

"Oh, Danny. Don't give her a twisted ankle again."

"I promise she won't touch the floor."

"You're that sure of him?"
"I'm that sure."
"All right, my love. Then you have my blessing."

Hannah was just starting down the steps when she saw Neil Ryan anxiously coming toward her through the crowd.

Her breath caught with the sight of his rugged, raven-haired looks in the black-tie formal wear. And she nearly stopped breathing completely when she finally saw the look of open adoration in his shining blue eyes.

As she came down the last few steps, Hannah quickened her pace. Yet she was certain that her balance and footing had been just fine.

The fact was, Hannah never knew exactly how it actually happened. All she felt was the *swish* of a draft near her heels and then she was tripping forward, her body sailing through the air like a flying Wollenda.

Oh, my God! was all Hannah could think. *This can't be happening to me again!*

Below her, Neil's blue eyes widened at the sight of Hannah's flight. Without hesitating, he rushed forward, his arms opening wide. Suddenly, a flash of memory assailed him. Ten years ago, Neil had been working at Hannah Whitmore's coming-out party, serving guests from one of those ubiquitous silver trays. Back then, when she had tripped and fallen, Neil had been too far away to catch her.

But not this time.

Tonight he was right there for her, happy to hold out his arms— because this was one woman for whom Neil Ryan would always want to cushion any fall.

A few outbursts of "Ohs" and "Whoops!" warned that it would be a close call. But in the end, Hannah landed squarely in Neil's strong arms. And as her hands caught hold of his broad shoulders for balance, he embraced her, wrapping his arms tightly around her so he could hold her close.

"I've got you," he whispered into her ear.

"I'm glad," she whispered back.

A moment later, Holly was leaning in, patting Neil on the shoulder. "Nice catch, Captain."

"Thanks," Neil called, as she darted away.

Stepping back, Hannah recovered herself. With a brief wiggle, she straightened the skirt of her little black dress.

"Well, *Captain*," she teased, standing tall, "what do you think? Do I pass inspection?"

"Hmmmm. Let's just see, Whitmore." Neil took both of her hands in his and stepped back to admire her transformation. "You do realize this will require a *closer* inspection?"

"Closer?"

Neil's eyes danced with blue fire. "Much."

"Gee, I can't wait." She laughed, but then her voice grew soft and serious. "But what do you *really* think, Neil?"

The laughter left Neil's eyes. "I think you're stunning."

"Really?"

With sincerity, Neil nodded. "Dazzling. Gorgeous. A heavenly body . . . but then you always were beautiful to me, Hannah. Oh, look, I've made you blush again, too. I love doing that."

She laughed. "I love it, too."

Neil touched her cheek. "But do you love me?" he asked on a whisper. "Is that why you did this?"

He watched as Hannah lifted her eyes. Flecks of silver shimmered inside their gray depths like stars at twilight. It seemed as if she wanted to say the words, but she didn't quite trust her voice. Then, finally, she took a deep breath. "I—"

"Excuse me!"

Neil turned to find Herbert Peabody upon him again. The man was clearly furious. He tried grabbing Neil's arm and spinning him around, but the rigid rock of muscle beneath Neil's tuxedo sleeve seemed to give the man pause.

"You know, Peabody," said Neil in a slow dangerous tone, "wrinkles make me *very* angry."

Herbert released Neil's sleeve, taken aback for a moment at the level of grim hostility in his face. Instantly, he regrouped, shifting his focus to Hannah.

"My dear, do you realize what you're blowing?" sang Herbert in a sweetly threatening voice. "I'm sure your new look is quite becoming, but unless you change back, *pronto*, your career will be finished. And you'll be a laughingstock."

The second of uncertain hesitation in Hannah's eyes made Neil hold his breath for an instant. But then the determined gray fire flashed brightly, and it was clear to him that Hannah had made up her mind long before she'd descended the staircase.

"Herbert," she snapped briskly, "I don't care anymore what people think, or what they say. I'm through with living up to someone else's vision. It's time I had the courage to pursue my own—"

"And if you fall flat on your face?" barked Peabody.

"Then I *fall*," said Hannah sharply. "I'll just pick myself up again and start over. A few bruises won't kill me."

Neil found himself amazed, yet again, by the woman in front of him.

"Don't worry, sweetheart," Neil growled as his arm looped possessively around her waist. "I'll be there to happily put salve on whatever bruises that fine form takes. Oh, look, I've made her blush again."

"Who the hell are you, anyway?" asked Herbert.

"I'm *nobody*, Peabody. I recall you told me that yourself one day under this very roof."

"What?"

"I think I was taking your luggage up to your room—something like that."

"Wait a minute," said Herbert, squinting. "I *know* you. You look familiar."

"He should," said Hannah firmly. "He's the man I love."

For a few seconds, both men beside Hannah blinked at her in slack-jawed surprise. Neil recovered first.

"You mean that?" he asked quietly.

"Yes, of course, Neil. I love you. And I don't care who knows it."

With immense satisfaction, Hannah watched as Neil's grim expression slowly melted into the most wonderful, joy-filled smile she'd ever seen. It was as if his heart had finally found its way home.

"Wait a moment!" barked Herbert angrily, stepping between them and jabbing Neil's shoulder with his finger. "He's the man in the picture, isn't he? The one kissing you in the garden? That's right, what was that headline again, something about a Homemaking *Hussy*?"

Neil registered Herbert's words and slowly turned to face the man. Hannah gasped at the ferocity in Neil's eyes as he grabbed both lapels of her ex-husband's coat. "Just give me a reason, Peabody,'' Neil bit out in a low terrible threat. ''Just give me a reason.''

More than a few heads turned their way, and Hannah quickly began pulling at Neil's immovable arm. ''Neil!'' Hannah interrupted. ''I'd really like some champagne. *Now*, Neil!''

Neil reluctantly released an unnerved Herbert from his grasp. ''Fine,'' he said, watching Herbert instantly turn and vanish into the crowd. ''You lead the way.''

Chapter
Twenty-eight

"Welcome back to *Prime Insight*," announced the well-dressed New York anchorman. "And now, for our exclusive 'live-time' feature for tonight—"

In the hotel's cozy library, Neil Ryan stood behind the twentysomething cameraman with a bleached blond ponytail and tensely watched the small television monitor.

"—*Prime Insight* takes you to lovely Newport, Rhode Island, where our remote reporter, Sylvia Stone, talks with one of America's best-loved homemakers. Mrs. Hannah Peabody will tell us about her own happy home and successful marriage. . . ."

Crossing his arms, Neil tried like hell not to cringe. Obviously no one had informed the New York studio that their lead-in script needed some updating.

Hannah was sitting a few feet away on a small silk-covered sofa. Next to her was the *Prime Insight* reporter—a navy-suited, celebrity-eating barracuda if ever Neil saw one.

Neil tried giving Hannah his most reassuring expression, though he was so damned worried, it wasn't easy. Then Hannah smiled back with such warmth and affection that Neil

realized what was really going on here: She was the one trying to reassure him.

The truth was, Hannah looked as cool as a March breeze
off Newport harbor. With her long legs crossed attractively,
her posture relaxed against the back of the sofa, she appeared
more than ready for the onslaught.

". . . And now over to Sylvia."

"Thank you, Case," began the reporter, her smile flashing
to the "on" position right along with the remote camera's
little red light. "It seems I've got a real scoop for our viewers
this evening. Until tonight, millions of fans have known
'Homemaking' Hannah as *Mrs.* Hannah Peabody. This evening, however, *Prime Insight* has just learned that 'Homemaking' Hannah is breaking up her home and divorcing her
husband."

Neil tried to keep his smile in place, but his jaw automatically clenched, a small vein pounding with tension. If Hannah was going to be put through the wringer, he wanted to
be here for her—but it sure as hell wouldn't be a picnic to
witness.

"Mrs. Peabody," began the reporter, then stopped herself
with a little theatrical shake of her head. "I mean, *Miss* Whitmore. I'm sure I won't be the first one to make that mistake!
Anyway, can you tell us, what was it that took the final toll
on your happy home? Was it that tabloid story? Or was that
just a catalyst, the last straw for what's been rumored to be
your workaholic lifestyle?"

Neil was just about ready to strangle this reporter with his
bare hands. But when he saw Hannah's reaction, or rather,
her lack of one, he found himself amazed.

The reporter clearly wanted to rouse an emotional response
from her subject—she certainly had from Neil. But something
had transformed Hannah Whitmore tonight. She sat before
America as a woman who'd discovered her own mind, and
with it her own style, and temperament. The new Hannah
wasn't about to be put on the defensive—or to start hopping
about frantically to someone else's agenda.

"First of all, Sylvia," began Hannah in a warm, intelligent,
and perfectly composed voice, "why don't you call me *Hannah*? I'd prefer to be known that way, especially to my audience. And second of all, I'm sure that people in the media

would love to make hay about that ridiculous story in the tabloids, but the truth is, my divorce is nothing new.''

"What do you mean, 'nothing new'?'' asked the reporter, leaning in with the intensity of a hungry predator.

"I mean that I've *been* divorced from my husband for some time,'' explained Hannah. "The marriage didn't work out. It's a fact of life today for many, many people. No one wants to go through the pain and heartache of a failed relationship or a failed marriage—especially in full view of the public; but, when it happens, as it did for me, the best thing to do is accept the inevitable and get on with your life, as I've been trying to do.''

"But you've been using the name *Mrs. Peabody* for some time,'' pointed out the reporter. "Do you mean to tell your millions of fans that you've been divorced for years? That you've been misleading, some might even say *lying*, to your audience?''

"Yes.''

Neil watched with interest as the reporter simply stared at Hannah for an awkward moment. It seemed that Hannah's unpretentious honesty had actually *stunned* the woman into silence, realized Neil, a glow of pride brightening his eyes. The veteran reporter was probably so used to interviewing people who'd sing and dance their way around the whole truth that she didn't know what the heck to do when they simply confessed it outright.

"Well, ah,'' began the reporter a moment later, "you can't . . . ah . . . expect your audience to be happy about that.''

"No,'' agreed Hannah. "I expect anyone who's been lied to would feel angry and betrayed. But, you see, I don't doubt that, like me, many of my viewers don't have very happy homes, either; yet they may have also tried to put on a face to the world that they are happy. Whether we're married, divorced, or single, I think all of us very human beings can relate to trying to live up to some standard or expectation, yet feeling as though we won't ever do it. Feeling as though we're not good enough—that we don't measure up.''

"Uh . . . yes,'' said the reporter, her expression softening slightly. "I suppose I never thought of it like that . . . in fact, I do believe you received a Cable Ace Award for a *Homemaking* episode addressing that subject.''

Hannah nodded at once. "Yes, it was called 'Re-creating Your Home After Your Love Moves Out,' and I share the award with Greta Green, *Homemaking*'s very talented head writer. Greta and I both love doing the traditional *Homemaking* themes of decorating and entertaining—of creating the 'perfect' home. But it is our sincerest hope that we get the chance to expand *Homemaking*'s themes to include topics that are informative and insightful to people who live in an *imperfect* world."

"Like?"

"Well, like decorating a family home on a *limited* budget; cooking fun meals with children who don't get enough of your attention; tips for a single person on making a small living space homey; or easy ways to pull yourself together and feel good about yourself, whether you're a harried office worker or a stay-at-home spouse."

Neil noticed that one of the technicians with a headset was now signaling the reporter.

"That's quite fascinating, Hannah. I'm sure we'll all be watching with anticipation as your show makes its move from cable to this very network next month. Thank you."

"And thank *you*," added Hannah, "for the chance to explain everything to my *Homemaking* viewers."

The reporter smiled, then turned to the camera. "And now back to Case Cross in New York. . . ."

Neil felt a relieved breath escape his lungs as he finally relaxed his tensely folded arms. He waited until Hannah finished shaking hands with the reporter and her crew, and then he approached her.

Hannah smiled up at him as he snaked a strong arm around her waist and led her from the room.

"Well," began Hannah, looking up at him, "what did you think?"

"I think . . ." he said softly, "that I've never met a more courageous woman in my life."

"That's very sweet," said Hannah with a sigh, "but I hope you think that when I'm out of a job and crying on your shoulder."

"You really think your boss would fire you after that brilliant interview?"

"Neil, I signed a five-year contract with very little rights or protection. And, the unhappy fact is, I've just flushed Chip Saunders's arduously constructed image of Happy Hannah Homemaker right down the crapper.''

"I see," murmured Neil as his arm tightened around her. "Tell you what, why don't we worry about falling into that chasm when we come to it?"

Hannah smiled. "That's a deal."

The two were approaching the hotel's lobby. Most of the people from the rehearsal party had already gone up to their rooms or back to other hotels in anticipation of the next day's events. But about thirty or so guests were still laughing around the bar and the large stone fireplace.

"Do you really want to go back to the party?" asked Neil.

"No," said Hannah softly. "I told Holly she could find me in my suite if she needed me. Let's go up there."

Neil nodded and started forward, but Hannah stopped him. "Neil, would you mind if we just used the side steps? I'd rather not see anyone but you just now."

"I'm shocked, Miss Whitmore," teased Neil. "You'd stoop to using the *servant's* staircase?"

Hannah touched Neil's cheeks. "Whatever gets me into your arms faster is first-class travel by my estimation."

"Well, then, my dear," said Neil, sweeping her into his tuxedo-clad arms, "I believe your transport has arrived."

"I don't know what the fuss is all about," complained Tiffany Townsend at the hotel's bar. "So she cut her hair and put on some lipstick. She's still a skanky scarecrow who's probably frigid in the sack."

Clark Von Devon blew a smoke ring with one of the bar's complimentary cigars and picked up his martini glass. "Oh, cuz, you're just tanked again. Not to mention obscenely jealous."

Tiffany turned sharply on Clark. "Screw you, you little ungrateful parasite, whose side are you on, anyway?"

Clark looked horrified that he'd let the booze loosen his tongue. "Y-yours, of course, Tif, I was just pulling your chain, that's all. Lighten up, will you? I think you're way too obsessive over this guy. After all, he's just some nobody jarhead guard, right?"

Tiffany's eyes narrowed. "I don't like your attitude, Clark.

Obsessions make life interesting, and"—she poked him in the shoulder—"you're *supposed* to be arranging an ironclad way for me to get his undivided attention."

"Right, of course," put in Clark quickly. "Got it all figured out. Tomorrow's the day it'll all happen."

"*What* will all happen? Burglars, kidnappers, assassins?"

Clark stalled for time by taking a long sip of his martini. "Kidnappers," he said quickly. That sounded good to him.

"Really," purred Tiffany, suddenly pacified. "Tell me what you've got planned."

"Oh, Tif, that would be giving away the surprise," cooed Clark. "And your *surprised* reaction is what will help convince that jarhea—uh, I mean, uh, Ryan that you're really in grave danger."

Luckily for Clark the vodka martinis were starting to dull Tiffany's claws. She smiled in a fuzzy kind of way and put her arm around Clark's shoulder. "Wow, I underestimated you, sweetie."

"Just be patient," whispered Clark. "I'm not even sure when those kidnappers will strike. Could happen early in the day or late in the evening, after the reception. It's their call."

God, I'm good, thought Clark. His cousin was buying it all, hook, line, and sinker. And by the time she figured out that nobody was going to kidnap her prissy butt, Clark would be on his way to Palm Beach with some college friends— along with a few carefully filched bills from Tiffany's tasteful Chanel bag.

"Okay, Clark, honey. I can't wait!"

"Jimmy," said a pleasingly low male voice nearby, "give me two frog waters to go."

Tiffany turned at the familiar voice. "Why, look who's here, the junior Ryan. And doesn't he clean up nicely!"

J. J. tried not to blanch when Tiffany strolled over to him and ran her hand up and down his tuxedo-clad arm. He'd been so enamored with Holly all evening that he'd barely even noticed Tiffany was at the party, too.

"Oh. Hello, Tiffany."

"Hello yourself, Ryan junior," she purred. "You know, I might just need a little midnight snack tonight. I'll even throw in a few bills to make it worth completing the job this time."

Artfully, Tiffany turned just enough for J. J. to glimpse a

cascading string of antique and, no doubt, obscenely expensive pearls. The accessory was clearly there to emphasize the dramatic dip in the back of her slinky red dress, a feature that exposed a tantalizing length of perfectly tanned flesh.

"What do you think, junior Ryan? Wanna special deliver yourself in an hour or two?"

J. J. sighed. The girl certainly had no shame. Or else she just assumed he was a complete moron. Either way, he didn't have the stomach for Tiffany's brand of "romance."

"Maybe I'll catch you later," said J. J.

"What do you mean, *maybe*?" whined Tiffany with a pouty little lift of her chin.

"I *mean*, the sad fact is, you're beneath my standards, Tiffany Townsend."

A few minutes later, as J. J. strode toward Holly Whitmore, he decided that the look on Tiffany's face was more than worth the price of getting his tuxedo dry-cleaned.

Actually, a martini in the face did make the eyes sting. But what the heck, thought J. J., as his ma always said, if you want to dance a jig, you've got to pay the piper.

J. J. approached Holly cautiously. He'd noticed her standing alone by one of the lobby's tall windows, and he couldn't help but slow his steps, just to have the time to admire her.

Her white dress with the satin collar and cuffs outlined a charming figure, making her appear both innocent and alluring at the same time. It was an intriguing combination in the woman herself—one J. J. found rare and very special.

Though he preferred to see her shoulder-length chestnut mane loose and free, he did like the stylish way she'd twisted it up off her neck tonight. It seemed to accent the auburn highlights, letting them shimmer under the room's romantic lighting to give her hair an even more lustrous richness. And it exposed her pretty neck—an area of flesh he longed to taste.

"Excuse me, Holly," J. J. finally said softly, trying to keep his intense feelings under control, "I thought you might like more champagne."

The sound of a man's low voice at her ear nearly made Holly jump through the glass.

"Oh, J. J.!" she blurted, half-turning toward him. "You

startled me. How are you? Are you having a nice time at the party?''

"Yes, of course," said J. J., extending the champagne flute. "Are you?"

"Oh . . . what?" asked Holly, feeling a little flustered by his sudden appearance. "I was just standing here remembering those parties my parents used to have at the mansion."

"Sure . . . my ma used to go on and on about them, especially the staff picnics." J. J. glanced forlornly at the proffered champagne glass. "Please, Holly, if you don't take the champagne, I'm sure to look like one of those two-fisted drinkers. Not such a rotten image if you've got a man's drink," he added with a wry smile, "but this is froggy water."

"Oh, I'm sorry—" Holly said with an amused smile as she reached out. "Thanks."

"Anyway," J. J. continued, "those parties were usually big barbecues, weren't they? The whole staff would bring their families to the mansion for the day."

"That's right," jumped in Holly. "The third Saturday of every August. I used to love playing with everyone's kids. We'd run around the grounds, and swim, and take turns on my swing . . . but I don't remember playing with you, J. J. Why is that?"

"I was afraid of you."

"Afraid of *me*? You're kidding! Why?"

"You were . . . different. Rich kid, you know. I thought . . ." J. J. wanted to be honest with her, but it wasn't easy. His gaze swept away a moment.

"Come on," she prompted, her small hand lightly touching his shoulder. The light touch nearly undid him. "What did you think?"

J. J. took a deep breath, less for courage in being truthful than to steady his wildly beating heart. "I, uh . . . I thought you'd get angry at me or something and have my mother fired."

"Oh, my God, J. J., that's ludicrous!"

J. J. shrugged. "It had happened to a friend of mine in Middletown. Chauffeur's kid had a beef with an owner's kid and before you knew it, chauffeur's out of work."

"Oh, I see." Holly stared out the window a moment. "Is there that much of a gulf between us then?"

"I don't know, colleen," teased J. J. as he touched the lip of his crystal flute to hers with a pretty little clink, "I made it over here, didn't I?"

"Yes," said Holly. She had been trying hard not to look into J. J.'s warm green eyes, but for a moment, she made the mistake of doing just that. They held such open affection for her that she nearly lost her composure.

Instantly, she glanced away, back toward the darkened glass, which reflected her own image back to her.

"Where's your fiancé?" J. J. suddenly asked softly.

Still looking toward the glass, Holly couldn't escape the uncomfortable truth of the sad expression that crossed her face. But by the time she turned to J. J., her practiced smile was back in place.

"He's around," she chirped.

"Where's your fiancé?" he asked again, his tone as disturbingly calm as if he hadn't asked the first time.

"I said, he's aroun—" Holly stopped herself then. *He wants to be my friend*, she realized. "Reggie said he had some business to take care of," Holly finally confessed. "He needed to pick up some faxes from his cigar plantation and get them to potential investors. Very important."

J. J. studied Holly's pensive face as it, in turn, studied the disappearing bubbles in her champagne. His hand itched to touch her chin, to tip her face toward his and lightly kiss her lips. To give her something that would put the sparkle back in her eyes, the bubble back in her laugh.

Brother, he'd never wanted a woman this much in all his life. It actually hurt.

"Holly, would you do me one favor tonight?" asked J. J., his eyes burning brightly in the romantic lighting of the beautiful hall. "I want to show you something. It's just on the edge of the grounds."

Holly didn't answer. She seemed to be holding her breath.

" 'Twill only take a wee amount of your time," added J. J. with as harmless a smile as he could muster.

Holly hesitated another moment. Finally, she gave the slightest nod, and J. J.'s smile broke into an elated grin.

"Come on," he said and took her hand.

Without another word, he led her to the rear door of the mansion's lobby. The night was a mild one, and as they crossed the dewy lawn, J. J. pointed out some of the brilliant constellations overhead—the ones he'd learned from his older brother.

Holly breathed in the scents of the spring blossoms and the salty freshness of the sea air. She liked the way her hand fit into J. J.'s, liked the way he shortened his strides so that she wouldn't have to gallop to keep up—Reggie seldom took the trouble anymore.

"Where are we going?" Holly finally asked as they neared the edge of the mansion's grounds.

"You'll see!" J. J. felt the excitement mount within him. Joe Stokes and Charlie Baxter had helped him with the surprise earlier in the day, and he couldn't wait until Holly saw it.

Finally, they were within sight of the old oak tree. Holly stopped when she saw J. J.'s surprise. She actually rubbed her blue eyes a moment to make sure she was seeing clearly.

"My swing," she whispered in disbelief.

"Yes," said J. J., squeezing her hand.

"You did this? For me?"

"Yes," said J. J.

The look on Holly's face was all the thanks J. J. needed, because he knew in that moment he'd done what he'd set out to do. He'd touched her heart.

"Well, John James Ryan, I guess I've only got one thing to say to you now."

"What's that?"

Holly hesitated for only a moment before she kicked off her heels and launched herself toward the old oak tree.

"Race ya!" she cried, the bubbling back in her laughter.

J. J. was more than ready to take off in pursuit.

Back inside the mansion, in the glowing light of the carved stone hearth, a pair of ice-blue eyes were watching the movements of a woman in red.

"Tiffany Townsend, Tiffany Townsend . . ." Herbert had been chanting the young woman's name over and over to himself for ten minutes, ever since he'd witnessed her little martini-throwing scene with the tuxedo kid.

For a moment there, Herbert actually sympathized with the kid; after all, he himself had endured his share of bar baths to know that vodka stung when it hit the eyes. But it *had* been an amusing little event, not to mention a lucky one.

After all, with Hannah clearly out of the picture financially, he'd have to get some ducks in order again. Sure, he had that other project hatching, but you could never really count on anything these days—unstable economies around the globe, and all. It always paid to keep options open.

So, when the kid pronounced the young woman's name, Herbert's mind couldn't help but click into action. A few discreet inquiries was all it took to confirm his suspicions with glee. Tiffany Townsend was the daughter of one of the biggest real estate tycoons in the nation.

"Ah, yes," murmured Herbert to himself as he sauntered toward the exposed back of the girl's scarlet gown. "Fresh meat, at long last."

Chapter
Twenty-nine

"Okay, so I heard the one about the wedding dress, and the wedding bouquet, is there one about the cake?" asked Neil with a smile as he stroked Hannah's hair. "I love to eat cake."

"Well, let's see . . ." Hannah snuggled against him under the goose-down bedcovers in her lovely suite, her cheek against his naked chest. "There's one about the wedding cake. They say if an unmarried woman sleeps with a piece of wedding cake under her pillow, she'll dream of her own wedding."

"Kind of a messy tradition, isn't it?"

"Not if you use enough plastic wrap."

"Ah, I see . . . and did you ever try that one yourself? The cake under the pillow, I mean—not just the plastic wrap."

"Yes. It was my second cousin Veronica's wedding—in Boston. I guess I was about twelve, so you must have been fifteen. You were working a lot with Benji then, weren't you? Helping him maintain the cars?"

"Mmmm, yes, I think so."

"I used to spy on you constantly. And you just treated me like a little kid."

Neil laughed. "You were a little kid." For a moment he was silent, his fingers playing with the newly cut strands of her silky golden hair. "I remember how light your hair would get by the end of the summer back then. Golden, like it is now."

"It's lucky I fell down the grand staircase that night ten years ago," said Hannah with a laugh, "or you might never have taken pity on me, let alone noticed me."

"It wasn't pity," said Neil, amazed that she'd use such a word. "And I've got news for you, sweetheart, I noticed you long before your coming-out party."

"What do you mean?"

"I mean, a few years after that cake sleeping episode, when you were fifteen, about to turn sixteen, you had taken a long stroll alone along the Cliff Walk. You had on this pretty yellow sweater and a tight pair of blue jeans, and you stopped by a hillside to pick some daisies."

"Neil!" Hannah rose onto her elbow to look at him. "How can you remember something so trivial?"

"It wasn't trivial, that's what I'm trying to tell you, Hannah. It was the moment I fell in love with you."

Hannah's gray eyes widened. "But I was alone. How could you have—"

"Your father asked me to follow you, at a distance. He wanted me to keep an eye on you.... Actually, now that I think about it," he added with a laugh, "you were my very first protection job."

Hannah shook her head, astonished. "He never said a word."

"You'd unsettled him the week before by disappearing on a long walk. He knew how headstrong you were, and your penchant for wanting to explore things by yourself. He didn't want to tie you down, and he didn't want to argue with you, so he simply decided, for his own peace of mind, to ask me to look after you—without letting you know, of course."

"Heaven help me . . ." Hannah murmured as she collapsed back into Neil's arms. "You did one heck of a good job. I never even suspected."

"I watched you from a distance. You found this hillside of wildflowers tucked between the cliffs, so you climbed up and began picking out the daisies until you had this pretty little bouquet.''

Neil began to stroke her hair again. ''I remember how you tucked one behind your ear and brought another to your nose to smell. Then you just sat on the hillside and looked out at the ocean for a long time.''

''Why didn't you say something?''

''I promised your father I'd keep my distance. That day, anyway.''

''I wish you'd broken that promise.''

''No, Hannah. I'm not a man who breaks promises.''

''Yes,'' said Hannah softly. ''I know that about you, Neil. In fact, that's one of the things I love about you.''

Neil placed a soft kiss at the top of Hannah's head. ''Lovely, bright, and unpretentious,'' he whispered.

''What?''

''That's what I thought about that fifteen-year-old girl on that sunny day. There she was among all those wildflowers, and I thought, she's just like them—just like the daisies she's gathering. Lovely, bright, and unpretentious. A good person. A good girl . . . and now, a good woman.''

Neil met Hannah's eyes as she moved to look at him. ''And you're a good man, Neil Ryan.''

''I'm glad you think so.''

''You know, Neil, I never told you, but I used to chart the summer by the Big Dipper in the night sky. When spring would flow to summer and summer to fall, the cup turned on itself. It felt to me as if it were spilling its contents—all the good things going with it. Summer's end would come, and the cup would be empty.''

Neil searched Hannah's eyes in question.

Finally she explained. ''I don't want the summer to end for us, Neil.''

''Does it have to?''

''You said that love doesn't change anything. But that was wrong, I think. Love can transform people—it can change whole lives.''

''Change isn't always easy,'' warned Neil.

''I know, and neither is love.''

Neil sighed and leaned back against the pillows. He studied

the mural on the ceiling for a moment, pink clouds of dawn against the blue promise of a clear sky.

"So what was it you dreamed all those years ago?" he found himself asking. "When you were twelve and put the wedding cake under your pillow . . . did you dream of your elopement with Peabody?"

"No, Neil," said Hannah plainly. "I dreamed of you."

The ring of the phone interrupted the couple, and Hannah found herself debating whether to answer. But that only lasted three rings; by the fourth, Neil had picked up the receiver himself.

"Miss Hannah Whitmore's suite," said Neil politely.

His expression seemed puzzled as he listened to the voice on the other end. "Yes . . . but she's right here, let me put her on—"

Hannah reached out for the phone. It wasn't necessary, the phone conversation was already over. The caller had delivered his message and hung up.

Neil replaced the receiver, then slowly met Hannah's questioning eyes. "He didn't want to speak to you," said Neil, the blue of his eyes looking much less bright than it had a few moments before.

"Who was it?" asked Hannah, a knot of tension forming in her stomach.

"Chip Saunders," said Neil.

"Well? What did he—" It hit Hannah harder than she thought it would. The message was as clear as the miserable look on Neil's face.

"I'm fired, aren't I?" whispered Hannah.

"Yes," said Neil softly. "As of tonight."

Holly swung her legs up and back as J. J. pushed her gently in her old swing. The night seemed like an old friend now, the sea air a pair of welcoming arms.

She could hardly believe J. J. had gone to the trouble of digging her little wooden swing out of the mansion's store-rooms. It was just the same as she remembered it, too—hard pine with little blue flowers painted around the edges. In fact, it looked as though someone had refreshed the paint recently. She wouldn't be surprised if J. J. had done it himself this afternoon.

"Is that really true?" asked Holly as J. J. pushed her back gently, his warm touch like a subtle caress.

"It's absolutely true. Cross my heart. This swing was not *always* yours."

"But I carved my initials under the seat! It has to be my swing."

"It *was* yours, but it wasn't *always*. Someone had the swing before you."

"Who? It couldn't have been Hannah because I found the swing myself when I was five."

"See what I mean, you *found* it—in storage probably, just like I did."

"Yes, but whose swing was it?"

"There's an older man who works here, Joe Stokes. He once worked on these grounds decades ago, and he told me that your grandmother Edith was the one who'd wanted the swing put up. Apparently she even helped Joe do it one afternoon."

"You're kidding!" cried Holly in delighted astonishment. "Grandmother *Edith*? God, I can hardly believe it."

"Why?"

"She's always been such a . . . well, a snob, I'm sorry to say. I just can't picture her ever doing something so wonderfully simple."

"All of us have kids' hearts at one time, Holly. Even if it's only for a short time."

"Well, this really brings *me* back." Holly kicked her legs out as she swung. She was finally tall enough now to touch the lowest branches with her feet. "God, I was so happy here."

J. J. could tell. Her voice was even lighter, bubbling with more joy with each pass of the swing. He felt mesmerized by the image of Holly in white satin, first gliding toward him and then away, a luminous image against the night's darkness. Like a ghost, she seemed to float before him, an elusive spirit that he could reach out and touch one moment only to lose again in the next.

"Holly, remember what we talked about this afternoon?"

"You mean my worries about moving to England? Or your teaching aspirations?"

"Actually, what I have to say would encompass both. Remember when I mentioned John Lennon—how he'd studied art and I wondered what his teachers thought of him?"

"Yes?"

"Well, did you know what John Lennon's aunt told him when he was living with her?"

"No."

"She told him to give up the guitar. Said he'd never make any real money at it."

"Good Lord!" Holly laughed. "I guess he was smart not to listen to bad advice, huh?"

"That's right," said J. J., suddenly catching Holly's swing and bringing her to a stop. "Or to give up what he really and truly wanted."

Holly's blue eyes looked up to J. J. as he moved to stand in front of her. With exquisite care he brought his hand to her face and touched her cheek.

"J. J.—" whispered Holly, but that's all she said. She didn't try to stop him as he slowly leaned down and touched his lips to hers. The kiss was wonderful—chaste yet clearly full of passion and yearning for them both. In fact, the chemistry was so palpable between them that it actually frightened Holly. And, after a few moments, she forced herself to break away.

"I-I've had too much champagne," she said, trying to laugh as she rose from the swing and straightened the skirt of her dress. "J. J., you'll have to forgive me for acting so silly. You won't mind if we go back to the mansion now?"

It took J. J. a moment to find his voice. "Course not, colleen," he said, trying his best to alleviate her embarrassment. The last thing he'd wanted her to feel at the touch of his lips was embarrassment. " 'Twill be me pleasure to escort ya."

J. J. helped Holly to find her shoes. She quickly stepped into them, and, within another few minutes, they were within sight of the mansion's back door.

"Holly," said J. J. softly, touching her arm and leading her a few steps into the shadows of a nearby weeping willow.

"Yes, J. J.?"

"I know you're getting married tomorrow, but it seems to me, if I don't say it now, I'll go through the rest of my stupid life wondering 'what if.' "

Holly's brow furrowed. "J. J., please don't—"

"No, just listen to me. You have to know how I feel." J. J. stepped closer, his hand reaching out to finger an escaped chestnut curl at the nape of her neck. "I lied earlier this evening."

"Lied? About what?"

"When I said I was afraid of you because of your being the owner's daughter—that wasn't entirely true. I was also afraid because I had the worst sort of crush on you."

"God, how could you, J. J.!" exclaimed Holly with a laugh. "I was such a ratty little tomboy, then. All I ever wore were jeans and T-shirts, and I was such a god-awful plain little girl."

J. J. shook his head. "You were full of laughter and joy. It just shined from your face. And I swear to God the first time I saw you I thought I was struck by that cupid at the back of the mansion."

"Oh, J. J., that's so sweet."

"It's much more than sweet. Even in this little time we've spent together, I feel the same. And I *know* you're having doubts about this marriage."

Holly took a deep breath and expelled it. "I don't know what to say, J. J. It's just too much for me right now."

"Is this too much, too?" asked J. J. as he leaned in and touched his lips lightly to hers again. When he lifted his head, her robin's-egg eyes were shimmering like blue silver in the moonlight. J. J. was certain that no matter what happened, he would carry that image to his grave.

"The British Crown may not have given me a title, Holly," he whispered, "but I'd be a knight for you."

"Oh, J. J . . ." She wondered how it was possible to be engaged to one man while feeling so much for another. Was she making a mistake? She just didn't know, and the confusion made her feel even worse than the idea of hurting the wonderful man declaring himself in front of her.

Holly's gaze fell to the damp grass, one salty wet droplet descending with it. "I do care for you, J. J., but I can't . . . I just can't stop what's already started. Please try to understand."

J. J. sighed heavily, knowing there was nothing more he could do. Anything else would just sound like a pathetic attempt at begging—and the last thing he could bear right now on top of Holly's rejection was her pity.

"No chance then, colleen?" he asked, forcing a lightness back into his weak voice.

Holly looked back into J. J.'s face and gently touched his cheek. "In another life, maybe," she whispered. "I just think it's too late . . . so many people are expecting the wedding. And I made a promise. I won't go back on it now."

With a sad but resigned nod, J. J. leaned close and touched her lips again. This time in farewell.

Holly closed her eyes for the kiss, and realized that the intense passion behind it was making her shiver from the top of her head to the tips of her Italian shoes. The kiss was so magnificent, so powerful, Holly actually kept her eyes shut after it ended, hoping to prolong the feeling. She sighed softly, wondering yet again why Reggie's kisses no longer touched her so deeply—or if, in retrospect, they ever had.

"J. J., I have one last question for you. Do you think—" she began a few moments later. But when she opened her eyes, he was already gone.

Chapter Thirty

"Danny?"

"Yeah, Daisy?"

"Have you noticed something a little peculiar about Sir Reggie's behavior tonight?"

"Yeah, Daisy."

It was well past one in the morning. Holly had gone up to bed, and the ghosts of Dan and Daisy Doyle were hovering above the lobby bar. Carraway was there, drinking and talking with his three golfing buddies he'd met just that morning—wealthy American businessmen interested in investing in Carraway's cigar factory.

"Why would a man neglect his bride on the night before his wedding?"

"Your suspicion's in the ballpark, Daisy, but you'll get nowhere on deductions if you look at the situation from the romantic angle."

"What's that supposed to mean?"

"Just try asking the question another way: What's a man with title, money, and connections doing hustling up investors the night before his wedding?"

"Hmmm . . . yes, you're right, I see what you mean."

"I'm often right, sweetie, you know that."

"Don't get cocky."

"So I know Ryan did a standard check on the man," continued Dan, *"but I think we ought to get involved."*

"I agree—as long as there'll be no more faxing yourself across the ocean."

"Oh, Daisy, don't start getting the vapors about that again!"

"I mean it! What would happen if the circuits got jammed halfway through the transmission? You'd be stuck two miles under the Atlantic!"

"Calm yourself, kitten. Let's just start with a routine tail and see what we see."

"Oh, all right."

It was past two in the morning when Herbert Peabody tiptoed out of Tiffany Townsend's room and back to his own. When he stepped inside, he found that a folded piece of buff-colored hotel stationery had been slipped under his door.

Herbert read the note and went to the phone, slipping out of his lipstick-stained jacket before he sat down on the side of the bed and dialed a room on the second floor.

"Gareth, it's me," said Herbert quietly. "Got your note. What's going on?"

Herbert listened intently for a moment and then sighed. "No, don't come to my room. Just take a casual stroll outside—act as if you need a walk and a smoke. There's a large oak tree on the northeastern edge of the rear grounds. Meet me there in ten minutes."

After hanging up, Herbert went to his briefcase and checked an address book for a number. Quickly, he dialed, then waited a good thirty seconds before the ringing line was picked up.

"Sweeney? It's me, Parkinson," began Herbert. "Don't give me any lip. I'll call you when I call you if it's two in the afternoon or four in the morning, have you got that? . . . Good.

"Now listen to me, I have the information you need to get into this wedding. Listen carefully and, for Christ's sake, *write it all down*. Ready? . . . All right.

"There are over a dozen guests who received invitations but declined on the RSVP. Their names will still be on the pass list at the front gate, so be sure to say that you've had a last-minute change in plans and are able to attend. Have you got that?

"Use the names Simon Kingsfield and Wes Pratt . . . What? No, *two* T's, you moron. Now get some fake IDs done, just in case . . . What's that? No, I've never met the woman you're grabbing, but like I told you she's supposed to be the queen of kitty litter. Remember her name is Edith Channing Williamson, and about five years ago she was worth close to thirty million—she's probably worth even more now."

Herbert listened to his hired gun go on for about ten seconds then broke in. "Look, I've got an appointment. But it's like I told you, if the woman *does* show, it'll be easy money. She's already so paranoid about kidnapping, she'll write out a friggin' check within the first hour you take her. Okay, that's it. See you tomorrow."

Herbert smiled as he hung up the phone. He had so many potential little moneymaking projects going he was starting to feel like the friggin' Wall Street wheeler-dealer whiz his tight-wad parents had always wanted.

"Gee, Mom and Dad," murmured Herbert as he grabbed a pullover sweater and headed for the door, a pompous little smile upturning his lips, "too bad you can't see me now."

"I've got to hand it to you, mate," murmured the tall, bearded man as he stood in the shadows of the big oak tree. "You were spot on with this particular game."

"I know what I'm doing, Gareth," snapped Herbert. "I told you that back in Monte Carlo."

"So you did. So you did."

"All right, then, where are they?"

The man who Holly knew as Reginald Carraway placed his lit cigar in his mouth and reached a hand into his jacket to retrieve three personal checks. His golfing companions from that morning had each made them out to what "Reggie" said was his company.

"Here you go, mate, all made out to H. P. Ventures, just like you told me."

Herbert's teeth flashed in the night after he checked the

notations. "My-oh-my, Gareth, just look at all those lovely zeroes."

"Bloody beautiful."

"I'll tell you what else will be beautiful," said Herbert. "Your wedding night."

"Righto!" cried the bearded man with a lewd laugh. "You know, the girl's been pretty much stiff-arming me as far as the sack goes. Claims she's a virgin, what! But she's not so hard on the eyes, so I won't mind a go at her tomorrow, know what I mean?"

"You idiot, I'm not talking about the sex—screw her, don't screw her—that's your affair. I'm talking about the wedding presents. The *money*!"

"Of course, of course."

"Fifty-fifty, Gareth, like we agreed. And don't hold out on me, or I'll be very unhappy."

"No problem, governor—"

"And watch the Cockney, will you? Christ, it took me three months to get you ready for this, don't blow it now."

"No, no, Herbert." Gareth stepped backward awkwardly and felt something bump his leg. He jumped around in terror that someone had come upon them only to see he'd backed up into a child's swing.

"Gareth, what the hell are you doing?"

"Christ, it's just a bloody child's swing," said Gareth in disgust. Angrily, he reached a hand up and yanked as hard as he could, determined to tear it down. But it didn't budge.

Someone had tied the thing very securely. Tied it to one of the sturdiest branches of the old oak tree. Gareth tried yanking again, but his efforts were in vain. It disturbed him for some odd reason.

"Gareth? Gareth! Just leave the swing alone, would you?" said Herbert impatiently. When the tall man's attention was finally back, Herbert continued.

"And remember, you can't cut out right away. You've got to put in at least two weeks with the girl. Get through most of the honeymoon and do your best to weasel some of the two million inheritance from her bank account. I've given you a laundry list of ways already."

"No prob. I'll use the old family illness thing like you said, then I'll disappear. Meet you in London, like we planned."

"That's right. Listen, Gareth, take a deep breath, all right? The hard part's over. And those investors won't know what's hit them until the first quarter when they'll be waiting for reports that never come. But H. P. Ventures will be out of business by then. It's a beautiful plan, isn't it?"

"That it is, mate," said Gareth as he glanced once more at the rope of the swing. "That it is."

"Hannah."

Beneath the bedcovers, Hannah tossed in her sleep, partially twisting her white silk nightgown around her legs.

"Hannah . . ."

She turned again, this time onto her side. When her slender body collided into Neil's solid form, she half awakened. Groggily, she draped her arm over his naked torso, just brushing the elastic top of his briefs.

"Hannah!"

"W-what?" Hannah's eyelids parted slightly. "Neil?"

Rising on her elbow, Hannah saw that Neil was sound asleep. With a yawn, she snuggled back down next to him and shut her eyes.

Just above her, Daisy Channing Doyle blew a frustrated chill into the room. *"Dan, what do you propose now?"*

Dan flitted about the suite in thought. When he spotted Hannah's laptop on her desk, he got an idea. *"Try calling her again, Daisy. And don't give up till she's awake."*

A few minutes later, Hannah was on her elbow again, looking down at Neil and wondering why she kept dreaming of someone calling her name. She was about to collapse back again when she realized something seemed amiss.

There was a glow. And it seemed to be coming from the middle of the room.

Hannah sat up higher in the bed and saw that the glow was coming from the antique desk, where she'd been working earlier. The screen of her laptop computer was fully up and on.

"That's really odd," whispered Hannah to herself. She had turned it off and lowered the screen hours ago, after that awful call from Chip Saunders had led her into phoning Greta Green.

With care, Hannah moved away from Neil and tossed the

edge of the bedcovers from her legs. After pausing a moment to straighten her twisted silk nightgown, she walked to the laptop and reached her hand out to flick it off. But something made her fingers hesitate.

"What the—?" she whispered again into the dark, not noticing the rustle of bedcovers across the room.

"Hannah?" called Neil sleepily from the bed. "Is something wrong?"

"Oh, Neil, I'm sorry I woke you. But it's my laptop. I could have sworn I'd turned it off."

"You did. I saw you."

"But now it's back on and . . . something must be wrong with it. I know it sounds crazy, but the laptop seems to be typing, um, *by itself*."

In the next second, Neil was sitting up and tossing the covers away. "Typing by itself, you say?"

"Yes." Hannah tried not to be distracted by the muscular male legs walking toward her, or those well-defined biceps, so she turned her eyes back to the computer screen. And what she saw there left her dumbfounded a moment.

"Neil, d-do you see what I see?" she finally asked, a shiver coming over her.

"Yes."

"The computer. It's not malfunctioning. It's typing *words*!"

"So I see," said Neil, his eyes skimming the screen with intense interest.

REGINALD = GARETH.
CIGARS MAY BE REAL
BUT HE BLOWS
SMOKE.

"What the heck does it mean?" whispered Hannah

"It's obviously a reference to Holly's fiancé," said Neil as he folded his arms across his chest then rubbed his chin. "Remember I told you about his cigar plantation—"

"Yes, of course, in the Dominican Republic. But what has that got to do with—"

"Wait," said Neil, gently touching her shoulder. "There's more. Look . . ."

Both Neil and Hannah watched and waited as more letters seem to type themselves onto the screen:

WEDDING A SCAM.
PEABODY IN ON IT.

"Oh, my God," said Hannah, her palm going to her forehead. "What the hell is this? Some new way of sending e-mail?"

Neil's eyebrow quirked. "You might say that."

Hannah frantically moved to the laptop. "But I don't have this plugged into a modem!" she cried as she saw the only wire running from the laptop was the kind that fed into an electrical outlet.

"Yes, Hannah. I know."

Suddenly, she stopped. "Neil, *why* are you so calm? What do you know about this? Is it some kind of prank?"

"No, Hannah. The thing of it is, I've gotten messages before like this . . . on my own computer, I mean. It's one of the ways they've, uh . . . communicated with me."

"They?" Hannah stared in confusion for a moment at Neil. And then her eyes slowly widened in shock. "Oh, my God," she whispered, backing up from the computer. "It's not—"

"Yep. It is."

"The ghosts," rasped Hannah with an unconscious shiver. "It's Dan and Daisy Doyle again, isn't it? They're trying to communicate with us!"

"Calm down, sweetheart. I'm certain they're on our side. They're trying to help."

"But help with *what* exactly?"

Neil studied the screen in thought. "Like I said, it's clearly about Reginald Carraway. But I already checked him out. His fortune is real, his assets are real. Nobody can falsify that much informa—"

"But who's *Gareth*, then?" interrupted Hannah, reading over the ghost-writing again.

"Well, Gareth seems to equal Reginald, according to Dan and Daisy, which means . . . Oh, no—" Neil stopped and crossed the room, sitting down heavily on the edge of the bed. "God, it can't be," he lamented to himself, shaking his head. "But it's the most logical conclusion."

"What is, Neil?" Hannah followed him to the bed and stood before him.

"Hannah, Sir Reginald Carraway checks out legitimately because he *is* legitimate, just like his cigar plantation."

"Then where's this supposed scam that Herbert is in on?"

"It's the man himself, honey. He's the scam. Whoever he is, he isn't the real Carraway. Maybe he has access to the real Carraway's accounts, his personal information, or maybe he's just gotten access to some expertly forged IDs. But my guess is that he's simply posing as Carraway."

"Oh, no," breathed Hannah, her face draining of color as her every nightmare was coming true. "I have to tell Holly."

"Wait," said Neil, catching Hannah's arm as she began to turn for the door. "We need evidence before we can accuse anyone."

"Yes, that's true," agreed Hannah. She sat down next to Neil on the bed. "Now that I think about it, Holly's sure to ask me where I'm getting my information. Then what will I tell her? That two ghosts typed it out on my laptop!"

"Let me call someone at Scotland Yard," suggested Neil. "They can get us a picture faxed as soon as possible."

"Yes, that's a good idea."

"Unless . . ." Neil sat down a moment on the bed.

"Unless this Gareth *looks* like Carraway," guessed Hannah.

"Right . . . in which case, since we've got"—Neil checked the bedside clock—"a little more than eight hours till your sister says, 'I do,' I suggest we try for something that can't be disputed."

"Like?"

"Well, for instance," said Neil, rubbing the back of his neck, "a fingerprint would work."

"But how would we get one? We can't exactly ask the man to roll his hands into police ink."

"No."

"How about his room's doorknob?" asked Hannah.

Neil shook his head. "Too many other fingerprints. We need something that he alone may have touched—or, at the least, only one or two other people."

Hannah paced the room and paced the room but could think of nothing—until she passed by the antique desk again. She noticed the notes she'd been scribbling on a tablet earlier in the day. She'd been working on a sidebar for her book about weddings. The notes were on the traditions of giving toasts . . . *toasts*!

"I've got it, Neil!" cried Hannah.

"What, honey?"

"Wedding toasts! They're accompanied by drinks from champagne glasses. Get it?"

Neil shook his head. "I don't know what—"

"I bought Holly and Reggie special gold-rimmed flutes for their wedding. I gave it to them tonight for their rehearsal party."

"Bride and groom flutes, right? I remember," said Neil quickly, the excitement now evident in his tone.

"Yes, all we have to do is get to Reggie's groom glass before the kitchen staff washes it."

"Holy cow, let's go!"

"Wait, Neil!" cried Hannah as he went for the door.

"What?"

"You may want to put on your pants first."

Chapter Thirty-one

"Holly?"

Hannah opened her suite's front door to a young woman bearing little resemblance to the fashion plate that had waltzed into the hotel two days before. Wearing old, worn blue jeans and a flannel shirt, Holly looked like her old self again, complete with hair tied back in a messy ponytail.

It would have felt refreshing to Hannah if her sister's eyes hadn't betrayed serious strain and her face hadn't seemed so pale.

"Holly, is everything all right?"

"Sure, Hannah. I'm just a little confused, you know? Would you mind talking a little?"

"Of course not, come in. Sit down. Have some coffee. . . ."

In the suite's bathroom, Neil had just finished turning off the shower. As he stepped out of the large marble tub and began to towel off, he realized that Hannah was speaking with someone.

"Thanks," came Holly's voice. "You know, Grandmother Edith really *is* coming. She actually phoned me from Boston to apologize for missing the rehearsal party, but she said she'd be stepping into her limo right after she hung up with me.''

Neil wrapped a towel around his waist and stepped closer to the bathroom door, opening it just a crack to hear better.

''I'll believe it when I see it,'' said Hannah. ''But what's this about being confused? Are you okay?''

''I didn't sleep very well. Actually, I was up thinking for most of the night.'' Holly sighed and was silent a moment. ''I tried to tell myself it was nothing. I was hoping to feel differently this morning. But I don't, and it's got me very confused.''

''Whoa, slow down. *What's* got you confused?''

''I have all these feelings for him, Hannah, and I feel so strange marrying Reggie today when I think I've . . .'' Holly's voice trailed off.

''When you're what?'' prompted Hannah. ''What are you trying to say?''

''I think I've fallen in love with J. J. Ryan.''

''J. J.!'' exclaimed Hannah in delighted surprise. *''Really?''*

''It's such a mistake, and I feel so ashamed. It's like I've turned into some fickle little airhead or something. And I hope you can talk some sense back into me.''

Neil closed his eyes and clenched his fists, forcing himself to keep still and stay silent. He wanted nothing more than to burst into the room and tell Holly to stop her marriage—tell her that his little brother was a true knight, while her present fiancé was certain to turn up with tarnished armor. But, lack of evidence aside, his attire wasn't exactly appropriate for the encounter.

Just let Hannah handle it, he told himself as he folded his arms tensely across the muscles of his bare chest.

''Holly, I don't think you're being an airhead. Or fickle. I think you're having serious doubts, and you should call off the wedding.''

''No, I promised Reggie—and I promised myself. This is what I've always wanted, Hannah. I can't call it off now.''

''You *can* Holly, everything will be all right. Just tell Reggie that you need more time to think.''

''But, Hannah, what if he won't give it to me? What if he gets angry? What if my little episode of cold feet ruins everything?''

"I don't think Reggie is who he claims to be, Holly. The man's not worthy of you."

"Oh, Hannah, how silly. What makes you say such a thing?"

"I—I have my reasons, you just have to believe me. After all, the man doesn't have any family or friends here for us to meet. Don't you find that peculiar, Holly? Don't you find it suspicious?"

"*Suspicious?* Hannah, are *you* feeling all right? Reggie has very little family still alive, I told you that already. And his friends are planning a reception for us in England, after our honeymoon."

"But . . . don't you even trust your own feelings, Holly? Listen to your heart. Listen to what it's trying to tell you."

Holly sighed again. "I'll think about it all a little longer. But, Hannah, until you hear differently from me, please don't do a thing to call the wedding off, okay?"

"Oh, Holly, how can you—"

"*Promise* me?"

Neil's jaw worked in frustration as he listened intently at the door.

"Okay, Holly," Hannah's voice finally consented, "I promise."

"Good. I think what I need to do is talk to Reggie. Maybe I just need him to reassure me—"

"NO! You can't do that!"

"My God, Hannah, don't get hysterical. Why can't I?"

"It's, ah . . . bad luck! Bad luck for the bride and groom to see each other before their wedding."

"Get a grip, Han. You must have been working too hard on that book of yours. Believe me, this is one time when seeing the groom before the wedding might just bring the bride *good* luck."

Geez, lamented Neil, clenching and unclenching his fists behind the bathroom door, *now I know how the ghosts must feel. Able to listen, but unable to say a damn thing!*

"But, Holly—"

"I'll see you later, Hannah. And remember your promise."

After Neil heard the front door close, he stepped out of the bathroom. Hannah stood in the middle of the suite, a white silk robe wrapped around her, her eyes cast down, her ex-

pression defeated. Finally, she looked up to find Neil staring
at her from across the room.

"You heard?" she asked.

"Yeah," said Neil. "If Holly goes to see 'Reggie,' I guar-
antee you she'll marry him today."

"Why?"

"Your sister's obviously very confused. In her heart she
may feel something for J. J., but her mind is telling her she's
obligated to another man. If Reggie truly is an impostor, he'll
use every charming trick in his book to get her down the aisle
today."

"There's got to be *something* I can do!"

Neil walked to Hannah and placed his hands on her shoulders. "Just be patient, sweetheart. We got the fingerprints last
night, they're already in the hands of my contacts. I've got
calls being made by my staff, trying to contact Carraway's
homes. Now all we can do is wait for something to come up
before the ceremony, then we'll have some real proof."

"But what if the proof doesn't come *today*?"

"Patience, Hannah. All we have now is our own suspicions."

"And the ghosts'."

"Yes. But a man's reputation is on the line here. We can't
start making accusations without proof."

"Even if it means that tonight my sister might be giving
her innocence to a man who's anything but?" asked Hannah
miserably, feeling as though she were being forced to relive
her own terrible choice in marrying Herbert Peabody.

Hannah turned from Neil and walked to the window. Why
did it feel so much worse now? wondered Hannah. Her own
anguish she could live with, but she could hardly bear to
watch its infliction on someone she loved.

Suddenly Hannah stopped. *This is what Neil must have felt
when he'd heard about my own elopement with Herbert Peabody*, she realized with a jolt. *Miserable and helpless.*

"I'm sorry, Hannah," said Neil. "But she's a grown
woman. In the end, this is her choice."

"I know it is," rasped Hannah, her eyes meeting Neil's
with level determination. "But I swear if that man hurts my
baby sister, I'll shoot him."

*   *   *

A few hours later, the guests began to arrive.

Limousines came, shiny black stretch ones, complete with bars, phones, and small-screen televisions. There were Mercedes, Rolls Royces, and BMWs, too, almost always chauffeur-driven, while the sportier models, usually Porsches and Astin Martins, were taken out by the owners themselves, who considered breaking speed limits one of the more exhilarating forms of weekend recreation.

At the ready were the polished, brightly smiling troops of Château du Coeur. As each guest entered the beautiful mansion, coats were taken, drinks served, and lounges pointed out with military efficiency.

The agenda looked elegantly simple for the afternoon. Hannah had gone over it with Maura about fifty times already. First there would be the receiving of guests in the lobby, then the assembling in the garden for the vows.

After the ceremony, a gourmet sit-down dinner would be served, followed by dancing to an orchestra in the grand ballroom and a more modern band on the lawn, where the hotel's tent was to be magically erected during the dinner. In the lobby, a harpist would lull the more mellow groups by the hearth. The wedding cake would also be displayed there for the entire day.

As Maura Ryan passed by that five-tiered, smoothly iced confection and made her way through the well-heeled crowd gathering in the lobby, she put in a quick pass by the table of cold hors d'oeuvres at the side of the room—just to make certain it was still a work of art.

As expected, the bowls of jumbo shrimp were being continually replenished, as were the imported caviar and freshly shucked Pacific oysters, flown in the day before along with fat juicy scallops that deep-sea divers had just harvested. And, thank goodness, the large ice sculpture of a cupid with his bow—a chilly little copy of the one on the hotel's rear grounds—was no longer leaning to one side or the other.

When Maura was satisfied that everything was running like clockwork and looking its level best, she searched out Hannah. The poor girl had been standing near the front door, shaking hand after hand, for over an hour. Maura saw the unwavering smile on Hannah's face and wondered whether she'd used toothpicks to keep the edges of her mouth fixed so well for so long.

"Everything's going smoothly, my dear," reassured Maura softly into Hannah's ear. "Chef Antonio sends his congratulations and says he will prepare, and I quote: 'de most sumptuous feast dat has ever come from my keechen.' "

"That's touching, truly," said Hannah.

"Are you all right?" whispered Maura, noticing the signs of worry in Hannah's gray eyes.

"Sure. Although, if I shake any more hands today, I may need a few skin grafts," Hannah whispered back, even as she found herself extending her palm yet again. "Oh, hello, Mr. Wallace, Mrs. Wallace, so glad you could make it."

"Good afternoon, Miss Whitmore," broke in a familiar male voice from behind her.

"Oh, Mr. Stokes, isn't it?" asked Hannah, turning to the gentleman who'd just greeted her.

"That's right," Maura affirmed. "Hello there, Joe."

"Good afternoon, Mrs. Ryan, at your service," said Joe with a slight bow. The older man appeared as dapper as ever in his black tuxedo, the red plaid vest and bow tie bringing out the ruddiness in his smiling sailor's complexion. But something was different today, realized Hannah.

"You shaved your beard, didn't you, Mr. Stokes?"

"Right you are!"

"You look even more handsome without it," said Hannah. "Doesn't he, Maura?"

"Indeed he does."

"Thank you kindly, ladies. I won't keep you. But, if you please, Miss Whitmore, I was wondering if your grandmother Edith has arrived yet? I'm quite lookin' forward to seein' her again."

"Again?" Hannah glanced at Maura then back to Joe Stokes.

"Yes . . . y'see, I was, ah . . . acquainted with your grandmother . . . many years ago, when I worked the grounds here for the Doyles. I was a very young man then, a ways more agile and strappin' sturdy then, o' course. Doubtful she'll remember me, but . . . well, I remember her, y'see?"

"Oh, I see," said Hannah solemnly. "Well, I hate to disappoint you, Mr. Stokes, but I wouldn't count on Grand-mother Edith being here today."

"Why is that, miss? If you don't mind my asking?"

"She's become a recluse," said Hannah with a shrug. "I honestly don't know why. She used to be so overbearing; but since her husband's death eight years ago, she never leaves her town house. She *says* she's afraid of kidnappers, but I think she's just isolated herself for so long that . . . well . . . I think she's just afraid, period."

Joe nodded his head gravely. "I'm truly sorry to hear that. But please do let me know if she does come, I'd be honored to make sure she has a pleasant day—whether she recalls me or no."

"Thank you, Mr. Stokes. That's very sweet."

After Joe departed, Maura tapped Hannah's shoulder. "Can you step away a moment?"

Hannah nodded and followed Maura into the hallway near the small library that was now being used as a coatroom.

"Neil told me that there's a bit of a problem with Holly's groom—one that you're *both* investigating?"

Hannah nodded again. "We're still waiting for some in-formation, but Holly's been having some doubts, too. . . . I expect you've dealt with this kind of thing before?"

Maura nodded reassuringly.

"Well," said Hannah, "I guess we'll just have to . . ." She shrugged, though her eyes were still filled with worry.

"Musicians call it improvisation," said Maura with a little smile. "And only those who've already practiced the standard tunes can do it the best."

"I know you're the best, Maura. So I won't worry."

Maura touched Hannah's shoulder. "That's precisely what I wanted to convey, dear. I'll do what I can to keep everyone calm and comfortable, no matter what happens."

Hannah sighed and kissed Maura on the cheek. "Thanks."

"You're very welcome," she said as she walked her back to the front door.

"Hannah!" a female voice suddenly called. Hannah turned from Maura to find a very tall, strong-shouldered woman with a curly cap of red hair. "You're sure a pretty sight for jet-lagged eyes."

"Greta Green! You actually made it!" Hannah exclaimed

as her best friend in the world gave her a tight hug.

"Let me look at you!" cried Greta. "Your transformation really stuck, huh?" she teased, taking in Hannah's shimmering golden hair, her exquisitely made-up face, and her figure-hugging ice-blue satin gown. "Baby, I still can't get over your guts."

"Thanks, Greta. But, like I told you last night on the phone, love changes everything."

"Aww, now you're sounding like a Top-40 song again."

"You want to meet him?"

"Of course."

Hannah took Greta's hand and led her through the lobby to the small office hidden behind the antique reception desk. Neil was back in his black tux and standing just inside the lobby, where he could keep an eye on the party and still be close to his security office—in case any word came in on Carraway.

"Wow," whispered Greta as they approached Neil. "You weren't exaggerating about the hunk factor with this one, were you?"

"Sometimes it just hurts to look at him," said Hannah sighing theatrically.

Both women giggled uncontrollably as they made their way to Neil, who looked decidedly uncomfortable having two giggling grown females on his hands—even if one of them was Hannah.

"Hello," he said awkwardly.

"N-Neil," began Hannah, pausing to giggle between words, "this is . . . my friend . . . from the *Homemaking* . . show. . . ."

"Greta Green," said the redhead in the evergreen linen suit, recovering from her fit a little quicker than Hannah.

Neil extended a hand. "Nice to meet you. Hannah's told me so much about you."

"Everything but the prison time, I hope!"

Neil stared at the woman grimly. "You're joking."

Greta turned to Hannah. "A bit of a stiff, isn't he?"

"He's *much* better than he used to be," said Hannah with a smile. "He just doesn't joke about criminal records."

"Really?" asked Greta, feigning seriousness. "Even yours?"

"Hey," broke in Neil, his blue eyes narrowing. "Are you girls *playing* with me?"

"Is that an invitation?" Greta asked Hannah, who started breaking up again. A few heads began turning their way.

"Sorry, Neil," said Hannah finally, "must be the tension. If I don't crack up, I'm sure I'll—"

"Crack up!" shrieked Greta.

Neil rolled his eyes as the two women began laughing yet again. Finally, Greta calmed down and turned to Hannah.

"Listen," she said, taking her friend's hands in her own. "I have some news from Chicago."

"I'm *not* fired?" asked Hannah. "Chip's call was a practical joke, right?"

"Well, no."

"Why is it I'm not surprised?"

"You should have seen him watching your interview. The guy got so worked up, I think he actually crushed his Iso-flex ball beyond repair. But after it was over, he *did* get on the phone and try to convince the network that *Homemaking* would be the same show it always was—even with a revamped hostess."

"You're kidding? Chip went to bat for me?"

"Well, for you and for him. He didn't want to lose his contract with the network. But, in the end, the network executives said they'd cancel Chip's contract unless he fired you." Greta shrugged. "He felt he had no choice."

"I see. Well, I can't really blame him."

"But wait. There's more. This morning, the network brass saw the overnight numbers on your interview. They were outstanding, Hannah, everyone was tuning in! And the network received thousands of phone calls, and tens of thousands of faxes and e-mails. Your fans thought you were very brave to be so honest, and people who never saw your cable show say they're looking forward to the network debut!"

"Really! Then I'm rehired?"

"Well, no."

"Greta! You're driving me nuts! Didn't you tell Chip about the idea we came up with last night?"

"I'm getting to that! Don't you know anything about telling a story—"

"Greta!"

"Okay, okay. Here's the thing. The network called Chip this morning and told him to create a *new* show for your new image. And there I was already sitting in his office with our *Life Style* idea, which he was in the middle of turning down, I might add. But when the network called, he changed his tune. Turned right around and pitched them on it. They bought it, Hannah! They want an entire year's worth of shows!"

Neil felt a surge of pride and pleasure at this news, and his gaze went from Greta to Hannah, expecting her to be thrilled. But she didn't look thrilled. Or happy. She simply stood silently for a moment, then said, "So Chip is going to exec produce our new *Life Style* show. Just like *Homemaking*?"

"Sure, Hannah," said Greta. "Aren't you happy? I thought this was what you wanted?"

"I do, Greta, I do. But don't you wish there were some way that you and I could produce this show ourselves? It's our idea, and you and I will be the ones who put the time, effort, and creative energy into making it work."

"Hannah, we can't produce our own show unless we have moola, you know, cash on the barrelhead, and plenty of it. And even if we did, we'd be stuck. Chip never shares ownership of his shows. It's his hard-and-fast rule."

Hannah sighed. "But it isn't *his* show. Maybe *Homemaking* is, but *Life Style* certainly isn't. I called you about it *after* he fired me, for Heaven's sake."

"That's true, but—"

"And what's to stop him from pushing us around all over again?"

"Nothing. But it's another chance for you, girl. Think about it, would you?"

Hannah nodded. "I will, Greta, and thanks for coming. You're a real friend."

"Couldn't hear a nicer compliment than that, honey, thanks. And listen, I know you've got a lot going on today, so I'll see you later. Don't worry 'bout me. Maybe I'll get lucky with one of these rich dudes."

As Hannah hugged Greta, the redhead gave a quick wink at the grim-faced head of security. "Just be sure to warn your guy to be careful about that hysterical laughing of his. He might bust a gut."

The edge of Neil's mouth quirked as Greta threw a smile at him. "I'm *watching* you," he warned.

"You do that, sweet cheeks, and if there's any more guards that look like you around here, *please* send them over to arrest me. I'll be by that lovely ice sculpture stuffing caviar into my bag—look, he's actually starting to smile, Hannah."

"So he is."

After Greta left, Neil turned to Hannah. "I like her."

"I'm glad," said Hannah as the smile in her eyes slowly faded. "Have you heard anything yet?"

"No."

Hannah nodded stoically, then turned to go back to greeting guests.

"Hannah," called Neil before she departed.

"What, Neil?"

"I think I know where you can get the money you need."

Hannah stared at him, perplexed.

"To produce your own show," explained Neil.

"Oh, Neil, that's sweet. But if you're going to suggest my grandmother, forget it. That woman wouldn't part with her precious assets in a million years."

"I'll tell you later. Just trust me, okay?"

Hannah didn't know what he could be talking about but she nodded just the same. "Okay."

"Hannah!"

God, now what?! thought Hannah as she stepped up to Maura, who was rushing toward her with a face that looked as though she'd seen a ghost.

"It's your *grandmother*. She's actually come!" cried Maura. "She's *here*!"

Chapter
Thirty-two

"My *grandmother*'s here?"

Hannah couldn't believe it. She rushed to the vestibule and looked out the front door for herself. What she found there was a smartly dressed chauffeur stepping up to the back door of a sleek black limo.

As the door opened a fiftyish woman emerged in a beautiful peach gown, dripping with embroidery. Her ears held diamonds, her neck a glistening string of jewels.

"That's not my grandmother!" cried Hannah in shock.

But then the chauffeur went to the passenger door in the very front of the limo. He opened it and handed another woman out of the car. This one was slender, close to seventy, with coiffed gray hair and a crisp black maid's uniform.

"Grandmother Edith?" Hannah felt a little woozy. Was she seeing things?

The two women walked toward her, and Hannah rubbed her eyes. *The tension must be getting to me.*

"Is that my dear Hannah? Is that Lilian's elder daughter?" asked the woman in the maid's uniform, her regal bearing and haughty demeanor unmistakable.

"It *is* you!" shrieked Hannah. "Grandmother, what in Heaven's name are you doing in that outfit? And *who* is this woman wearing your jewels?"

"Shhhhh," said Edith Channing Williamson with a finger to her lips. "This is my maid."

"But—?"

"Can't be too careful these days. Crime, crime, everywhere you turn! I would take no chances on stepping foot from my home unless precautions had been implemented!"

"So you dressed as your *maid*?"

"Of course," affirmed Edith with a lift of her chin. "Any kidnappers afoot would have been completely deceived!"

Oh, God, thought Hannah. *She's gone batty on me.* With everything that had happened today, it was too much for Hannah to take. She was just about ready to break down and cry, when, all of a sudden, she felt the warmth of a strong hand touch her shoulder.

"Good afternoon again, Miss Whitmore," came a familiar male voice. "Won't you present me?"

"Oh!" exclaimed Hannah, turning toward the man who'd reappeared at her side. "Grandmother, may I present a wonderful friend of our family's?"

"And who might that be?" demanded the grand dame haughtily.

"Joe Stokes, Miz Edith. Could you possibly remember me?"

"Joe Stokes . . . Joe . . . *Stokes*?" whispered Edith, stepping closer to the older man. "My goodness me, it *is* you. I-I can't believe it . . ."

And then Hannah watched something she'd never seen in her entire life. Her grandmother's unshakably haughty demeanor actually began to melt away. In the space of a heartbeat, the chilly pride of her expression gave way to the glowing light of welcoming warmth.

"It's me all right, Edie," said Joe with a dashing smile. "What's the matter, cat got your tongue?"

The nickname and once-familiar teasing nearly undid the woman. And Hannah watched with amazement as the hard-hearted matriarch of her clan began to giggle. *Giggle.* Like a little girl.

"Oh, you rascally rascal, Joe! You remember how shy I was."

"I remember many things about our time together, Edie. How you used to like dancin' on the lawn to your aunt Daisy and uncle Dan's old records—"

" 'Ain't We Got Fun!' " exclaimed Edith. "And 'Yes, We Have No Bananas,' and what was that old ballad that Daisy used to play? 'Eternal' was in the title, I think."

Joe nodded. "Remember how you used to sneak away and meet me at the Cliff Walk's forty steps? How you'd leave me bundles o' wildflowers on my work gloves—"

"That's right!" interrupted Edith. "Just inside the carriage house out back. Is it still there? Oh, and do you remember my swing? The one you helped put up?"

"I remember," assured Joe. "Would you like to see the grounds again? Maybe after the ceremony?"

"Oh, Joe, yes, I'd love to see it all again . . . with you."

"Excuse me, ma'am," said the maid at Edith's side, who was dressed to the nines. "What would you be wantin' me to do now?"

"Oh, my," lamented Edith, a hand to her mouth. "I didn't think that far ahead."

"Why don't you have the woman enjoy herself, then, Edie?" suggested Joe softly. "It is a party, after all."

"Why, of course you're right, my old friend. Have fun, Mary! Just have fun! And bring Roy in, too. No use having the driver stay out with the car the whole time, is there? Have him join the party!"

Hannah watched this entire scene with a rare mix of awe, delight, and shock. "Holly will never believe me," murmured Hannah, her eyes agape, as Edith took Joe's arm and strolled away. "Not in a million years."

From the shadows, just off the entrance to the lobby, Herbert Peabody carefully emerged with a smirking smile of satisfaction on his face.

This final arrival of Grandmother Edith—dressed as a maid, no less!—was as sweet as icing on a wedding cake.

Sometimes, you just get lucky, thought Herbert. It had happened on occasion in Monte Carlo, when just *every* spin of the roulette wheel went his way.

Of course, the two follow-through men he'd hired through his old contacts in Chicago had yet to arrive, but Herbert had no doubt they would. Probably during the ceremony, which seemed to be getting under way out on the lawn.

What else is there to do? wondered Herbert, glancing around.

Perhaps he'd corner Tiffany Townsend for a little fun in some broom closet, he thought, spotting her tanned little body in a skintight flesh-colored gown. She had been quite the acrobat the evening before, and Herbert knew exactly what would be up this girl's alley.

God, he had that one's number—a real kinky obsessive, for sure. And it would be smart to keep her hooked, too, just in case he needed an escape hatch.

But Herbert didn't think he'd need one today. Everything was working out so well. His carefully laid plans were blooming like rosebuds in the sun.

"Oh, yes," murmured Herbert to himself as he tailed the queen of kitty litter out toward the garden. "I'm so good I think I've even managed to impress myself."

"Holly, are you sure you want to go through with this?" asked Hannah as they approached the lawn.

The guests had assembled surprisingly quickly on white folding chairs aligned in the garden. Hannah saw the long, pristine silk runner, scattered with white and yellow daisies, and the tall British man who stood at the end of it, beneath a bower of spring wildflowers.

Hannah also noticed another man, dark-haired with green eyes, and looking about as miserable as a man could look. J. J. Ryan stood watching on the edge of the festivities, near the old oak tree. It seemed her younger sister was refusing to look in that direction.

"Stop asking me that, Hannah," whispered Holly. "You've done it at least a dozen times since noon, and my answer is still the same."

Hannah sighed and helped her sister with her train. The snow-white wedding dress, dripping with Italian lace, looked gorgeous on the girl, and Hannah was actually beginning to hope that Carraway was not, in fact, an impostor.

After all, she wanted Holly to be happy. Maybe she was

simply allowing her own ugly experience with Peabody to stain the belief that her sister could find bliss.

"Okay, Holly," said Hannah finally. "If this is truly what your heart wants, then I'll be completely happy for you."

"Oh, Hannah!" Holly turned to hug her sister. "Thanks for all you've done."

And then the two women started toward the crowd.

"Mr. Ryan?"

Neil was standing on the lawn at the back of the assembled guests when he heard the voice over his walkie-talkie. His hand brushed by the handle of his .38 as he pulled the little radio out.

"Yeah?"

"Houston here, at your office in the carriage house."

"What have you got? Don't waste my time."

"A fax is coming through, but it seemed to jam on the second page."

Neil took off immediately for the carriage house. "What's the first one say, Houston? Read it to me."

"From: Inspector McDrury, Scotland Yard," said Houston between bursts of static. "Regarding your inquiry about Sir Reginald Carraway. We have run the fingerprints and found some interesting results . . ."

In the carriage house office of Ryan Investigations, Neil heard the start of the wedding march on the lawn outside. It began just about the moment he'd pulled the jammed paper from the fax machine's rollers. But the pages were unreadable.

"Dammit!" cursed Neil. "Houston, call McDrury's office and have them resend the fax *immediately*!"

"Yes, sir."

"Dan Doyle!" cried Neil a moment later into the air of the office.

"What, sir?" asked Houston.

"Dammit, not you, Houston. I gave you your instructions. Go to it!"

"Sorry, sir," said the young man, jumping toward the phone.

"Dan Doyle!" called out Neil again, his young guard lookıg at him as if he'd gone nuts. "I need your help!"

The music was swelling to a crescendo, and Neil realized
ıat the bride must have started down the white runner on the
awn.

"Do anything you can to stall that wedding!" cried Neil,
oping to Heaven the ghosts were within earshot—or what-
ver the hell they had instead of ears.

"Ooooh, Danny, an invitation to mischief!"
"And for a good cause, too."
"Twenty-three skidoo!"
"Sing it, gal. Now, what shall we try first?"
"Well, no tripping of the bride—or her maid of honor.
lannah's had enough falls in one lifetime."
"How about we pick on the groom, then?"
"Oh, my, honey! This should be fun!"

"Dearly beloved," began the minister. "We are gathered
ere in the sight of God and in the face of this congregation
ɔ join together this man and this woman in holy matrimony,
vhich is an honorable estate . . ."

Hannah stood beside her sister, trying her best to keep her
nind on the ceremony, but her eyes kept straying to the car-
iage house. *C'mon, Neil! Where are you?*

She'd seen him dart away before the ceremony began, and
he was certain he was getting some news on Carraway. If
nly he would reappear, thought Hannah worriedly. If only
e would nod and smile and reassure her that Carraway's
ngerprints had checked out fine—that he was the man he
laimed to be. Then she could finally breathe easily again.

". . . and therefore is not by any to be undertaken lightly
r wantonly, but reverently, discreetly, advisedly, soberly, and
n the fear of God—"

Suddenly, the minister paused. "My son?" he whispered
oftly. "Are you feeling all right?"

Hannah glanced to her right to find Carraway listing like a
acht in a choppy harbor. First he leaned one way, and then
he other, and then he started swatting at the air.

"Reggie?" whispered Holly, alarmed. "What's wrong?"

"You've got a bloody evil lot o' mosquitoes here, that's
vhat's wrong."

"Mosquitoes?" asked the minister. "I don't *see* any."

"Well, they're buzzin' by my head like a logger's saw. . Oh, just get on with the service, will you?" barked Regg in frustration. "And hurry it along."

"Yes, of course . . ."

As the ceremony began again, Edith Channing Williamsc turned to her very old and dear friend, Joe Stokes.

"I'll be right back, Joe."

"Where are you going, Edie? Would you like me come?"

"No, no, just the little girls' room."

Joe smiled warmly as Edith rose and worked her wa across the row of chairs.

She passed a young woman in a daring flesh-colored gow Tiffany Townsend noticed the maid going to the john, ar thought it was a marvelous idea. It was bound to be muc more exciting than watching this tiresome ceremony.

Rising, Tiffany worked her way to the end of the row, to And in another minute she was walking toward the rear do of the mansion's lobby.

Hannah half-listened to the minister's words as her eye strained to see into the carriage house.

Suddenly she heard a sound behind her—a shocked, "O) my!" followed by the sounds of a crowd of people murmu ing in dismay.

"Reggie!" came Holly's cry a split second later.

Hannah's head turned back to find Carraway on the groun Clearly, he had abandoned the listing in favor of falling c his best asset.

"My son, I'm sorry," whispered the minister in alarr "but are you *drunk*?"

"No!" cried Reggie, quickly rising to his feet agai "Somebody bloody *tripped* me!"

"Tripped you?" repeated Holly. "Reggie, no one's eve *moved* around you!"

"I'll have none of your lip, girl."

"But, Reggie!"

"Get on with the vows!"

Hannah's eyes narrowed at the man's tone to her sister, b

she held her tongue. Even the minister looked less than happy
to go on. Nevertheless, the gray-haired man turned a page in
his small leather book and began the vows.

"Join hands please. . . . Do you, Reginald Bernard Geoffrey Carraway, take this woman, Holly Lilian Whitmore, to
be your lawfully wedded wife—"

Inside the mansion, Herbert Peabody had already tailed
Edith Channing Million-Dollar–Heiress until she'd reached
the ladies' lounge and disappeared inside.

Where are those hired guns? thought Herbert as he checked
his watch impatiently. *This is the perfect opportunity.*

In frustration, Herbert walked toward the front door, not
even noticing Tiffany Townsend slipping into the ladies'
lounge behind him.

Suddenly, he saw two men in tuxedos stepping from the
coatroom, one with short brown hair, another with black curly
hair. Herbert had never met these men before, but he knew
at once they were the men he'd hired out of Chicago. It was
the way they looked—both very tall and strong. Both with
hard, suspicious eyes.

"Excuse us, sir, I'm . . . uh . . . Simon," said the first one,
and Herbert knew it was Sweeney, the man he'd spoken with
the night before.

"I'm Wes," said the second.

Herbert smiled, careful to mask his voice. "So very nice
to see you, gentlemen." *At last.* "Come on, follow me."

"Sorry, we, uh, seem to have come a bit late," said the
second in nearly a whisper. "But could you tell us where we
might find one of the guests here, an Edith Channing Williamson? We have a little message for her."

"Sure," said Herbert, smiling with the knowledge that the
two still didn't know who he was. *Great, and I'll keep it that
way, too. No use getting myself more involved than I have to.*
"She's in the ladies' lounge. If you wait right here, she should
be right out."

"Thank you so much."

Herbert left quickly, hoping to avoid any entanglement in
what was about to take place.

*   *   *

Out on the lawn, Hannah thought she was going to have a heart attack. No sign of Neil and they were almost done with the vows. She watched in torment as the minister turned to her sister.

"Do you, Holly Lilian Whitmore, take this man, Reginald Bernard Geoffrey Carraway, to be your lawfully wedded husband—"

"Stop the wedding! Stop the wedding!"

It was Neil Ryan, running full speed from the carriage house, waving a small stack of papers in his hand.

Thank Heaven, thought Hannah as the crowd of guests murmured among themselves.

When Neil finally stood, a bit breathless, before them, the unhappy minister turned to him. "Do you have some objection to this union, sir?"

"I do," answered Neil.

"What the hell's the meaning of this?!" cried Reggie, clearly outraged.

"Oh, Neil!" lamented Holly, pushing back the fine pearl-encrusted netting of her wedding veil. "What are you doing?! You're ruining everything!"

"No, Holly," said Hannah, gently touching her sister's shoulder. "Listen."

"What are your grounds, sir?" asked the minister.

"My grounds are legal. Holly, this man can't take you as his wife. Not as Sir Reginald Carraway—"

"I don't understand."

"His name is Gareth Henner, Holly. He's a con artist with a long record. He only *resembles* Carraway, a man on whose house staff he once worked—"

"That's a lie!" cried the man in question. "This man should be arrested for barging in here like this and accusing—"

"And by the way, Gareth," broke in Neil as he waved the faxes he'd received, "Scotland Yard is looking for you. And so are the states of New York and California. I told the authorities you'd be happy to wait right here for them."

"You, sir, are gravely mistaken!"

"Neil, how can you be so sure?" asked Holly.

"We got his fingerprints," piped up Hannah. "I'm sorry, Holly, but it's true," she said, then turned to the con artist.

"You see, Gareth, we lifted them from your groom's glass late last night."

The look of arrogant outrage on Gareth's face slowly transformed before Hannah's eyes. Horrified shock came first, and then a kind of raging panic.

"Reggie? Is any of this true?"

A sweat had broken out across the man's brow. "I-I w-won't s-stand 'ere and be bloody insulted!" he wailed before launching himself in the direction of the rear wall.

Neil didn't follow. And when Hannah sprang forward Neil grabbed her arm. "Oh, no you don't, Hannah. The man's dangerous. He's wanted for murder. Let my staff take care of it. I've already alerted them."

Hannah looked at the shocked, devastated face of her sister and considered her options. "Neil, I told you what I'd do if that man hurt Holly."

"What?" he asked, but before the syllable was even out of his mouth, Hannah had reached into Neil's jacket and grabbed the gun from his holster.

"Hannah, no!"

But she was already in hot pursuit of the fugitive, her ice-blue satin shimmering in the sunlight as she knocked over a huge arrangement of blossoming rosebuds and ran full speed across the lawn.

Inside the ladies' lounge, Tiffany Townsend barely noticed the old bag in the maid's outfit. Such people were beneath her, after all. Yet the maid seemed quite comfortable with herself, nodding and smiling as if she owned the place.

Tiffany threw the woman a half smirk and turned back to perfecting her lipstick.

Outside the door two men were waiting. When the door swung open, they closed in.

But the first man grabbed the second one's arm and shook his head. "It's just a maid," he said. "Look at the uniform."

"Oh, right. Guess the heiress is still in there."

The two didn't have long to wait. The door swung open again and a pretty young woman in designer duds, dripping with diamonds, practically walked right up to them.

"Excuse me," said the man with black curly hair, blocking her exit. "We'd like a word with you."

The brown-haired man came up instantly behind her.

Tiffany put a hand on her hip. "And *who* are you?"

"A friend."

Tiffany's eyes suddenly brightened as she realized she'd been cornered. "Are you here to kidnap me?" she whispered. "Because I've been waiting *forever* for you to show up!"

The two men looked at each other.

"You were looking *forward* to this?" asked the big, brown-haired man behind her.

"Of course, you idiots! What did you think?!"

The first man looked at the second a moment. "Isn't she too *young* to be this Williamson broad?"

"What's your name?" asked the man behind her.

"Oh, you two are *so* tiresome!" exclaimed Tiffany. "*Kidnap* me, already, will you?!"

Dressed in her maid's uniform, Edith Channing Williamson had just turned the corner to the lobby when she could have *sworn* she'd heard the word that she'd been living in fear of for years. With extreme care, Edith peeked back around the corner.

"So you won't put up a fight if we take you to our limo and catch a ride out of here?" questioned the man with the black curly hair in front of Tiffany.

"Well, *I* won't. But I've got a bodyguard assigned to me everywhere I go. Today's lucky winner is standing just inside the lobby waiting for me."

"Then we'll have to make sure we don't make a sound. Okay?" whispered the brown-haired man in her ear.

"Okay," said Tiffany with a little giggle. "Let's go!"

But the little trio's progress was halted an instant later.

"What's going on there?" called an older woman in a maid's outfit from down the hallway. "Are you men bothering that young woman?"

"Hannah, for God's sake, stop!" called Neil, taking off after her across the mansion's lawn.

Hannah didn't need Neil's command to stop her. She came to a halt the moment she met the sight beneath the old oak tree.

"J. J.," she whispered. "Good job."

Neil jogged up to Hannah and immediately took the gun

from her slackened fingers. He was about to give her a lecture when he saw her staring dumbfounded at something on the lawn.

Neil turned and gasped. "J. J.? What the hell happened?"

"I don't think he's dead or anything," said J. J., standing over an unconscious Gareth Henner. "I just tripped him up, you know, then knocked him flat with this."

Hannah looked at Neil and they both burst out laughing.

J. J. had laid out the notorious con man with the seat of Holly's little wooden swing.

Chapter
Thirty-three

Neil put an arm around Hannah's shoulders as three members of his security team rushed forward to help J. J. with Gareth Henner.

"C'mon, honey," he said, "let's get back to your sister."

Hannah nodded.

The wedding guests looked suitably alarmed, but, true to form, an unflappable Maura Ryan had already come to the rescue, calming people down and keeping them seated. And all hell would have most likely been contained, too, until a hysterical older woman in a maid's outfit came running up the center aisle.

"Kidnappers! Kidnappers! Help, help!"

"Good God, now what?" murmured Neil as they approached the crowd.

"It's Grandmother Edith!" cried Hannah, breaking into a run. "Oh, please don't tell me she's gone delusional!"

"Kidnappers! Kidnappers! Help, help!"

"Edie!" cried Joe Stokes, jumping from his seat to comfort his dear friend. "What's wrong? Calm down, tell me," he urged, taking her hands in his.

Neil and Hannah got to Edith in time to hear her panting explanation. ". . . two men took a young woman in a beige gown by the arm and pushed me down. I thought I'd broken my hip for a moment there."

"I'll kill 'em!" snarled Joe with ferocity as he put a protective arm around her shoulders.

"My goodness no, Joe, they're terrible men!" cried Edith. "A nice, clean-cut boy tried to help. He'd been waiting in the lobby for the girl. But one of those terrible men hit that boy in the head with the butt of a gun! A gun! Knocked him out cold!"

"Where did they go?" asked Neil with quiet calm. "Which direction? Can you recall?"

"Yes," said Edith. "There was a commotion near the front of the lobby—so they turned toward the passages that lead to the kitchen below stairs."

"We'll cut them off from the back, Mrs. Williamson. Thank you," said Neil politely, and then he was off and running, not even noticing Hannah right on his heels.

As he moved across the grounds, Neil automatically reached for his walkie-talkie. He knew his entire force of security guards was already scrambled in pursuit of Carraway. They didn't yet know he was out cold, decked by a girl's wooden swing.

"Code Red. All guards. Carraway subdued. Search on now for two men with a young woman in a beige gown. Men armed. Code Red. Last seen headed toward kitchen. I'm cutting them off at the rear door."

Hannah watched Neil running toward the far end of the mansion. "Neil!" she called, but he was talking on his radio and didn't seem to hear.

Without wasting time for explanation, Hannah ran to a hidden little door in the other direction. She'd known as a child how to get right into the kitchen through a cellar. It was much quicker this way, and she was determined to warn Chef Antonio and his staff of the danger.

"Oooooh! This is fun!" exclaimed Tiffany. "Where to now?"

The two thugs looked at each other. They were extremely

displeased that their hastily made plans had been altered so severely and so fast.

This Heathcliff Parkinson character who'd hired them had said the job was "a piece of wedding cake." The guy had gone over the front gate procedure well enough, but he'd said nothing about other guards on the premises.

"If I figure out who this Parkinson is," said the first man to the second, "I'm gonna wring his neck."

"What the hell kind of maze is this?" cried the second man.

"How the hell do I know?! We were supposed to be able to waltz out the damn *front* door, not make a run for the back! Christ, this whole place is *crawling* with security guards! Parkinson never mentioned that little detail!"

"Maybe he didn't know."

"Shut up! And pick a door!"

Suddenly, the men burst into a bustling kitchen. They stopped dead as a few tense faces in white chef's jackets glanced up for a moment, then went back to their duties.

"Okay," said the first thug to Tiffany. "Just play like there's nothing special going on and we're just passin' through."

"Sure, whatever!" said Tiffany with a giggle.

"Is this chick *on* something?" asked the second thug.

"Can it and move," commanded the first.

They were just about to the middle of the kitchen when a short man in a white chef's jacket and traditional chef's hat confronted them.

"What you want here in my kitchen?" demanded Chef Antonio with arms crossed. "Dis no dance floor!"

A few feet away, Hannah popped out of a small hidden doorway. It took about three terrible seconds for her to realize she'd stepped right in the middle of the kidnappers' escape plans.

"Chef Antonio!"

"Hannah! Why you not at de wedding of your sister?"

"That's it!" cried the brown-haired thug, drawing his gun. "Clear the hell out of the way, or I'll have this do it for me!"

"Wow, this is too much!" exclaimed Tiffany, clapping her hands in delight. "Like I'm in the middle of that Marlon

Brando mob picture, what was it?'' she asked the curly-haired thug. *''The Grandfather?''*

''Shut up and move!''

''Okay,'' said Tiffany with a little pout, ''but I don't like your tone of voice.''

It all happened very fast. Hannah couldn't stand seeing the barrel of that gun pointed at her dear friend, Chef Tony. So, when she thought the brown-haired thug was distracted, she leapt for it.

''What the hell!'' cried the thug, lifting the gun faster than Hannah could have imagined. She tripped and fell at his feet.

''Take her, too,'' barked the first man, ''she looks worth a few bills.'' Then he turned his head about the room. ''All of you people freeze or I'll shoot both of these broads!''

And then Hannah was being shoved along at gunpoint through the kitchen.

''Do not you hurt our Hannah!'' threatened Chef Tony. And, as the angry eyes of the executive chef's devout followers tracked the progress of the quartet across the very large kitchen, a chilly breeze suddenly stirred the steamy air.

Neil had just rounded the corner of the outside doorway when he heard the last few threats being issued inside the kitchen. With gun drawn, he carefully peaked around the corner of the door frame.

Dammit to hell. His heart nearly stopped when he saw one of the perps pointing a gun at his beloved's head. As he waited silently, sweat actually began beading on his brow, something that seldom happened to this veteran soldier and hardened detective.

Neil knew he'd have to move with absolute precision, pulling Hannah out of harm's way and laying out the thug in one movement. He honestly didn't know if he could do it—though he'd done similarly difficult maneuvers in his career.

But this time there were mitigating circumstances: two men had to be taken out at once. And it was his Hannah whom Neil had to save—which meant emotions were now involved. A horrific understatement, thought Neil, because in that moment he realized just how much he loved this woman whose life was now endangered.

He loved her with all his heart. He loved her with all his

soul. And if he'd have to exchange his life for hers, he was ready and willing because there was no greater duty than love commanding him now. And maybe, just maybe, realized Neil, there was no greater duty in all the heavens—or on the Earth.

Swallowing nervously, Neil tried to prepare himself. *Heaven help me,* he prayed, a droplet of sweat stinging his left eye.

Then, something odd assailed him, and oddly familiar. It was the strange sensation of electricity in the air. No sooner did he feel it, than he witnessed an amazing feat.

As the two thugs moved a gleeful Tiffany and an unnerved Hannah past one of the largest chefs in Antonio's little army of white jackets, a heavy steel skillet began to levitate.

The big chef they called Minnow never moved a muscle. But the skillet hanging two feet behind him and one foot above him suddenly moved. In fact, it *floated* by itself through the air and then levitated right in front of the man's gaze.

Minnow adored Hannah. And he didn't care much for interlopers in his boss's kitchen, either. So he never even questioned *how* the skillet got into his hand. He simply took it and swung with all his might.

"Mon Dieu!" cried Chef Antonio in a shocked outburst.

Hannah wasn't distracted. Her eyes had been steadily fixed on the back exit of the kitchen, with unwavering faith in Neil. And sure enough, the moment Minnow's swinging skillet connected to the curly-haired thug's head, Hannah saw Neil step quickly into the room and level his revolver.

Instantly, Hannah dropped out of the way and the thug who'd been holding the gun on her was now a target at point-blank range.

"Drop it now," said Neil calmly.

The thug obeyed, realizing he was trapped. A moment later three more security guards rushed into the room.

"I will spit in deir face!" announced Chef Antonio, rushing up to the thugs.

"Stand back, Antonio," warned Neil, as his guards moved in to handcuff the thugs.

"I will boil dem in olive oil!" insisted the chef. "Hannah, my Hannah! Are you well?"

"Yes, Tony," she said, giving him a hug. "Thank you. And thank you, Minnow!" she exclaimed, wrapping her arms around the big man's neck and kissing him on the cheek.

"S'okay," mumbled the big man with a furious blush to his cheeks.

No one questioned how the skillet floated into Minnow's hands. In the commotion that followed, there was hardly time. But Hannah knew who to thank, so she silently threw a kiss into the steamy kitchen air.

Two hours later most of the wedding guests had departed, and the police had carted away the two perps. Finally Neil and Hannah found a quiet moment alone.

"So, is there enough evidence to prove Herbert Peabody was at the center of all of this garbage?" asked Hannah as they strolled out onto the lawn.

"Yep. Peabody, Parkinson, and Princeton are all wanted men now."

"All three rolled up into one," said Hannah.

"Yeah, one stinkin' piece of filth."

"I still can't believe he managed to slip away."

"Oh, he won't get far."

"Why do you say that?"

"He slipped out with Tiffany Townsend. It seems, at the airport, she left a little message on her father's phone machine, telling him she fired her bodyguard service and is heading for Rio de Janeiro. She wanted him to wire her money there. Seems her cousin Clark Von Devon, who also slipped away, cleaned her wallet of credit cards and cash."

"So the police know where Herbert is headed?"

"Oh, yes, and so does Tiffany's father, which is much more dangerous for the man."

"I don't understand."

"Tiffany's father is the toughest SOB in American real estate. I've already talked to him about who Peabody is. He's not about to let his little princess stay in the presence of that creep for long—although my guess is that when it comes to scruples, Tiffany and Herbert are pretty well matched. Nevertheless, I expect Vincent Townsend will arrange a nice South American prison for Herbert to take up residence in for the next few years."

"Either that or the two will end up married."

"Fine with me," said Neil. "As long as they pick any hotel

on Earth to recite their vows but Château du Coeur.''

"Funny, Ryan."

"Yoo-hoo, young man!"

Hannah looked to see Grandmother Edith walking briskly toward them. Joe Stokes was slowly bringing up the rear.

"I'd like a word with you, young man!"

"Yes, ma'am," said Neil, sounding a bit like a teenager again, riddled with anxiety over a grown-up's displeasure. Hannah stole a glance at his face and noticed the familiar stoic curtain coming quickly down over his expression.

"I understand you're the man responsible for the security around here!" announced Edith.

"Yes, ma'am," said Neil with the ghost of a sigh. It was hardly detectable, but Hannah had gotten to know him—and love him—so well, that she could now sense things she hadn't before.

"I know who you are, young man," snapped Edith. "You're Neil Ryan, the man I called a gold-digging gigolo all those years ago."

Neil's teeth clenched, but he said nothing.

"Well, I was darned wrong, I can tell you. And I apologize to you," said the older woman. Then she turned to her grand-daughter. "Hannah, this young man is a hero. A hero, I say! If not for him, and his well-trained staff, my worst nightmare would have come to pass. I tell you this day has helped me change my life."

"Grandmother?"

"I've decided my money is too great a burden. It's kept me a blasted prisoner in my own house for Heaven's sake. I'm giving every last cent away. As of today. It's all arranged. The ASPCA will get a good deal, and, of course, the Preservation Society of Newport. I'll tell you right now I'm not leaving a cent to you girls. It's a curse, I say, and I wouldn't wish such a plague on members of my own family!"

Hannah glanced at Neil, who suddenly seemed to be—Hannah couldn't believe it. He was *laughing*.

"Grandmother," said Hannah earnestly, "are you sure you shouldn't think about this? What will you live on?"

"I'll take care of her," said a man's voice softly.

Hannah had almost lost track of Joe Stokes standing nearby.

"Joe, do you have the income?" asked Neil. "I thought you were working here to make ends meet?"

Joe shook his head. "I was lonesome. Wife's been gone, and I guess I came back here for the memories mostly. Maybe, in the back of my mind, I was hoping to see Edie again. And here, I have. It's a right nice turn of events, I'd say. She can live with me."

"Joe's got one point three million in T-bills and stocks," said Grandmother Edith matter-of-factly.

Hannah's eyes widened. "Mr. Stokes! When I said you looked like a million, I never thought—"

Stokes shrugged. "Ah, it's only money. Can't buy happiness. Can't buy memories of friendship—or love," he said with a wink. "That stuff's what's priceless. Eh, Edie?"

Edith didn't answer. She simply took Joe's face in her hands and gave him a wet sloppy kiss.

"And she used to be shy!" he said with a laugh, putting his arm around her and leading her away.

"Well, what do you know," murmured Neil, the laughter still in his eyes.

"Edith's about-face?"

"Naw, I was just thinking that life's ironic as hell, if you're alive long enough."

"Neil?"

"Hannah, do you remember earlier today, when I said I had a solution to your money problem? You said you needed investment capital if you wanted to produce and own your own show with Greta Green?"

Hannah's eyes narrowed. "Neil? What are you up to?"

"Nothing. I'd just like to be the one to provide the start-up cash."

"But, Neil, we're talking—"

"Can't be more than ten million. I can spare that, I think."

"Stop teasing."

But Neil wasn't laughing. Instead he was reaching into an inside pocket. Silently he presented her with a letter from a prestigious law firm.

"Oh, my God, Neil. This says you're Cornelius Vandenburg's biological *son*?"

"That's right."

"Then the rumors?"

"They're true," he said softly. "Maura had an affair, very brief, right after Vandenburg's first wife died. Apparently, Maura had loved him from afar when she'd worked in the household. And, according to her, Vandenburg cared for her, too.

"But when she discovered she was pregnant, Maura fled. Said the gossip and scandal would have ruined him. He didn't know until years later, after both were married to other people, that she'd had me. And nobody ever knew, not even me and Maura, that the man put a conservative sum in trust—to be given to me upon his death—"

"Which was just last month, wasn't it?"

Neil nodded. "Some of Vandenburg's family tried to sue, but the will is ironclad. The trust is twenty years old."

"Neil, did you know he was your real father?"

Neil shook his head. "All I ever heard were the rumors, just like you—just like everybody. Maura would never talk to me about it. She said it was the past, and she didn't want it dug up in her lifetime. Doesn't even want to know how much he left me."

Hannah stared at Neil, amazed.

"Don't *you* want to know?" he asked.

Hannah kept staring.

"With interest accrued, a little over thirteen million dollars. . . . Hannah? Hannah? Are you okay? Sit down."

Neil helped Hannah backward toward one of the white folding chairs that were still set up on the lawn. And then she began to laugh, and laugh, and laugh, and so did he.

"You're wealthier than the lot of us now, Neil!" she shrieked.

"I *told* you it was ironic."

"It's more than ironic . . . it's . . . it's . . ."

"Rich?"

And then they were both doubled over with laughter again.

The sun was beginning to sink toward the horizon and, as Neil's laughter began to fade, he caught a play of sunlight on Hannah's golden hair and joy-filled face. He gazed down at the radiant sight for a wonderful moment, seeing her all over again, like the first time, in that field of wild yellow daisies.

"So, Whitmore?"

"Hmmmmm?" Hannah saw the look in Neil's deep blue es, and felt herself go woozy again.

"You never did tell me about that wedding you dreamed —"

"What?"

"You know, when you put that cake under your pillow."

"When I was twelve?"

"You said you dreamed of me," Neil reminded her.

"And so I did," whispered Hannah, wistfully looking over e empty lawn, the abandoned trellis. "On a beautiful day e this one. With a bower of wildflowers and daisies—"

"Like this one."

And a Jazz Age wedding gown, thought Hannah, but it unded silly to say.

"So," whispered Neil, facing her, "what do you say we ke advantage of this dreamy opportunity?" Neil had come close to losing her again, first to a lie and then to a bullet, could hardly bear to let more time pass.

"What do you mean, Neil? You can't mean—"

Neil stared intently at Hannah. And then, taking her hand his, he dropped a knee to the ground. "Will you marry me lay, Hannah Daisy Whitmore?"

Hannah's eyes widened. "Neil! Today?!"

"The minister's still here. And Château du Coeur knows st how to get a marriage license *tout de suite*."

"Well, then, what can I say?" Hannah laughed. The sound emed to carry high into the air, rising beyond the tops of e trees.

"You can say yes. And then I can say—"

"Yes," said Hannah, her voice direct and clear.

Neil's smile was fairly dazzling.

"Then welcome home, Hannah Whitmore," said Neil be-re giving her the sweetest kiss she'd ever known. "Wel-me home."

Epilogue

"Hannah, my dear, I want you to see something we ca[me]
across in the hotel renovations."

It was a half hour after Hannah had agreed to marry N[ick]
and, while the groom-to-be was taking care of the licen[se,]
Maura was leading Hannah to a cedar closet in the corner [of]
one of the hotel's private offices.

Hannah's eyes widened when Maura pulled a beautifu[lly]
preserved wedding gown from among the garments. It ha[d a]
drop waist and beading and came with a headbanded veil[.]

"Someone in your family obviously used it back in [the]
twenties," said Maura. "We thought of donating it to [the]
Preservation Society. But I wanted you to have a chance [to]
see it first."

Suddenly, Hannah felt a chill . . . and then the wisp o[f a]
woman's voice was whispering in her ear. *"It's your 'si[ngle]
little girl's dream dress, isn't it, Hannah?"*

Hannah moved forward and took the gorgeous garment i[n]
her hands.

"Look beneath the hem, my dear."

The voice in her ear was strong and sure, and Han[nah]

334

beyed it. She laid the dress out and lifted its hem.

"What are you looking for?" asked Maura.

Hannah saw it, the small embroidered flower—a daisy.

"Hannah?"

"Nothing, Maura." Hannah smiled, a liquid sheen of joyful surprise glimmering in her eyes. "Something that came in a dream. Something I already knew."

"Do you think it will fit? Would you like to wear it?" asked Maura, checking her watch to make sure they didn't miss sunset.

"It will fit," said Hannah.

"You're certain?"

"I've never been more certain in my life."

The wedding of Cornelius Patrick Ryan to Hannah Daisy Whitmore took place on the rear grounds of Château du Coeur. The vows were recited just as the beautiful red-orange ball of sun slipped beneath the vast waiting sea, and the first shine of Heaven's silver promised light through any darkness.

Around the happy couple stood a smiling hotel staff, maids and chefs, waiters and security guards. Chef Antonio, and Minnow, Charlie the gardener, and Sally Ellen Grady, were all there, too, faces whom Hannah had known and loved for years.

Of course, Maura Ryan was there, crying softly. And Holly was happy to stand as a witness, no worse for the wear. A brave raven-haired young man stood close by her side, where he'd been since the afternoon's ordeal—and where, it seemed, he was destined to be for the rest of their lives.

Two more faces were there for the ceremony, older faces, who'd seen their share of weddings. But after the ceremony was over, Joe and Edith stole off quietly as the happy newlywed couple and their cozy party stepped inside to a table filled with more gourmet food than they could possibly devour.

Strolling the grounds at twilight, after so many years apart, was now a priceless thing to the older pair, an opportunity they could not let pass. And, likewise, when they spotted the swing by the old oak tree, they naturally had to give it one more try.

* * *

"*A dreamer can awaken to a Heaven on the Earth . . .*"

"*Sing it, gal.*"

"*Oh, Danny, how I love happy endings.*"

"*Of course. You're a romantic.*"

"*So are you, Danny . . . when the heart is finally taken by a love that knows its worth . . .*"

"*I'm a realist, Daisy. And a solver of mysteries.*"

"*You're the ghost of a realist. Which means, you're a romantic.*"

"*So what does that mean? I should start resolving romances?*"

"*Start, Danny? I think you just finished.*"

"*For now, sweetie.*"

"*Yes, my darling love. For now. . . .*"